THE HOT COUNTRIES

Also by Timothy Hallinan

The Poke Rafferty Series
A Nail Through the Heart
The Fourth Watcher
Breathing Water
The Queen of Patpong
The Fear Artist
For the Dead

The Junior Bender Series
Crashed
Little Elvises
The Fame Thief
Herbie's Game
King Maybe

The Simeon Grist Series
The Four Last Things
Everything but the Squeal
Skin Deep
Incinerator
The Man With No Time
The Bone Polisher

THE HOT COUNTRIES

Timothy Hallinan

Published by
Soho Press, Inc.
853 Broadway
New York, NY 10003

Library of Congress Cataloging-in-Publication Data

Hallinan, Timothy.
The hot countries / Timothy Hallinan.

ISBN 978-1-61695-446-8
eISBN 978-1-61695-447-5
I. Title.
PS3558.A3923H68 2015
813'.54—dc23   2015020054

Printed in the United States of America

10 9 8 7 6 5 4 3 2 1

THE HOT COUNTRIES

Part One
MONOLOGUES

The Cave of the Ancients

THE DUSTY BRAID of Christmas lights in the tiny window has been there for decades and has been plugged in all year round. The original bulbs are long burned out, but not even the occasional, irregular replacements, glowing in faded red and green, can compete with the prisms of light and color created by the big beads of rain on the outside of the glass. Rafferty is looking at the prisms, intentionally facing away from the man who's talking, and trying not to check his watch.

"You just hop on the equator," Arthur Varney is saying. "Ride it like a train." Standing next to his stool at the far end of the bar, one foot hitched up on its rail, he gives the impression of a man who's about to mount a horse, but by contrast with the other men in the room, most of whom seem to have been welded to their stools for decades, it's not difficult to look energetic.

Varney allows the pause to stretch long enough for him to take a pull on his beer. He's a wide, but not fat, olive-skinned man of medium height in his late forties with a square face, heavy eyebrows, and a bandit's bushy mustache. His medium-length black hair is straight and parted on the left, so badly that it looks experimental. Despite an incipient gut, he gives the physical impression of a hard, shiny, almost insectlike solidity, with the overdeveloped chest and shoulders of a vain gym rat. When he puts down the mug, his blue eyes roaming the room, there's a line of foam, like frosting, like Christmas-tree snow, on the bottom half of his dark mustache.

No one fills the silence. No one leaps in to interrupt. The men in the Expat Bar have been telling one another the same stories, complaining about the same weather, comparing the same assets of the local female professionals, for forty years and more. There are no conversational surprises waiting to be flourished, no unheard punch lines. The group is thinning as its members burn out, although it—unlike the Christmas lights—has seen few replacements: Patpong's most lurid days are long past, and the younger sex tourists have taken their small talk—and very small it is, too, Rafferty thinks—over to Soi Cowboy and Nana Plaza, offering the same stale goods in brighter boxes. Here in the Expat Bar on Patpong Road, Arthur Varney is the flavor of the month. Nine days here, according to the regulars, and he's hardly stopped talking except to take a drink.

"Like a train," he repeats, wiping his mustache with a broad, tan hand. "Look out the left window, look out the right. What do you see?"

"Lot of water," mutters Bob Campeau from his immemorial stool near the bar's end. Campeau's been a fixture there for so many years that he fancies his longevity has made him a sort of all-purpose nightlife expert, a sage with a specialty. His wide, thin-lipped mouth is downturned at the corners, and he's barely spoken all night. Poke thinks he might be sulking.

From his stool near the door—the only stool with a silvery plate bearing its occupant's name—Leon Hofstedler drives a nail into Campeau's self-regard by saying, in the German accent that invests even his simplest sentences with the threat of blitzkrieg, "Don't interrupt, Bob."

"No, no, *please*," Varney says, swiveling on his stool to turn his bright, interested blue eyes on Campeau. It reminds Rafferty of the reaction of a fan at a dull baseball game when the pitcher hits a triple. "You were saying?"

"Uh." Campeau balls a fist loosely and bounces it lightly on the bar. "Nothing. Just there's . . . you know, a lot of water. That you'd see." He nods at the surface of the bar. "From your train."

"*Absolutely*." Varney beams approvingly at Campeau, watching the muscles at the hinges of Campeau's jaws bunch and relax as though he's chewing rocks. "*Lot* of water. Let's see, Atlantic Ocean, Pacific Ocean, Indian Ocean, Molucca Sea." He closes his eyes and touches the tip of his index finger to an invisible map in front of him. "Lake Victoria in Africa, the Karimata Strait, the Makassar Strait, Gulf of Tomini." His eyes open. "Might be a couple more. I disremember. As you say, Bob, lot of water."

"The Halmahera Sea," Rafferty says, with a satisfying twinge of malice. He's been listening to Varney for three days now, escaping the marathon of Brits in costumes whose stiff upper lips have filled his new wide-screen TV night after night. "You know. Between Malaku and West Papua."

The flicker in Arthur Varney's eyes would be enough to make a timid man take a step back, but he smiles and says, "Good catch. Thought I'd said that."

"Maybe you did," Rafferty says. They hold each other's gaze just a little too long to be polite.

"But water is water," Varney says, once again addressing the room. He squares the big shoulders as though he's readjusting their weight. "When you get to land, what do you see? Holes in the ground where the gold and diamonds and tin and oil used to be, the crumbling ruins of colonialism and empire, grand buildings where people now make campfires on the floors and dig holes for toilets. Straits and beaches seized and armed and bristling with new cities to protect and multiply the plunder. The spices taken, the rubber taken, the hardwoods taken, the mountains scalped to make mahogany coffee tables for liberals in Greenwich Village." He shaves an imaginary mountain slope upward with the edge of his palm. "Brown- or black-skinned hot-country people living under the thumb of light-skinned cold-country people. The equator," he says, drawing a big horizontal circle in the air, "is a trench of destruction all the way around the globe. The burial trench of the hot countries. Except, Bob, for the water. Hard to dig a trench through water."

"You're talking about colonialism," Campeau says with new confidence; he's recognized something he's heard of. He throws a *Watch this* look at the Growing Younger Man, Hofstedler, Rafferty, and a silver-haired guy whose name might or might not be Ron. "Thailand was *never* conquered, *never* colonized. That mean it's not hot?"

"No, no, no, *no*," Varney says with a froth of delight in his tone that says this is the very question he was hoping for. "I could be pedantic and point out that Thailand, hot as it is, isn't *on* the equator, but actually, if you want, you could *broaden* that swath of devastation from the Tropic of Cancer to the Tropic of Capricorn, all the way around the globe. You'd get most of Southeast Asia that way, more of India and Africa, too. But then, to examine your specific question, who runs Thailand?"

Campeau looks for the hook, fails to see it, and says, "The Thais?"

"The people who *actually* run Thailand, *Bob*"—Varney deepens his voice very slightly each time he speaks Campeau's name, an inflection that might be either unintentional or ironic—"are the same people who run Cambodia, Laos, Vietnam, Malaysia, and Singapore—the *Asian* whites: the Chinese. Everywhere you look here, paleface Thai-Chinese lord it over darker-skinned people. The Chinese own *everything* in Southeast Asia while the people who were here first fight over crumbs and the rockier bits of the back forty. Light over dark, it holds true all across the tropics: when people from the cold countries come to the hot countries, they rarely mean to do anyone any good."

"Really," Rafferty says. "And what brings *you* here?"

"The travel writer," Arthur Varney says, showing a row of big square teeth, so yellow that Rafferty wonders if he grew the black mustache to make them appear whiter. "Always looking for a story."

IT'S BEEN A couple of minutes since Varney checked his watch—one of the thick, heavy steel ones that would probably still be ticking after the asteroid hit—and left, at about the same time he seems to leave every night, around ten. Rafferty checks his own watch, and from her station in front of the bourbon the barmaid, Toots, who has been pouring these men's drinks since the late 1960s, says, "Why you not home? Kwan have baby, yes?"

Kwan is Rose's Thai name, which, like Toots's, has receded so far into the mists of time that it takes Poke a second to understand the question. "Not yet," he says. "Six months more."

With the air of someone forced to state the obvious, Toots curves her arms a few inches from her stomach and says, "Have in *here*."

"Yes, right. We're at the throwing-up stage."

"Three month," Toots says. She pokes the inside of her right cheek with her tongue, searching for something, and sucks at a tooth. "Should stop now."

"She'll throw up as long as she can," Rafferty says. "She's hanging on to every phase. This may be the world's first two-year pregnancy."

Toots shakes her head, and her hair, graying, permed into thick, Brillo-stiff curls—black when Rafferty met her—wobbles a tiny bit, like molded Jell-O. "So why you come here? Should be at your house. Taking care."

"I'm hiding from the television," Rafferty says. "She and Miaow have bought bootlegs of every DVD the BBC ever made about English people who live in big houses and hate each other. *Downton Abbey*, *Upstairs Downstairs*, *The Forsyte Saga*, *Pride and Prejudice*, practically the complete works of Anthony Trollope. Just one well-bred snub after another."

"Yes?" Leon Hofstedler says, his eyebrows tied in a knot of puzzlement. "For what purpose? This is not what Thai girls watch. Thai girls, they want to see that . . . that doll with the knife—"

"Chucky." Campeau accompanies the information with an apparently involuntary glance at the door, as though he's afraid Arthur Varney will barge in from the street to contradict him.

"Not *my* Thai girls," Rafferty says. "What they like is *servants* and people with *titles* and huge dinners with eight courses and gowns and big, clunky jewelry and feathered hats. And Colin Firth, can't forget Colin Firth."

"Be a great setting for the next Chucky," the man who might be named Ron says. "*Chucky Abbey.*" He runs his fingers self-appreciatively through the silver waves of his hair, something he does often. The hair, Hofstedler said once to Poke, is all the man has left.

"Anything would be an improvement," Rafferty says. "The people in these shows are asleep when they're awake. They sneer at their own reflections. Rose is developing a British accent."

"But yes," Hofstedler says, nodding as he catches up to the conversation. "This is true. Rose is with child, and Miaow is in school. What year she is in now?"

"Eighth," Rafferty says.

There's a silence while these men, who have been on the edges of Rafferty's life for more than seven years, consider the implications. Rafferty uses the time to look, without much nostalgia, around the room. It's shaped like an ambitious bowling lane, no more than fourteen feet across and about fifty deep, its shape dictated by the fact that it was wedged by a voracious developer into what had been a sliver of space between two go-go bars, My Big Honey and Yellow Bellies, both long gone. One of them is still offering go-go, now under the name Miles of Smiles, while the other sells plastic leather goods to the easily fooled. The room is so narrow there's barely room for the stained, battered bar with Toots behind it, plus the usual mirrored display of mislabeled whiskeys, the beer and soft-drink taps, a small sink, and a blender that's used almost exclusively for the Growing Younger Man's complicated smoothies, mostly uneasy mixes of alcohol and health-preserving algae. The place smells of old beer, neglected dentistry, and, thanks to the rain, wet wool.

Eight stools crowd the bar. Shoved against the opposite wall are four tiny tables that have been turned into booths by the addition of high-backed, plastic-covered, pumpkin-colored banquette seats of conspicuous cheapness. When Rafferty arrived in Bangkok, one of the booths was essentially reserved for a guy named Mac, the only openly gay member of the Expat Bar regulars, but Mac has been dead for three years now. Just as Rafferty thinks of Mac, whom he had liked, Bob Campeau puts into words the thought that was triggered in many of them by the information that Miaow is an eighth-grader.

Campeau says, "Goddamn, I'm old." He carefully pats his baroque comb-over as Ron, if that's his name, rakes his gleaming silver locks again and Hofstedler picks up a giant brandy snifter with a loose scattering of paper money in it and slides it down the bar with a grunt. He's been putting on weight again, which, for someone with his medical history, is dangerous.

"Five hundred baht," Hofstedler says. "Two-fifty for the swearword and two-fifty for talking about age."

Campeau says, and it's close to a snarl, "You were thinking the same thing I was. And 'goddamn' isn't fucking swearing. There, *now* I said something you can fucking fine me for." He pulls out some paper money and drops it into the snifter. It looks short even from where Rafferty's sitting, but nobody calls Campeau on it. These men, who once considered themselves the kings of Bangkok, are running out of money.

"Eighth grade," the Growing Younger Man says. He takes a drink of something that's way too green for everyone else's comfort. "Hard to believe."

Rafferty hoists his own glass and drains the warm beer it

contains, gone flat now. "I know. I still think of her as four feet tall with a part in her hair, and there she is, sitting at home watching *Debrett's Peerage on Ice* and planning to be an actress."

"That's a rough life for a kid, acting," the guy with the hair says, and the solemnity of his tone suggests that the thought has never before been put into words. "There's a lot of rejection."

"Yeah, well, we give her a lot of acceptance. In fact, she's got a play coming up."

"When?" This is Hofstedler, who actually sounds interested.

"I don't know. What day is this?"

"Thursday?" the man who might be named Ron suggests.

No one disagrees, so Rafferty says, "A week from tomorrow. At her school. It plays Friday through Sunday."

"This play is named what?" Hofstedler asks.

"It's an old one. *Small Town.*"

"But I know this play," Hofstedler says. "The girl dies at the end, yes? So sad."

"Well, that's who Miaow's playing," Rafferty says. "The girl who dies. Julie."

"I seen it, too," Campeau says. "A million years ago."

"We should go," Hofstedler says. "Show our support for Miaow. An *actress*, she is. You must be very proud."

"I'd go," the Growing Younger Man says. The guy with the hair who might be named Ron emits a syllable of enthusiasm, and Campeau mutters something.

Hauling the denizens of the Expat Bar to Miaow's play is not on Rafferty's bucket list. He says, "We'll talk about it next week, see who still wants to go," and raps his knuckles on the bar. "Can I have a check, Toots? It's about time for me to be allowed into the living room again."

"Raining," Campeau says without looking out the window.

Rafferty gets up, pulling baht out of his jeans. "I've been wet before, and I'm still here."

The door opens, announced by a bell on a string, and Pinky

Holland tentatively looks in, most of him remaining outside in case a retreat is in order. "Is he gone? Did I miss him?"

"Gone," Hofstedler says, lifting his personal stein. "Toots, please? Another, yes?"

"What was the topic tonight?" Pinky says, coming the rest of the way in. He's a small, narrow-shouldered, professionally tan man of seventy or so with deeply creased laugh lines and a smooth bald head that Rafferty suspects he polishes. "No, lemme guess. Was it voting out every American politician and electing—who were they?—hair dressers and street mimes? Or the great Tulip Mania? Or was it—"

"Something new," Campeau said. "The equatorial trench, I think. Exploitation in the tropics."

"Sounds like a pip," Pinky says. "Has he said where he comes from yet?"

"One can only ask so many times," Hofstedler says, watching Toots fill his stein. "Then it becomes rude, yes?"

"What's *rude*," Pinky says, mopping his shining head, "is not answering the question."

"He's got something to hide," Campeau says grimly.

"Well, jeez," Pinky says. "He's in *Bangkok*." To Rafferty he says, "So how do *you* like him?"

Poke says, "I'd like him better if he came with a remote. When he looked at that nine-pound watch, I saw something yellow, a tattoo, on his wrist. Anybody know what it is?"

"It's that rattlesnake," the Growing Younger Man says, "although I don't know why it's yellow. From the Gadsden flag?"

"Which flag?" Hofstedler asks. Hofstedler has an interest in flags that Rafferty privately classifies as Germanic.

"Gadsden. From just before the Revolutionary War. Bright yellow, the coiled rattler that said 'Don't tread on me.'"

"That's making a comeback," Rafferty says. "Lot of people on the American right are flashing it around, as though the liberals are coming after their country-club memberships and incandescent bulbs."

"They are," says Campeau, who hasn't set foot in America in forty years.

Pinky Holland says over him, to Rafferty, "First time he was in here, he asked about you, you know."

Rafferty regards Holland for a few seconds. "No," he says. "In fact, I didn't know." He turns to Hofstedler, the Repository of All Knowledge in the Expat Bar.

"He didn't," Hofstedler says. "Pinky leaps to his conclusion yet again. About travel writers he was talking, asking who wrote best about Bangkok."

"And who does?" Rafferty says.

Campeau says, "Christopher G. Moore."

"Those aren't travel books, they're mysteries. Was that it? He asked, and that was the answer?"

"No," the Growing Younger Man says. He pulls the straw from his drink and licks a formless clot of powdered blue-green algae off its tip while everyone looks elsewhere. "We said, you know, about Chris Moore's books, and then the guys named half a dozen other writers, and then someone thought of you."

"No prophet is honored in his own land," Rafferty says. "It didn't occur to you, Leon—it didn't occur to any of you—to mention this to me?"

"He has always been here when you were here, yes? So who could tell you about it?" Hofstedler pulls his stein back across the bar and studies the level of the beer, probably comparing it to ten or twelve thousand others. "And he did not exactly leap to his feet when your name was finally mentioned."

Pinky says, "Toots, I'm going to stay where I am and drip for a minute. Can I get a double?"

"Jack Daniel's or Crown Royal?" Toots says.

"Oh, come on," Pinky says. "Everybody knows they're all really Mekong."

"Jack, then," Toots says. "More cheaper."

"You know," Rafferty says, "I don't remember anyone calling me by name in here during the past few days."

Hofstedler takes a sip, looking like he expects to find an insect floating in the suds, and says, "But why would we? We know who you are."

"But tonight your Arthur Varney called me a travel writer, which means he knows what my name is," Poke says, pushing his stool back into position against the bar. "I think that's kind of interesting." He pulls a baseball cap out of his pocket and slaps it open on his jeans. "Would you drip a little to your left, Pinky? I'm on my way out."

"Gonna get wet," Pinky says, sidestepping.

"We have explained this to him," Hofstedler says. "But he is young and foolish."

"Gee, thanks, Leon." Rafferty says, pulling the hat on. "I haven't been feeling very young lately."

"In here," Hofstedler says, "you are a child. *Ein Kind.* This is the Cave of the Ancients." He holds up a hand, as though in benediction. "Miaow's play. We all go, yes?"

2

Like an Ice Cap

AFTER THE AIR-CONDITIONING in the Expat Bar, set for the internal thermostats of people from Varney's cold countries, the rain feels like a hot shower.

Rafferty zigzags his way across the packed sidewalk, holding his breath against intermittent clouds of tobacco smoke. He inserts himself into the slow-moving snarl of pedestrians, almost all men, who are doggedly working their way up Patpong and then crossing over to the other side and going back down again. For people who have traveled thousands of miles to do precisely this, they don't seem to be having a very good time. They're mostly drunk, and grimly drunk at that. Some of them are walking as though they learned the skill on a planet with much weaker gravity and they can't get used to how much their feet weigh. They've stopped in multiple bars without choosing a temporary companion among the five or six hundred young women who are dancing there, which means that either they're just browsers or, Rafferty thinks—with a nod of acknowledgment to Joni Mitchell—they're discovering the craziness that comes with too much choice. Voices are cranked up, gestures border on the operatic, faces are red. The ripe, nose-assaulting smell of spilled beer, half yeast and half piss, fights for dominance with the cigarette smoke and the body odor that's so often a by-product of the interaction between Caucasian armpits and the all-enveloping heat of the tropics.

The rain is a type that's found, in Rafferty's experience, only in Thailand. It combines two kinds of rain at the same time: big, sloppy, splatting drops slanting down through a misty drizzle that hangs halos around the bright lights dangling above the booths of the Patpong Night Market. The Chinese-made junk on sale is roofed against the weather by sheets of blue plastic, some of which have probably been hanging here for decades.

He feels a faint shadow of the thrill that used to come over him when Thailand was new to him, every time he remembered where he was: in the *tropics*. The distance he had traveled from the sun-scraped desert of Lancaster, California, to the steaming excess of Thailand—an overstuffed tangle of plant and animal life with this teeming city at its core—never presented itself to him as a matter of miles or kilometers. It seemed to him not so much a journey as a rebirth. And, he thinks, the men in the Expat Bar probably once saw it the same way, before it turned into the place where they simply grew old, the place that witnessed the indignity of their infirmities: their swelling guts, their limps, their spotted baldness, their forgetfulness.

To the extent that Rafferty actually paid attention to Arthur Varney's soliloquy, it sounded both accurate and dishonest, with the mix achieving an almost political level. It was accurate in that the hot countries have been ravaged for centuries, dishonest in that Varney omitted colder places like North America and the northern regions of Japan, where the native populations had been subdued and either wiped out or marginalized by relative late-comers. So what Varney says is true of the tropics, but there's no geographic monopoly on exploitation.

It's an undependable argument made by a man who, at first glance, struck Rafferty as undependable to the marrow of his bones.

And why, he wonders, is Varney interested in him?

If he is. And even if he actually *is*, it's probably no cause for alarm. If the man's best shot at finding Rafferty was claiming a stool in the Expat Bar, how formidable can he be? If it weren't for Miaow and Rose's marathon of British programs on their new flat-screen, purchased the night he learned Rose was pregnant, Rafferty wouldn't have gone anywhere near the place. Until a few nights ago, he hadn't been there more than two nights in a row for years.

Still, he does a quick mental fact-check. No one in the bar actually knows where he lives.

When he first came to Bangkok, the Expat Bar had appalled him in a limited way—in a way that felt like it might be interesting in a book. Crowded into that little room was a tiny, tightly focused society, a sort of antimeritocracy, made up of resolutely, even defiantly flawed men who had abandoned their homes, their work, and their families so they could drown themselves in the cut-rate flesh of Patpong. At the time they must have felt like they were buying a ticket to an earthly version of the jihadists' heaven, an endless supply of renewable, or at least plausible, virgins for the rest of their lives. But Rafferty has come to believe that time is essentially a slow-motion joke, and in this case it's a dilly: the street's bars have deteriorated; the bar fines and the bar workers' "tips" have gone up as the men's incomes dwindled, a dynamic that Campeau bewails endlessly; and the men themselves have grown old and vast-waisted. Women who work in bars, like women who work pretty much anywhere, generally prefer young, slender men to old, fat ones, especially old, fat ones who are running out of money. These days the Expat Bar's patrons grouse endlessly about the way the "girls" have changed, without ever looking at themselves.

And they're dying.

It hasn't struck him until now how much that bleak, single-minded little world has shrunk. It's melted away like an ice cap. At least eight of the twenty-five or so men he'd met when he arrived in Bangkok eight years ago have passed away, thousands of miles from home, creating awkward problems for their embassies and prompting imprecise but deeply felt memorial ceremonies in the bar: approximately Jewish, approximately Catholic, approximately Buddhist. Nine months ago, it had almost been Hofstedler's turn. He'd gone down like a tree, slammed to the pavement by cardiac arrest, outside the Queen's Corner bar. He survived only because four bar girls, with a lot of profanity and perspiration and a great many soprano grunts, had hauled the big man up to Surawong Road and jammed him into a cab, and four of them had hopped in and directed the driver to the nearest hospital. They'd told the hospital staff extravagant lies about how the fat *farang*, whose name they didn't even know, was a millionaire. Hours later, when he opened his eyes beneath the harsh fluorescents of the recovery room, Hofstedler had experienced a long moment of very complicated gratitude as he realized that his beautiful rescuers were actually a quartet of thickly made-up ladyboys. They'd saved his life, they'd created a prolonged and highly dramatic scene until the doctors, in self-defense, examined him and immediately opened him up and put in a stent, and they'd waited for hours, their *moneymaking* hours, to make sure this perfect stranger had come through, and they were ladyboys. It was their hospital; it specialized in breast embellishments and male-to-female metamorphoses.

Hofstedler had always loathed ladyboys.

Somebody bumps Rafferty from behind, and he automatically checks his hip pocket, which still has a wallet in it. Six or seven years ago, one of the guys in the bar, an Italian named Enrico, had slapped his pocket exactly as Rafferty had, and when he got home, he discovered a cheap plastic "Hello Kitty" wallet stuffed with currency-size pornographic manga, which he'd brought into the bar and shown around to warn the other guys to be on guard. So Rafferty removes his wallet, glances at it, and shoves it down into a front pocket, since those are harder to pick.

Enrico, he thinks. He'd practically lived in the bar, and he had loved classical music with Italianate fervor. And he'd died a year

or two back. So that's another one gone. Make it nine. Age had
had its way with the bar's patrons in other ways, too. Buster
Fielding, one of the men Rafferty met all those years ago, has been
hospitalized with dementia, and another, a Vietnam veteran
named Wallace Palmer, has grown vague and intangible. Being
with Wallace these days is like sitting next to a shadow. Sometimes he knows who Poke is, sometimes he mistakes Poke for
someone he knew in 1969. Leon, Pinky Holland, and the Growing
Younger Man take turns checking on Wallace every night, making
sure he's found his way home from wherever he goes, taking him
food, hauling him into the bar occasionally for an evening among
the living. After the last drink, one of them will escort him home,
because otherwise he'll direct a *tuk-tuk* or a motorcycle taxi to an
apartment over a shop front that was demolished twenty-five years
ago. Hofstedler has slipped a card with his name and phone
number on it into Wallace's wallet for the police, when they find
Wallace lost and he can't tell them where he needs to go. Wallace
had been tall and still physically vigorous when Rafferty met him,
with a face like a Greek ruin—destruction failing to mask flawless
structure—and he'd been the first of the men in the bar to befriend
Poke. Rafferty had been wandering the city with his mouth
hanging open, trying to cope with the sensory overload and find a
center for his book. Wallace had helped him get an apartment,
taught him how to cross streets without getting killed. He'd moved
Rafferty to the stool next to his at the Expat Bar, brought him into
the conversations, and ushered him into the small and fiercely
defended circle of Hofstedler's goodwill. Once Rafferty was okay
with Hofstedler, he was okay with everyone except Campeau, who
liked no one on earth but the bar girl of the moment. These days
Campeau doesn't even have one of those to soften his heart.

The Expat Bar had been one of Rafferty's keys to the city. Out
of what he heard there, he had written tens of thousands of words
for his book, had begun to construct a lattice of understanding
about how the sex trade and, beyond that, the city itself worked.

Without the bar, without Wallace, he would have had no way of understanding who Rose really was the night he first saw her dancing at the King's Castle bar. Without Rose he never could have adopted Miaow. Together, Rose and Miaow form the center of Rafferty's life, and without the Expat Bar he wouldn't have either of them. And especially, he thinks, without Wallace.

Who hasn't been around these past few nights. He should go see Wallace.

Rafferty is most of the way to the point where Patpong ends in a T-junction with Silom, lost in thought and letting the crowd carry him along, when he hears a bottle hit the ground, followed by a shout and a long string of profanity. He turns to see a beefy, balding guy in what Rafferty thinks of as the Aussie beach uniform—knee-length shorts and a wet, once-white, wifebeater now stained with God only knows what—backing through a puddle of beer until he bumps against a market stand, endangering a glinting array of fraudulent designer wristwatches, as a much smaller Thai woman in her mid-twenties raises a hand glittering with cheap rings to slap the cheek the man is already rubbing. The woman leaps across the distance between herself and the retreating man so quickly that Rafferty hardly sees her move; once there she plants a knee in the center of the Aussie's shorts. The man bellows like a water buffalo, and the crowd parts to allow two more men in similar outfits to emerge. They charge the girl as their friend sinks to his knees, pulling with him the cloth that has the watches on it. The girl backs up quickly and wheels around to fade into the crowd. Short as she is, she'll be invisible once she insinuates herself into it.

Before she does, for just an instant, her eyes meet Rafferty's and widen when she sees him looking straight at her. She's gone in a blink, but it's obvious to him that she'd known he was there, known *exactly* where he was. Had, in fact, confirmed his location. With two furious drunks in wifebeaters about to grab her, she had taken the time to check him out.

A plausible explanation: she was following him when she tangled with the Aussie. And as she fled from his friends, she remembered Rafferty and confirmed that she hadn't lost him.

Scanning the crowd for her, he thinks, *First Varney and now this woman*. Putting together his impressions of her, he realizes she was probably a bar girl dressed for the street. Long, looping curls hanging down like gift-wrap ribbon, rouge as bright as bougainvillea, a tight red dress from the Tart Shop or wherever the women in the trade buy their street clothes. Something odd about her face, visible even through the thick impasto of stage makeup: a smudge of some kind to the left of her mouth. A port-wine birthmark, maybe. No one has been interested in Rafferty for months, and suddenly there's this pair.

But right now he's not interested in being interesting. Rose and Miaow are at home, and Rose has their child taking shape within her. Treasure, the third female in his life—at least in the sense that he feels responsible for her—is safe and in good hands, for now. He's reconnected with Arthit, his best friend in Bangkok, and he's even forging a relationship with Anna, the woman who almost drove them apart and with whom Arthit is living and whom he might even marry.

And in the apartment, Rose and Miaow's Brit parade will finally be over. The television will be off.

He's about to cross the street at Silom to walk home when he feels, or thinks he feels, eyes on his back. He turns and scans the crowd, reflecting on all he has to protect at this time in his life. Even though he sees no one who is obviously watching him, he steps off the curb and flags a taxi. If he takes an indirect route, looking out the back window the whole way, he'll be able to get home knowing that no one was behind him.

Not that anyone would actually be behind him, of course.

3

The Bamboo Telegraph

THE PREVAILING COLOR is the fraudulent, slightly chemical purple that jelly makers have chosen to represent grapes, but the hue has faded. In fact, it's had time to fade so much that he asks himself why he never noticed the prints before, when they were fresher.

There are half a dozen purple ghosts, slowly disappearing into the general grime of the elevator: quite clearly handprints, and in defiance of reasonable expectations when one is confronted by grape-jelly handprints, the hands are adult size and too high for children. Two distinct sets, perhaps a man and a woman, who got into this elevator after, apparently, eating grape jelly with their bare hands. The sight of the prints is so dismaying that he checks for other signs of decline as the elevator climbs toward his floor.

They're *everywhere*: a sticky sheen of finger dirt around the buttons; a name in Thai, "Kaew," chiseled into the cheap wood above the control panel; a cobweb draped like an elf's cape over one of the fluorescents; chipped corners on the square black-and-white floor tiles. Mottling the white tiles are spills that might be coffee and red wine. Ancient cigarettes have left their vile wisp in the air. How could he not have noticed all this—this *decay*—before? His family lives here.

Ever since Rose realized she was pregnant, they've been talking about getting a bigger apartment. Rafferty, who had traveled his entire adult life looking for a home, had dug in his heels: he was here now and happy about it, and he wasn't moving. Rose had put his hand on her still-flat belly and walked through his resistance as if it had been a patch of sunlight, and now they both take it for granted that a move is in the future, although Rafferty has been assuming that they'd just choose a different unit in this building, where they've lived together as a family. But as the doors slide open, he's made a decision. You don't bring a clean baby into a dirty building.

In keeping with the theme of the moment, the light in the hallway seems dimmer than usual, the carpeting a bit sticky under-foot. Before he puts his key into the lock, he presses an ear to the door, listening for a British accent or the upswelling of romantic music that usually signals tears and lace and candlelight, some man patting a woman's shoulder or saying something stiffly reas-suring and missing the emotional boat altogether. Eighty percent of British literature, he thinks, and ninety percent of British tele-vision, is based on how little men understand women.

He knocks twice, fast—his signal—waits a polite moment, and goes in.

Miaow looks up from the white hassock, a thin paperback book in her lap. She's got her back to the flat-screen, so it's off. She gives him the tiny eyebrow raise that's her current greeting. Minimal, nothing overboard: *You're here, now what?* He returns it to her and gets the grin he's fishing for, although it looks a bit like charity, since they both know that no one is as cool as a kid. Still, he'll take it. For a while there, a few months ago, Miaow had smiled so seldom that it was almost possible to forget she was Thai.

He says, "So what's happening?"

She closes the book, her finger marking her place. "Mr. Slope is going after Eleanor, who's clueless, like all nice girls. Mr. Slope is such a grease spot."

"Mr. *Slope?*" He locks the door. "You're watching *Barchester Towers?*"

Her lower lip pops out, and she gives him a little shrug, acknowledgment that he's surprised her by knowing the title. "Sure," she says. She reaches up to scratch her shoulder, and he sees that she's wearing black nail polish. Scratching furiously, she says, "Mr. Slope?"

He waits. "What about him?"

"In this show he's Alan Rickman—you know, the one who played Snape in the *Harry Potters*."

"From Snape to Slope. What a stretch."

"He's the best actor in anything he's in," she says, with some heat. "Always."

"Fine. You want something from the kitchen?"

"Whatever you think I'd like."

"Oh, *sure*," Rafferty says over his shoulder. "You bet. *Whatever I think you'd like*. That'll work out great. Is he better than Colin Firth?"

"Colin Firth belongs to Rose," Miaow says in her almost unaccented school English. "The one I'm standing in line for is Benedict Cumberbatch."

"If you've learned to pronounce it," Rafferty says, "you must be serious." He opens the door of the refrigerator to find that Rose has once again rearranged its shelves into her preferred supermarket-after-an-earthquake mode. It takes him a moment to locate a landmark. "Vanilla yogurt?"

"Yogurt tastes like something a cow couldn't keep down."

He secretly agrees, but Rose, after a lifetime spent, like many Thais, avoiding most dairy products, has recently developed a pregnancy-inspired mania for yogurt, and the refrigerator is jammed with it. "How about some grapes that are kind of flat on one side?"

"That sounds *fabulous*. You try one first."

He says, "No, thanks," and pushes aside some tall items so he can see behind them. "Where's your mother?"

"In the bathroom. She has to pee a lot lately."

"Well, if you had a little weight lifter sitting on your bladder, you'd have to pee a lot, too. Got some mango slices."

"Cool. And some of the yogurt, too, I guess. Maybe on top of the mango."

He pulls out Miaow's requests, fans the mango slices on a plate—quite artistically, he thinks—and then grabs a big Singha for himself. With the bottle chilling his hand, he administers a brief sobriety field test and then puts the Singha back. For a count of three or four, he stands irresolute and then reaches for a small bottle, pops the cap, gets a spoon and the carton of yogurt and Miaow's plate, and carries all four items, intentionally making it look harder than it is, back into the living room. "Slop your own yogurt," he says. "What are you reading?"

"The play. *Small Town*, you know?"

"Still? You're opening in a week. If you don't know it by now . . ."

She watches him make a production of juggling the food, but she doesn't try to help. "I've been ready forever. But then Dr. Srisai asked me what the play was about, and I said it was about a young girl who dies." It had amazed Miaow when she landed the role of Julie, the young female lead in the school play; she'd assumed it would go to the beautiful Siri Lindstrom, the school's most obvious future movie star. Rafferty knows the play because, when he was in high school, he'd played Ned, the boy Julie falls in love with. He worries vaguely about the boy playing opposite Miaow in this production, because Poke himself had spent much of his senior year tied in a series of adventurous *Kama Sutra* knots with *his* Julie.

Putting the dishes on the glass-topped table, he says, "I thought it was about a boy who has to survive the death of the girl he loves."

"See?" Miaow says. "We were both doing it. We were both looking at the whole play like it was all about our character." With her right hand, she flicks her index finger on the cover of the book with a solid *thwack*. "But it's not. It's about everybody. Dr. Srisai says we make the same mistake with life—we think it's just about us, but it's about all of us. We're all part of everything."

Rafferty says, "Mmmm," and pushes the plate with the mango slices closer to her.

"So I'm reading it like I would if I was going to play all the characters," she says. "And you know what it's really about? It's about how people don't know how many blessings they have, and how sad that is."

"Wow."

"I knew you'd go all gooey about it."

"Mango?" he says, and when she reaches for the plate, he stretches out the hand with the beer in it and touches its base to her fingers. "What's this?"

She turns the back of her hand to him and wiggles her fingers. "Nail polish."

"I got that far."

She drags a black-tipped finger through the yogurt and licks it. Makes a face that's mostly wrinkled nose. "It's to see how it makes me feel. Dr. Srisai has been talking about a kind of acting from the 1800s or sometime, and the idea was that a movement or a piece of clothing was supposed to bring up the emotion you need for . . . for whatever you're doing."

"The Delsarte method," Rafferty says. "Cross your hands at the wrists and raise them to your mouth, and it'll summon up horror. Okay, what's this?" He stands with his left leg behind him and extends his arm parallel to it, fingers extended and palm aimed downward, then turns his head in the opposite direction.

He's just beginning to feel silly when Miaow says, "Rejection?"

"I have talent after all," he says. "There was a pose, a physical attitude, for every emotion. Most classical actors worked that way until—I think—the late 1930s, when Stanislavski started to become influential outside Russia."

He gets a dubious look. "How do you know that?"

"I read a lot. So I guess Dr. Srisai is working out."

Rose glides in, glances at Rafferty's beer, and sticks her tongue out at him. No alcohol and no cigarettes for the past three months, with another six months stretching bleak and thorny before her, have given her some new issues. She pads past the two of them, barefoot, and heads for the kitchen, looking, to Rafferty, as wastefully beautiful as a sparkler in the sunlight.

"He's great," Miaow says. She drags a slice of mango through the yogurt and sniffs it. "He was in the theater for years and years in England. I mean, he actually *did* things. Mrs. Shin says he was in plays with *everybody*. Alan Rickman, even." Mrs. Shin, who teaches English, Korean, and drama at Miaow's international school, is the director of *Small Town* and also directed the former semester's production of Shakespeare's *The Tempest*, which Miaow stole in the role of Ariel. When his daughter was at an emotional low point and needed some distraction, Rafferty had promised to find her an acting coach. Mrs. Shin recommended Dr. Srisai.

"So does it work?" he says. "Do the black nails make you—"

"Not really." She looks at her fingernails again, her mouth pursed critically. The mango slice in her other hand drips yogurt onto the glass table. "I chose the wrong thing. It was supposed to make me feel sad about, you know, Julie dying, but it's sort of like my hair, when I dyed it red, remember? It's just a girl who wants attention. It reminds me of me."

"Of the way you used to be."

"It was *only* a few months ago." She waits, glancing up at him quickly and then giving her attention to wiping up the yogurt spill with her fingertip, knowing he has more to say and that it's about her.

"You're not the same person," he says. "You took something that hurt, and you *used* it." He doesn't want to get specific, doesn't want to push what he and Rose privately call "the Andrew button"— named in honor of her first real boyfriend, Andrew Nguyen, who is no longer in Bangkok—but Rafferty's been waiting for an opportunity to say these things, and this one is too good to pass up. "You didn't sit around and sulk or feel sorry for yourself. You took all that crap energy and you turned it into good energy and used it to do something creative. You're working on acting, you're working on yourself. You've changed."

"She has, hasn't she?" Rose says, coming in with a glass of water and a small dish of deflated grapes.

"Because I've been watching Maggie Smith," Miaow says. "She's so good it's sick."

Rose says, "Which one is Maggie Smith?" To Rafferty, who's sitting in the center of the couch, she says, "Scoot."

"The dowager countess," Miaow says. "The Countess of Grantham. Professor McGonagall."

"Oh, yes," Rose says. She touches her finger to the tip of her nose and tilts her head back haughtily. "*That* lady."

Moving over, Rafferty says to Rose, "*Scoot?*"

"You taught me that," Rose says. She sits and leans toward him, gives him wide, earnest eyes, and puts a hand on his arm. "The things you've taught me," she says, in very slow, dramatic English.

"Like this," Miaow says, pressing the back of her hand to her brow and closing her eyes halfway. "The *things* you've taught me."

"Oh, Peter," Rose says, *oh* coming out *euh*. "Euh, Peter, Peter, Peter."

"Peetah," Miaow supplies.

Rose says, "Euh, *Peetah.*"

"This is exactly what I was afraid of when I bought the television," Rafferty says. "How are your grapes?"

"Poor little things," Rose says, prodding one. "How was your night out?" She touches her index finger, cold from the grape, to the back of his neck.

"Girls galore, just lining up right and left, pushing each other out of the way to reach me. Took half a dozen cops to get me out safely."

"Next time don't take any money. They won't even see you."

Rose picks up a grape, examines it, and puts it down again. To Miaow she says, "Give me your spoon. You're not using it."

"I was at the Expat Bar again," he says. "It was kind of sad." They look at him without replying, so he goes on. "They're getting old, and some of them are dying, and, you know, they don't have anyone except each other, and they don't even like each other very much." Rose sits back, putting a little more distance between them, her eyes still on him. Miaow is watching Rose watch him. "And they're a million miles away from their real homes, their families, people who speak their language . . ."

"Whose fault is that?" Rose asks. She dips the back of Miaow's spoon into the yogurt and licks it.

"I'm not talking about *fault*."

"Why not?"

"Why *not*? I'm not judging them. I'm not qualified to judge them. Jesus, I might have *been* one of them."

"Never," Rose says, skimming the yogurt's surface with the back of the spoon again.

"Because I met you."

"A *lot* of men met me," Rose says, in Thai that sounds as if the words have been clipped apart with tin snips. "But you knew what you were looking for, not like those old fools." She sips her water and makes a face. "They're elders now. They should be earning respect and balancing their life's karma and setting an example, and they're still chasing their dicks around."

Miaow follows the conversation like someone watching a boxing match. They've rarely talked about this in front of her before, at least not so frankly.

"I know," he says. "And that's sad, don't you think?"

"No," Rose says. She plants the spoon deep in the yogurt and lets go of it. "Name one of them."

Rafferty pauses. "Why?"

"I want to see if I remember any of them. Just name one."

"This is silly."

"So I'm silly. One name."

"Okay. Bob Campeau."

Rose looks past him, riffling through the bar girl's mental Rolodex. Most of the women who work the bars—the successful ones anyway—can dredge up years later the name of a man they met for ten minutes. "Mouth like . . . ?" She draws an upside-down U in the air with the tip of the spoon and then mimes a comb-over, brushing her hand forward and sideways above her head. "Hair . . . ?"

"That's Bob."

Rose shakes her head. "He was old when I started working."

"Yeah, well, he's older now."

"And you like him?"

"I didn't say I *liked* him." Rafferty feels like a tourist who's accidentally violated some esoteric cultural taboo. "I'm not defending him. I'm not defending any of them. I just said—"

"Right, you feel sorry for them." She takes a handful of hair on the top of her head and yanks on it, something he has often seen her do when she wants to focus her thoughts. "Well, then, *Bob*, let's talk about Bob. At my first bar, when the girls on the stage saw him come in, nobody would look at him, because they didn't want him to point at them to come sit with him. But *somebody* had to sit with him, so a game of rock-paper-scissors would start at the front of the stage and go all the way around, and the girl who lost had to sit with your *friend* when she got off the stage."

"He's not my—"

"At my second bar, no one would sit with him at all unless it was a new girl who didn't know anything and another girl was mean enough to say he was okay." She's avoiding Poke's eyes now, and Miaow is watching her with her mouth partly open. "So the poor, dumb new girl would get Bob. Or some older or uglier girl who hadn't been bought out all month and needed to get the bar fine or she might get fired. And do you know why nobody wanted to go with him?"

Rafferty says, "He's not very pleasant, but—"

"Because Bob, your friend Bob, he thought he was Wonder Man. He liked the girls to *call* him Wonder Man. Miaow, put your fingers in your ears."

Miaow says, "Oh, come on."

"Do it loosely, then. Just satisfy me." Rose waits until Miaow's fingers are in the general vicinity of her ears, and then she says, "He had to do it three times. Because he was Wonder Man. Every time he took a girl. She couldn't leave until he'd had his three wet little pops."

Miaow's eyes have doubled in size.

"And then, after all that work, he paid her *small money*. She spent practically the whole night to get this old wreck up and keep him there. She lost two or three other customers, and he gave her eight hundred baht, a thousand baht. And if she argued, if any of them argued, he shouted at her. He slapped two or three of them."

Miaow says, one finger still in an ear, "How do you know?"

"The Bamboo Telegraph," Rose says, not looking at her. "That's what the *farang* used to call it. Everybody in the bars knows everything. A customer tells a girl he's going to go only with her, and early the next night he goes butterfly with a girl from another bar. By the time he walks into his sweetie's bar at midnight, it's like the two of them were on TV. Or a customer is a pincher or a biter or wants something disgusting. Every woman in every bar district knows who the good and bad customers are. Some girls try to keep the best ones to themselves, but sooner or later they brag to a friend, and the next time the guy comes in, the friend is sitting on his lap, and at that moment every girl in the bar makes a note. Bob, he's famous. He's been a mean, bad-hearted cheap Charlie for years and years."

"I don't like him any better than you do," Rafferty says, wondering how he got himself into this position. "But it's still sad. The whole *group* is sad. I mean, they sold their lives for something they probably outgrew or got sick of or can't even *do* any more, and now they're stuck here. And the ones who haven't outgrown it, they're the saddest of the bunch."

"You can have all of them," Rose says. "You can tie them together with a rope and push them into the river."

"Fine," Rafferty says. "My, my. This bottle of beer is certainly empty." He gets up and heads for the kitchen.

Miaow says to Rose, "When you were working there, you didn't like the customers?" Rafferty keeps going, but figuratively cocks an ear.

"It was *business*," Rose says. "Some of them were better than others. But most of them! I hated them."

"But you had to pretend you liked them, right?"

"What is it you want to know, Miaow?"

Rafferty stands in the kitchen with the open refrigerator pouring cold air onto his feet.

"You hated them, but you had to act like they were handsome or something. You were *acting*. Isn't that right?"

"I hadn't thought of it that way," Rose says. She raises her voice. "Poke, get your beer and close the refrigerator. I can see your reflection in the sliding glass door, just standing there with your big ears sticking out."

"A guy can't even eavesdrop in his own apartment." He picks up the big beer and opens it.

"Acting," Miaow repeats. "In front of a live audience."

"More or less," Rose says. It sounds like she'll elaborate, but she doesn't.

"Improvising," Miaow adds. She's not giving up.

"What does that mean?"

"No script. Making it up while you were doing it."

"Oh, no," Rose says. "There was always a script. *Poke* may think these men are interesting, but when they get into the bedroom, there are only four or five kinds of them, and there's a script for every one of them. Do we have to talk about this?"

"You were up close," Miaow says without a moment's hesitation. "It had to look real. Didn't it?"

"Not very." She's shaking her head. "They weren't really looking at me. They were looking at something they wanted, a brown girl who would do what they wanted her to, or the whore who would fall in love with them. See them as different from all the others, prove to them they *were* different from all the others, which they weren't. Or they were looking back at the money they spent to get me out of the bar, waiting to see what it had bought. Most of them forgot my name before I left."

Miaow says, "But still."

"*Yes*, Miaow, it was acting. All right? Some of them really needed to believe I thought they were . . . whatever they needed to be—romantic or sensitive or sexy or . . ." She looks up at Rafferty as he comes in. "Or like Bob. They needed to feel powerful."

"Dr. Srisai says that the only way to make the audience believe something is to believe it yourself. You have to . . . to feel, inside you, the way your character feels."

Rose nods slowly. Wherever she thought Miaow was going, this clearly isn't it.

"It's the opposite of that other way, the Del . . . Del—"

"Delsarte," Rafferty says, sitting beside his wife. "The Delsarte method. In that approach the gesture, the exterior, creates the emotion. You look like you're afraid and bang, you're afraid. In the approach Miaow's talking about now, it's the other way around. The emotion inside creates the exterior."

"That's exactly it," Miaow says.

Rose says, "I want some of that beer."

"Tough," Rafferty says. "Laurence Olivier—you know who he is, right?"

Miaow says, "Yes," and Rose shakes her head.

"Olivier, in a Shakespeare play, had a scene in which he learned that his character's daughter had been murdered. Every reviewer talked about the scream he let out when he heard the news. He said later that he made the scream by remembering when he was a boy and he touched the tip of his tongue to a frozen metal flagpole. It stuck, and he had to rip it away."

"Ohhhh." Miaow looks thrilled. Rose raises her eyebrows and ostentatiously licks the spoon.

"So," Miaow says to her, "when you had to make them think you liked them, what did you use? I mean, what did you think about? It had to be something powerful, didn't it?"

Rose gives her a long look and says, "I thought about being alone."

BY THE TIME they finally go to bed, Rose seems resigned to the idea that the patrons of the Expat Bar will continue to share the world with her and breathe her air until they're all dead and that Rafferty is entitled to his own feelings about them as long as he doesn't mention them by name. They share a slightly perfunctory and not very aerobic romantic workout to put the tension behind them and smooth the surface. Rose, as usual, is asleep and breathing deeply by the time Rafferty rolls over.

He's been reading Greek poetry lately, and a line from Sappho surfaces as he drifts: *He was handsome then and young, but eventually gray age overcame him, the husband of an immortal wife.* The men in the Expat Bar have grown old, but the women on the stages have remained immortally the same age, even if they weren't the same women. It is, he thinks, a cruel metric: losing your beauty and vitality among all that youth and seeing your faltering present-day self reflected in their uninterested eyes. Seeing the way they reserve themselves, even commercially, for younger men when, inside, you still feel the way you always did—youthful, vigorous, attractive. But, of course, Rose is right: these men signed up all those years ago for the full five-course meal, including the bitter dessert, and they got to this point without ever doing anything to push back from the table and use their lives to accomplish something useful.

Trying for the tenth or fifteenth time to get the lumps in his pillow arranged just right, he sees the eyes of that bar worker, finding him across the crowd, and hears Arthur Varney call him "the travel writer."

4

An Inactive Post

"VARNEY," RAFFERTY SAYS, dropping his fork and scowling at the slop on his plate. "V-A-R-N-E-Y."

"And *what* is it you want me to do?" Arthit says. The misunderstanding that divided the two friends during Rafferty's head-on collision with the lethal former soldier and freelance troublemaker Haskell Murphy has dissipated to the point where they can get exasperated with each other without giving offense.

"Hell, I don't know." Rafferty pushes his chair away from the table to put a safe distance between himself and the food. They're sweltering in a badly air-conditioned restaurant near the station to which Arthit has been assigned by a superior whose ass Arthit pulled out of the fire and who is uncomfortable with the memory of his near humiliation, which he's erasing by banishing the person who witnessed it. Arthit claims that his boss chose this station because it's surrounded by the worst restaurants in the city.

"At any given point in time," Arthit says, picking through his food as though he expects to find at least one insect, "the range of possible actions facing an individual, while quantifiable, can feel almost infinite. Rather than you sitting there while I try to eliminate the things you *don't* want me to do, why don't you narrow it down a little? So far you've communicated a name, 'Varney,' which you thoughtfully spelled out for me, and a vague feeling of unease." He looks up and gives Rafferty a smile that's more muscular than cheerful. "How, exactly, would you like me to abuse my powers to help you with whatever it is?"

Rafferty scrapes the surface of his tongue against his front teeth to scrub the grease off it, with no improvement. He swabs his sweating face with his shirtsleeve. "Since you put it that way, let's change the subject. The last thing I'd want to do is impose on a friend, and I *especially* wouldn't want to make work for a friend who has essentially been transferred to an inactive post—a concept that is uniquely Thai, by the way—and has probably fallen far behind with his report on how many paper clips, staples, and empty ballpoint pens his new police station has." His irritation, which he's barely bothered to mask, bubbles all the way to the surface. "Forgive me for thinking you might actually want something to do during your workday."

Arthit idly moves a mystery chunk from one side of his plate to the other and looks longingly out the window, as though he'd prefer to be outside, under the powder-gray sky. "You're in fine spirits today."

"It's nothing. Well, no, it's something, obviously. This guy Varney—have I mentioned Varney?—is bothering me. There's something wrong with him, with the way he appeared at the bar. And, of course, then there's life. At home, Rose has stomachaches all the time, and her gums are swollen, and she pees every twenty minutes, has a bowel movement every four days, and wants a cigarette every other second. We're all living on yogurt. Miaow is studying the Delsarte method of acting, and she goes around with one hand pressed to her brow, emoting with an English accent. This food is wretched. I'm hot. It's going to rain until the end of time. And, goddamn it, we have to move." He rocks his chair back until he's leaning against the wall, earning him an urgent *tsk-tsk-tsk* from the waitress, which he ignores. "I've been *happy* in that apartment. I've never been really happy anywhere else in my life, and now there are grape-jelly handprints in the elevator and the building is getting sticky and fly-paperish. It's haunted by decades-old cigarettes."

Arthit passes a broad, dark hand over his mouth, literally wiping the smile from his face. He looks out the window again, assessing the day, which has grown alarmingly dark. "She's in the second trimester?"

"Well, you know, no host of angels barged in to sing the Annunciation, or if they did, I missed it. Near as she can figure, it's the thirteenth or fourteenth week."

"Well, see this?" Arthit says. He holds up his left fist, clenched. "Your child is a little smaller than this." He wiggles the fist back and forth. "He or she has fingernails. Here's something nice. The tail has disappeared."

"The *tail*—"

"The embryo had a tail for a while. That's the main thing that whole 'ontology recapitulates phylogeny' idea came from, the old theory that an embryo, as it develops, goes through the evolutionary stages that humans went through: fish, reptile, and so forth. There was the tail, and there were supposed to be gill slits—"

Rafferty brings his chair back down and says, "Since when are you an expert on pregnancy?"

"Since you told me about Rose. I didn't know anything about it before, but Anna has a son, and she's walked me through Rose's pregnancy a week at a time."

"You guys *talk* about this?" Rafferty is surprised at how touched he is. "When we're not around?"

"You have no idea," Arthit says. "I've been shown charts and graphs. Ultrasounds on YouTube. You're the second person today to tell me that your wife is constipated."

Rafferty says, "Gosh."

Arthit reaches across the table and taps the back of Rafferty's hand with his index finger. "I've wanted to say this for months. Becoming . . . well, friends with Rose has meant a lot to Anna. Even though they're at different—excuse me—social levels."

"It's not just different," Rafferty says. "It's a gulf." Anna was born into an old, if not rich, family, while Rose is the daughter of an impoverished farmer in the northeast, and she moved even further down the scale when she became, for a year and a half, a sex worker.

"But they're reaching across it, to some extent," Arthit says, "and it's made a difference to Anna. The deafness sealed her off from people. Her husband's family took the child and threw her away. Now she feels like her world is bigger. There's Rose, you, the kids at Father Bill's. There's Treasure." He opens his mouth to say something, closes it again, and—it seems to Rafferty—says something else instead. "It's . . . it's . . . well, it's been good to see." He sniffs in an aggressively masculine fashion that no one could mistake for the sniffle of someone who feels a little misty. Picking up a fork, he spears something with it, puts it into his mouth, and then takes it out with his thumb and forefinger and puts it back on his plate. "This is *awful*," he says.

"So you can't help me out with Arthur Varney."

Arthit pushes his plate to the center of the table and drinks some creamy-looking iced coffee. "If I wanted to, which I don't, I could probably go to immigration and find out what his birthday is, where he comes from, and what occupation he lists on his passport. But it wouldn't be worth the effort it would take and the favors I'd owe. Especially since, as we both know, there are passports and there are passports."

"Why do countries have to be so official?" Rafferty says. "Why can't they be more like high schools or book clubs? You've got a question, you figure out who to ask, and you ask it."

Arthit flips his heavy watch on its too-big band so that it's faceup, and he looks at it. "You don't actually want me to answer that, do you? I mean, even *your* time is worth something."

Rafferty sits back and lets his shoulders slump. "I guess."

"And I don't understand what all the agitation is about. A guy you instinctively dislike knew your name and seems to have asked about you—a bit obscurely, if you want my opinion—when you weren't around. Maybe he really *is* interested in writers. Maybe he's secretly a fan. You must have some fans *somewhere*. And a bar girl looks at you on Patpong. Looking at men is their job."

"It was the *way* she looked at me."

"Maybe she was trying to figure out what you are. Thais like to know who we're dealing with, and you're kind of confusing. Thanks to your mother's Filipina blood, you could almost be Asian, but you could also be *farang*. It's like you're wearing two different uniforms—let's say police and army—at the same time. Everybody asks themselves, 'What the hell *is* he?'"

"I've gotten those stares for years," Rafferty says. "This was different." The light in the restaurant goes even dimmer, and he looks out the window to see a world submerged in a yellowish gloom. The passersby have picked up the pace, many of them glancing at the sky. "Listen, we'd better hurry or we're going to get soaked."

"I need to talk to you about something," Arthit says. He takes a breath and then blows it out and shakes his head. "But it'll wait."

"Until when? Is it important?"

"It is to me. But I don't want to discuss it with someone who's disappointed with the world. It's a topic that requires optimism. Go home, look at your wife and daughter for a while. Think about the baby. When you've stopped feeling sorry for yourself, call me, and we'll set a time."

"Why not now? Look, I'm all cheered up."

"Can't now," Arthit says, getting up. "I have to get back, but more urgently than that, I need the toilet. The guys at the station call this place the 'Magic Restaurant,' because you always seem to get rid of more than you eat."

"It wasn't *that* bad," Rafferty calls after him, although it had been. Seen from behind, Arthit has love handles, something Rafferty has never noticed before. His friend—the closest friend of his adult life—is putting on weight, bad restaurants notwithstanding. Anna, Rafferty guesses, must be feeding him pretty good.

He's eating, Rafferty thinks gratefully. And then he thinks, *He must be happy*.

5

The Closet of Wonders

HE DAWDLES OVER dinner, hoping Rose and Miaow will call an evening's time-out in the Brit Twit Marathon, but they're already anticipating a comeuppance for Mr. Slope, the hypocritical clergyman who blots the nostalgic Eden of Anthony Trollope's Barsetshire. Rafferty could spoil it for them, since he's read the novel twice, but what would he get out of it? They'd just hate him for a few minutes and then decide he's got it wrong and watch it anyway.

Still, he stretches out the chitchat, and for a while he thinks he's snagged Rose's interest as he tells her how Arthit and Anna are following her pregnancy. She's got her chin on her knuckles, her long fingers curved under her palm, her elbow propped next to the bowl of yogurt with orange slices in it, her enthusiasm for yogurt having been supplemented with a craving for oranges that borders on druggy. What he's saying even gets Miaow to look up from the spicy noodles with crisp pork and chilies he picked up for the two of them on the way home.

Miaow says, "*How* big?"

Rafferty says, "Make a fist," and when Miaow does, he says, "Say hello to your little sister."

"Or brother," Rose says.

Looking at her fist, Miaow says, "Hard to believe I was that little."

"Your body was," Rose says in Thai. "Your spirit was the same size it is now."

"You think?" Miaow says.

"Of course." Rose uses a big spoon to dredge an orange section from the bowl and lifts it to study its color. "Your spirit never changes. In one lifetime after another, your spirit is the light you're wrapped around."

"So," Rafferty says, at a loss. He feels unqualified to participate when they discuss spirit; his parents' generic, workday Protestantism didn't give him the vocabulary for it. "According to Arthit, that's what you're toting around this month. Something that big."

Rose says, with a glance in his direction that's so quick he's not even sure he saw it, "Could be two." She puts the orange into her mouth.

Rafferty says, "Excuse me?"

Rose shrugs, straight-faced, but he sees the flicker in her eyes. "It runs in my family," she says around the piece of orange, as though they've talked about it for weeks. "My father was a twin, and so was my mother's father."

Miaow, who not too long ago had hated the idea of even one new child coming into the family, says, "Cool."

Rafferty says, "This is nothing you thought was worth bringing up before?"

"It never seemed like the right time." She's still speaking Thai. "How are your noodles?"

"Who cares about my noodles? How can you tell? We should find out. What about, you know, whatever it is, where they take a picture of it with—"

"Ultrasound," Rose says. "I don't want one. I want to be surprised." She picks up her napkin and folds it in half, then passes the crease between her fingernails to sharpen it. In English she says, "Don't you *want* two?"

"Well," Rafferty says, "I mean, sure, two sounds fine, I mean, it sounds like . . ."

Rose uses the folded napkin to blot her lips, although she's not wearing lipstick. "Like?"

"Like a lot of babies," Rafferty says. He holds up a hand. "Wait. Just wait. You can't just tell a guy that he's suddenly got armfuls of children when—"

"There are triplets on my mother's side," Rose says.

Miaow laughs a mouthful of noodles onto her plate.

"*Right,*" Rafferty says. "Why not quints? Why not nine? We could have a baseball team."

"The twins aren't a joke," Rose says. "I might have twins."

"Well," Rafferty says.

Now they're both looking at him.

"Sounds exciting," he says. "Really. Honest."

Rose is watching him closely, as though, after all these years, Mr. Hyde is finally beginning to emerge. "You don't *want* two babies, do you?"

"Sure I do," Rafferty says. "I just thought we'd have them one at a time, like other people."

"Will they be identical?" Miaow asks. "You know, like a set?"

Rose says, "My mother's father looks just like his brother."

"My, my, my," Rafferty says. "Isn't life *interesting?*"

Miaow snickers in a way she knows he finds irritating.

Rose has lowered her eyes, closing him out, as she fishes in the bowl for another bit of orange. "Are you going back to that bar tonight?"

Even *this* is safer ground. "Depends. Are you going to watch *Barchester Towers?*"

"Sure," Miaow says.

Rose says, "I like the bad priest."

Rafferty says, "Then I guess I'll go hang with my posse."

"It was inevitable," Varney is saying, waving the hand with the beer in it, "that people back then would have created the Delsarte method, or something like it." He's picked up a shred of conversation Rafferty fumbled, and he seems dead set on carrying it all the way to the end zone. "It's acting *pre*-psychology. Pre-Freud, pre-Jung. It was the age of phrenology, when a head doctor analyzed character by the bumps on the outside of the skull. The *outside*."

"Outside," Hofstedler responds politely, but the glance he gives Rafferty isn't a grateful one. The men in here can relate to the hot countries; nineteenth-century acting isn't even on their horizon.

Thanks to the downpour, the bar is almost empty—no guy whose name might be Ron, no Growing Younger Man, none of the occasionals: just Rafferty, Campeau, Hofstedler, Varney, and Toots. The rain is hammering down outside, the night-market vendors perched on their molded plastic chairs beneath the blue tarp, blowing smoke into the rain and peering down the deserted street.

Varney says, "People knew *how* their friends and enemies behaved, but not *why*, right? No complexes, no subconscious, no past trauma. People were defined from the outside, by their roles in life: noble, peasant, servant, merchant, mother, soldier. You acted on a stage by doing an imitation. The very word 'act' suggests imitation, not insight. Put the character on like a costume. The Friar's robes. Lear's crown. The villain's mustache," he says, tugging on one end of his own. "If you're a boy in Shakespeare's company, Juliet's gown."

Rafferty says to Hofstedler, not making much of an effort to lower his voice, "How's Wallace?"

"Not good," Hofstedler says, sotto voce, politely keeping his eyes on Varney. "Forgets where he lives, yes? Talks always about some girl from sixty years ago. Name is Jah. Jah, Jah, Jah."

Varney says, "Sorry?"

"I was agreeing only," Hofstedler explains. "I say, '*Ja, ja.*'"

"'Cause, I mean, I'd hate to bore you." Varney shows his big yellow teeth in a smile that demonstrates how much he'd hate to bore them.

"*Nein,*" Hofstedler says. He gets more German when someone opposes him. "Acting from two hundred years ago, very interesting. Yes, something I wonder about frequently."

The door opens, letting in the rattle of rain and a tiny climate of hot, wet air, and everyone in the bar turns to see a small boy drip his way in. He's eight or nine, hunger thin, wearing a sopping, too-big T-shirt that makes his neck look even frailer than it is. His amateur buzz cut, possibly self-inflicted, is all different lengths and sparkles with drops of water. He gives the room a quick glance, goes straight to Rafferty, and lifts himself on tiptoe to slap something down on the bar. A second later the door closes behind him.

"Your birthday?" Campeau says.

"It's not *just* from two hundred years ago," Varney says, as though there's been no interruption. He's responding to Hofstedler, but his eyes are on Poke. "It was the way the Greeks acted their plays. It's the style you see in silent movies. It's Noh, it's Kabuki, it's the style of temple dance, all over Asia."

Rafferty tries to open the envelope in the conventional way, peeling back the flap, but the paper is too cheap, and the whole thing pulls apart in his hands. He has to worry it away from the folded sheet, thicker and heavier, inside.

"Nineteenth-century ballet, opera—it's all Delsarte," Varney says, apparently armed with a month's worth of material. "Classical painting and sculpture. The *Pietà*. The pose is everything."

Rafferty recognizes the heavy piece of paper as coated stock, meaning it has a slightly shiny layer of clay on one side of it, which allows colors to be printed brilliantly but turns into a kind of stickum when it gets wet. While it's still folded, Rafferty can see that whatever is written on the other side is in black and seems to be a single word in reasonably large type. Varney's voice drones on, something about the vocabulary of emotion and how so many of the expressions we still use—"stiff with fear" is the one Rafferty catches—are external descriptions of internal processes.

He pries the paper open, a bit at a time, until he's looking at the type. It says:

$3,840,000

A sort of high-blood-pressure hiss fills his ears, drowning out both Varney's voice and some quarrelsome interjection from Campeau, who's been acting increasingly fed up. The number is a sum Rafferty has thought about a hundred, two hundred times since the night a house belonging to a man named Haskell Murphy caught fire and blew up. A house that had contained plastic explosives, three-dimensional models of well-planned atrocities to advance some obscure political agenda, a brutally abused child, and six hard-sided military briefcases, battlefield rated and practically indestructible, each stuffed full of tightly banded hundred-dollar bills. The cases had been stacked tidily on the floor of a closet, next to a cache of explosives wrapped in some kind of rubberized sheet.

The number on the sheet of paper is Rafferty's estimate of the total in the six cases, based on the one briefcase he'd taken with him, which had contained exactly $640,000.

The cases had all been packed identically, the band around each stack of hundreds helpfully announcing the total as $10,000. He's found himself doing this multiplication in the middle of the night, while making coffee, walking on a sidewalk, having a conversation. It always comes out the same.

He sits back from the bar, looking not at the number but the paper. The fold is precise, letter style, creating equal thirds. The numbers are centered on the page.

The *numbers*—

Campeau says to Varney, "Jesus, you got a lot of crap in your head." It doesn't sound like a compliment.

"Guilty," Varney says cheerfully. "It's a curse, I suppose."

"Buncha useless fucking knickknacks," Campeau grumbles.

—the numbers are very black. They have the resolute unambiguity of a computer printout, which is what they are. They read three million, eight hundred and forty thousand dollars, and nothing else. Three million, eight—

Hofstedler says, "You are saying what, Poke?"

"Sorry," Poke says. "Nothing." He folds the paper, watching his hands shake and trying to still them.

Varney is saying, " . . . like the old cabinet of curiosities, just a room full of stuff, not categorized, not classified, something feathery here, something shiny there—"

"The *Kunstkammer*," Hofstedler offers. "The closet of wonders. The paw of a monkey, a map of hell, a footprint from a million years ago, books, clockworks, paintings, the twisted horn of a narwhal—"

"That's it," Varney is saying. "The museum before there were museums. Odds and ends, this and that. Facts, ideas, fantasies. Rocks and bottles."

Rafferty is half listening and half back in that night of flood and death and flames, the battered girl Treasure running into Murphy's burning house, reflected upside down in the black water until the moment it breathed in for the last time and blew, pieces thrown a hundred feet into the air, fire raining down around him.

When he had finally clawed his way out of there that night, away from the heat and smoke, he had that one briefcase in the trunk of his car. The money, most of it, is still hidden in a hundred places in the apartment he shares with Rose and Miaow. He had thought it was over.

He had been wrong.

"Having a bag full of facts," Campeau says. His voice sounds like the scratch of a striking match. "What's it mean? It ain't the same as wisdom."

"No, *Bob*, it's not the same," Varney says. "Facts are just things—any kind of thing: could be a handful of cards, a couple pieces of metal, a wad of cotton, some black powder."

There's something in Varney's voice, the edge of something just barely concealed, a razor beneath a sheet of paper, and Rafferty glances up, his hands folded on top of the wet envelope, to find the man's bright blue eyes on him. The moment Rafferty looks at him, Varney's gaze skitters away, fast as a drop of water sizzling across a hot pan.

It suddenly seems to Rafferty that the paper with the numbers on it warms beneath his hands. He's certain that Varney knows what's written there.

"But *wisdom*, Bob," Varney says, "at least in my opinion, wisdom is knowing how to *take* those things, the cards or the metal and the powder and the cotton, and put them together in a way that turns them into something. A royal flush, for example." He looks at Rafferty again, holds his gaze for a moment, and then turns back to Campeau and says, "Or a bullet."

Rafferty swivels his stool to the left until he's facing Varney directly. The stool squeals, and he finds Varney regarding him with what seems to be a mixture of curiosity and amusement.

Varney says, "Get a letter?"

Rafferty slips the wet paper into the pocket of his T-shirt. Something is squeezing his chest, and he recognizes it as a blend of fury and fear. He says, "Do you ever shut up?"

"Have I gone on too long?" Varney's tone is mild, but the amusement in his face has hardened into an expression that shouldn't be caught in freeze-frame. And, Rafferty thinks, Varney knows it and shows it to him anyway.

"This is my fourth night here since you showed up," Rafferty says, the anger putting a steel rod between his shoulders, stiffening his neck, "and the only thing I've heard is your voice."

Hofstedler says, "Poke," and puts a hand on Poke's arm.

"I know," Varney says, cocking his head slightly to one side as though he's curious. "It's a terrible trait. I was alone too much as a child."

"And I can see why," Poke says. Without taking his eyes off Varney's, he says, "Check, please, Toots."

"Early," Toots says. "They still looking TeeWee."

"There are worse things than English actors," Rafferty says.

"Kid must have brought you bad news, huh?" Varney says. He's still smiling.

Campeau says, "You know what, sonny? I heard enough, too."

"I also would like to talk sometimes," Hofstedler says deferentially.

"Well, *fine*, Leon," Varney says. There are tight red highlights at his cheekbones. "We're all eager to hear it. Go right ahead." He rests an elbow on the bar, puts his chin in his hand, and waits. Drums his fingers, once. No one says anything, and Toots puts a check in front of Rafferty.

"Need a topic?" Varney asks Hofstedler. "Wagner, maybe? Nietzsche? Why Shakespeare is better in German? Who was it who translated him again?"

Hofstedler says, "Goethe." The back of his neck is turning a dark cherry red.

"*Much* better in German, with Goethe and all," Varney says. "The Bauhaus school? Caspar David Friedrich? Eugenics? Nerve gas? Aryan bloodlines? Innovative operations for changing eye color?"

"This is enough," Hofstedler says.

"Guess it is." Varney gets up. He reaches over and turns his glass on its side, flooding the bar with beer.

Campeau gets off his stool.

"Come on, Gramps," Varney says. He takes a step back. "Tote that old bag of bones over here."

"I'm buying your drinks," Rafferty says. "Get out of here."

"Too bad," Varney says. "I was just beginning to work the room." His eyes, fixed on Poke's, are bright with something that might be glee.

The door opens, letting in a gust of wind, bearing the ghosts of many cigarettes, and Pinky Holland puts his head in. He says, "Whoops," and starts to back out.

"Come on in, Pinky," Rafferty says. "Mr. Mustache here is just leaving."

"Naw, that's okay," Pinky says. "Just . . . you know, popping in. Maybe later." The door rattles when he closes it.

"Thanks for the drinks," Varney says. He puts on a shiny black slicker, very deliberately, taking his time. "Quite a mood change there. You ever think about medication?" He takes a step in Poke's direction.

"You're big," Rafferty says, stepping toward him. "But I fight dirty."

"Pitty-pat, pitty-pat," Varney says, tapping his chest with a flat hand. "Guess we'll have a chance to find out sooner or later, won't we?" He pushes his stool over, and it hits the floor with a bang that sends Toots eight inches into the air. "Be seeing you."

He walks the length of the bar, and Campeau sidles around behind his own stool.

Just before Varney reaches the door, Rafferty says, "Why were you looking for me?"

"Looking for you?" Varney says without turning back. "Why the fuck would I look for you?"

He leaves the door wide open, and Rafferty gets up and closes it. When he turns back to the bar, everyone is staring at him. He says, "He *has* been looking for me, and he's had someone watching me. It's a bar girl, and I need to find her. Short, wide face, late twenties, long, loopy spiral curls. She's got a . . . a birthmark or something, above her mouth. Left side, I think." No one responds, and he adds, "I think this might be important."

Campeau says, "No one like that comes to mind right off the bat."

"Thought you knew everyone."

"Slowing down," Campeau says, looking embarrassed. "Losing the old moxie."

"Anybody?" Rafferty says to the bar at large. "Come on, this isn't a very long street."

Hofstedler says, "Tomorrow. Just before the bars open." He looks around the bar and swallows, someone about to reveal a secret. "Meet me here and we talk to my ladyboys."

6

Not the Shophouse

WALLACE PALMER AWAKES to darkness, the only light a somewhat-less-dim rectangle that indicates the window. He peers at it and shakes his head to clear the fog; the window is on the wrong side of the room. Is he sleeping with his head at the foot of the bed? His sleep these days is thinner than the worn sheet that covers him, laundered almost out of existence. He couldn't have moved around that much without waking up. Or could he?

He can't remember. Has he done this before? He knows that the window should be over—

Oh. Not the shophouse. The new apartment. The *new* new apartment. The one he still can't navigate in the dark without bumping into things. Not the place above the shop where he lived for all those years, his first home in Bangkok when he came back after the war, fifty-some years ago: the two rooms with the wooden shutters over the windows that you could prop open. Concrete walls two feet thick, cool wooden floors, the smell of cooking from downstairs. In the shophouse he could put his hand on anything no matter how dark it was, since no one but he ever moved anything. Living there alone while he ransacked Bangkok for Jah. Because he'd destroyed things with Jah.

He hears rain, spattering against the tin housing of the air conditioner.

He sits up with a soft grunt, swings his long legs over the edge of the hard little bed, and puts his feet on the floor. *Carpet*. Not the shophouse, then, the apartment. The second apartment, or maybe the third. What had happened to the shophouse*!*

Now that he knows which room he's in, which year he's in, his hand can find—after a couple of timid sweeps—the surprisingly heavy little brass lamp on the table beside the bed. He spiders around its base with his fingers to find the chain and tugs it. The bulb puts out just enough piss-yellow light to show him a low-ceilinged, heavily shadowed room, with a wide recessed closet yawning open in one corner, one of its sliding doors derailed and leaning at a seasick angle against the wall. His clothes, what remain of them, hang any old way, not so much organized as abandoned. The air conditioner sits idly in the window with the rain banging off it. He decided long ago to live with the heat. After all, he'd *chosen* the heat. The bathroom is over there, through that grimy door. He reminds himself again to take a sponge to the door.

One of these days.

With his sight restored, the world tilts slightly and snaps into place with an almost audible click. Time reintroduces itself, as it has a way of doing lately. The shophouse had been demolished years ago, along with the whole neighborhood, a cluster of two- and three-story structures of inky, mildewed concrete webbed with thick electrical wires, the whole thing built on either side of a narrow *soi* paved over one of Bangkok's lost canals. A genuine *neighborhood*, the remnants of one of the small villages Bangkok had devoured, a place where he was the only *farang* among people who'd known one another for years. They'd raised one another's children, each woman automatically picking up and soothing the nearest crying child. He'd spent months looking out the window and trying to pair the kids with their biological mothers. People who took the time to stop and talk when they met, whose grandparents had been friends, who shared old jokes, who had accepted him with smiles.

All gone now, scattered apart and blown through the big city.

Living now among strangers. All the buildings lost, even the spirit houses, knocked into dust and chunks of cement.

You don't see many spirit houses in the city now, he realizes, except for the big commercial ones with all the gilt paint. When Wallace thinks of a spirit house, he thinks of a small wooden structure on a platform, a miniature old Thai-style village house, the paint long bleached away by the sun and the wood a dry, pallid ash-gray . . .

How *noisy* it had been when they destroyed the place, the machines growling at the buildings like big dogs before taking bites of them, the residents staring dolefully from across the *soi*, like attendees at a cremation. The funeral of an entire village, all its smiles and stories wadded up and tossed away to make room for something *useful*.

He gets up slowly, straightening carefully through the sudden grab of pain in his lower back, always there and always a surprise, and launches himself toward the bathroom, feeling a slight fizziness in his head. He stops abruptly, trying to remember where he left his shoes. For the last ten years or so, after one too many panicky, flailing, full-length falls over one of his own shoes in the dark, he's made a point of creating a clear path between himself and the bathroom.

But wait. He's got enough light to see. This is not, is not, is *not* the shophouse.

And what time is it? His wrist is bare. It's been weeks, and maybe a lot longer (maybe *years?*), since he could find the heavy steel Rolex his father had given him to take to 'Nam. He promised his parents he'd keep it on California time so he'd be with them whenever he looked at it, but that hadn't lasted. Nothing had lasted. Not even the Rolex. When he'd lost track of it, whenever that had been, he'd bought a counterfeit at a street market, and as he turns on the bathroom light, the watch gleams fraudulently at him from the edge of the sink and informs him it's 11:21 P.M. So he's slept through the day's heat and dust, and outside, the Bangkok he loves best is once again camouflaging the city's dirt and dreariness behind the bright nightly tangle of neon and steam.

The bathroom mirror shows him the grandfather or great-grandfather of Wallace, never Wally, Palmer, shockingly old. In place of his thicket of bright, curly hair, a few long, iron-gray strands, inexplicably straight, paste themselves across his scalp, which is mottled like a faded map of countries no one wants to visit. He's played a few times with the strands, trying to comb them lower on his forehead to simulate a real hairline, but the last time he'd done it, Ernie's phrase, "turban renewal," flashed through his mind, and he'd laughed and abandoned the effort.

Wallace says, "Shit." He looks away from the mirror, avoiding the sight of his neck or the slope of his once-broad shoulders, and picks up his toothbrush. Sees the yellowness of his nails, the spots on the backs of his hands.

Someone knocks on the door in the living room.

"It's always something," Wallace says aloud, although he's aware that lately it hasn't been. He leans heavily against the sink, closes his eyes, and waits for whoever it is to go away, but then there's a triplet of knocks, louder this time, and a basso profundo voice calling, "Wallace? You are in there, Wallace?"

Leon, Wallace thinks with a minor surge of despair. Leon Hofstedler, the most boring man in Bangkok, which is saying a lot. So boring, Leon's friend Ernie had once said, that if you'd just come out of a cave where you'd spent a year alone and saw Leon, you'd turn around and go back into the cave. What happened to Ernie? Ernie always made him laugh. He again sees Ernie's grin, white in the dark face, the gap between his teeth—

The knocks sound once more, loud as kicks. "Wallace? I need to hear you talking. Everybody in the bar asks is Wallace okay. Even *Poke* says hello to you."

Leon isn't going away. Leon has nothing better to do with his life than to stand in that hallway, kicking Wallace's crappy door and singing German opera for everybody in the building to hear. A fucking menace. The German Peril.

The idea of Leon being dangerous makes Wallace laugh as he heads toward the living room. Wallace lived with *dangerous* day and night for three tours of steaming, blood-stinking duty. The only thing Leon had ever killed was time. He'd like to say that to Ernie, Wallace thinks. Ernie always looks surprised before he laughs, as though it startles him that other people are funny.

"Coming, Ernie," Wallace calls. He looks down at himself and is reassured to see that he'd gone to sleep fully dressed.

"*Ernie?*" Hofstedler bellows though the door. "This is not Ernie. Ernie—*mein Gott*, Ernie is a thousand years dead. You should not be alone so much."

"I'm not alone," Wallace says, undoing the door's assortment of locks—a joke, given that the door itself is made of soda cracker. "You're here." He opens the door on the mountain that is Leon Hofstedler.

Hofstedler, his magisterial bulk draped in one of his many-pocketed safari shirts, narrows his eyes as if trying to sight Wallace through a fog. He says, "Ernie?"

"Been thinking about him," Wallace says.

Hofstedler continues to study Wallace's face. After a moment he gives a grudging grunt. "I will tell them you look okay."

"Of course I'm okay," Wallace says around the sudden bloom of irritation in his chest. "Why wouldn't I be okay?"

Hofstedler shrugs. "They worry, you not coming, night after night. You know, thinking maybe . . ." Whatever they're thinking, it's too dire for Hofstedler to voice it. "Tonight," he says, "tonight we almost had a fight. In the bar. You remember this man Varney?"

"Sure," Wallace says, wishing he could shut the door. "Varney."

"You would have liked it." Hofstedler is looking past Wallace, into the apartment. "Talks, the man talks all the time, and tonight Poke—do you remember Poke?"

"Leon," Wallace says, and it's close to a threat.

"So," Hofstedler, says, lifting placating hands, "Poke, he had enough, and he asked the man, Varney, if he ever shuts up. And I said that I *also* would like to talk once in—"

"Sounds great," Wallace says. "I'm a little busy."

"Yes?" Hofstedler sticks his head around the door as though to make sure no one is standing behind it. "You are alone?"

"Writing my memoirs. Before I forget them. Funny, huh, Ernie?"

"Ernie is—" Hofstedler shakes his head. "Tomorrow, eight o'clock, I will come for you. Take you to the bar. Will you remember?"

"I've got a memory like a . . . like a . . ." He scratches his head shocked, as always, at the bare skin beneath his fingertip—but he manages a laugh. "That's a joke, Leon." He puts some weight on the door, forcing Hofstedler back. "You tell them I'm fine and say hello for me, 'kay?"

"And tomorrow," Leon says. "Eight. Do not forget."

"Yeah, yeah, tomorrow." He pushes the door closed on Hofstedler, completing in his mind the sentence . . . *whatever is supposed to happen tomorrow*. Through the door he hears Hofstedler sigh and then the man's heavy tread drawing squeaks from the cheap plywood flooring.

A shower. That's what he needs, a shower and some clean clothes. *Jah*, it's Jah he wants to see, he realizes with a jolt of electricity. Whip-thin, tousle-haired Jah, who went with him to Don Mueang Airport the first time he flew back to 'Nam and cried inconsolably at the departure gate. And was there, jumping up and down like a teenager, when he came back. Running at him from thirty yards away and leaping on him, her legs twined around his waist, as all the other guys stared.

Jah.

In 'Nam the women and children had been terrified of him, afraid to meet his eyes, and he understood why. His very idea of who he was had been shattered, that easy, cheerful California boy broken into pieces one death at a time and reassembled wrong. Six months in country, his feet rotting with the damp, whole colonies of exotic parasites claiming his intestines, his soul knotted with death. The girls in the villages they defended, sometimes by burning them, looked at Wallace and the others in his platoon with the terror and revulsion the Americans occasionally earned: Twice, men Wallace knew well had turned bestial on the floor of some thatched shack, impatiently taking turns on a girl barely out of childhood. Leaving behind on the packed earth the sobbing remnant of a human being.

And then his first R&R furlough. After a copter out and an hour or two in a plane, he was here, in the city of joy. Smiles everywhere, food everywhere, everything cheap and easy, and girls who *loved* him, or at least seemed to. Girls who looked at him and saw a young, handsome man, not a beast. Girls like nutmeg, girls like cinnamon, girls who blended into a single smile, a single "No problem" as he took them, in threes and fours at first, like a starving man sweeping a whole tableful of food toward himself, feeling like some fool out of *Playboy* but finding, in the crowded beds, a kind of life that flowed into him and filled him back up. And then one night, the bed too full to give him room to turn over, he got out and slept on the floor, waking in the morning to find that he'd been layered over with towels from the bathroom and that sleeping next to him on the carpet, curled into a ball against the chill of the air conditioner and uncovered except for a hip-length cascade of tangled hair, was a slender dark-skinned girl. When he smoothed a towel over her, she opened her eyes and smiled at him as though he were the God of Morning, and Wallace, for the first time since leaving 'Nam, felt his heart unlock. Her name was Jah, and after that it was Jah, just Jah, always Jah. Staying with her for days on end. Falling asleep beside her on clean sheets in a cool room. Warm breath on his chest. Smooth cheek against his. Crossing the river once in a long-tail boat to sleep in a musty-smelling, lantern-lighted wooden shack, not a vertical wall anywhere and overhead the dry scrabble of rats as she breathed her way into sleep. He was safe. Writing her letters from 'Nam, letters he never sent. She couldn't read a word of English.

But she could read him.

Hansum man, Jah called him. *Teerak*, Jah called him, Thai for "sweetheart." *Wallet*, Jah called him, and he'd thought it was a joke about his money until he realized that Thais can't pronounce a sibilant at the end of a word, and she was trying to say his name. He took to calling himself Wallet, appreciating its appropriateness even if Jah didn't understand it.

The airport's name nags at him. *Don Mueang? Do military flights come through Don Mueang?* It sounds wrong, but he shrugs it off, along with his shirt and trousers, and pads toward the shower. *The women may be professionals*, he thinks, *but they're still Thai, and Thais are clean. It shows respect when you come to them fresh from the shower.*

He steps into the shower still wearing the cheap watch and sees it just as the stream of water hits it. In seconds he's out of the tiny stall, scrubbing at the watch with a graying towel, holding it up to see whether the second hand is still jerking forward in the one-second increments that mark the watch as a fake. He dries it a final time, puts it to his ear, and slips it back on his wet wrist, then sees what he's done and yanks it off again to pat the skin dry, and a few minutes later he's back on the bed, drying his shoulders and toweling away the drops of water that hit the top of his head. He checks the watch again, sees the second hand lurching from silver numeral to silver numeral, and asks himself, *Weren't these luminous?* Asks himself, *Wasn't "Rolex" written in gold?* What watch is this? How many of these has he bought since he lost the Rolex?

He leans back against the pillows, sees in his mind's eye the face, the hair, the timeworn, destroyed Wallace he'd seen in the mirror. *Jah*, he thinks. *She'd be seventy by now.* A kind of deep-sea pressure settles on him, squeezing out a long sigh. He hears Jah's laugh, as though she were in the living room.

The light in the living room is on. Wallace thinks, *Leon. Leon was here, wasn't he?* And then he pulls the thin blanket over himself and closes his eyes, and he's asleep.

7

A Rat on a Sharp Stick

"HE'S AMERICAN," RAFFERTY says. "No regional accent, could be from anywhere."

"We get about three-quarters of a million Americans every year," Arthit says, rubbing his eyes. "And we've got another twenty, thirty thousand living here." He's wearing an industrial-gray T-shirt and a pair of khaki shorts, baring short, hairy legs. It's Saturday, and he'd obviously planned to sleep in, although Anna has already left for the homeless-children's shelter. On Saturday she teaches her special class of nonhearing children. On the weekdays they're mixed in with those who can hear. Coffee is dripping in the kitchen, but Rafferty, who was up most of the night— stewing, as his mother would have said, in his own juices—has already downed a pot and a half and is feeling the persuasive, strumming adrenaline of anxiety.

Rafferty says, "Thank you for the statistics, but he's not like most of the tourists and expats. He stands out. He's after the money, Arthit, Murphy's money. He tracked me down in that bar somehow and set the whole thing up. He was in the bar when I arrived last night, talking, of course. About ten minutes after I came in, he said he forgot something. So he goes back outside for a minute or two, just long enough to make a phone call or give an instruction. When he comes back, he's not carrying anything I can see, so maybe he didn't forget anything after all. Half an hour later, the kid barges in and gives me this." He taps the piece of paper on the table, now stiff and dry. "He was *watching* me as I read it. He wanted to see my reaction."

"And how did you react?"

"I don't know. I have no idea. It was like I'd gotten caught between a pair of cymbals, and all I could do was wait for the ringing in my ears to stop."

"I'm not going to minimize any of this," Arthit says. "But who could he be?" They're in the living room, wan morning light filtering through the windows, the sky outside flashing a few optimistic, misleading patches of blue like fake watches gleaming inside a con man's coat. The house is silent and immaculate but wrong to Rafferty's eyes—Anna's pictures are on the walls, and her small ornaments and prizes litter the tables, spaces that had been decorated with the things that Noi, Arthit's wife, dead now for a year and a half, had kept there. Still, it's immeasurably better than it had been in the months following Noi's death, when Arthit had closed the door on the world so he could drink uninterrupted, his loneliness a beacon he defied anyone to acknowledge. "Who would know Murphy had all that money?" Arthit interrupts himself with a yawn. "Who'd know how much it was? Most important, who'd know you had anything to do with him?"

"Someone exactly like Varney," Rafferty says. "Someone who was involved with Murphy. He's the same kind of man Murphy was. There's nothing soft in him anywhere. You should have seen his face when he lit into poor old Leon, practically calling him a Nazi. Tormenting him like a rat on a sharp stick. You know as well as I do that Murphy had to have a network, probably a loose group of sociopaths he could call on when he needed them. He'd survived as a fixer and a strong-arm man for the US government and whoever else would pay him, all over Southeast Asia ever since the Vietnam War ended. My guess is that Varney was closer to him than most of them, close enough to know about the money, maybe even working with Murphy on whatever operation the money was for—that bombing operation down in the south, for example. Not just a hired hand. Closer than that."

"If that's the kind of guy he is, you know what it means." Arthit leans forward, stretching his lower back, his palms on his thighs, seesawing his shoulders up and down. "He could be connected, he could be official or semi-official. Murphy was working with the Yanks, and he had the private phone numbers for our internal spook corps. Major Shen, for example."

Rafferty says, "He doesn't feel military. Murphy was ex-military, using his army connections and experience to work as a fixer. Frighten some farmers off their land, arrange to break some heads if a bunch of peasants protest the fact that they're being poisoned by a gold mine. He probably knew dozens of thugs, guys with skills. Ex-CIA, ex-whatever. They're all over the place. As Varney would say, they're drawn to the hot countries."

"But too young to have been with Murphy in Vietnam," Arthit says.

"That's what I mean. Not military. Maybe a contractor who worked in Kuwait, Iraq, Afghanistan—some war of the week— through one of those fake soldier outfits, Axe or Whisker or whatever they're called. But you know, Arthit, the fact that he wasn't actually military isn't very comforting. Some of these guys are worse. I've got a pregnant wife and a daughter, and these aren't the kinds of people I want coming through my door."

"You don't know any of this for sure," Arthit says.

"I do." Rafferty puts his fingertips on the note and slides it back and forth on the table. "I know *with certainty* that Varney sent that kid in with that note. He knows I've got the money, Arthit. And he wants it."

"I'll do what I can," Arthit says, "but it's not much." He grabs the edge of the table and pulls himself to his feet. "Coffee?"

"Oh, hell, why not?" Rafferty says, getting up. "Black, okay?" He follows his friend through the dining room. When Noi was alive, the table had always been lush with flowers, but Anna doesn't have Noi's magical sway over plants, and now the center-piece is a pair of antique Thai fish traps, weathered, elongated baskets with reeds pointing inward around the opening so the fish can swim in but not out again. They're from the largest and poorest region of the country—Isaan, in the northeast, where Rose lived with her family until she ran to Bangkok to avoid her father's plan to sell her into the sex trade.

"I can only get so much information from immigration," Arthit says. He opens a cupboard, stares into it, closes it, opens another one, and takes down two thick mugs. "Noi kept them over there," he says, nodding at the cabinet he'd opened first, "and I *always* look there." He shakes his head. "Still getting used to things," he says. "Anna also puts the utensils in a different drawer from the one I'm used to." He opens a drawer and pulls out a splotchy, wooden-handled knife that has a blade about twelve inches long and two inches wide, with no point but a gleaming edge. "This was Noi's favorite knife," he says. "Hand-forged Japanese sword-quality steel, about three hundred US. So sharp you could use it as a straight razor."

"It's not exactly a dazzler," Poke says. "Looks like it was brought up from a shipwreck."

"It's not stainless. Stainless chips when it gets thin, so it can't take an edge like this. Look." He slides the knife edge down his forearm, and when he shows it to Poke, it's got little hairs on it. "Anna's thrown it away three times." He wipes it carefully on his shirt and puts it back into the drawer. "Getting used to things," he says again.

Poke says, "Immigration."

"Right, right. I can find out when he entered the country, what kind of visa. I can find out what he wrote on the immigration documents: where he arrived from, his passport number, whatever occupation he's claiming."

"And where he's staying. There's a blank on the form for—"

"Don't be silly." Arthit pulls the carafe off the hot plate and pours. "Anyone can write anything he wants on those things. You can make it up out of thin air."

"Wouldn't his home address be on his passport?"

"He could have moved a dozen times." He hands Rafferty the mug. "Or, if he's the kind of guy you think he is, who knows if it's really his passport?"

"Still," Rafferty says. He sips the coffee. "It's better than nothing."

Arthit says, "Let's assume you're right. Let's say he's after the money." He goes to the door that opens into the tiny yard behind the house and pulls it open, and the room fills with the edgy, new-rain scent of ozone, one of Rafferty's favorite smells.

"He is," Rafferty says. "He knows somehow that I was there, in Murphy's house when it blew up, and he *wants the money.*"

Arthit is standing at the small kitchen table, loading sugar into his coffee. "Kind of a shame you can't just give it to him."

"You know I can't. It belongs to Treasure. As badly as he treated her, she's still his daughter, and the only thing I can do for her is make sure she eventually gets that money."

"Of course," Arthit says. He takes a big breath. "Listen, about Treasure—"

"And here's the real issue," Rafferty interrupts. "Even if I did give it to him, it wouldn't solve the problem."

"Why not?" Arthit sits down and stirs his coffee.

"Because," Rafferty says, "he obviously thinks I have *all* of it. All three million eight hundred and forty thousand dollars of it. Which makes me more than three million short."

Two cups of coffee later, Arthit says, "I need to change the subject."

"By all means. This is what you wanted to talk about, back at that restaurant?"

"It is." He looks down into his empty cup. "How long since you've gone to see Treasure?"

A pang of guilt yanks Rafferty's spine straight. Treasure is the thirteen-year-old daughter of Haskell Murphy, who had tried brutally to transform her into a version of himself, bullying her, deriding her, and even beating her while half attempting to train her in the tactics of sabotage and terror. When Rafferty met her, the night Murphy's house exploded, she'd been fiercely feral; when her father had been shot, she'd cried out, "Again, do it again!" Rafferty had assumed she'd died in the explosion, but in fact she'd taken refuge in a hedge behind the house. Two months later she'd been found, feverish and nearly starved, in an alley by two street kids who had hauled her to a shelter.

And now Anna, the new love of Arthit's life, is teaching at that shelter.

"I haven't seen her in more than a week," Rafferty says. "The thing with Rose—"

"Anna says Treasure has asked a few times where you were."

"Aaaahhhh, hell. I'll go later today."

"She's becoming a thirteen-year-old child instead of a small, violent adult," Arthit says. He touches his wet spoon to the surface of the sugar in the bowl and then to his tongue. "I have to admit, I thought you were crazy when you decided she should stay at the shelter. I was thinking doctors, professionals, you know. But you were right. What she needed was kids. She'd never been around other children, and she didn't trust adults, except for you. And now she's hardly the same person."

"Thanks to Anna and Dok and Chalee," Rafferty says. Dok and Chalee are the street children who found Treasure and got her to the shelter. They'd stayed with her through the first and hardest days and became the first friends she'd ever had.

"Not so much Dok lately," Arthit says. "He and Chalee had a fight a few days back. And Treasure's got . . . well, an admirer."

"You mean since I was there? In a few days?"

"He had a head start," Arthit says. "It's the kid whose face she scratched. He calls himself Tip."

"The one who sneaked in to look at her when he thought she was asleep?"

"That's the one. He's got an eye. She's beautiful."

"Her mother, Neeni, was gorgeous, even when I saw her, doped on codeine. Does Treasure reciprocate?"

"She talks to him a little bit," Arthit says. He shrugs. "Anna says she won't cross the room to sit near him, but she stays put when he comes near her."

"Poor Dok," Rafferty says. The scrawny little boy with the two big, ratlike front teeth is his favorite. "I think he was in love with Chalee."

"There will be other loves," Arthit says. "Even with those teeth." He's put his cup on the table in front of him, and he's turning it right and left, looking into it as though there's someone down there signaling up to him.

Rafferty says, "What is it?"

"She's different from the other kids in the shelter," Arthit says. His face pales for a fraction of a second, reflecting a white flicker of lightning on the other side of the open kitchen door, but he doesn't seem to register it. He's choosing his words slowly, obviously picking his way across a subject that matters to him. He waits out a brief rattle of thunder before speaking. "Yes, she was abused physically and emotionally, and yes, her mother lived in a bottle of cough syrup and barely remembered her own name, but still, Treasure was—is . . . accustomed to a level of material comfort that the other kids can hardly imagine, and she reads and writes at a much higher level than they do. Anna is essentially running two classrooms at the same time: one for Treasure and one for everybody else."

Outside, Rafferty hears the rain begin to fall.

"So," Arthit says, and pauses. "Well, sooner or later I have to say it out loud: we're thinking of asking her to come live with us."

Rafferty says, "Permanently?"

"If she wants to," Arthit says quickly. He looks past Poke, at him, and away again. "We're considering adopting her. If she did decide to . . . to live with us for a while, sort of a trial period on both sides . . . well, it would give her everything at once. She'd have a nice place to live—here, I mean—and every day she could go back to the shelter with Anna and see her friends."

"She'd have a mother and father," Rafferty says. He experiences a twinge of uneasiness at the idea of Treasure being able to relate to a father figure, even one as benign as Arthit, but a smile is called for, and he produces one. "It's a wonderful idea."

Arthit returns the smile, although it mirrors some of the anxiety Poke thought he'd concealed. "And later we could see to college and all that. Just, you know, a real life for her." He reaches out and covers Rafferty's hand with his. "I'm glad you think it's all right. We were a little worried about you."

"Why?"

"No, no, I said that wrong. I mean we were worried about *both* of you, Treasure and you. You were the first adult male she ever trusted. You were the first one who ever treated her like a child—like a human, for that matter—and you were the one who ended her relationship with her father—"

"By killing him," Rafferty says.

Arthit makes a loose fist and raps the back of Rafferty's hand, a call for attention. "He needed killing, and she knew it. And then, when she finally said something at the shelter after all those days, the first word she spoke was your name. You were the only person in Bangkok she asked for."

Poke says, "And?"

"And I think she's had it somewhere in the back of her mind that she might eventually be able to live with you and Rose and Miaow."

"Not possible," Rafferty says. What Arthit said is no surprise. "I've got Rose and Miaow and the baby or babies to think about, and I can't bring Treasure into all that. She's still too unstable."

"Babies?"

"You don't even want to know."

Arthit tilts his head toward the door. "Listen to that come down."

"Flooding up in Rose's village," Poke says.

They sit there, smelling the freshness of the rain. Poke says, "Arthit, I *know* how Treasure feels about me. It's been bothering me, too, but I don't know what to do about it."

Arthit says, "It's a tough one. So does this . . . interfere with anything you had in mind?"

"Only in the sense that I might be able to stop worrying about her."

"Then you think it might work? Treasure and Anna and me?"

"I think if anybody can make it work, you can." He sips some cold coffee. "But she's a complicated kid."

"Anna loves her."

"Well, then, that's about half of it, isn't it?"

Arthit says, "She'll do everything she can to make Treasure happy. And I'll be wise and fatherly, if I can figure out how." They sit there in the warm, shining room, two friends who have come through a rough period and found each other again.

And then Rafferty says, "Holy shit."

"What?"

"Varney."

Arthit says, "Why would Varney—" He breaks off, and the rain outside crescendos. "We're idiots. We haven't given it a—"

Rafferty is shaking his head. "He has no way of knowing she's alive. Even if he thinks she might be, there's . . . there's no possibility he knows where she is. But if he wants the money, he might also want—"

"Major Shen?" Arthit says. "Let's say Varney was connected to Major Shen through Murphy—" He says, "No, no," and shakes his head. "Even if Varney is in contact with Shen, Shen doesn't know that Treasure turned up alive." He's looking at the back door again but not focused on it, nipping at the tip of his tongue. "Her mother?"

"I suppose he might find her village," Rafferty says. "If he knew Murphy well enough, he might know where in Laos she came from. But I never told Neeni that Treasure surfaced. It was so obvious that all she wanted to do in the world was drink herself to death. And Hwa—the Vietnamese maid who took care of Neeni when I was trying to get her off the dope—Hwa had no idea where Treasure was. And Varney would have to find Hwa even to learn that."

Arthit gets up. "Well, I'll tell you what. This is the prod I need. Even if we're certain that no one knows where she is, in light of all this . . . this *bother*, it seems like a good time to move her. And to check out Mr. Varney." He picks up the cups and totes them to the sink and runs water into them.

"Listen, Arthit."

"What?"

"This isn't . . . I mean, this thing with Treasure, with adopting Treasure. It isn't going to be easy."

Arthit turns off the water. He says, "Easy is the last thing I think it's going to be."

8

Talks, Talks, Talks

"No," Anna says, packing a lot of opposition into the syllable.

Arthit looks at Poke, who shrugs and looks at Boo. Rafferty has good reason to trust Boo's judgment: Years ago, when Miaow was abandoned on the pavement by her parents, Boo—then using the street name "Superman"—had taken her into his gang of runaways and protected her. Just a few months ago, he acceded to Rafferty's request that Treasure be allowed to stay in the shelter, even though Boo felt she might be a danger to the other kids. He seems to feel Rafferty's eyes, and he glances over at him before he says, in Thai, "I think she can handle it."

"You don't know who this man is," Anna says to him. "You don't know what their relationship was, if they had one. Even Poke doesn't know. What if he's like her father? What if she goes back . . ." She swallows, leaving unspoken the words they all hear: *to the way she was.*

When, after a lifetime of deafness, Anna worked up the courage to abandon the sheaf of blue cards she had always written on and chose instead to speak aloud in front of strangers, her voice had seemed to Rafferty to be flat and mechanically unpleasant. She had never heard the way people emphasize some words and drop others, and she had to take many pronunciations on faith. Even now her sentences have a kind of chewed-and-swallowed sound to them, the stresses coming seemingly at random. But at the moment he doesn't really register any of that. He just hears the love she so clearly feels for the child.

It's the tone Rose uses when she talks about the baby.

He says, "I think he might be a danger to her." Anna, watching his lips, starts to speak, but he holds up a hand. "We don't even know if Varney is his real name. We don't know much of anything. The less we know about him, the harder it's going to be to protect her. Maybe she can give us the information we need."

Boo, sitting behind his rickety old desk in his little office at the shelter, a space that's walled off by movable hospital-room dividers, says, "Up to you if you want to ask her about this man, but I don't think you should say anything about adopting her until I talk to Father Bill and get him to say yes."

Arthit says to Boo, "What do you mean, 'get' Father Bill to say yes?"

"He'll start the process if she wants to do it," Boo says. "But it's complicated, and it takes a lot of his time. I don't want to surprise him with it. He's not good with surprises."

"I'm a *policeman*," Arthit says, sounding stung. "Anna's a teacher. We'd be great parents."

"I'm sure you would," Boo says. "I'm just telling you how it is." They're all speaking Thai, Rafferty following along a couple of syllables behind and Anna turning to watch people's lips. Now she reaches over and puts a hand on her husband's shoulder, gives him a single calming pat that tells Rafferty quite a bit about how the intimacy between them has grown.

"Sorry," Arthit says. "I'm nervous."

"He is," Anna says. She smiles at Arthit as though he were a child who just needs a little understanding from the grown-ups.

Boo raises his voice and calls, "Chalee? Chalee, are you out there?"

A thin girl with a strikingly angular fox face and quick, bright eyes pokes her head into the opening between the movable room dividers. "Now in here," she says in English.

"Can you get Treasure for us?"

Chalee says, "Can," and starts to retreat.

"Wait," Rafferty says, and Chalee freezes on the spot, her eyebrows raised inquisitively. "You know her better than anyone," he says.

Chalee looks down at the floor, considering the sentence. "I guess."

"Have you been listening?"

"Sure." Chalee is giving her English some exercise.

"Well, what do you think? Is she . . . I mean, has she gotten stronger?"

Chalee says, "Yes."

"What if this is someone who frightens her? Do you think she can handle that?"

Chalee looks at Boo and says, in English, "Boo say okay."

Boo says to Chalee, "You know her better than I do."

"You can't ask a child to make this decision," Anna says tartly. "You're the expert."

"You're the *teacher*," Boo says. Chalee's eyes go from one of them to the other.

Arthit says, "Poke is the only one who knew her before."

Poke says, "Anyone else want to pass the buck?"

Chalee says, "What's a buck?"

Rafferty says, "It's a . . . it's a something people . . . uh, pass to one another when . . . when—"

"When they don't want to make a decision," Arthit says. "Like now."

"Well," Chalee says, looking at Poke, "up to you."

"If it's up to me," Rafferty says, and takes a deep breath, "bring her in."

Chalee looks at Boo and then at Anna, sees no disagreement, and disappears between the partitions.

After a moment's silence, Arthit says to Boo, "If she says she wants to go, Father Bill will let us have her?"

"It's not that easy," Boo says. "There's legal stuff, and he'll want to talk to both of you, too."

"About what?"

"I don't know. Whether you know what you might be getting into. Kids are a full-time job."

"*I* know that," Anna says. "I understand children."

"I know, I know," Boo says, "although Father Bill would say there's no such thing as *children*, there's just one kid at a time. Look, there's nothing we can do about it now. We should all just relax."

"Right, right," Arthit says, sitting back in the chair, his spine rigid. He notices his bouncing leg and quiets it, but he's still radiating tension as Chalee comes in, followed by Treasure.

At first sight it's difficult for Rafferty to see in this girl the furious, terrified child in the filthy nightgown he'd met that night in Murphy's house. She'd carried her shoulders in a tight, permanent flinch, arms pressed to her sides as though to make her smaller. Her thick, dark, reddish hair had been a concealment, a tangled thicket that she pulled forward to surround and hide her face like a snarl of thorns. She had moved with the tamped-down, ever-present wariness of someone who expects a slap to be waiting around every corner. At the height of the violence that had erupted that night, she'd run from the room and methodically soaked the house with gasoline. Then she'd set it ablaze. Her movements now are fluid, not precisely confident, but without her former hesitation. The stiffness in her neck and back is mostly gone, just a hint of rigidity in the set of her shoulders. She's gained weight, and her hair has been tamed, pulled back from her face and pinned in place by two red plastic heart-shaped clips, something he never would have associated with her, even more surprising than the used, street-child shorts or the bright T-shirt featuring four guitar-carrying anime Japanese teenage girls. Looking at her now, Rafferty realizes that he might not have recognized her in the street.

She surveys the room quickly and—out of habit, Rafferty

thinks—holds no one's gaze. She nods respectfully at Anna, who has become her teacher. Her eyes slow when they reach Rafferty, and she gives him a small, almost unintentional smile, ducking her head a bit awkwardly, and then she stops, just a few steps inside the room, waiting.

Rafferty says, "Hello, Treasure."

She looks at him again for a split second and then away, and Boo breaks into the moment, saying, "Sit down, Treasure. We want to talk to you for a minute. Thank you, Chalee." Chalee, looking disappointed, goes out of the room, although probably not out of earshot. Boo parts his long hair with his hands, snags it behind his ears, and waits, looking at each of them.

Rafferty says to Treasure, "How are you?"

In spite of Boo's invitation, Treasure hasn't taken a chair. Instead she stands beside one, keeping it between her and the others, her hands grasping its back with one raised knee resting on the seat. Although Rafferty asked the question, she looks first at Boo and then at Anna, who smiles encouragement at her, and she says, very softly, "I'm fine." She seems to search for words for a second, rocking the chair a little on its back legs, and then surprises Poke by saying, "How are *you?*" She's speaking English, her father's native language. She glances at Anna again and gets a nod of approval.

"I'm fine, too," he says, unprepared for the question. He clears his throat. "We want . . . I mean, we need to talk to you about something."

Her voice taut, Anna says, "I still don't know about this."

The moment Anna says it, Rafferty realizes that he agrees with her. He says, "Maybe we don't need to talk about it yet."

Treasure says, "Did I do something wrong?" She turns to Boo so quickly that the chair squeals on the floor. "Do I . . . do I have to leave? Can't I stay here?"

"No," Boo says, both hands upraised. "Nothing like that. Nobody wants you to leave."

"Then what?" Treasure says. She swallows loudly enough for Rafferty to hear her across the room. "What did I do?"

"Okay," Rafferty says. "Listen, the first thing you need to know is that you haven't done anything wrong and that we all love you and we're all going to stay with you and . . . and take care of you."

She says, "Then what is it?"

With absolute certainty that he's handling this badly, Rafferty says, "Did you ever meet a man named Arthur Varney?"

Treasure's gaze drops to the floor, and she's still for the space of several breaths, seeming to work the question through. Then, without looking up, she says, "You mean, with my, my—" She shakes her head as though clearing it. "My father?"

"Yes."

"Arthur Varney," she says experimentally. She looks at each of them and says, "No."

"He's shorter than I am," Rafferty says. "Kind of . . . not fat, but . . ." He spreads his hands. "Wide. Like he's got muscles, like one of those guys who's into showing off his muscles. Forty years old, maybe a little more."

Treasure relaxes a bit, leans away from the chair, her hands grasping the back. "American?"

"Yes. He *sounds* American anyway."

"My, my, my father, he didn't have friends. Only people he yelled at. I don't know who you mean."

"He's American, a little older than I am but younger than your father, black hair. He's got a big mustache—"

He breaks off because Treasure's head has snapped up. Now she's looking past him, as though at a light over his shoulder, a long distance away. Her mouth is slightly open. After a moment she rubs her right index finger over the skin of her left forearm, just above the wrist. She says, "Snake?"

He nods.

With no warning at all, she plants both feet on the floor and drags the chair a few steps back, keeping it in front of her, tilted so that its rear legs point at them like gun barrels. The self-possessed girl who came into the room is gone. Her shoulders are raised and rigid, almost as high as her ears. The knuckles on the fingers curled over the chair back are paper white. She tilts her face downward as though she still expects the tangled curtain of hair to drop forward and hide it, glancing at them, one at a time, out of the corners of her eyes.

Everyone in the room can hear her breathing.

Rafferty says, "Treasure," and she hauls the chair another quick step back, its legs making a ragged noise against the floor. Anna is up and moving toward her, but Treasure stops her with a glance. So deliberately that it looks mechanical, she turns her face toward Rafferty again, showing him the expressionless mask of muscle she had worn in the presence of her father. She lifts her right hand and uses the side of her index finger to blot her upper lip. Her hand is shaking. "Talks, talks, talks?"

"That's him."

"Not Arthur," she says. The only thing moving in her face is her lower lip, which is trembling. "Name is . . . is . . . is P-P-Paul. Paul something." She turns to look through the doorway Chalee just left through. "He's . . . he's *here?*"

"No, he's nowhere near us. Please. Sit down."

"He can't come here," she says.

Rafferty says, "He won't."

"Maybe," she says, "maybe I should go."

"You're safe here," Anna says, and Boo says, "We won't let anyone—"

"You *don't know,*" she says, her voice scaling up.

Arthit says, "Don't know what?"

"Don't know who . . . don't know who . . ."

"You need to tell us," Rafferty says. "We're going to keep him away from you."

She makes a sound that it takes Rafferty a moment to recognize as a laugh. He says, "Who is he?"

"My, my, my . . ." Her jaw is trembling so violently that Rafferty can hear her teeth chattering. He goes to her, turns the chair around, toward her, and kneels beside it. After a long moment of looking down at him, she sits. Anna starts to say something but cuts it off and swallows.

"Look at us all," Rafferty says. "We're all here, we're going to take care of you." He's ransacking his mind for the thing he should say. "We promise. I'll . . . I'll get more people here."

"He . . . he won't care," she says. "If he . . . if he . . . he *wants* me, he'll come. He'll take me. I belong to him now." She's up from the chair, shaking her head, moving as aimlessly as a butterfly for a moment and then turning her back on them and heading for the door.

From across the room, Arthit says, *"Treasure."* His tone stops her. She angles her head toward him, not turning her body, her eyes on the floor at a point midway between them. "I'm a policeman," Arthit says. "We can protect you."

Treasure has both fists clenched and pressed against her thighs, "He's not the same as you. He doesn't care. He doesn't hurt. He can't be hurt, he just *wants*. He wants, and he . . . he . . . he won't care, won't care if you're there or if you have a gun, he doesn't care about guns. If he—" She turns away again. "I should go."

Boo calls, "Chalee."

"No." Treasure says, *"Not Chalee,"* as Chalee comes in, her wide eyes making it clear that she's heard everything. "Don't let him see Chalee. Or Dok. Not Dok, not Tip, not any of them, not *any* of them, not any, any, any—"

Still kneeling next to the chair, Rafferty says, "Treasure."

The sharpness in his voice cuts her off and brings her eyes down to him.

"He is *not* going to hurt you. He doesn't know where you are. No one will tell him, ever. Everyone here promises you that. All of us, and we'll bring in more people to protect you. Other policemen, right, Arthit?"

"There will always be someone here," Arthit says. "If he tries to get near you, we'll kill him."

Chalee says, "Why would he want to hurt Treasure?"

Treasure says, "You *have* to kill him. You can't hurt him. He doesn't . . . he doesn't hurt."

"What does that mean?" Arthit says.

"My father said he didn't hurt, not ever. I didn't believe him, so Paul held a lighter under his hand until I could smell it cooking, but he just looked at me until my father told him to stop, and when he did, part of his hand was black and it had cracks in it, like dried mud, and he held it up in front of my face and then slapped the burned part with his other hand. Then he laughed at the way I looked."

The room is silent. Chalee's eyes fill half her face, as though something has just come through the wall at her.

Treasure says, "He told my, my *father*, he told my father he bit off p-p-part of his tongue when he was a kid because he didn't feel it. He had to learn to . . . to talk all over again, and now he talks *all the time*. He can do *anything*." She knots Rafferty's T-shirt in her fist. "My . . . my father was *afraid* of him. You have to kill him."

"We'll find him," Arthit says.

Boo says, "Is that possible? Not to hurt?"

"I read something about it in a newspaper a long time ago," Rafferty says. "A little girl, eleven or twelve, who couldn't feel pain. She couldn't imagine what it felt like to hurt. Her parents found out when the little girl was helping to make pasta and she dropped the spoon into the pot, and she reached into the boiling water and pulled it out while her mother screamed at her. She spent the rest of her childhood padded like a mummy." Everyone is staring at him. "Most people who have this thing, like a muta-tion to a certain gene, die in childhood because they don't know they've been hurt."

"This man, Paul," Arthit says to Treasure, "Why was he at your house?"

"They did things together," Treasure says. "The things my, my father did. Blow things up. Kill people, hurt people. Fright-fright-*frighten* people. When my father was angry at me, he, he used to say he would give me to . . . to Paul."

"Is that what you meant," Poke says, "when you said you belonged to him?"

"Not—no, no." She breaks off to swallow, and she is looking directly at Rafferty. "He said if he ever died . . . my father said, if he ever died, I would be-belong to Paul. Paul would . . . would come for me."

Rafferty gets up, and for the first time since he met her, he puts an arm around the girl's shoulders. She starts but then holds still, allowing it. He says, "That's not going to happen."

"YOU'RE GOING TO stay with us," Arthit says. He and Boo have been out in the alley for the past five minutes, arguing loudly enough to be heard, and he's just returned to the room.

The look that Treasure gives him is just short of terrified. Seeing it, Anna begins to get up, but Treasure says, almost in a whisper, "Chalee."

"Fine." Arthit looks at Anna, who makes a tiny shrug, although Rafferty sees Chalee register it. "Chalee, too. Will you . . . I mean, would you like to come, Chalee?" Chalee looks away, and Treasure doesn't respond, so Arthit says, "Does that sound better?"

Treasure nods. She seems to be examining the room as though looking for an escape route. Standing beside her, Chalee flicks her upper arm with an index finger, and Treasure says, quickly, "Yes."

"And you'll both come back with Anna for school every day."

"I'll have a few people here, keeping their eyes open," Rafferty says, trying to think of who they might be.

Treasure lets her gaze settle on him, and then her eyes drift away, and he has the feeling that she's assessed him and found him wanting.

"And I'll come over," he says. "I'll tell you what, I'll come over to Arthit's every evening around eight o'clock. If that's okay, I mean."

She nods, and Chalee gives him the smile he was hoping for from Treasure.

Sitting behind Boo's cracked laptop, Anna says, "Could he smell?" She looks up at Treasure.

"Smell?" Treasure says. "Oh. Oh, *smell?* He couldn't. He said so. And my, my father asked what would happen if he . . . if he were in a house where the gas was—" She takes a sudden breath and breaks off, and her eyes make a quick circuit of the room, and then she's looking at the floor again.

"The gas?" Rafferty asks.

"If the gas was leaking." She says the words very quickly. Her eyes go to everyone in the room for an instant, but at chest level. "And he . . . he . . . he said he'd probably get blown up." Her hands are fists.

"'Congenital insensitivity to pain,'" Anna reads aloud, stumbling a little over the words. "You were right, Poke. It's a problem with a gene, or maybe three genes. Most of the people who can't feel pain can't smell things either."

Treasure says, "I'm frightened."

"I know," Poke says. "But we're not just going to keep you away from him. We're going after him, and when we find him, you'll never have to think about him again." He looks at his watch. "In fact," he says, getting up, "I might learn something about him right now."

9

Lutanh and Betty

IT'S A SURPRISE to open the door of the Expat Bar and smell perfume instead of beer and old-fashioned hair oil. The source of the fragrance is easy to identify, since the bar is empty except for Toots and the two ladyboys, one seated on either side of Leon.

At first glance Rafferty decides that the pair of them represent opposite ends of the commercial ladyboy spectrum. The one on Hofstedler's left is almost childishly small, slight, delicate, conventionally pretty in such a feminine way that Rafferty doubts his own eyes. The only real tip-off is a shadowy Adam's apple, which suggests she's new to the game. The surgical reduction of this telltale is a specialty at the hospital to which Leon was dragged after his heart attack, but it's usually one of the later touch-ups.

The ladyboy on the right is almost as tall as Rafferty and probably a few pounds heavier, with a linebacker's shoulders, a private eye's square jaw, and, even through makeup as thick as stucco, a charcoal smudge of beard shading her chin. Her nose is as blunt as a thumb, and her lips have obviously never been plumped. She's in her unapologetic fifties, and Rafferty instinctively likes the look in her eye. It says, *Fuck you if you can't take a joke, and maybe even if you can.*

Rafferty is not a connoisseur of ladyboys, but his guess is that the little one is for men who want to persuade themselves they thought they were going with a woman until, *Good Lord*, it was too late, and the big one is for men who are just shopping for a guy dressed like a girl. In between these extremes are the ones fishing for clients who just want ladyboys.

"Ah, here is Poke," says Leon, who has never shied from stating the obvious. "We have just been seated, yes, Toots?"

"Still pouring," Toots says, and indeed she is, upending over a glass a bottle of some kind of orange soda that Rafferty's never seen in here before.

"Lutanh," Leon says, indicating the smaller one without actually touching her, "does not drink. But Betty—"

"Betty drink all the time," says Betty, hoisting a double of mislabeled Mekong. "Betty like drink too much." Betty's voice is of a piece with her general appearance. If there were a ladyboy production of *Showboat*, she'd be the one to tackle "Old Man River."

Rafferty says hello to both of them and gets a truck driver's laugh and an elbow in the ribs from Betty when he repeats his first name. He takes the stool next to Lutanh for safety's sake and says, "Thanks for setting this up, Leon." He's speaking English in front of the girls because Leon has resolutely declined to learn Thai.

"This is not a problem," Hofstedler says. "This man, I don't like him myself."

"Man?" says Lutanh in a voice wispy enough to have issued from a column of steam. "I think you say *girl*."

"It is a girl," Rafferty says, "but I think she can lead me to the man Leon was just talking about."

"Bad man?" Betty licks away a droplet of whiskey sliding down the outside of her glass, the steel ball stuck through the tip of her tongue making an alarming *clack*.

"Actually, yes," he says. "In fact, both of you need to know that he's a very bad guy indeed, and I strongly suggest you stay the hell away from him. And, Leon, if I'm not in here tonight, please tell Bob and the other guys to do the same."

"You think he will come back?" Hofstedler looks unsettled by the idea.

"Last night I would have said no," Rafferty says. "He's done what he needed to do. But that was before I knew he was crazy. And I'm not just throwing the word around. He's as crazy as a shark on methamphetamine."

"*Yaa baa*," Lutanh suggests, using one of the Thai names for crank.

"Good-looking?" Betty asks as Lutanh takes a hummingbird sip of her orange soda. Lutanh's nails, curved around the glass like a circular stairway, are at least two inches long and have been painted an orange that complements the drink.

"I don't know," Rafferty says. "Not much."

"Not," says Leon.

"Some crazy man, very sexy," Betty says, dismissing both of them.

"Don't get near him. I mean it, he's dangerous."

"Look like what?" Betty says.

Rafferty describes Varney—*Paul*, he silently corrects himself—and when he gets to the snake tattoo, Lutanh says, just above a whisper, "I see him before."

"Where?"

"He come my bar."

"Which one?"

"This or That Bar," she says. "Patpong 2."

Leon says, "Not the Queen's Corner?"

"I change," Lutanh says. "Have better customer at This or That Bar."

"Did he take anyone?"

"No. Come three time last week, then not come. Buy me drink. Have watch, big like steering wheel. Have, have *ngu*."

Betty says, "Lao for 'snake.'"

"Me," Lutanh says, pointing at herself. "Me Lao."

Hofstedler says, with a faint blush, "Lot of ladyboys from Laos now."

"We pretty," Lutanh says.

"Have *you* seen him?" Rafferty asks Betty.

"No," Betty says. "But I look, just for you, okay?" She shows him two rows of big, even teeth.

"Okay. But don't do anything that might tell him you're . . . you know, interested, not in any way. If he even glances at you, you go in another direction."

"And lady?" Betty says. "Lady you want to know about?"

Rafferty describes her, and when he gets to the birthmark, Lutanh says, "I see *her*, too. I see in street, about six o'clock, two, three times." She pronounces it "sick o'clock," which had bewildered Rafferty when he first arrived in Bangkok.

"Which end?" Rafferty says. "Was she coming from Silom or Surawong?"

"Surawong, same as me."

"Six o'clock."

"Maybe sick thirty. Sick, sick thirty."

"Could you tell where she was going?"

"Other side," Lutanh says, lifting her chin toward Patpong. "Other side of night market."

"Got it," Rafferty says. He reaches into his pocket and pulls out a thousand-baht bill. "Can you two split this?"

"Oh, no," Lutanh says. Suddenly she looks shy. "I do for you. No money."

"I'd rather—" he begins, but Betty, moving so fast he doesn't see her hand, snatches the bill.

"Lutanh, she like you," Betty says. She gives him the big teeth again, but this time it looks like she's thinking about taking a bite. "She think maybe you like ladyboy, but me, I know. You like lady. Yes?"

"Yes," Rafferty says. He looks at Lutanh, feeling obscurely guilty. "I'm sorry."

Barely audible, Lutanh says, "No problem." She doesn't look up.

"I give her five hundred later," Betty says. "Eight o'clock tonight, nine o'clock, she forget you."

Lutanh laughs, covering her mouth with her hand, Japanese style. "Come to my bar," Betty says. "We have real lady, too."

Rafferty starts to reply, but Hofstedler speaks first. "These . . . girls," Hofstedler says, and he surprises Rafferty by leaning back on his stool and putting his arms around their shoulders. Even Toots, who has seen literally everything, looks surprised. "These girls saved my life." His blush deepens to a fierce red. "These wonderful girls saved my life."

IT'S NEARLY SICK o'clock, and Rafferty heads up Patpong to Surawong, almost the lone male swimming against the tide of young women streaming into Patpong to report for work. They come in twos and threes, most of them, some with their hair gleaming from a recent shower, either holding hands or interlocking elbows with this week's best friend. Rose has told him how deep and how short some of these relationships are. In an environment where it's essential for someone to have your back, the climate is rich for sudden, intimate friendships and unforgivable betrayals.

The majority of them wear the universal Southeast Asian street uniform of T-shirt and jeans, and most of them are not made up yet, saving that task to be done among their friends and not-friends on the benches that will be crowded with men only ninety minutes later. It's an evening ritual, chatting and painting their faces beneath the flat fluorescents that will snap off at 7 P.M. in favor of glittering disco balls and the primary-color spotlights that will airbrush the women's flesh into a smooth, blemish-free, marketable commodity. For now what he sees are the unadorned faces of the northeast, the rice basket of Southeast Asia, where for decades farmers and their families have methodically been cheated by private industry and the government alike, scraping along at subsistence level and, when even that is beyond them, sending their sons and daughters south to the bars, brothels, massage parlors, sidewalks, and escort services of Bangkok.

The sex trade, like the rice trade, drives up the nation's gross national product for the benefit of the sleek and the fat, so these impoverished farm families are making a double contribution—their rice *and* their children—to support the rich men in their billion-baht houses and to pay the cops and soldiers who are called into action when the squeezed rise up in protest. It is, he thinks, a system in which the prey funds the dental work that preserves the teeth of the predators.

The woman with the birthmark had come in from Surawong, according to the wispy-voiced Lutanh. The problem, from a surveillance perspective, is that the high roofs of the night-market booths running down the center of Patpong block the view of whichever side of the street the watcher isn't on. Rafferty can't just stand around in plain sight, because she'll probably see him before he sees her. The last thing he wants to do is tip Varney that he's on the hunt; if he has any advantage at all, it's that Varney doesn't know that the quarry has turned around to sniff the air.

The thought of Varney, an outlier if there ever was one, brings to mind Rafferty's concept of circles of reality, which he originally formulated as a boy in the desert outside Lancaster, California. Of all his early ideas about how the world works, that was the one most altered by travel. Everyone, he has long believed, lives more or less comfortably in the center of a circle of reality, circumscribed by culture and geography and expectation. It may be challenged and reshaped occasionally by an unforeseen tragedy or a windfall blowing into it like a meteorite, yet by and large it changes slowly, with time and experience. But travel made it inescapably clear to Rafferty that the circle of reality for a middle-class American desert boy has little in common with that of an Indonesian rice farmer, which has little in common with that of Rafferty's Manhattan book editor, which in turn has little in common with the circle of reality of a terrified child bride in Pakistan or an African woman stranded in the midst of a tribal war.

And yet, as widely different from each other as those circles are,

Rafferty is certain that Varney orbits a space far beyond the sharp edge of improbability that borders every one of them. However varied the circles are, there's one way in which they're all identical: they all exclude Arthur Varney.

On the far side of Surawong, he sees what he needs—a foot-massage shop with a big plate-glass window. He crosses the road carefully, and for two hundred baht he buys twenty minutes in the chair nearest the window. He tips the masseuse to leave his feet alone.

For a few minutes, he loses himself in the street scene. Then his attention is drawn to a couple on the other side of the glass, a middle-aged *farang* and a younger Thai woman, arguing. Their faces are intense and hard, but Rafferty thinks he could sense the argument even if they were headless. The man's arms are crossed defensively across his chest, and the woman has one hand on her hip with the elbow angled sharply back, away from the man. *Hands on hips*, he thinks. It can mean several things. One hand on the hip, with the elbow pulled back like that, is anger pure and simple. It's as easy to read as a face.

He hears Miaow's voice in his ear, saying *Delsarte*, and he realizes that he's eavesdropping visually and that the Delsarte method is a terrifically valuable asset to someone who wants to do exactly that. And he's suddenly conscious of the position of his own body, leaning toward the window with one hand clasping the arm of the chair, a posture that announces, *I'm watching*. He turns back into the room and finds three of the masseuses watching him watch the street. *Attention draws attention*, he thinks.

So he smiles and sits back and exhales, doing the Delsarte version of a guy relaxing in a comfortable chair, and when he turns idly to the window again he sees the woman he's been waiting for climb out of a cab on the other side of the street: the long spiral curls, the smudge above her mouth. She's wearing full makeup an hour before she's due on the stage, and he thinks, *She probably always wears it.*

He's up in a shot and through the door as the women in the shop laugh behind him, one more *farang* who's spotted the woman of his dreams. On the sidewalk he's hit by the wet heat and the smell of exhaust, and at that precise moment it starts to rain. Hunching his shoulders and squinting against the dazzle of moisture, he dives into the traffic, weaving between headlights across the shining pavement.

But the traffic demands attention, and by the time he's at the entrance to Patpong, she has disappeared. On the verge of diving into the crowd, he becomes aware of his posture, spine bent, neck craned forward, a parody of the searching man, and he straightens and relaxes and moves forward, just fast enough to thread between people who are moving more slowly than he is, but trying not to project the concentrated attention that will draw notice.

He thinks again, *Delsarte*. How could he have forgotten this for all these years?

He wipes rain from his face. What had she been wearing? Something blue, he thinks; he'd been distracted from her clothes by the distinctive, long, Lillian Gish spirals of curls, something out of a silent movie, although the style seems to be coming back lately. In fact, he immediately spots a similar hairstyle ahead of him, but the curls are shorter and darker, and when he draws up beside her, it's a different woman. She answers his look with a bright, professional smile, and he gives her a tamped-down version in return as he moves past her, hearing the immemorial bar-girl question, "Where you go?"

"He go *here*," someone says, and slaps him loudly on the shoulder. He's face-to-face with Betty. Up close she looks even more like a man, like a weight lifter who's accidentally wandered into a comedy and finds himself in drag. She says, "You come my bar?"

Rafferty gives up. By now he has no chance of catching up to the woman with the birthmark. If she's making better time than he is—and it would be difficult not to—she could be most of the way to Silom by now, except that she's probably vanished into a bar. And he's not going into a bar to look for her, because she'll see him first, with the radar that allows bar girls to keep one eye on the door at all times.

"I was trying to follow that girl," he says in Thai.

Betty points a finger at a spot above and to the left of her mouth, and Rafferty nods. "She just go by," Betty says in English. She bats her lashes at him. "Go in bar."

"Which bar?"

With a sidelong glance that looks like it's gotten a lot of use, Betty says, "Lutanh like you." She lifts her head as though to confirm it's raining and grabs his shirt and hauls him out of the wet, beneath the blue plastic roof of a booth that's selling, of all things, baby clothes.

Dutifully, Rafferty says, "I like her, too. I like both of you. But I'm married."

"Many men who like ladyboys are married," she says, speaking Thai now. "If there were no married men, we'd all be selling makeup."

"I'm not that kind of married. What bar?"

"Cowgirl," Betty says. She attempts a pout, but it looks so silly that Rafferty laughs, and she joins him. "I'll tell Lutanh to forget about you," she says. "You have no spirit of adventure."

"Cowgirl is a big bar." He hasn't been in it for years.

She wiggles her head side to side, a gesture he associates with India. "Thirty, forty ladies."

"Not so bad," Rafferty says. "I'll see if I can pick her up when they close."

Betty brushes some rain off Poke's shoulders. It feels maternal. "What will you do when you find her?"

"I don't know," he says. "Follow her home. Eventually I want her to lead me to the man, if she can."

"This is not actually a great plan," Betty says.

"No, it isn't," Rafferty says. "If you think of anything better, call me."

10

He Was Supposed to Kill Me

THE FIVE OF them sit at the table, moving food around on their plates, in a silence so thick and so lengthy it makes Rafferty's ears pop. The only one who's eating is Chalee, and she looks up at everyone else and stops chewing, her fork halfway back down to the plate, which is piled with *pad see-ew*—rice noodles, gravy, and chicken.

"Isn't it good?" Anna asks anxiously.

Chalee nods, finishes chewing, swallows, and glances at Treasure for a cue. Treasure says, "Yes," and looks down at her plate again. Chalee nods in agreement.

The clock in the living room ticks a couple of times, and Rafferty thinks, *I'll never get those seconds back.*

Arthit clears his throat. Everyone regards him expectantly. He clears his throat again.

Rafferty says brightly, "I like the fish baskets."

Anna says, "I bought them at Chatuchak." Chatuchak is Bangkok's biggest open-air market.

Chalee says, "You bought them? But they're *old*. We had new ones in my village."

Rafferty says, "They turn a beautiful color when they get old," and is rewarded by a twist of Chalee's mouth that makes him feel like an idiot.

Chalee says, "How much?"

Anna says, "I'm sorry?"

Chalee tilts an imperious chin at the fish baskets. "How much did you pay?"

Anna says, "I don't remember."

"You don't know how many baht?" Chalee says with some incredulity. She's speaking Thai.

"It was a long time ago," Anna says, and Rafferty can practically see her wishing she had her blue cards back.

"Huh," Chalee says. "New, maybe sixty baht."

"Old ones are—" Treasure says. It's the first sentence she's begun since they sat down. Her glance at Anna is so quick that Rafferty isn't sure he saw it. "Old ones cost more."

Treasure's Thai isn't quite as assured as her English and Vietnamese, but it's better than Rafferty's. While Treasure was still at the age when children absorb language through their pores, her father's retinue had moved all over Southeast Asia and many of the maids who had raised her had been Thai.

Chalee says, "Why?" She pokes a finger through a tear in one of the baskets. "A fish would swim right through this."

Anna waits to see whether Treasure will reply, and then she says, "Some city people like old things."

Chalee shakes her head. "When I have money, I'll never have anything old."

"Here is . . . different," Treasure says. She licks her lips, and her gaze drops to the table's surface for a moment as she organizes her thoughts. "You know those store windows where everything is old?"

"Oh," Chalee says, her face brightening. "*That* kind of old."

Treasure says, "*Antiques.*" Then she goes silent, her head cocked slightly, one ear turned toward the direction of the living room.

For the forty or so minutes he's been here, commanded to come to dinner by a desperate-sounding Arthit, Rafferty has seen that Treasure is always listening for something. It's in the straightness of her spine, the angle of her head. She goes motionless whenever there's a sound from the street, and her eyes keep straying to the living-room windows. At the moment her head is lifted and her mouth is very slightly open. All he can think of is an animal that's scented something.

When the knock at the door breaks the silence, she drops her spoon onto her plate with a clatter that makes Chalee jump.

"Don't worry, Treasure," Rafferty says. "This one's mine." To Arthit he says, "May I answer the door?"

Arthit is already standing. "With me behind you."

The two of them go through the living room, and when they reach the front door, Arthit steps in front of Rafferty and moves aside to pull the door open so that he's standing partway behind it, and Rafferty is surprised to see the automatic in his hand.

The man filling the doorway is almost cumbersomely big, tall for a Thai, with a thick neck, broad shoulders, and a belly that's obviously had its way for some time. His face is a mismatch of features that might have been intended for several other people: small eyes, too close together, and wide nostrils, the nose short above a long upper lip, jaws so broad that his head narrows at the temples. Despite the unusual features, if Rafferty hadn't known that the man was coming, he doesn't think he would have recognized him; his once-black hair is frosted with gray, and he's added at least ten or twelve kilos of solid-looking bulk since they first collided with each other, five or so years ago.

"This is Sriyat," Rafferty says, stepping aside to let Arthit emerge from behind the door. Sriyat takes a step back at the sight of the gun, and Arthit tucks it out of sight. Rafferty says to him, "May I invite Sriyat in?"

Arthit says, without a lot of conviction, "Please."

Rafferty introduces them, stressing Arthit's rank, and Sriyat follows the two of them through the living room, moving as if he expects to break something at any minute, to the wide opening into the dining room. Treasure has already risen, looking like she's got one foot in the air, but Anna and Chalee are still in their chairs. Anna gets up hurriedly, swallows self-consciously against the embarrassment of speaking aloud to someone new, and says, "Have you eaten?"

The big man makes a *wai* and says, "Yes, thank you," in an unexpectedly soft voice.

"I've known Sriyat for a long time," Rafferty says. "Well, that's not really true. We *met* each other a long time ago, but this is the first time we've seen each other since then."

"Really," Anna says, every inch the hostess. "How did you meet?"

"I think he was supposed to kill me," Rafferty says, and Chalee's jaw drops. Treasure is as still as a carving. Arthit looks at Sriyat appraisingly.

Sriyat ducks his head and says, "Only beat you up."

Anna says, "My, my." She sits down again, the social levels having been firmly established.

"I'm assuming there's a reason for Sriyat being here," Arthit says.

"He's going to be outside all night, heavily armed," Rafferty says, "and tomorrow night, too, and on Monday morning he'll follow you to the shelter when it's time for school. And in the daytime he'll be replaced by a friend of his."

"My friend's name is Pradya," Sriyat says in his tissue-paper voice. Then he says "Pradya" again, as though he doubts anyone got it the first time.

Arthit says, "Both of you are good shots?"

"We're all right," Sriyat says modestly.

"Our late acquaintance, Colonel Chu," Rafferty says, and Sriyat tenses slightly at the sound of the name. "Chu could afford the best, and Sriyat and Pradya are the ones he chose. You actually talked to Sriyat once, on the phone when my father was in Bangkok with half of China chasing him. Sriyat and Pradya were supposed to take me out of the equation."

"Only beat up," Sriyat says.

Arthit says, "And you got his *phone* number?"

"I got everything," Rafferty said. "Every piece of ID, his numbers, address, everything. It was insurance. He thought I was going to turn them over to you."

"You were a cop," Arthit says. "I remember now."

Sriyat ducks his head in apparent embarrassment. "Yes, sir."

Arthit says, "Mmmmm." It's noncommittal and disapproving at the same time. "Do you need a thermos of coffee?"

"I have one."

"Something to—" He remembers that Anna and the girls are in the room. "To do . . . you know, into? A jar or something?"

"Got one of those, too."

"Good, good. Well . . ."

"Yes, sir." To everyone else, he says, "I'll be out there."

"What color is the car?" Arthit says.

"Dark purple. Looks black at night."

"I'll come out with you so I recognize it later." Arthit gives Rafferty a parting glance that says, *We'll talk about this*, and leads the larger man back out.

There's a short silence, and then the front door closes.

Treasure says, "Paul could kill that man with his teeth."

"It's what I could think of," Rafferty says.

Arthit says, "How do we know which side that man will be on a month from now? And now a crook—a fired ex-cop—knows where I live." He's on the couch, sitting forward with his palms on his thighs. Rafferty can't help seeing the impatience and frustration behind the pose. "You should have asked me."

"I know," Rafferty says. "Did I already say I'm sorry?"

"No."

"Well, then, I'm sorry."

"Oh, well," Arthit grumbles. "I wasn't actually looking for an apology."

"Too bad," Rafferty says irritably. "I needed someone fast, and he's who came to mind."

Arthit waves it off. "Why do you think you can trust him?"

"Because what he really wants," Rafferty says, "is to be back on the police force."

"Well, good luck to him." Arthit sighs and sits back. Anna, Treasure, and Chalee are in the kitchen, banging dishes around and cleaning up, although there's not much talking. Rafferty is, as always, taken aback by the fact that Arthit never offers to help. He, Rafferty, is up to his elbows in soap after every meal.

Arthit says, "Have you got any more surprises for me?"

"This isn't *about* you." Rafferty hears the frustration in his own voice. "It's about *Treasure*, okay? It's about trying to make Treasure a little less frightened. I didn't actually need to spend time doing this, Arthit. I have a pregnant wife and a daughter of my own to think about, and they're probably in danger from Varney, too."

Arthit says, "And what are you doing about that?"

"*Worrying* about it. What else can I do, hire a platoon of hit men? I only got Sriyat here tonight because Treasure was so frightened."

Arthit regards him for a moment, and then he sighs, and Rafferty can practically see the tension flow out with the breath. Arthit says, "And of course it never occurred to you that easing her mind might make this whole evening, this whole *situation*, a little easier for Anna and me."

Rafferty says, "No. Never gave it a moment's thought."

"I knew it was going to be difficult," Arthit says, lowering his voice, "but not like this. What am I supposed to *say* to her? To either of them? I know how much Anna wants this to work, but ever since we got here, I've been stiff as a board. And she can barely look at me. She's *afraid* of me."

"She's afraid of every adult man in the world. You know what she went through with her father." He reaches out and touches his friend's arm. "Just let Anna take the lead for a while, and you stay in the background until the kid can relax." He feels a little hypocritical, offering his friend platitudes. "Look," he says. "It's not going to be easy. But if it works out, it'll be the best thing that could happen to Treasure."

"And Anna," Arthit says.

"And the thing about talking to them? Just do it the same way you'd talk to an adult. Ask them what they *think* about things. I can guarantee you no one ever asked either Treasure or Chalee for an opinion and then listened to it."

"Is that what you do with Miaow?"

Rafferty almost laughs. "Among many, many other things. You'll see."

Arthit says, "I hope so." Then he shakes his head and says, "Miaow. Maybe you *should* be home."

"Maybe she and Rose should be somewhere else. Listen, you'll be okay with all this. You'll work it out."

The noise level in the kitchen drops, and Arthit lowers his voice. "If Chalee wasn't here, I don't think Treasure would stay in this house for a minute."

"Having Chalee here is a good idea," Rafferty says. "Except—"

"I know, I know." Arthit leans forward within whispering distance. "You think I haven't been worrying about that? How is Chalee going to feel when we adopt Treasure but not her? I mean, *if* we—"

"She's had a hard time," Rafferty says over him, but now they're both whispering. "Her sister's suicide, her family dissolving. She survived all that."

Arthit says, "It's so awkward. She's a wonderful kid. She deserves a good life. But Anna—Anna has taken Treasure to heart in a way I don't completely understand. I'm not saying I don't . . . care for Treasure, too. Of course I do. But to leave Chalee, and Dok—"

"I'd take Dok in a minute," Rafferty says. "If Rose weren't pregnant, if I knew how Miaow would react, if I were rich, if, if, if." He sits back but promptly leans forward so he can whisper again. "In the end, I guess, you'll just have to accept that you can't rescue everyone."

"It's one thing not to *rescue* them," Arthit says between his teeth. "It's another thing to wave it around under their noses and then yank it away, and that's what I feel like we're doing with Chalee."

"Let's just think about one thing at a time," Rafferty says, and then he lifts a finger to his lips, and Chalee comes in with a silver tray. On it are two mugs of coffee.

"These are for you," Chalee says proudly. "I made the coffee myself. I had help, but I did most of it. I poured *all* the water."

Arthit's glance at Rafferty says, essentially, *Shoot me.*

"It smells so *good*, Chalee," Rafferty says. "Which one is mine?"

"The one you want," she says.

He squints at the cups, looking racked by indecision, "Mmmmmm, no. I can't decide. You pick one for me."

"Okay," Chalee says with certainty. "The blue one."

"That's the one I really wanted," Rafferty says, taking it. "How did you know?"

"I just did," Chalee says, looking pleased with herself. "So is this one all right with you . . . uhhh, sir?" she says to Arthit, holding out the tray with the remaining cup.

"That's the one *I* wanted," Arthit says, glancing at Rafferty as though for approval. He takes the coffee, and Chalee wheels around and runs out of the room, balancing the tray on her head.

Rafferty says, "You'll learn," and as the tray clatters to the floor in the dining room, his phone rings. He fishes it out of his pocket and holds up a *Just a second* finger. "Hello?"

"Poke. This is Leon talking. You are coming?"

"I hadn't planned on it."

"But Wallace is here. I *told* you Wallace would be here. And the other one, Varney. Varney was here and left something for you."

"What is it?" He looks around the room, surprised to find himself on his feet. Arthit is staring up at him.

"It is an envelope," Hofstedler says primly. "Sealed."

"I'll get there as fast as I can." He repockets the phone and says, "Varney. He left something for me at the Expat Bar."

Arthit gets up, nodding in the direction of the living-room windows. "Maybe you should take the killer out there with you."

Rafferty says, "Maybe I was right before. Maybe I should hire a dozen of them."

11

Only Half Blind

THE RAIN, WHICH had taken a break for a smoke or something while Rafferty was at Arthit's, has made a reappearance, and in the taxi he flags down, the wiper on the driver's side has lost its rubber blade, forcing the cabbie to lean sharply to his left to see out of the far half of the windshield. In Thai, Rafferty says, "Why don't you get out and switch them?"

"I'd get wet," the driver says, steering around a bus and missing it by a couple of coats of paint.

"Better than being killed."

"I am very good driver," the driver says in English.

"I'm sure you are," Rafferty says. "But think how much better you'd be if you were behind the steering wheel."

"Every time have rain," the driver explains, "I think I should change. But then rain stop and I forget. Do something else."

"So don't switch them," Rafferty says, still in Thai. "Buy another one. That way they'll *both* work. Listen, I'll get out here."

"Two block more," the driver says.

"This is fine," Rafferty says, opening the door while the car is still moving. He reaches over and drops some bills on the driver's seat, and the cab comes to a stop. "Fix that thing," he says, climbing out into the rain, too far from the curb and directly in front of an oncoming motorbike. Rafferty slams the door and leaps out of the bike's path, landing between two cars idling at the curb, and stops there, taking several long, deep breaths. He knows he's been apprehensive, even nervous, ever since the moment in the bar when he opened that note with the number on it, and this is not a state of mind that's optimal for survival. He needs to be calm and, to use a phrase he's borrowed from Rose, within his center. At the moment his center feels like a swarm of gnats.

So the thing to do is to be where he is, *right now*, to steady his breathing and his attention, to open himself to what's happening around him. To be as dispassionate and observant as a camera so he can see whatever's coming in time to jump out of its way.

He allows himself to feel the rain hitting his face and his bare arms. He listens to the sounds of the traffic, breathes in the distinctive monoxide bouquet of the Bangkok night. Lets the people on the sidewalk flow by, paying enough attention to them to resolve them into individuals without allowing his attention to snag on any of them. Inhales and exhales slowly and regularly, feeling his heart slow, the muscles in his shoulders and neck relax, his mind quiet itself. A long time ago, watching Rose as she diced vegetables with a large, razor-sharp knife, the blade moving so fast it was a gleaming blur, he waited until she paused and then asked her how she avoided cutting herself, and she said, "This is the chopping meditation." *And now*, he thinks, *time for the walking-and-watching meditation*, and he takes his first step, up onto the curb and into the river of people on the sidewalk.

It's just another bright, garish, noisy, drunken Patpong night. The rain hasn't put much of a dent in the crowd, even though it's still relatively early: only a little before ten. In unusually clear focus, he sees the same night-market vendors he's seen a thousand times, flogging the same cheap crap in the booths, the same bar girls arm in arm with their interchangeable sweethearts, heading for the night's first or second hotel. He's momentarily distracted by a sudden certainty that Rose's story about Campeau could have been told more accurately in the first person, Bamboo Telegraph or no Bamboo Telegraph, but he waves it aside; it's been years since he's stopped taking personally all the things that happened to Rose, although the addition of Campeau—someone he knows and has never much liked—gives the topic a kind of fresh immediacy. He'd worn his attitude smooth, and suddenly it's gritty again.

Still, that has nothing to do with the walking-and-watching meditation, so he lets it float past like a puff of smoke and reorients himself, just in time to intercept a sweet smile, apparently genuine, from an extremely pretty girl in a short, swirly dress the color of violets. He's returning the smile when he realizes that the girl is Lutanh and that the guy who's got his arm wrapped possessively around her shoulders is giving him the stony eye. Rafferty turns the smile on him and says, "Be nice to her," and steps aside to let them pass. The man, who just *might* be pushing the masculinity a bit, bristles at him reflexively but then gives him a sudden, surprisingly sweet, co-conspirator's grin, and Lutanh stretches up and kisses the side of the man's neck in approval. As they move away, she leans her head against her companion's chest, wiggling bye-bye fingers at Rafferty behind her back, and he finds himself hoping the evening works out for her.

Whatever that means. Rose was with *Campeau?*

Two doors away from the Expat Bar, he steps up onto the sidewalk and sees Pinky Holland slouching toward him, folded forward against the rain. His bald head, beaded with water, makes him look wetter than anyone else on the street. Pinky extends a hand, palm out, to stop Rafferty from coming any farther. He tiptoes to the window and cups his hands around his eyes so he can see past the dismal little Christmas lights, another of which has burned out, and then steps back, looking satisfied. He says, "Coast clear," and opens the door. Rafferty waves Pinky through first and catches the door one-handed as it swings shut so he can pause and take a last sweep of the street. There's no bar girl with a birthmark, no bright blue eyes above a black mustache. Everything seems to be normal, or at least *Patpong* normal, which would qualify as headline-quality bizarre anywhere else in the world.

But he sees nothing he's reluctant to turn his back on, so he pushes the door the rest of the way open and goes in.

And has the sense, as he so often does when he first enters this room, that all motion in the place has been frozen since he was here last, that it's been as inert as the inside of a refrigerator. Now that his arrival has broken the spell, they can all resume the long-suspended moment: Toots mixing a drink behind the bar; Campeau, sitting and scowling where he always sits and scowls; the Growing Younger Man sipping something green enough to have been skimmed from the surface of a fetid pond; the silver-haired guy who might be named Ron resting his chin on his fist, like Rodin's *Thinker*, probably minus the thought; Pinky sliding into his pumpkin-colored booth; and, on the stool beside Leon, the only real change in the room: the slumped, once-powerful form of Wallace Palmer.

Wallace's hair, which had been curly and receding when Rafferty first met him, is now sparse and long and pasted so tightly across his scalp that it might have been ironed there. Its loss is cruelly offset by tufts of hair that seem to have taken refuge in his ears, from which they bristle aggressively. He's still slender and fit-looking, except for the slope of his shoulders, and his chin remains square and angular, but the skin below it falls in tight little accordion folds to an Adam's apple that protrudes as sharply as a chicken's beak, and the strong bone structure of his face seems to be surfacing, emerging as though it might soon push its way through the skin altogether to reveal the bony grin beneath. Everyone in the bar has grown older, Rafferty thinks, but Wallace seems to have been picked up by time and hurled forward, through several stages of hale old age, directly into infirmity.

"Hey, Wallace," Poke says, pulling up the stool beside him.

"*Look*, Wallace, here is Poke," Leon says, too loudly and with a kind of ghastly geniality, accompanied by a smile as empty as a pumpkin's. "You remember Poke, Wallace, yes?"

The look Wallace gives Rafferty doesn't seem to contain

anything that could be mistaken for recognition, but he says, "Sure. Good to see you." The voice is still deep, although there's a slight quaver that hadn't been there before. "Uhhhh, long time, right?"

Hofstedler gives the pot a determined stir. "Poke has been asking and asking about you, haven't you, Poke?"

"Sure have," Poke lies. "All the time. Wondering what you were up to."

"Yeah?" Wallace says. "I been . . . busy." He glances at Toots, like someone seeking confirmation, and then beyond her to the mirror. He squints at it for a moment, and then his face clears and he says, "Your . . . your beautiful wife. How is she?"

"She's wonderful," Rafferty says. "She's going to have a baby."

"*Rose,*" Wallace says, with the air of someone discovering gold. He taps the center of his forehead with his index finger, as though nailing the fact in place. "Her name is Rose. So beautiful." He holds up a huge hand, indicating height. "*Big.* Big and beautiful."

"She's all those things," Rafferty says, and he suddenly wants to weep. "Smart, too."

Hofstedler, beaming at how well Wallace is doing, raises his voice and says, "A *baby* she will have."

"I can still hear, Leon," Wallace says. "A boy or a girl?"

Rafferty shakes his head and realizes he's overacting for Wallace, who doesn't seem to need the extra effort. He sniffles and clears his throat. "All I know at this point is that it's going to be a baby. Or maybe two."

Way down the bar, Campeau says, "You kidding? Two?"

"Runs in the family," Rafferty says, pushing a perfunctory smile past the resentment he feels toward the man. "Hers, not mine."

"You're married, you're gonna have a kid," Wallace says slowly, his eyes scouring the bar in front of him. He pauses, his mouth open, clearly searching for something, and he nods as it arrives. "When you came here, you didn't know *anything.*"

"This is true," Hofstedler says. "He comes to write a guidebook, and in the dark he can't find his own pocket."

"You were my first guide, Wallace," Poke says. "To this particular part of Bangkok, anyway. I'd never seen anything like it."

"You sure as shit made up for it," Campeau grumbles. "What with Rose and all." He's never been happy that Rafferty took Rose off what he thinks of as "the market."

"Somebody had to keep her away from people like you," Rafferty says, trying to make it sound light.

Campeau hoists his beer and looks past it at Rafferty. "Little late for that."

"Bob," Rafferty says, and suddenly he's standing. "What you want to do right now is shut up."

"Come now, come now," Hofstedler says. He reaches across Wallace and pats the seat of Rafferty's stool, an invitation. "Everyone here is friends, yes?"

"Sure," Rafferty says. He sits again, looks down the bar, and says, "Buddies, right, Bob?"

Campeau holds up his index and middle fingers, side by side. "Couple of fucking brothers," he says. "And don't push that fucking jar down here, Leon."

"Anger disrupts the adrenal system," the Growing Younger Man observes.

Pinky Holland, safely out of the conversational line of fire in his booth, says, "Is that right?"

"Strictly speaking," the man who might be named Ron says, "there's no such thing as the adrenal system." He pats his hair as though making sure it's still there. "There are two adrenal *glands*, but they're part of the endocrine system."

"*I* know that," the Growing Younger Man says, just barely avoiding a snap. "System, my ass. The *point* is that anger can contribute to adrenal fatigue, and adrenal fatigue affects—"

"You said Varney left something for me," Rafferty reminds Hofstedler.

"—everything, it affects everything," the Growing Younger Man says. Then he says, with remarkable vehemence, "*System.*"

"If I said that Varney left it, that is not exactly what I meant," Hofstedler says to Poke.

"Varney is the . . . the thug with the mustache?" Wallace asks. He's rubbing his eyes with the heels of his hands, and it makes him look exhausted. "The one who talks?"

"He is," Hofstedler says, hoisting his stein.

"Something wrong with that man, bad wrong," Wallace says, blinking to refocus. "I've seen him before."

Rafferty says, "Where?" and to Hofstedler, he says, "Wait, what do you mean, that's not exactly what you meant?"

"Not this guy, not him personally," Wallace says. "Never met him until tonight. I mean, I don't think I have." His eyes are focused on the middle distance, looking at someone no one else can see. "But people *like* him, I've seen them before. Not many, but some."

To Rafferty, Hofstedler says, "I mean he did not leave the envelope for you himself." He glances at the others, as though seeking support. "He came in and talked of this and that—what was it tonight, Bob?"

"I don't care what he talked about," Rafferty says. "Just tell me where the envelope—"

"I *am* telling you," Hofstedler says. "I think it is all one piece. Astronomy, he was talking about astronomy, about how something with great gravity can bend space into a . . . a—"

"A lens," the Growing Younger Man supplies.

"Just so." Hofstedler nods slowly, as though it requires an effort, and frames a large circle in the air with both hands. "A lens. A curve of space like one in glass, so that light, when it passes through this space, is bent. Imagine this, space curving."

"For Christ's sake, Leon," Wallace says, coming back into the room from wherever he's been, "tell him about the envelope."

"So he talks," Hofstedler says, as though Wallace were in a soundproof booth. "But all the time he talks, I think he is looking for you. Waiting for you."

"That's right, come to think of it," the Growing Younger Man says. "He kept staring at the door."

"Guy's got balls made of brass," Campeau says. "Last time he was in here, we practically kicked him into the street, but he comes in tonight like we were his fucking fan club and just starts talking again, but you know what, Poke? They're right. He was waiting."

"Yes," Leon says. "He talks and talks, and finally he says, 'Is Rafferty coming?'"

Rafferty says, "He did, did he?"

"And I say I am not in charge of your schedule, maybe tonight you stay home, and then he asks where you live."

"And you said?"

Hofstedler gives him both hands, palms up, Delsarte for *How would I know?* "I said I have no idea, yes? Nobody here knows where you live. We are friends, but we do not go home with you."

"What did he say when you told him you didn't know where I lived?"

"Something about the red shift," maybe-Ron says. "How a gravitational lens can distort the red shift."

Rafferty says, "The red shift."

"He said the red shift is how we know which things in the universe are close and which are far away. He said it was very important to know what was close and what was far away."

"And whether it's coming toward you or going in the other direction," the Growing Younger Man says.

"Listen to me," Wallace says, breaking in. He blinks heavily a few times, and Rafferty thinks he might have lost the thread, but Wallace says, "It was his *tone*. When you've lived with violent men, you learn to listen to tone. He was being personal."

Hofstedler says, "This is why I was telling you what he—"

"Until then he'd been bullshitting," Wallace says, "but this was different. That thing about needing to know what was close and what was far away, that was a threat."

"Yes," Hofstedler says. "He said if something is coming toward you, you need to know how far away it is and how fast it is coming. So you can get ready for it—is this not right?" He doesn't wait for an answer. "Then he said, 'Tell Poke I'm sorry I missed him,' and he left."

Poke says, "The *envelope*."

"Yes, yes." Hofstedler reaches into his shirt pocket and pulls out the kind of envelope that might hold a greeting card. "Two minutes after Varney went out, that child, the same one from before, came back in and put this on the bar and went away again. So you see, he didn't exactly give it to you, but—"

"Got it, Leon." The envelope says *Philip Rafferty* on it in an expert calligraphic script, done freehand in black ink. Unlike the first envelope, which had been soaked through, this one is almost completely dry, just one circular splotch from a raindrop that hit dead center in the curve of the capital *R* that begins Rafferty's last name, diluting the ink to create a dark circle, a little like a bullet hole.

Rafferty slides a thumb beneath the edge of the flap and pops it open. It's a commercial card for a person who's suffered the loss of someone close, and on the front is a photograph of gently rolling green hills with a fading sunset in the distance, all seen through a tidy, somewhat fussy typeface that says, *With Sympathy*.

Wallace, looking over Rafferty's shoulder, says, "Somebody dead?"

"My guess is, not yet," Rafferty says, unfolding the card. There's no preprinted message inside, but three lines have been handwritten there, in careful, even precise, block letters. It says:

YOU'RE PROBABLY WONDERING,
OR WHAT?
COMING RIGHT UP.

"What the hell does that mean?" Wallace says.

"It means he wants something from me, and there will be

consequences if I don't give it to him," Rafferty says. He's keeping his voice level, trying for an easy tone, but he feels as if something very large has squeezed itself into his chest, its knees folded against his lungs. He closes the card, putting a lot of effort into keeping his hands steady, and tries three times to slide it into the envelope before he succeeds. He feels Wallace's attention on him and turns to see the old man watching the care with which he's closing the flap. Wallace's face is so empty he might be sitting alone in the dark.

"Wallace," Rafferty says, "you said you'd known people like Varney before. Who were they?"

He has the feeling the question has to travel a considerable distance before it reaches the part of Wallace's mind where the answer is stored. Wallace takes a deep breath and closes his eyes for a moment, and when he opens them, he says, "Guy's a back-shooter." He puts a straight index finger on the bar and draws it slowly toward himself like someone tracing a trail on a map. "If he'd been in my squad," he says, turning the line into an arc, "I would have led him straight into a minefield." All five fingers snap up from the bar's surface, and he says, "*Boom.*" His eyes come up to Poke's, and there's no question that a much younger Wallace is looking out through them. He says, "Never let him get behind you. Never."

12

He Does Not Share the Stage Well

ROSE AND MIAOW will have absorbed their two hours of the dreadful Reverend Slope and *Barchester Towers* by now, and Rafferty wants their company as intensely as he can remember ever wanting anything; he needs them to help him shrug off the anxiety that's wrapped itself around his chest. So he begs off Leon's request to help him take Wallace home, promising to do it next time, even as Wallace dismisses the idea, saying Poke will be no help getting him home, since he barely knows Bangkok at all.

"Yes, but the parts Poke *does* know are the Bangkok we now live in," Hofstedler says. "You, you know the Bangkok of the ghosts."

Wallace pushes his stool back from the bar and says, "Some of my best friends are ghosts."

"Well, Rose would say you should be nice to them," Rafferty says, getting up. "If you've managed to get on a ghost's good side, you want to stay there."

"Ghosts are the only people who can still make me laugh," Wallace says. "You got my leash, Leon?"

"You are joking," Leon says. "I go with you because I enjoy your company."

In the end Rafferty's guilty conscience compels him to wait the long moments it takes Leon and Wallace to organize themselves and get through the door. As he walks them onto the sidewalk, he can't help noticing that Hofstedler keeps a pinch of Wallace's sleeve firmly between his thumb and forefinger.

They stand under the bar's meager awning, looking through a sparse sparkle of rain at the activity in the street. "Remember," Wallace says, "when they put the night market in and that old guy Trink went on and on in the newspaper about how thousands of people would be burned to death if the government didn't listen to him and knock the whole thing down?"

"Old guy," Hofstedler says. "He was old when I got here, and he's still alive."

It was before Poke's time, but he knows about Bernard Trink, a diminutive Belgian who wrote, for years, a sort of sex-trade roundup in the *Bangkok Post* each Friday, complete with snaps of particularly lissome "demimondaines" and tips about which bars were allowing the dancers to "show." The guys in the Expat Bar called the column "The Tart Mart." Eventually an epidemic of politically correct sanity broke out among the *Post* editorial staff, and Trink was put on book reviews.

Wallace says, "And that fucking Dinty Moore beef stew." To Poke he says, "He's in the country with the world's greatest food, and the guy could *not* get enough Dinty Moore canned stew. Wrote about it all the time: 'Foodland is no longer selling Dinty Moore beef stew.'" He's smiling broadly, and he looks more like the man Poke first knew. "Town was a lot funnier back then," Wallace says, and the three of them let a moment pass in silence as the crowd parades by.

Poke is about to say goodbye when Hofstedler clears his throat and says, "Look at them. They think it was invented for them."

"They're young," Wallace says, watching the men in the rain. "They can have it." He turns and registers Poke standing there. Confusion clouds his face, and Poke realizes that Wallace has forgotten who he is. Poke gives him a parting smile anyway, and Wallace surprises him by snatching his arm away from Hofstedler's pinch and throwing it around Poke's shoulder. Wallace is a few inches taller than Poke, so Poke has to look up at him to see that Wallace has recognized him again and is smiling. "You grew up good, kid," Wallace says. "Give my love to your wife, to Jah—" He shakes his head as though something has gone loose inside. "Not Jah, *Rose*, to Rose."

"Will do," Rafferty says, knowing he won't. He's not going to have *that* conversation again.

"Beautiful girl," Wallace says. He gazes past Poke, at the street. "So many beautiful girls."

HOFSTEDLER AND WALLACE are barely out of sight when Poke's eye is caught by rapid movement to his left. He freezes midstep, seeing people scatter as the small boy with the dreadful buzz cut shoves his way through the crowd, breaking into a full-out run, slowing slightly when he sees Rafferty and then picking up his pace as though one of the more persuasive Buddhist hells has yawned open and its demons are right behind him. Rafferty ducks behind a pair of slow-moving drunks, thinking, *Could be Varney chasing him*, but when no pursuer materializes from the crowd in pursuit, he does one fast, final survey and takes off after the kid.

It's too crowded for him to run, but he can track the boy by the trail of pissed-off drunks and the occasional off-balance woman, the second of whom is sitting on the pavement surrounded by the scatterings of a very full purse and swearing a sort of Ingmar Bergman stream of Swedish syllables. A bit farther on, he pushes past a slight young man in shorts who's making a disproportionate fuss about a skinned knee.

The Patpong area is shaped like a capital H, with the two uprights of Patpongs 1 and 2 bisected in the middle by the cross street, which runs through a gap in the night-market booths. The cross street is to Rafferty's right, and the relative disorganization of the crowd in that direction pulls him in.

As he emerges from the area between the booths, the neon of the Queen's Corner gleams to his left. A pair of ladyboys from the

Betty end of the spectrum stand at the entrance with open umbrellas, smoking like a couple of jazz drummers and halfheartedly trying to wave a few customers in from the rain. Directly in front of Rafferty, the short stretch of pavement leading from Patpong 1 to 2 is relatively empty. To his right and left, Patpong 1 is jammed, but whatever groove the boy might have cut through the crowd has had time to close itself behind him, or else the boy went straight across, toward Patpong 2.

"A kid?" he calls in Thai to the ladyboys in front of the King's Corner. One of them makes a little hitchhiking gesture with her right thumb, directing him toward Patpong 2. He waves thanks and starts to run again, then thinks better of it and slows to a brisk walk.

Among the inbred cluster of Bangkok's "adult entertainment" districts, Patpong 2 is the cousin nobody likes, the family member who gets the room without the window. It's right there, just a few dour meters from Patpong 1—which, while it's decades beyond its rancid peak, continues to attract throngs of gawkers who don't know any better. Still, Patpong 2 is a marathon dud, even though it shares the Patpong name and offers the same shopworn attractions, plus an assortment of spuriously upscale "cocktail lounges," where wannabe executive punters sit at tables, drink hard liquor, and hit on the waitresses, who have shown up solely to be hit on. There's also an all-boy go-go bar that seems to have wandered several blocks down Surawong from the gay stretch that's blossomed there in the past eight to ten years, known as "Soi Katoey" in honor of the ladyboys who decorate it each evening. Other than these minor variations, the family resemblance to Patpong 1 is marked.

But no one comes to visit. There's one person here for every fifteen on the other street. From where he stands, Rafferty can see both left and right almost to the intersection at each end, and there's no kid with a bad haircut. The rain has thoughtfully lightened, so visibility is good. He steps up on the sidewalk, and, hearing Wallace say "back-shooter," he peers through the plate-glass window of the cocktail lounge on the corner before he leans his back against it as he reviews how he got here and what might be next.

The boy had been running, but no one had seemed to be chasing him. So, two possibilities. First, whoever was pursuing the boy—for argument's sake, let's say it was Varney—had seen Rafferty and stopped, melting into the crowd. Second, of course—and it's suddenly so obvious it feels like a whole tray of ice cubes poured down his back—there may have been no one at all after the boy. He may have been sent to draw Rafferty out, may have been running solely to *get* Rafferty to follow him—maybe to Varney—and Rafferty has, brainlessly, fallen for it. That means that Varney, or whatever surprise Varney might have arranged, is in front of Rafferty, not behind him.

Perhaps the surprise is an explanation of what Varney means by "Or what."

It feels like a ripe moment to stand still. Wallace, he suddenly thinks, probably knew how to size up the most logical spots for ambushes, trip wires, and punji pits in a jungle. Rafferty believes he's developed an equivalent eye for the streets of Bangkok. This seems like an appropriate time to put it to work.

To his left is a row of outdoor bars, just pink-lighted tables sharing a single long, thick, dripping concrete roof, from which hang a few flat-screen TVs tuned perpetually to the soccer game of the moment. Rafferty has come to the conclusion that there's a soccer game being televised somewhere in the world at every second of every day of the year and that Bangkok sits at the very bottom of a kind of digital valley, down into which every single one of these games rolls, ripe for television. On the far side of the outdoor bars is the sidewalk, and on the far side of the sidewalk are the doors to the indoor bars. The kid isn't visible in the outdoor bars, and he wouldn't be allowed into the indoor ones. With his back comfortably pressed against the solidity of the cocktail lounge, Rafferty studies this nocturnal little cityscape until he's reasonably certain he can discount it as suitable to Varney's purposes.

Just to the left is the first of the indoor bars, the infamous Star of Light, whose slogan could be "Decades of Oral Satisfaction." Movement catches his eye, and he sees a woman in the black clothes favored by the bar's specialists leaning against the wall with an expression that suggests she's projecting her personal movies onto the rain. She catches his eye for a second, sees nothing to engage her attention, and returns to her reverie. No one else is visible in the stretch of street beyond her. So scratch the left.

To the right are a couple of cocktail lounges like the one he's leaning on and a massage parlor, and then there's a slight elbow curve that leads the last twenty or thirty meters to Silom. There's some kind of fetish club there, beneath a big sign that says, helpfully, FETISH CLUB, although Rafferty has never been able to imagine what kinds of fetishes are so trivial or so wholesome that their practitioners would walk boldly under that sign and through the door. He thinks it's probably people who don't alphabetize their bookshelves or intentionally wear mismatched socks and want to be mildly reprimanded. Beyond the fetish club are a couple of stores selling cheap luggage that are open until 2 A.M., and beyond those is the busy sidewalk of Silom. He figures he can dismiss the street to the right, too.

So that leaves the area more or less directly across the street.

It's a teensy bit of middle-class life, a snippet of Pleasantville dropped into Gomorrah: two respectable-looking restaurants and a big, shiny supermarket, a Foodland, bright enough inside for a person to get a fluorescent tan. It's so pragmatically Thai, he thinks: towing the kids past the Fetish Club, the Star of Light, and two or three more of the most disreputable bars on the Asian continent to buy them a Tootsie Pop in Foodland. Look, kids, here's *this* part of life, *that* part of life, and here's your Tootsie Pop, and when you grow up, you'll have to decide which door to go through, so pay attention.

Foodland and the restaurants, he believes, can also be struck from the list of the likely destinations Varney might have chosen to explain the specific nature of his *"or what?"*—perhaps accompanied by a short, painful, and memorable teaching aid.

Rafferty feels like he's been here too long.

What remains, when the right, the left, and most of the area across the street have been eliminated, is the thing he hasn't wanted to think about: a narrow, dreary alley in between the restaurants and Foodland, a little dead end with a curve to it that leads perhaps ten meters to a door, once the entry point to a dodgy girlie bar that seemed to change its name every few weeks and took advantage of the alley's length to provide enough time so the patrons could stow the dope and the women could get up off their knees and wipe their chins, before the cops came in. The space is empty now, and, Rafferty thinks, one way God could demonstrate his or her existence would be for it to remain empty until the end of time.

Surely Varney can't think Rafferty is stupid enough to enter that alley in pursuit of the running boy moments after getting a message about "or what."

Well, how stupid *is* he? Stupid enough to come this far.

Varney is selectively capable, Rafferty thinks. Probably much more dangerous in a small, dark space than Rafferty is, especially since, as Treasure says, he can't be hurt. But he's got one obvious drawback: he talks, but he doesn't listen. And then Rafferty hears one of Miaow's acting terms: *monologue.*

Varney is a monologist. He does not share the stage well. The entire relationship between the two of them has, so far, been a monologue with Varney getting all the lines, setting the parameters, and calling the shots. It's been a bravura performance in bits and pieces, and it's been allowed to flow largely unchallenged. And when Rafferty *had* challenged it, in the silliest possible way, with the Halmahera Sea, Varney hadn't liked it at all.

So challenge it again. Walk away right now, leaving Varney waiting to spring his surprise on no one. Just remember to keep checking your back. Take the most obscure and counterintuitive route home to your wife and child and soak yourself in the atmosphere of love, liberally seasoned with amused tolerance, that they've created for you.

And write yourself a part. Turn the monologue into a dialogue, one that Varney doesn't control. One with some surprises in it. Take some immediate precautions for those you love and for Treasure, and then kick this thing into act 2, in which Varney no longer has all the good lines.

So he does. He turns and walks away, looking back every few steps. He's not running away, he tells himself, he's making a strategic retreat. It takes him almost forty minutes and two taxicabs to get home, but when he's there, he knows he's arrived alone. *Upper-Crust Theatre* is over, the television is dark, and the people he loves most are there. He kisses both of them, eats some leftover take-out food, listens to Miaow's imitation of Alan Rickman, and goes to sleep feeling that tomorrow he'll go to work on the second act.

And in the morning he reads that a male street child has been found dead in an unused and partially burned Patpong bar, and at around ten that evening, after a day spent in a kind of stunned self-loathing, he gets a call from Leon, who says that there's a new note, and when Rafferty insists that Leon read it to him over the phone, he learns that it consists of three words: *Where is she?*

Part Two

THE BANGKOK OF
THE GHOSTS

13

Thai Heaven

THE CANAL THAT parallels New Petchburi Road is the worst-smelling waterway in Bangkok, a town notable for noisome canals, a vast, interlacing network of open-air sewers. The people who live beside the canals poop directly into them, and hundreds of underground pipes carry waste from the more distant and more socially elevated neighborhoods straight into these slow-flowing diversions of the Chao Phraya River. There are places where weeds grow on the water's surface, rooted in the floating night soil. Walking on Wallace's left, Ernie says, "Whoever called this place the 'Venice of the East' was born without nostrils."

Wallace had laughed the first time Ernie said that, as though he'd known what Ernie was talking about when in fact Wallace had no idea that anyone had ever compared Bangkok with Venice. He'd never seen Venice either; Wallace's Venice was a vague, misty, postcard vision of crumbling old buildings afloat somehow on a flat gray sea with a bunch of movie extras pushing boats along with poles and singing. A Californian's Europe, steepled with churches, stripped of color, full of foreigners, and cold.

Even though he'd heard the joke before, Wallace laughs again now. It's become automatic for him to laugh when Ernie uses that flat, uninflected voice that says, *This is nothing special*, and means he's thought of something funny. Wallace turns to say something to him, but Ernie's not there anymore, although Wallace is sure that Ernie just made a joke and that it had been Ernie, a minute or two ago, who'd first spotted the lights of Thai Heaven, where Jah is waiting.

But when Wallace looks ahead again, the lights aren't there. Nor is the smaller constellation of lights that signals Rhapsody, the bar across the way from Thai Heaven. Instead the road stretches away in front of him, a straight black line paralleled by the leaden gleam of moonlight on the thick, stinking canal water to the left. On the right side of the road, he sees the indistinct shapes of foliage. Here and there a kerosene light gleams in one of the small, wooden, stilted houses that alleviate the flatness of the riverine semi-swamp on which Bangkok is built, still dark and unbroken in this area, as empty as it would be if the nearest city were a thousand miles away. But just then the swamp shimmers and wavers for a second, and here's Ernie again beside him, but not looking the same, looking dead, which, Wallace remembers, he is; Ernie has been dead for years. And the canals have been cleaned up for years, and the swamps have been built over for years, pressed beneath the weight of skyscrapers and tunneled through for subways, but here Wallace is, walking a dark road through the swamp with the stench of the canal—the *klong*, they call it—to his left.

The moonlight on the canal breaks into circular ripples as though a stone has been thrown, although there's been no splash, and Wallace realizes that this version of New Petchburi Road— the "Golden Mile," they call it—shouldn't be this empty: there should be other guys walking, there should be smaller bars here and there, and he should have passed Jack's American Star Bar, where the black guys hang out to the sounds of live jazz and rhythm and blues, and the girls have permed their long, straight Thai hair into Afros.

But those things are absent, and Wallace senses that the edges of this moment, of this place, are more flexible than usual, that space is twisted so that it might be a kind of Möbius loop where he'll soon come upon his own footprints in the road and then see himself up ahead, trudging away into the distance. The margins to the right and left feel fluid and permeable, like a page off of which the words might heedlessly run or onto which sentences from a different page, or a different book altogether, might suddenly push their way, a train wreck of meaning.

Ernie says, "It's something, ain't it, kid?" and when Wallace looks at his friend this time, it's apparent that death has almost finished with him: Ernie's uniform hangs in rotting tatters, and his face seems to have melted a bit, so that the bone beneath the skin of his forehead gleams through, smooth and white and somehow unthreatening. With the expertise of someone who has dreamed profusely since childhood, Wallace realizes he is dreaming.

Wallace spent his childhood in a nightmare-free zone, probably because the days were so benign. The ocean was right there, serving as the western margin of the small town of Carlsbad, California—a blue, sparkling margin that advanced and receded, but on a regular basis and not enough to be alarming—and the sun was a permanent fixture in the sky, supplying the gold in a color scheme that was dominated by the harmonizing blues of the sea and the sky, the white of the sand, and the eye-piercing orange of the California poppies that carpeted the hills, soft as folds of cloth, as they tumbled toward the water.

To be sure, there were monsters out there in the deep, and once in a great while something lifted sharp teeth toward Wallace's helpless feet, coming up out of the deepwater darkness of a dream. But when he woke up, he knew where he was: in a safe bed, in a safe house, in the bosom of a safe family who lived in a safe town. The real monsters were kept at bay . . .

. . . waiting for him in Vietnam, where he found them all. He found them in the enemy, in his friends, in himself, in the sudden death of his comrades, and in the hell his platoon created in the villages. In the dead children, the weeping women, the small, dark-skinned men standing stunned with their hands secured behind them, waiting for the bullet.

His dreams went very, very bad during his first tour, and one night he was awakened because he was making too much noise in his sleep. The person who woke him, Ernie, taught him a secret. When the dream goes wrong, Ernie said to Wallace, swing your fist, as hard as you can, at the nearest solid object. When you don't break your hand into a hundred pieces, you'll wake up.

It took Wallace dozens of hair-whitening dreams before he remembered how to find that exit, but when he did, he learned it deeply enough that after a while he could play with the bad dreams, see how far they could take him, how unendurable they could become, before he swung at the nearest tree, the nearest wall. In Carlsbad he had ridden the mostly mannerly waves of the Pacific. Now he surfed fear in his sleep, and there was nothing mannerly about it: he was riding ten-footers, twenty-footers, tsunamis of fear, daring it to get bigger, then bigger still, and ducking out of the wave when it did.

So, trotting along a dark, unrealistically empty New Petchburi Road beside his dead friend, with a stinking *klong* to the left and a haunted swamp to the right, with the lights of Thai Heaven having disappeared in front of him, Wallace figures he's got five or six more numbers on the volume knob before it's time to bail. Remembering Ernie's question, he says, "*What's* something, Ernie?"

"All of it," Ernie says. "The whole fucking mishmash. Every one of us who got dropped into that meat grinder, on both sides, to fight a war that never should have been fought. A million people dead, and I've met a lot of them by now, and what did we accomplish? I mean, why am I rotting here?"

"Guys in suits," Wallace says. It had been their answer back in 'Nam.

"Dead now, most of them," Ernie says. "Of course, *they* died on silk sheets on top of mattresses stuffed with money, or in intensive care in some hospital that was like a medical country club. But I have to tell you, Wallace, I hope some of them writhed with colon cancer, screaming in some white room while the nurses poked them for fun and told each other jokes. I hope some of them wound up pushing their swollen scrotum in a wheelbarrow, listening to people say, 'Hey, Jack, how's the balls?' when there they were, big and bright as day, the size of watermelons, fire-engine red, and hurting like a nail through the toe."

"Well," Wallace says mildly. He burned through his anger long ago, but Ernie died with his at its zenith. It was what had kept him going when he was alive, it was what had sharpened the edge on the jokes. "As you said, they're dead now."

"Fuck that," Ernie says. "You know what? Doesn't make any difference if they're dead. No difference to the world, I mean. They're like the girls on Patpong: they're immortal, one generation replacing another so you hardly notice. The fatsos in their suits, they're always there, they always look the same. In the big offices, in the goddamn capital cities. All dressed alike, all keeping their eyes on the big cake, all with the fucking flag pins in their lapels. 'Make money, shore up our power, by killing people? Sure. No-brainer. Next question.'"

"Look," Wallace says. Up ahead the night thins as though water has been poured into ink, and the lights of Thai Heaven shimmer toward them. Inside, there will be music and drinks and the famous sky-blue dance floor and dozens and dozens of women, but however many women there are, he'll be looking for Jah. "Ernie," he says, "why are you here? Just a visit?"

"A *visit?*" Ernie says. "You don't think I've got things to do?" He looks at his watch, and Wallace looks with him, seeing the skin disappear to reveal the bones of Ernie's wrist.

"Well, then," Wallace begins.

"Remember Hartley?" Ernie says, and when Wallace, surprised at the name, looks over at him, he's Ernie again, his uniform pressed and neatly buttoned, the same expression, the one that says, *We have to find something funny about this or we won't get through it,* and Wallace hears quite clearly the last two things Ernie ever said in life, sitting thunderstruck beneath a tree with his insides spilled into his lap. He'd looked down at himself and said, "If you're going to take my picture, I need a minute." And then he said, "Hold my hand?" and slumped sideways, and while he was still falling, he made his escape.

"Hartley," Wallace says, pushing the memory away. "That motherfucker."

"You just met him again," Ernie says. "You know who he is. And you need to be careful."

Music reaches Wallace's ears, but it's the wrong music, not the Beatles and Beach Boys and Doors songs that keep everybody dancing in Thai Heaven, but some kind of marching music, all brass and drums, trombones and tambourines. Ever since 'Nam, Wallace has thought that the phrase "military music" is a perversion of language, an evil oxymoron along the lines of "sadistic sex," taking something that should be constructive and peaceful and chaining it to aggression and discord. He says, "The guy with the mustache."

"Bingo," Ernie says, and then he says again, ". . . ingo," but he sounds farther off, and then, farther away still, he says, "*Ingo, going go, going to go*," and the lights of Thai Heaven flicker and die, and Ernie's gone, and the music gets louder, and the water in the canal rises up like a wall, black and putrid, as the sky shimmers and brightens with the false dawn of exploding ordnance just over the horizon, and there's nothing for Wallace to swing his hand against, so he drops to his knees and punches the road with all his strength and sits up in bed.

The window is on the wrong side of the room, he thinks, and then he says out loud, in a voice that's all breath, a voice that sounds like he's been kicked in the stomach, "*Ernie*. What does Varney have to do with *me*, Ernie?"

14

Showing You Who He Is

STIFF-FACED, ARTHIT GLARES at the little white card for
the fourth or fifth time, turning it over again, checking the back,
just as he has every time he's picked it up, as though he might have
missed something there. He's wearing plastic gloves in spite of the
fact that they're probably useless; half the people in the Expat Bar,
plus Rafferty and Rose, have handled the damn thing. Still, he'll
take it in for prints when he reports to the obscure substation to
which he's been exiled.

"*Where is she?*" he reads aloud, and as though on cue, there's a
burst of laughter from the room that Treasure and Chalee are
sharing, the room that Anna is in now, too, getting the girls ready
to head over to the shelter for school. It's early Monday morning.
The daytime thug, Pradya, is waiting in his car just outside, and
Rafferty has prevailed on the nighttime thug, Sriyat, to follow
them a couple of cars back, looking for anyone else who might be
trailing along, and do a quick check of the shelter's neighborhood
before he goes home to bed.

Arthit glances at his watch. "They should be on their way. It's
getting late."

"Class won't start until Anna gets there."

"It's *Father Bill,*" Arthit says, and there's an edge to it. "We're on
tiptoe, trying to show him how dot-the-i's we can be."

They're at the dining-room table, the fish traps pushed to a corner to make room for the papers that Arthit brought home from the station on Sunday evening and spread all over the surface. Anna and the girls had eaten breakfast in the kitchen, and the strain among them seems to have thawed somewhat, because the girls had chattered and Anna had joined in, and every now and then they'd dissolved into giggles. Rafferty can only imagine how hard Anna must be working to keep up with the kids' words. "Father Bill has a lot on his plate," he says.

"He's a saint," Arthit says, raising both palms to rebuff the implication that he'd meant anything negative about Father Bill. "I have no idea how he does what he does. I've only got *two* of them here, and it's all I can—" He breaks off and smiles, a bit overbrightly, at someone behind Rafferty.

"We're ready to go," Anna says, coming in from the living room, dressed in the slightly official-looking dark slacks and blouse that constitute her teaching uniform. She widens her eyes as a call for attention and holds up one of her blue cards, on which she's written, *Say something about their clothes.* Then she says, out loud to Poke, "We all went shopping last night after you left. Your big friend followed us."

Arthit says, "He fit right in, especially in the girls' clothing stores."

The girls file into the room. Treasure seems barely to be present—she's pulled back, Poke thinks, into the protective shell she wore at her father's. Chalee is aglow with pride, but behind it Rafferty senses a kind of frazzled desperation. Wearing a big smile, she looks rapidly from one of them to the other, never pausing to hold anyone's gaze, and then lowers her eyes to the clutter of paper on top of the table as though she expects to find something about herself there.

"Don't you both look nice," Arthit says, sounding like someone who's rehearsed the line a hundred times and is finally saying it in front of an audience and knows he's getting it wrong.

"Don't they?" Anna says after a moment's silence. The girls' clothes are so new that Rafferty can practically hear them squeak.

"Let me guess," he says, diving in. "You two switched your shirts."

Chalee gives an enormous blink, but Treasure's gaze is steady, and she turns her head a few inches to regard him from the corners of her eyes. Chalee says, "How did you *know?*"

"I see all those orange ruffles on Treasure's . . . uh, blouse and I think *Chalee.* I see the little blue anchor on the pocket of yours and I think *Treasure.*"

Looking at her feet, Chalee says, "I never went to a store before. I think I picked out things that were too fancy." Her face is red. "When I see Treasure wearing that blouse—"

"It's a beautiful blouse," Treasure says. She glances at Rafferty and instantly away again, then clears her throat. "I talked you into letting me wear it."

"*All* my stuff looks like that," Chalee says despairingly. "Like they're in a cartoon. When I look at Treasure's clothes—"

"You chose lovely things, Chalee," Anna says. She's kept her eyes on Chalee's lips as the girls spoke. "But if you want to trade them, we can go back this afternoon."

"I want clothes like Treasure's," Chalee says.

"Well, I'm keeping this," Treasure says. She tugs at a random ruffle. "I like it."

"Let's go, let's go," Anna says. "We're going to be late." She shoos the girls out of the room.

"How did you know that?" Arthit asks. It's half whisper, half hiss.

"I didn't. I just guessed. That blouse was a poor kid's idea of fancy. But if I'd been wrong, they both would have jumped all over me, and they'd have liked it even better. Kids love to be right."

"It pisses me off that you know how to talk to them," Arthit says. "I say hello, and I feel like I'm doing an interrogation."

"Arthit. I've had *seven years* of Miaow. It took me a year to get anything out of her except yes and no."

Arthit lifts a hand and focuses on the table in front of him, clearly listening. In less than a minute, the front door opens. "Goodbye!" Anna calls, and then the door closes again.

Rafferty says, "Classy gesture on Treasure's part, trading blouses or shirts or whatever they are."

"They're like sisters, and that's both good and bad," Arthit says. "I already doubt that I'm up to it. Treasure, I mean. She works so hard to seem confident, on top of things. But she jumps whenever there's a loud noise, and last night she had a bad dream, woke up screaming, and wet the bed. It took Anna an hour to calm her down, and then she climbed into bed with Chalee." He rubs the bridge of his nose with his thumb and forefinger, his eyes squeezed shut. "I'm not supposed to know that happened. I didn't dare go into the room with Anna."

"It's who she is, Arthit. Actually, I think she's behaving pretty well, considering what her father put her through. And it's not going away anytime soon."

"When you first took Miaow in—" Arthit begins.

"Not the same. Miaow was very complicated, and she didn't trust either of us, but the street had made her . . . I guess the term is 'self-sufficient.' On a practical level, she could take care of herself, dress herself, feed herself, defend herself within reason. I think it was a year before she said thank you for anything. Emotionally, she was a wreck. No one had ever loved her. Her parents weren't even a dim memory. But Treasure had it even worse. There were two people who were *supposed* to love her. But her father beat her, terrified her, treated her like a ventriloquist's doll, and her mother hid in bottles of whiskey and codeine, so loaded she had a maid whose main job was to make sure she didn't burn the house down. So Treasure's problems are, maybe, deeper than Miaow's were."

Arthit says, "But look at Miaow now."

"Rose has been pouring love into her for years. And Anna will do the same for Treasure, and eventually, or at least possibly, if everything goes right and everybody's karma is good, it'll bring about a miracle. You don't have to take the lead. In fact, you shouldn't get anywhere near her physically until she comes to you. Essentially, you can do what I did—hide behind your wife during the really rough periods and then come out and be cool when the kid's put herself part of the way back together."

"Even if that would work, which I doubt," Arthit says, "I've never been good with kids. And I have no idea how to be cool."

Rafferty raps his knuckles on the table. "Then let me ask you the big one. If she stays, do you think you could learn to love her?"

After a silent moment, Arthit says, "Ah."

"Yes," Rafferty says. "That's pretty much it."

"But . . ." Arthit says. He takes a deep breath, makes a big, popping *P* as he blows it out, and moves some papers around in front of him. "Even if I can, how am I supposed to show it?"

"You just feel it. If you do feel it. And when you discover that you do, focus on it and let it fill you up, because it will. Believe me, she'll notice."

Arthit shifts uncomfortably in his chair. "I see."

"Arthit—do you *want* to do this?"

He takes a stack of papers, squares them, and raps the stack's edge against the table. "Anna does."

"That's not the same—"

"She misses her son so desperately," Arthit says. "And that human hangnail she was married to won't let her see him."

"Treasure is *not* Anna's son," Rafferty says. He pushes himself away from the table and thinks for a moment about how to frame what he wants to say. "Look, I don't usually give advice, but when you've got a kid who doesn't know who she is, it's not a good idea to wish she was someone else."

"You want to know the truth?" Arthit says. "The whole thing scares me to death."

Rafferty gets up and picks up both of their coffee cups. As he goes through the kitchen door, he says, over his shoulder, "Good. It should."

Pouring the coffee, he hears Arthit say hopelessly, "And then there's Chalee. What *are* we going to do with Chalee?"

"VARNEY WANTED US to find the boy fast," Arthit says. "He wanted to get the message out." He's sitting straight now, in his professional posture, and he's been organizing the documents into rows. Looking at the sheet squarely in front of him, he says, "Foodland manager got a call around three twenty Sunday morning, maybe four hours after you left, saying there was a fire in the closed bar, the Suction Cup, I think it used to be."

"Male or female?"

"Female. Thai. 'The bar next to you is on fire.' Then a hang up. There's only one bar that shares a wall with the market, so the manager ran down the alley to . . . to whatever it was."

"What it was, was a pit."

"And sure enough the door's ajar and there's smoke pouring out. So he kicks it the rest of the way open, the manager does, and finds two big wastebaskets on fire, filled with compressed trash, just restaurant and supermarket litter—bags, food cartons, torn-up cardboard boxes, stuff like that, but really pushed down, like an adult had stepped on it."

"To keep it burning longer," Rafferty says.

"The room was almost empty—just a few tables and broken chairs and the bar. The boy was in plain sight, on top of the bar." He takes a deep breath. "His neck had been broken."

"So he died fast."

"Yeah." Arthit scrubs at his mouth with an open hand, as though trying to scour away a bad taste. "I'm sure it was terrifying, but it was quick."

"But, you know, I'd been thinking that Varney killed the kid because he was angry. Because I hadn't shown up, I mean. He was furious, and he took it out on the kid. But—" He clears his throat. "But four hours later? I could see it if he'd done it right away, in a rage, but—"

Arthit says, "But he didn't."

"Are you sure? Maybe he killed the kid and then sat there for a while, trying to figure out what to do next."

"No," Arthit says. "Body temperature was too high. Almost normal. The boy died less than an hour before we got there."

"So he took his time, keeping the kid there, maybe to let the streets clear so people wouldn't see him leave, and then he killed him," Rafferty says.

Arthit says, "In cold blood. And then he called attention to it. You know where this is going."

Rafferty feels as though his coffee might come back up. "I do."

"You didn't come when he wanted you to, and he *thought* you might not, and he had an alternative plan in place." Arthit pushes his chair away slightly, measuring Poke's reaction. "He's showing you who he is."

"Yeah." Rafferty finds he needs the chair's back, and he slumps against it. "The note he sent me Saturday night said I was going to learn what he meant by 'or what.'"

"Maybe just the beginning," Arthit says.

"He's telling me he's willing to murder a child to get my attention. A *street child*, and I'll bet you anything you want that he knows that my daughter used to be a street child. Showing me his fucking credentials. And if I don't give him what he wants, there'll be more."

Arthit says, "He did a lot of work to draw your attention to it." Shaking his head, he picks up the card again and again reads it aloud. "*Where is she?* He wants millions of dollars. He wants Treasure, for some reason. He's saying he'll do anything to get her."

Rafferty says, "I have no idea how to deal with this."

"Well," Arthit begins, and then he tables what he was going to say. "Let's calm down for the moment. Here's what we've got. Using a coroner's picture of the boy and a description of Varney, we haven't found anyone who saw them together, and people would probably remember if they had, because that's a combination—adult foreign man and little Thai kid—that's not supposed to happen anymore, at least not in plain sight. But we do have two people who saw them a few feet away from each other for thirty seconds or so on the night the boy was killed."

"Where were they?"

"Silom end of Patpong. One of them was on door duty at the Thigh Bar, down near the end, and the other was a vendor, practically at the beginning of the street. She also saw—the vendor, I mean—she saw Varney leaving Patpong, on the run, the night you chased the kid. He took off in one direction and the kid in another, a couple beats later."

"He was heading for the empty bar," Rafferty says. "He ran the sidewalk on Silom and then turned left up Patpong 2."

"Probably waited with the kid until you came out of the bar, told him to count to ten or something, and took off to get to the bar ahead of you."

Rafferty says, "Did anyone on Patpong 2 see him go into the bar? When I got there, I saw a woman from—"

"The Star of Light," Arthit says. He touches three or four pieces of paper and pulls one toward him. "She's trying to quit smoking, and everyone inside was puffing away, so she went out for some air just as he charged past Foodland and into the alley. She couldn't describe him, except to say he had dark hair, because he was practically past her by the time she saw him, but who else could it have been? Anyway, about a minute later the kid streaked across the street and into the alley, and then she saw someone whom she described very accurately as you."

"She didn't wonder what a *farang* and a little boy were doing in a closed bar?"

"She did, actually, but one of her regulars showed up right after you left and dragged her inside with him, and then it got busy. She quit at two and went home, didn't think about it again until the next morning. When she heard the news, to her credit, she called the cops." He puts down the sheets of paper and paws through some others. "So four hours after Varney and the kid went into the bar, the Foodland manager calls the cops and the fire department. Our guys showed up first."

Rafferty gets up, just to move. At the far end of the table, he picks up one of the fish traps and turns it over in his hand, looking down at it but barely seeing it. "All this happens in that half of Patpong 1. That's the end I come in on, when I go in at all. He may not know where I live, but he knows what direction I come from. Oh, and besides the kid, there's the bar worker he had following me. I only really saw her once, the first night I met Varney, and she had so much makeup on over that birthmark that it was hard to see what she really looked like or how old she was. Christ, if someone else hadn't spotted her, by now I'd be wondering if her birthmark was makeup, too."

"Who spotted her, and where?"

"Ladyboy named Betty from King's Corner. Saw her going into Cowgirl. I was going to go back for her Saturday night, but I had to get home. And if she's the one who made the phone call to Foodland, I don't think she's got much of a future."

Arthit says, "Give me a better description." He writes as Rafferty talks. When he's finished, he says, "We'll scoop her up tonight." He looks up and asks, "Why does he want Treasure?"

"I don't know," Rafferty says. "Maybe that thing about her living with him if anything happened to her father was more than just talk. Maybe Murphy *promised* her to him." He sits back, blinking. "Or maybe she's Murphy's heir. Maybe he sees her as the way to get his hands on her father's estate."

The two of them silently think about that for a moment. Rafferty says, "Maybe, to look at the worst possibility I can think of, maybe Varney inherits if anything happens to her. And it could be a lot. A guy with three million in his closet might have money salted away all over the place."

"Well," Arthit says, "he's not going to get her." He pushes his chair back as though he's going to stand, but instead he sighs and sits still, his eyes on the rows of paper. "I'm going to work on this, unofficially," he says, "and it's all I'm going to do. The one good thing about being banished to the Nowhere Station is that I'm out from under Thanom's nose." Thanom is the superior officer who is embarrassed that Arthit saved his career. "So you and I will be holding hands, so to speak. And I know one or two other former cops whose services I can borrow to supplement your pair of hit men."

He gets up, and the two men face each other over the table. Rafferty says, "*Former* hit men."

"If you say so." Arthit holds up the card again. "I'd like Anna not to know for the time being that Varney wants Treasure. I'm going to put one of those cops on this house to reinforce your whatever-he-is when the girls are here, but I don't want them to know about it." He returns the card to the table and reaches for a sheet of paper that's at arm's length. "One more thing," he says, "just as a point of information. The vendor at the end of Patpong who saw Varney near the boy that night? She says Varney had a little camera and he took a couple of pictures, just before he ran off. He was pointing it up Patpong, which is to say toward you."

"Taking pictures of me," Rafferty says. "Why?"

"To give to someone you don't know?" Arthit suggests. "Might be another indication that he knew even then that he was going to kill the boy and he'd need to give a picture to someone else, someone you wouldn't recognize, so he or she could follow you."

"Maybe a *bunch* of people I don't know," Rafferty says. Then he says, "I'll feel a little better when you find that bar girl."

15

I Need the World to Hold Still

THE RAIN, WHICH had lightened on Sunday, has returned, bringing the wind along as an extra dividend. Rafferty's cheap umbrella has already been yanked inside out, so he tucks it under his arm on Arthit's front porch and resigns himself to getting wet.

He stands just far enough from the curb to be visible to the morning's oncoming traffic and raises the useless umbrella to flag a cab. There's a pothole about three feet in front of him, and a surprising number of cars manage to hit it as they go past, throwing a shin-high wave of oily water in his direction. He barely notices, just keeps waving his skeletal umbrella at the slow-moving stream of traffic and thinking about what he can and can't do.

One thing he knows he can't do is find Varney, if the man doesn't want to be found. Bangkok is just too big and too full of trapdoors and obscure corners. Arthit has put out a request for Varney's immigration paperwork, but they both doubt that it will contain any information about where Varney is or who he might actually be.

But Varney *needs* to talk to Rafferty. If Rafferty had gone in, that boy—

He shuts the thought down, blinking against the force of it, but it won't stay down. The boy *what*? Would be alive? Maybe, maybe not. Varney probably would have sent the kid away so he could make his demands without witnesses or just beat Rafferty half to death to get the information out of him. Up until now the man has done nothing in front of witnesses. The two of them have said something like four sentences to each other. Varney has made his demands through those anonymous notes, with nothing to link him to them except the boy.

So maybe he would have killed the boy later to eliminate the connection. And maybe not.

The boy had been seen too often. Varney must have been planning to replace him. Why else take the picture? Arthit's right—it had to be so someone new could spot Rafferty, someone waiting at the Silom end of Patpong with a photo in his hand. Maybe as a replacement for the other person who knows Varney, the bar worker with the loopy curls. He has an impulse to cross his fingers for her.

All that effort so Varney can find Poke. He *needs* to find Poke.

All right, then, Poke will make sure Varney can find him. That seems to mean hanging around Patpong.

A cab splashes to a stop in front of him. He gets in and says, "Patpong."

"Is morning," the driver says, in English, pulling into traffic. "Nothing open."

"I'm sorry," Rafferty says, wringing out the cuffs of his pants. "I was thinking out loud. Silom Soi Pipat."

They inch forward in silence for a moment or two, and the driver says, in Thai, "I hope that was a cheap umbrella." His eyes find Rafferty in the mirror to see whether he's been understood.

"Two hundred baht," Rafferty says, in Thai.

"Probably you could have gotten it for a hundred and twenty," the driver says, nodding agreement with himself. "It's cheap, so you'd still be wet, but for eighty baht you could buy a towel." He accelerates briefly and then brakes again, and Rafferty realizes it's going to be stop-and-start all the way home. "You want a girl?"

"I have one."

"Then why did you want to go to Patpong?"

"I didn't. It was a mistake."

"Patpong is always a mistake. Your girl, she's Thai?"

"Yes."

"Only one?"

"One is all I want."

Since they're not moving anyway, the driver turns partly around to take a look at the *farang* who only wants one woman. "How long?"

"Almost seven years."

"Married?"

"With a daughter."

"Good man," the driver says. "She can cook?"

"Who? The wife or the daughter?"

"Either one."

"Neither of them. They're good at getting things out of the refrigerator, but that's about it."

The driver sighs and fiddles with his window. "Must be beautiful, then."

"They are. Both of them. Smart and good-hearted, too."

"Those are important," the driver says. "But cooking matters."

Rafferty says, "Bangkok is full of food."

The driver sees daylight opening up ahead and sprints toward it. "You're a lucky man."

"I am," Rafferty says, and he thinks, *Time to move Rose and Miaow.*

ANNA REALIZES HER mistake the moment she, Treasure, and Chalee walk into Boo's office, which they're still using as a classroom. She shouldn't have let the girls wear their new clothes. The kids in this room have never worn anything new in their lives. Compared to them, Chalee and Treasure look like they're walking the red carpet.

Despite her efforts to get out of the house in time, they've arrived a few minutes late, so the other students are already in their seats when she follows the two girls in. Every eye in the room is wide, pasted to the bright new blouses. The store-fresh, unwrinkled jeans. The clean, unscuffed shoes. Most of these kids have spent their lives in mismatched flip-flops.

Anna can't hear the silence in the room, but she sees that no mouths are moving, although many are hanging open. She watches the blood mount in Chalee's face as she feels the attention being directed at her. Treasure seems oblivious. She has not allowed anyone but Dok and Chalee to get close to her. She's so separate from the others that she might as well exist three or four seconds in advance of them, as though if they reached out to touch her, she wouldn't be there anymore. Anna sees this attitude as a survival mechanism from Treasure's years in her father's house.

Treasure pauses just inside the room with the check-everything alertness she's demonstrated since she heard about Varney, and then goes in, surrounded by her invisible walls. A couple of girls snicker at the garish blouse Chalee bought. Treasure brushes past Tip, the boy with the crush on her, ignoring his smile as if the only one in the room she sees is Dok. She slows as she approaches Dok's chair, but he avoids her eyes, and she quickens her pace again to get to her seat in the front right corner of the room, where Dok and Chalee can keep the others away from her.

Anna sees Chalee follow Treasure in, her feet dragging in her bright new shoes, her eyes on the floor.

One of the boys puts two fingers to his mouth and makes a sound that Anna thinks must be a shrill whistle. Chalee straightens, and her face stiffens. A few other boys laugh, but the girls are silent. One of them reaches up and tugs at Chalee's borrowed blouse, but when Chalee pauses and glances down, the girl drops the cloth and wipes her hand on her own T-shirt.

In order to get to her seat, Chalee, like Treasure, has to pass Dok. Dok, still angry about their disagreement, pulls his chair back a few inches as though to avoid being touched, and Chalee stops.

Her chin dimples with the effort it takes to keep her lips pressed together as she stares down at Dok, who turns his head away from her. She looks around the classroom and finds everyone occupied with something else. When no one will return her gaze, she turns at last to Anna, searching her face for something. Whatever it is, she doesn't see it, and she lowers her eyes to break the connection and picks once, twice, at Treasure's new blouse with the blue anchor on it. Then her face crumples and she whirls around and pushes past Anna, out of the room.

Treasure waves an arm to draw Anna's eyes. "Let her go," Treasure says, even before Anna realizes that she'd been turning to follow Chalee. "What can you tell her?"

Dok pushes his chair back and stands. He says, "She's *still* my friend," and he's out and through the door in almost no time.

Anna feels like she's walked into a wall. The new clothes were a spotlight; Chalee had gone home with Anna on a Friday and returned on Monday wearing an outfit that cost more money than most of these children have ever had, clothes that announce as clearly as a trumpet fanfare that a change has taken place, that life will be different for Chalee now. Accidentally, Anna has built a wall between Chalee and the others. The children have always felt that Treasure was an exotic, a migrating bird that wouldn't be with them long, but Chalee was—*had* been—one of them.

And, of course, she still will be. Treasure will be gone, but Chalee will still be here. Homeless, with her useless new clothes. She won't even have anyplace to keep them.

Anna feels a hot wave of shame rise within her. As it heats her face, she feels Treasure's eyes on her from the corner. The girl's gaze is remote and empty of emotion or even curiosity. She's simply assessing Anna's reaction.

There's only one thing to do. She has a classroom of children waiting, most of whom have normal hearing while some are hearing-impaired. She walks to the whiteboard and waves up the child who can sign to the others. "Neung," she says, steadying her voice. She picks up a marker for the whiteboard. "Please come up and sign for me."

When Neung is halfway to Anna, Treasure shoves the girl aside, on her way out of the room.

NORMALLY WHEN ROSE is on the couch, Rafferty sits on the white leather hassock, now stuffed with Murphy's cursed money, so he can look across the glass table at her. But for this conversation, he wants to be beside her, preferably touching her. So he has his hand resting on her thigh when she says, in Thai, "How good a hotel?"

"First-rate," he says. "Four stars." No response. "Five?"

She lifts her chin, almost never a good sign. "I wanted my mother to come down."

Rafferty nearly groans; they'd talked about it, but it's slipped his mind entirely. He says, "We'll get her a room, too."

"How nice," Rose says. She takes a strand of hair and winds it tightly around her finger, watching it with what seems to be fascination. "Maybe we'll be on the same floor." She gives the hair a yank and says, "I don't suppose you'd like to explain it to me."

It takes him off guard, and he says, "I can't believe I haven't." He's about to go on, but she lifts a hand that says, *Stop.*

"This is the wrong time to uproot us," Rose says. She pats the air with her hand to indicate that he's to let her finish. "I don't bother you with this very often, but right now I need to be sure of things. I need the world to *hold still.* I get up every morning and think about the baby, looking at the place it will be born into. When we're talking to each other, I'm thinking about the baby, how you'll feel about everything when he—she—they are here. When I'm with Miaow, I'm wondering what kind of a sister she'll be for the baby. When we're watching TV, I'm wondering whether the baby can hear all that English so it can learn two languages at the same time." She brings an index finger up and blots beneath her eyes. "And what it's all really about is keeping the baby *safe*, and here you are—"

"You don't *bother* me with it?" Rafferty sits forward, trying to see into her eyes. "Don't you think I do the same thing? Maybe not as much as you do, but every day—"

"But here we are," Rose says. "And you're asking us to move."

"I'm frightened," he says. "You know that I don't usually waste time getting frightened, but right now I'm scared to death."

She pulls her leg out from beneath his hand, her arms crossed tightly over her belly, gazing down at her lap. The space that opens between them seems to be filled with clear, cold air. Through the sliding glass door to the balcony, clouds, edged here and there with pewter, glower sullenly at him, but Rafferty can see just the top half of the door from the couch because of the big flat-screen, which continually surprises Rafferty by its presence in the room. The apartment is quiet in the way it is only when Miaow isn't in it.

Rafferty says, "I want you and Miaow out of here." He tells her about Varney, about the demands for Murphy's money and Treasure, and about the boy's death. "He doesn't know where we live," he says, "but I don't think that's going to last very long."

Rose says nothing.

"I can call your mother," he says.

She waves it away. "She's not the problem. The baby is the problem, Poke, because that's what I *do* now, I think about the baby."

Rafferty's cell phone rings.

With what sounds like resignation, Rose says, "Answer it."

"I don't want to answer—"

"Does that mean that you know what you want to say to me?" Now she's looking straight at him. "After what I just said?"

"It's complicated."

She gets up. "Answer the phone."

The display reads ARTHIT. Rafferty gets up and says, "Hey."

"Hey yourself," Arthit says. "Bad time?"

"Need you ask?"

He watches Rose go into the bedroom without a backward look, a fist closing around his heart. She shuts the door behind her.

"Well, I've got good and bad, or at any rate interesting," Arthit says. "Good first?"

"Sure," Rafferty says, fighting an impulse to kick the flat-screen over. "A little variety is always welcome."

"Everyone's safe at Boo's place. Your guys prowled the area, and no one's there who shouldn't be. Your night guy is gone, and my day guy has arrived."

"Great," Rafferty says. "And the interesting thing?"

"Arthur Varney came into the country twice. First time was a little more than six weeks ago, second time was about two weeks ago. First time from Australia, second time from Phnom Penh. This was easy to find out—his embassy has been making some noise about him because he was supposed to be back four weeks ago."

"He doesn't sound Australian."

"Well, he wouldn't. Arthur Varney's body was discovered in Pattaya nine days ago. About the age and the size of the guy you describe. He'd been dead a little more than two weeks. And two weeks and a couple of days ago, someone with Varney's passport, undoubtedly doctored, went to Phnom Penh and got a new visa for Thailand, since Varney's original visa was good for only four weeks. And then, despite the fact that he's dead, Arthur Varney came back into the country."

"Well, well."

"So he's keeping that identity viable," Arthit says. "He may be using it at his hotel."

"You think so? After the cops identified the body?"

"They didn't. It was washed up on a beach, probably thrown into the water quite a ways offshore. He was naked, he'd been pounded into hamburger, and then the fish erased the rest of the things you use to describe someone. In the news stories, the body was a John

Doe. The Pattaya cops only got confirmation of his identity, through fingerprints from Australia, a couple of days ago."

"Will they sit on it a little longer?"

"Already set. To be modest, it's not as hard to get them to sit on something as it is to get them to do some work."

"So you can check the hotels."

"Already am. But don't get your hopes up too far. There are thousands of hotels, and some are going to be more responsive than others. Also, for all we know, Varney's passport might not be the only one your guy has in his possession. If he's done this once, he may have done it several times."

"Still," Rafferty says. The bedroom door opens, and Rose comes out with a long-sleeved blouse over her T-shirt and her hair tucked up. She sits on the couch and folds her hands in her lap, fingers interlaced. She has the most beautiful hands and wrists Rafferty has ever seen, hands that cry out for a musical instrument. "It's something, isn't it? And for now you've got an edge, because he doesn't know that the Varney passport is a magnet."

"Right. I'm not only sending an alert to the hotels but also pulling together a list of Western men who have recently been reported as missing and whose visa was renewed while inquiries were being made about them. Looking for new names Varney might use when this one wears out. And finally, if this thing isn't settled in two weeks, he'll have to make another visa run in order to keep that passport alive. If he does, we'll have him at the airport."

"Good," Rafferty says, mostly because a comment seems to be expected. "Good thinking."

"Well, I've got a stake in this, too," Arthit says. "Anna has her heart set on Treasure."

Rafferty says nothing because he can't think of anything, and Arthit adds, "God help us," and disconnects.

Rafferty ends the call and looks at Rose, who gets up and says, "Let's go find a hotel I want to stay in."

16

The Only Thing That Lit It Up

HUNCHED OVER THE rickety kitchen table where he eats his meals—when he remembers them—he slides his index finger across the sheet of transparent plastic. Beneath the plastic, blistered here and there by tiny bubbles of trapped air, are the flat patterns of black and white, actually black and yellow after all these years, that reopen the past. The plastic is stiffening, and it's turned a bit milky. Seen around the blisters and through the haze, the patterns resolve themselves into men.

Men face the camera, usually clustered in tight groups, looking as if the proximity is more about comfort than camaraderie. Not many smiles other than Ernie's, although here and there someone soberly makes rabbit ears behind someone else's head. In the biggest picture, centered on the page, one of the guys has a blurred face because he turned quickly toward a sound none of the others heard: Steve, who usually walked point, and for just that reason. The faces are young; the eyes, most of them, are old. Some of them already have the thousand-mile stare, and a few are glazed with dope. There are a lot of cigarettes. Here and there a thick, defiant joint. Here and there an upraised middle finger.

His own finger pauses on each face as the names float to the surface. Steve; Eddie; Big Mo; Horse; Ernie, with his grin on crooked; Antwone; T-Bone; Slack Jack; that kid who died before Wallace memorized his name; Wallace himself, looking very pissed off about something; Fat Frank; the Korean guy everyone called Soul, meaning *Seoul*, which amused some of the black guys; another kid who died before Wallace memorized his name. After a while you learned not to get close to the new guys, so it wouldn't hurt so much when they went down. And in fact the two unnamed dead boys went down on the same awful night, about three days after the photographer pointed his camera at them.

Your basic eight-man squad plus five drop-ins. Wallace's squad.

He slaps his pockets, looking for cigarettes, fails to find them, and forgets he was doing it. The picture in front of him, which he's hidden from himself for years and pulled out because of his dream about Ernie, has gathered potency. It's more real than the room he is in.

The shot was taken on the perimeter of a temporary camp bulldozed out of the bush, one of dozens. Two or three or four days after these men stared into the camera, Wallace's squad had moved out, into the ambush that killed the two new guys and Antwone. In their absence the camp had been targeted with surprising precision by a VC gunnery crew. Three of the drop-ins—T-Bone, Fat Frank, and Horse—had been in it when it was blown to bits.

The math is blunt. Out of thirteen people in the picture—thirteen? what were they thinking, was *everybody* loaded?—out of thirteen, six were dead within a few days. And Ernie was killed under that fucking tree a year or so later, during Wallace's final tour. So seven. Seven dead.

That he knows of.

He screws up his face, trying to remember who took the picture. Whoever it was, he'd used Wallace's camera, which is why Wallace has the photograph, but the photographer's face has been erased, as have so many of the faces from that time. Hundreds of them, gone now. Probably in self-defense; it's easier to think of the lost as numbers instead of faces, names, voices, hearts. People.

That's why he never looks at the photographs. They bring back the faces. And the voices, which are even worse.

Ernie's joke voice, dry as tinder. Slack Jack's slow Mississip' drawl. Or Antwone's, the deepest speaking voice Wallace ever heard, which he almost never used unless someone was hurt, and then the voice cradled whoever it was, for however long he lived. Soul, who wasn't even born in America but had volunteered anyway, whose Korean accent put the letter U at the end of many words; eventually the entire squad said "yesu" instead of "yes," and back in camp other guys stared at them. One of the two kids whose name Wallace never learned, a short, wiry guy with dramatically blue eyes, had a reedy, ephemeral voice that immediately led most of the others to brand him as gay until he caught the big, bad one the night of the ambush and died the way most of the men undoubtedly hoped they would: probably scared shitless but managing a kind of quiet, distant acceptance. And that was good, because other people were getting shot and no one could have fussed over him anyway. Not even Antwone, who was down himself by then, his spirit well above the trees.

All of them, just cards in a hand from a well-shuffled deck, dealt at random, straight into the grinder.

"Fuck 'em all," Wallace says aloud, meaning the men in the suits.

"They shoulda died twice," Ernie says.

Behind the soldiers but out of focus, an abstraction of alternating light and shadow, is the bush they hid in, hunted in, and were wounded and killed in, the steaming, malodorous, eternally wet bog of mud and red dust, trip wires, snakes, leeches, monkeys, guns, knives, punji pits, and panic: a stick cracking underfoot someplace near, a sudden squawk of radio noise, the glint of the lens on a distant gunsight. The villages, slapped together by the people who built them dead center in the clearings they created, as though they'd consciously chosen to live in a target.

Wallace reaches for his beer, but it isn't there. No beer, no cigarettes. Wallace says, aloud, "What have I got left, Ernie?" Ernie chuckles. Ernie was the only guy Wallace ever knew who actually chuckled, sort of half laugh, half cough.

A sudden knot in his lower back lets him know he's spent too much time bent over the album. With the surge of irritation that's never far from the surface these days, Wallace advises his spine to fuck off and leans even closer to engage Ernie's two-dimensional gaze. Ernie looks the way he always looked: as though he's a moment away from making himself laugh.

Wallace straightens in his chair and grunts. Runs his thumb over the album's upper edge, looks down at the line of grime on his skin, and wipes his thumb on his pants.

Wasn't he looking for his beer?

He gets up, pushing down on the edge of the table, which wobbles as it always does. The kitchen is the yellow of old butter, a color Wallace has always disliked. A lopsided pile in the sink announces the presence of every dish he owns, plus a few bowls, some foggy-looking glasses, and a couple of blackened frying pans. Utensils bristle out of the glasses. He says, "Gotta wash up."

But he doesn't. The refrigerator kicks into its low hum, like a bid for attention. Wallace realizes that going to the refrigerator was the reason he'd gotten up in the first place. He gives the squat little appliance a stern look, waiting for it to volunteer some information, but all it does is shut down its whir, as though daring him. Irritation rises again inside him and then flows out, leaving him empty. Purpose deserts him. He stands there gazing blankly at the refrigerator for a long moment, feeling like he's dangling lightly at a rope's end, a weightless husk, the air blowing him slowly back and forth. He can almost hear the toes of his slippers brushing the linoleum. A big shrug and a shake of his head bring his weight back, and he slips both hands into the pockets of his worn jeans. His thighs still feel reassuringly strong and ropy. He wanders into the living room, empty except for a long, scarred wooden coffee table standing patiently in front of a couch that seems to be undergoing a slow-motion explosion, with white foam popping through the edges of its cushions. Both pieces of furniture rest on an oval hooked rug that had been in his mother's bedroom in Carlsbad and may or may not have been made by her grandmother. The story changed depending on the level in the vodka bottle.

"Here's to you, Mom," Wallace says, replying to her favorite toast, and that reminds him why he got up. He says, out loud, "*Beer*," and yanks his right hand from his pocket to scribble the word on the air as a reminder. "Stay there," he says to the word, turning his back on it. Ernie chuckles. Since he's facing his bedroom, Wallace thinks, he might as well go to the bathroom. He doesn't particularly need to, but he's up and headed that way and he has to piss a lot lately, so why not now? He says aloud, "Economy of motion is our motto."

It's getting dark outside, and the rivulets of rain rippling the gray bedroom window take him off guard. For a few unmeasurable moments, he'd been back in Carlsbad, in the house he'd grown up in, and he had been expecting to see the eternal sunshine, pouring down on beauty and ugliness alike, spending itself as generously on the oily grime of a gas station as it does on a white curve of blue-edged beach. Looking at the gray rain wrapping itself around his building, he feels the sun's warm arm thrown over his bare shoulders as he runs down the path between the succulents and the poppies to the sea, his board tucked, feather-light, against his side, his body perfect and flexible, with a slender beauty he'd never appreciated until it was decades behind him. Wallace at seventeen, his hair a mass of curls bleached blond by the sun, a snarl of light. The Kid, the surfers called him.

The Kid.

What was I doing? he asks himself as he pees, remembering too late to lift the seat. *I was doing something. Before I got up for the beer, I was doing something.*

"Maybe you're right, Leon," he says. "Maybe I can't be alone now."

Alone. He's alone because he'd been a fool, because he'd been an idiot, because he'd been an *asshole*. Because, at the end, he'd been hopelessly outmatched, not so much by war as by love. War, he'd learned to prepare himself for, but against love he'd had no defenses, no map, no commanding officer, no half-forgotten briefing to orient his compass. It has taken him years to recognize that it had all been love with Jah, every moment of it, even at the end. *Especially* at the end, in the two or three seconds when he destroyed the only good, true thing that ever happened to him.

He hadn't known what to do with it.

And he can't allow himself to remember it all now, his self-destruction, as fresh as if it had happened only a few days ago. It's too much for him, it's more than he can handle. It reminds him where he keeps his gun.

Closing his eyes doesn't help. So he opens them wide, yanks himself toward the present, and finds the toilet handle by touch before turning back toward the bedroom.

He hears himself say aloud, "Jah."

On the other side of the streaming window, the city has grown darker. (The gun, an old revolver, is on the top shelf of the closet, beneath a never-worn sweater.) He sits on the edge of the bed, watching lights ripple on across the street. The Bangkok night: he had traded his life for the Bangkok night, and then he'd broken the only thing that lit it up.

(The bullets are all the way across the room from the closet, in the drawer of the bedside table. It had seemed like a safe distance when he put them there.)

He swallows something that feels as big as a softball. (The cylinder, carefully removed, is in the living room.) *Three steps*, he thinks. *Gun, cylinder, bullets. Three steps isn't so many.* And then he thinks, *Maybe I should throw away the bullets.*

Why is he alone?

Dodging the question, he puts his hands beside him on the mattress to prepare for getting up but can't think of anywhere that would be better. Maybe he'll call Leon. Go to the bar. The *bar*, he thinks. Poke. The guy with the mustache, Varney. Ernie saying, "You remember Hartley?"

Hartley.

He's up and moving, out of the bedroom, through the dark living room, switching on the kitchen light to see the roaches scatter, detouring to the refrigerator to grab a beer, and then he's flipping through the photo album, a cascade of young, mostly dead faces dragging names in their wake, and there it is: there's the picture he'd been looking for, and there's Hartley. At the edge of the group, always at the edge of the group.

There are a lot of reasons to join the armed forces, and the worst is because you purely want to kill people, and that's why Hartley had joined. Even the men in his own squad, a squad with a lot of blood on its uniforms, had stepped back from the intensity of Hartley's violence. In the picture he's turned partway to his left so that he finds the camera out of the corner of his eye. It seems to Wallace that Hartley looked at everything from the corner of his eye. The only thing the son of a bitch did straight-on was shoot. Son of a bitch could *absolutely* shoot. Problem was getting him to stop. Even after all his tours in 'Nam, Hartley was the worst person Wallace had ever met.

Well. Ernie had been right, and Ernie had been wrong. Arthur Varney wasn't Hartley. If Hartley were still alive, he'd be as old as he, Wallace, is now. But Varney and Hartley would have recognized each other on sight, would have picked each other out of a crowd of thousands. Varney, Wallace thinks, like Hartley, would never shoot head-on, at least not at anyone who was armed. Like Hartley, he'd find a perch, a blind, a place to wait until he could take a shot that wouldn't be returned. And he'd take the shot with joy.

He thinks, *I should warn Poke.*

He goes to find his phone so he can call Leon to come get him.

17

That Travesty on Her Face

VARNEY'S NOT GOING back to the Expat Bar, Rafferty is sure of it. Not after the boy's death. If Patpong is to be the meeting ground, Rafferty needs to find a place to hang his big fat face out in plain sight, at least until Arthit comes up with the hotel that Varney is hiding in. *If* he's using the passport with that name on it.

So: someplace Rafferty will be conspicuous. That narrows it down to several restaurants divided between Patpong 1 and 2. What they have in common is bright lights inside and big windows through which he'll be visible from the street. Varney will probably be more comfortable if the place is busy, a lot of people going in and out, competing for the attention of the staff. There are four possibles.

One of them is the RiffRaff, right at the top of Patpong. In addition to having a nice big window, the RiffRaff also serves decent food, if you stick with the Thai entrées the employees eat, and the thought makes Rafferty realize that he's hungry.

Late afternoon has dragged itself in, surprisingly sunny but with a gray slant of rain visible a mile or so away. The country boys who assemble the night market are shirtless in anticipation of the downpour as they fire up their forklifts and ferry up and down the street toting stacks of plywood and the lengths of steel pipe they'll turn into frames for the booths. Rose is at home, waiting for Miaow to finish packing for the Imperial, the hotel Rose liked. Five seconds prone on the bed in the suite they had chosen was a life-changing experience for her, making Rafferty's sagging old double feel like a field of stones by comparison. The Imperial, he thinks, could be an expensive proposition. After Miaow's finished, the day guy, Pradya, will drive them to the hotel and bribe the staff to let him claim a space where he can watch the front until he's needed or until he's replaced by Sriyat.

Rafferty pushes the RiffRaff's door open and walks into a wall of air-conditioning. The staff greets him with big, welcoming smiles. This was where he usually ate when he was roughing out his book, back in the days of early confusion, before Wallace came to his rescue. Most evenings he sat with his laptop at the window table, taking in the nightly transformation of a drab little street into a tarnished peacock, flashing its off-color feathers in a commercial mating display. He'd watched the night market blink into life beneath its dirty fluorescents as the sidewalks filled up with the voluntary homeless of all continents, their bonds cut, their promises forgotten, their common sense abandoned, looking dazzled to be in a no-rules zone where love, if not exactly free, was at least inexpensive and without apparent consequences.

In and out, in all senses of the expression, no harm, no foul. Except perhaps for the women, and anyway they seemed to have no real lives outside the bars, even though they could be surprisingly human in the morning. Still, look at 'em, they smile all the time (*everybody* smiles all the time), and they're probably doing better than they were in whatever dirt-road, dog-shit-spattered slum they'd escaped. They're doing okay, and if they aren't . . . well, whose fault is that anyway? Plane leaves in a few days, back to the real world, where the women, inconvenient though it might be at times, lead actual lives. And this isn't really a city, it's a theme park. Everybody's acting, everybody's fine. That's why they smile, isn't it?

The waitress rattles gossip at him in Thai—this cook was

stabbed by his girlfriend, that waitress's daughter got into college—and leads him to his customary window, the window through which, all those years ago, he'd first seen Miaow. He'd had his laptop open as he tried to find his way to a sentence he could believe, until he felt a presence and realized he was separated by about eighteen inches and a pane of glass from a very dirty little girl with severely parted, tightly pulled-back hair. The first thing that struck him, aside from the filthiness of her T-shirt, was the rigid control in her face: tight mouth, furrowed brow, betrayed eyes, an expression most people don't acquire until their beaten-down forties. A shallow wooden crate hung from a strap that ran behind her neck and obviously cut into her skin. The crate was full of chewing gum. She'd tilted it against the window, letting the glass take some of the weight.

He smiled at her and realized she was paying no attention to him at all. She'd been drawn by the glow of the laptop. He gave up on his sentence and swiveled the laptop toward her so she could see the screen better. Her eyes widened and came up to his, and then she backed away and took off at a run. She'd returned half an hour later, though, and then the next night and the night after, hypnotized by the luminous screen.

Now, of course—now that she's one of the two people he loves most in the world, now that she's played Ariel in *The Tempest* and is about to play Julie in *Small Town* and learned English and had her heart broken by a boy and replaced the boy with Benedict Cumberbatch and the entire British national repertory company—*now* he knows that she came back because that's who she is: she comes back for what she wants until she gets it. On the fourth or fifth night, he'd persuaded her, via Delsarte-style signs through the glass, to come in, and he'd bought her a Coke, which was all she wanted. Then he'd set up a game of pinball on the computer and abandoned her for half an hour after telling the staff she could have anything on the menu. When he came back from his stroll, the Coke was half drunk, the score on the screen was astronomical, and there were three packs of gum—all different flavors, just in case—stacked neatly on his plate.

That was a little less than seven years ago.

This street, he thinks. As wretched as it is, it gave him the two people he cares about, it gave him the only real home of his life.

He sees the first few bar girls of the evening, the early birds, filtering through the crowd, chattering like actual birds and flirting for practice. Rose and Miaow should be on their way to the Imperial by now, to the ridiculously expensive suite. Rose had been the most beautiful of all these young women once, the queen of Patpong, when he met her.

Looking at the bar workers, he realizes what he hasn't been thinking about: the woman with the birthmark. As he reaches for his phone to remind Arthit, it rings. And it's Arthit.

"I need you to meet me," Arthit says.

"Where?" Without waiting for an answer, Rafferty says, "That bar girl with the—"

"That's it," Arthit says. "I need you to identify her."

"Oh," Rafferty says. Then a huge amount of air forces its way out of him, and he squeezes his eyes closed and says, "Oh, *no*."

"You have something to write with?"

"Yeah, yeah, yeah." He wants very badly to break something.

"It's pretty awful," Arthit says. He gives Rafferty an address. "Have you eaten?"

"Not yet."

Arthit says, "Probably for the better." A moment goes by, and he adds, "And I'm pretty sure he left a message for you."

Rafferty's up, miming writing on the air to tell the restaurant staff he needs his check, even though the food hasn't come. "What is it?"

"You need to see it."

THE FIRST THINGS he sees, around Arthit, who's in front of him, are the fingers of her right hand, which are curved as peacefully as those of someone who's sleeping, But then Arthit steps aside, and he sees the rest of it: the blood on the bed, the garishly ornamented face. Against the rust-brown pool that surrounds her, and against the crude, mocking scrawls of makeup on her lips and eyes, the skin of her face is startlingly, angelically, white. Her birthmark, unsoftened by foundation, brings to Rafferty's mind the awful, fraudulent color of the grape-jelly handprints.

She had not put the cartoonish makeup on. Rafferty had seen her *real* makeup, and while it had been thick, it was artfully done. This was *slashed* on, crookedly and maliciously: big, uneven scarlet lips, hard-edged spots of rouge on her cheekbones, eyelashes drawn with an eyebrow pencil, so long they go straight through her eyebrows to her forehead and down her cheeks to her chin.

"It's her," he says. He swallows hard and turns away, feeling a rush of heat in his face and seeing gnats swarming the air in front of his eyes. He says, "And I'm going to kill him."

"I understand the feeling." Arthit takes Poke's arm and leads him from the tiny apartment, just a cement floor, a thin mattress, a limp little bouquet wilting in a glass jar on the floor near the pillows. On the wall hang a couple of birthday cards, a careful braid of cheap gift-wrap ribbons, and pictures of the girl taken years ago, her face village-girl clean, her smile broad and eager. The hand raised in each photo to cover her cheek might have looked coy if you hadn't already seen the birthmark. Happy forever, she's flanked by girls, probably the friends who young people think will be with them forever.

At the door Rafferty stops. People have gathered at one end of the hall, held back by two uniformed cops. The tenants, if that's what they are, are silent and curious. Some of the women give the flint-beneath-the-skin impression that says they might be bar workers or some other kind of pro. A crime-scene officer pushes past Arthit into the apartment with a curious glance at Rafferty's face and closes the door behind him. "The fucker spent the night with her," Rafferty says.

"Shhhh. They don't yet know, at least officially, that there's been a death," Arthit whispers. "The landlord asked us to soft-pedal it. Half of them will move out to avoid the ghost." He leads Rafferty down the hall, away from the onlookers. When they're a few yards farther away, Arthit says, "Why? Why do you say he spent the night?"

"Her face. Under that makeup her face was absolutely clean. Rose told me that when she was working, last thing she did every night was wash her face, and I mean she really scrubbed it, washing off the whole night and everything that went with it. This girl was sensitive about that birthmark, she's covering it in her pictures. She went to work already made up. If he'd knocked on the door in the morning, she would have at least slapped on some powder or something before she let him in. No, he was here last night, when she washed her face. She knew him well enough to let him see her without the makeup, to let him see the birthmark. He probably told her he liked the birthmark, that . . . that she was—" His throat seems to have closed, and he clears it forcefully and says, "He probably said she was beautiful." He kicks the corridor wall. "The sick fucker spent the night with her, made love to her, and then did *that*. And left me that message."

"I haven't shown you the message—" Arthit begins.

"The *makeup*. He turned her into a parody of a bar girl. Making sure I'd understand. He was killing Rose, metaphorically, same way he was killing Miaow when he murdered that street child. Didn't want me to miss the parallel, so he does that . . . that travesty on her face." He feels his voice thickening and forces himself to breathe and then swallow, but it doesn't help. "*Jesus*, Arthit, she was just a harmless young woman. She . . . she didn't think she was pretty, and she was self-conscious about it—she curled her hair, probably for hours every day, she tried to hide that mark on her cheek." He realizes he's pressed his hand to his own cheek and lowers it. "You know, she did what she had to do, day in and day out, not hurting anyone, just waiting or hoping for something good to happen. God*damn* him."

"I agree, I agree." Arthit is patting Poke's shoulder. "It's terrible."

"I need to see my wife," Rafferty says.

"First you have to look at something. It was clearly left for you."

"What?"

"The *message*." Arthit turns, gives the group of people at the other end of the short hall a brief, businesslike smile, and goes back to the apartment door. He knocks once, and when the door is opened, he says a few words and is handed a brown paper bag. Tucking the bag under his arm, he returns to Rafferty, pulling on latex gloves. With his back to the onlookers, he opens the bag and pulls out a bloodied copy of Rafferty's book *Looking for Trouble in Thailand*. Rafferty reaches for it, but Arthit pulls it away and shakes his head.

"I think it's extremely unlikely that this belonged to her," Arthit says. "He left it underneath her so we'd find it."

"Did he write something in it?"

"In a manner of speaking." Arthit opens the book, and Rafferty sees the piece of thicker paper—like an index card but bigger— that's just barely sticking out of the top edge of the pages. Arthit tugs it out and turns it to him. "What does this mean to you?"

Rafferty looks down at it and feels himself squint. The card is blank except for three numbers and two symbols. It's obviously another laserjet or inkjet printout; no one could ink them in so evenly by hand.

1 √
2 √
3

"Means the same to me that it probably does to you," Rafferty says. "He wants to tell me he's behind both of these killings and that there's a third on his list."

Arthit says, "I was thinking that, too, but then I wondered about the *three*, whether it might be an allusion to your family, the three people in—"

"I'm sure you're right. And you know what? He *wants* us to wonder. Because he's going to explain it. He's *burning* to explain it. This is just a topic for a speech. I know to the marrow of my bones that he wants me to obsess over it until he can take the stage again, and he's going to deliver that monologue if it kills him."

Arthit folds the bag down, tight against the book's edge. "Let's hope it does," he says.

18

The Stench of Men

ALL DAY LONG, ever since the dream at Arthit's house woke her up, Treasure has been smelling men again.

For a few weeks after Dok and Chalee found her and brought her to the shelter and she discovered—to her surprise—that she could escape and didn't want to, she had stopped being aware of the smell, she had stopped *scenting* them around corners or on the things they'd touched. But now it's back.

The stench of men, the heaviness of their smell, the reek that always makes them seem even closer than they are. The throat-jamming smell that had filled her nostrils when her father dragged her onto his knee and squeezed the pressure points on the sides of her neck to force her to open her mouth so he could imitate her voice and make her seem to say the words he wanted to hear from her. The smell of his friends. The sharp, ammoniac smell she associated with Paul, or Varney, or whatever his name was.

It was a new dream. She was in a big room, a kind of room she'd seen only in magazines, enormous and empty and dim, with marble floors and dark pictures on the walls. She couldn't see what the pictures represented, because when she looked at them, the patterns on the canvas shifted around. The meaning would almost declare itself when she looked just past it—a face, a figure—but when she tried to make it out, the image was gone and in its place was a vertiginous smear of color.

There was some kind of music playing somewhere, maybe one of those old instruments that was almost a piano, the little ones that sound kind of tinny, that were on the covers of the classical CDs her father sometimes listened to. The music her father liked was old and jittery and fast, a lot of instruments all at once and no voices, with notes all over the place. When she liked it, which wasn't often, the notes from the tinny little piano were like handfuls of diamonds thrown into a sunny room, hard and bright and full of rainbows. When she didn't like it, the notes were needles of ice, drilling through the air almost too fast to see, driving themselves into her skin.

She didn't like these notes. They made her want to put up her hands to ward them off. She couldn't tell which of the room's doorways they were coming through. There was a big open doorway in the center of each of the three walls she could see, and the space on the other side of the doors was velvet black. She was in the center of the room with her back to the wall she couldn't see, as far from the doors as possible. She was certain that something was going to come through one of the doors.

And then she knew, all the way to her gut, that what she was afraid of was already here, in the room with her. She wanted—she needed—to turn her head and look behind her, but her neck was rigid as though her—her father was squeezing it, and then the music stopped; it didn't finish, it just *stopped*, and she heard a noise behind her, the scrape of something hard sliding over something hard. As she tried to force her head around, the room flickered and brightened for a second, growing lighter and then the light dying down, and she sensed movement above her and looked up—it took no effort to look up; her head slid up and down easily but refused to turn left or right—to see a large spider shadow on the ceiling. The spider immediately resolved itself into the shadow of a hand with the fingers outspread, curling and straightening, and then the shadow was obliterated in a flare of light, and she turned her entire body to see Paul lifting his arms toward her, opening them to *receive* her, his hands balls of flame.

Smoke enveloped her, but it didn't smell like smoke. It smelled like men. The smell got stronger and sharper, edged with whiskey, and she knew that it was her father, that her father was right behind her, in his chair, and that one step back, one step away from Paul's flaming hands, would put her in her father's lap. She felt his fingers on her bare thigh.

"You were really screaming," Chalee says. "Even Mrs. Anna—"

"I still could smell him, after I woke up," Treasure says. Her heart is slamming in her chest again, the way it had the previous night. "And when she came in, when Mrs. Anna came in, I could smell her . . . her husband on her, like some of his smell had rubbed off."

Treasure and Chalee sit close together on a bare canvas cot, but Dok has claimed a wooden box a few feet away, as though he knows this is really a girls' conversation and they might at any moment kick him out of the room. Chalee says, "You didn't seem afraid of him this morning."

"I learned not to show it. My, my father *liked* it when I showed it."

Dok says, "Can you smell *me?*"

Treasure shakes her head. "You just smell like Dok."

"Yeah?" Dok says. He plucks his shirt to his nose and sniffs. "What do I smell like?"

"Like a friend, I guess."

Dok ducks his head and blushes at the floor.

The three of them are crowded into the corner farthest from the stairs on the building's second floor, where the girls sleep. Like the first floor, it's big—it can accommodate thirty cots in rows of six, with a meter separating the head and foot of each pair and aisles between the rows wide enough for two girls to walk through side by side. Like the first floor, it's dusty and hot and fragrant with mice. *Unlike* the first floor, it boasts faded curtains, actually old pillowcases, that hang limply over its windows,

Boo's instinctive recognition of female modesty and the fact that there are men out there who want to see the things the girls in the shelter are modest about. Because of the curtains, the room is dim except for the slashes of late-afternoon sunlight on the floor, light that has edged its way in through the gaps between the pillowcases.

Treasure can hear the buzz of the second floor's permanent population of flies. Other than the three of them, the room is empty except for one ragged new girl, eight or ten years old, dark-skinned and mosquito-bitten on her cheeks and forehead, who either sleeps or pretends to sleep on a cot halfway across the room.

"Can you smell all men?" Dok asks.

"Mostly. Some of them smell more. Young ones don't smell as much, or anyway not bad. Boo smells like a clean room."

Chalee says, "I can smell the stuff he puts on his hair."

"I smell through those things," Treasure says. "Perfumes and stuff. I smell right through it, to the man."

"What about Poke?" Chalee asks.

"Poke smells like . . ." Treasure squints and wrinkles her nose. "I don't know. Linen? He smells a little like girls, like his wife and daughter."

"Poke always looks so clean," Dok says. "I'd like to look that clean."

Chalee says, "*I* can't smell Mrs. Anna's husband."

Treasure wraps some of her hair around an index finger and tugs. "He smells like leather."

There's a long silence, broken by the girl on the cot, who sits up and says, "Leather?"

"Like a belt," Treasure says. "Or a . . . ummmm, a strap. A leather . . . a leather strap."

"I can't smell any of them, really," Chalee says.

The girl on the cot says, "*Everybody* stinks," and lies down again, her back to them.

Dok says to Treasure, "Are you really not going back with Mrs. Anna?"

Treasure closes her eyes and leans to the left, against Chalee's shoulder. Chalee smells to her like Mrs. Anna's soap. "I don't know."

"I'm not," Chalee says. "I wouldn't go back for anything."

"Then I won't," Treasure says. "I couldn't be there alone."

"That's silly," Chalee says. "They want *you*."

Treasure takes her head off Chalee's shoulder. "I can't be in the house with him if you're not there, too. And I like it here. I guess."

Dok says, "I don't."

Treasure looks at him for a long moment. "Then why do you stay? Why not go back to . . . to wherever you were before?"

Dok and Chalee exchange a look, and Chalee says, "It was no good." Treasure starts to speak, but Chalee cuts her off. "I mean *really* no good."

Dok says, "Men," and then he's blinking fast and staring at the nearest curtained window as though he can see straight through it.

Between her teeth Treasure says, "I *hate* men."

"Me, too," says the mosquito-bitten girl on the cot. "Every one of them."

"I like some men," Dok says. "I like Poke and Boo and Father Bill."

"I'd leave in a minute," Treasure says, "if I knew someplace safe."

To the girl on the cot, Dok says, "Where were *you* before you came here?"

"Street," the girl says. "Don't go."

"We've been," Chalee says. To Treasure she says, "Mrs. Anna loves you."

"Mrs. Anna doesn't even know me," Treasure says. "She wants a child, and she'll settle for me. And I don't want a . . . a father. Not now, not ever."

The girl on the cot says to Treasure, "Someone wants you? Is that what you said?" Her voice is hoarse, as though she's been screaming.

"Yes," Treasure says.

"Are they mean? Will they treat you badly?"

"Probably not."

"Will the man bother you?"

Treasure is silent for a moment, looking up at the closed curtains. "Probably not."

"Do they have a house? Would you have your own bed? Do they have enough to eat?"

"Yes."

The girl says, "Then you're crazy."

Treasure puts her hands together, palm to palm, and clasps them between her knees, leaning forward until she's bent almost double. As she straightens up, she says to Chalee, "*Will* you go back there with me? Please?"

"No," Chalee says. She looks away. "I can't. They don't really like me."

"Then that's it," Treasure says. She swallows loudly. "We'll stay here."

"But . . ." Dok says, and falls silent.

"But what?" Chalee says.

"But what about that man, you know, the one who wants to take you?"

Treasure is pressing her hands together so tightly her fingers are white. "I think I have to run."

In unison Dok and the girl on the cot say, "No."

The afternoon is far enough along now so that the slants of light pushing between the curtains stretch almost all the way across the floor to make bright, inviting paths to nowhere. Treasure follows one of them with her eyes and says, "I won't go back."

"The man," Dok says again.

"They can't protect me from him," Treasure says. "He'd kill them all—Mrs. Anna, Mrs. Anna's husband, that slow fat guy Poke hired. He could kill all of them in a minute. He could do it for fun."

Dok says, in a whisper so the girl on the cot can't hear, "We have hiding places, near here. Even Boo doesn't know about them."

Treasure says, mostly breath, "Show them to me." Dok pops his lower lip out and rocks a little from side to side, considering. "Tonight," he says. "When Boo's asleep. But just to look, not to stay."

Chalee says, "But how are you going to tell Mrs. Anna?"

"I know how," Treasure says, and she gets up. Chalee follows suit, and after a moment Dok gets off his box. The girl on the cot says, "*Pssshhhh,*" a sound of disgust.

As they go downstairs, the girl on the cot calls after them, "You're *all* crazy."

ANNA IS WRITING on the whiteboard when a sort of tingling in the back of her neck tells her the energy in the room has changed. She turns to see Treasure come back in, followed by Dok and Chalee. All over the room, kids sit forward.

Treasure and Chalee are wearing old clothes as they file between the other kids' seats. Girls look at Chalee assessingly, and a couple of them put their heads together to whisper. In the lead, Treasure holds a neatly folded brown paper bag, and Anna knows what it contains. Treasure puts it carefully on Anna's desk, says, "Thank you. I hope you can get your money back," and goes to her seat. Chalee has already sat down, without so much as a glance at Anna.

Dok is chewing on his lower lip, but when Anna looks at him, he stops and drops his gaze to the floor.

Anna's heart is pounding in her ears. She looks at Treasure, and when the girl won't meet her eyes, she turns back to the whiteboard, trying to read what she just wrote.

19

Face Powder

RAFFERTY IS ALONE in the empty apartment, taking advantage of the solitude and half hoping Varney will burst through the door so Rafferty can shoot him. His Glock gleams on his desk, loaded and freshly wiped clean of Rose's face powder, which has a way of sifting down through the tiny seams in their headboard and into the compartment concealed there, where the Glock is locked away when it's not needed. He wonders how many other guys' guns smell like face powder.

His suitcase, battered by hundreds of thousands of miles, yawns open on the couch. There's nothing in it, not even his shaving kit, but, he thinks, it's a beginning. He's actually pulled the suitcase out of the closet and carried it in here. He went into the bathroom and found the kit. While in there, he put into the kit the packet of moist paper towelettes that Rose uses on her face every night and had forgotten. Then he left the kit in the bathroom, but still. Surely all of that counts for something.

Rose's clean face. The scrubbed face of the girl with the birthmark, violently scrawled with makeup. Rafferty has a quick impulse to snatch up the gun and head out into the deepening dusk in the hope that Varney will materialize in his sights. He hates the man enough to pull the trigger and worry about the consequences later.

Five or six sheets of paper are littered any old which way across his desk. They all have lists on them, or rather they have variations of the same list, representing attempts to think ahead and plan for contingencies: if *this*, then *that*. So far they're rich in *if-this* entries and short on *then-thats*. Here and there a sketchy skull and crossbones occupies the space where a *then-that* is called for. The page with the most writing on it contains a rant he scribbled minutes ago to get it off his chest, using the kind of language that long ago would have earned him a slap from his half-Filipina mother.

He pulls back, gratefully, from the matter at hand to speculate idly how his mother is. She'd been abandoned twice in the little stone house in the desert outside Lancaster, California, where Poke had grown up—first by Poke's father and then, a few years later, by Poke, when he went into the wide world to find a place he could pretend was home. In their absence she's remade herself into a real-estate agent who enjoys surprising success hawking sandy acres in the desert to people fleeing the skyrocketing cost of housing in Los Angeles or in areas with other attractions to recommend them. Water, for instance.

The last time Rafferty saw her, she'd seemed like someone who'd been created to be viewed from a distance, her once-mercurial personality bottled firmly inside a surface so shiny it looked enameled. He'd meant to stay for a week, but it was evident after one eternal meal that he and his mother had little to say to each other, and he'd flown back across the Pacific the next day, without anything deeper than formal regret on either side.

She'd started life as Angela Obregon, and after eighteen crowded years as Angie Rafferty, wife and mother, she was Angela Obregon again, a steely solitary, and she didn't need anyone.

Unlike Poke. He knows exactly who he needs, he's got them, and he's not going to let anyone take them away from him.

He picks up a sheet he'd laid aside, which Miaow had found a use for. She'd been practicing her autograph in the Latin alphabet, wandering freely between ornate filigree and severe simplicity. There are multiple variations on each of her names: Miaow

Rafferty and, more often, Mia Rafferty, along with a new one (to him) Moira Swan, which he hopes is a passing enthusiasm. At the bottom, in her crimped, tentative, everyday hand, are the names *Philip Rafferty* and *Kwan Rafferty*. Each name is written three times.

When he'd first seen that his name and Rose's had shouldered their way into this hand-scrawled fantasy of fame, he'd been taken unawares. He'd had to blink a couple of times to clear his vision.

That was when he'd gotten up to get his gun.

The apartment *is* smaller than it should be with a baby on the way, but it's housed the only real family he's ever had. He'll say goodbye to it reluctantly, but everything that's been important to him here—that small, unbreakable unit of three (or four, or five)—will remain intact. Whenever he thinks about it, he's dazzled by the sheer improbability of the three of them finding and recognizing each other across distance, language, culture, belief, and expectations, and all of them realizing what they could have, what they might be able to build together. Rose would chalk it up to karma, but Rafferty thinks it was as random as winning a lottery.

So: the gun, face powder or no face powder, its easy pull, its matte-black ugliness, the weight of it in his hand. He's used it before, and the experience changed him forever, but he knows he can use it again. He has something he never thought he'd have, and no murderous son of a bitch with a mustache and yellow teeth is going to break it.

As he resumes packing, he thinks that Varney has at least made it clear to him what he'll do to protect the union between him, Rose, and Miaow. And what he'll do is anything.

20

A Starter Mansion for a Camel Trader

THE EMOTION HE'D experienced in the apartment had been an odd mixture, a sort of grim intent wrapped around love. The early-evening traffic, a series of long waits interrupted by short jerks forward, and the sight of Pradya, the daytime thug, looking out of place in an armchair in the hotel lobby and failing to notice Rafferty coming through the revolving door, brings the grimness to the fore. By the time he slips his card into the slot on the door to their room, he's feeling as if the ideal dinner would be something he'd personally killed.

"We want to eat upstairs," Rose announces the moment Rafferty drops his suitcase onto the thick carpet. "It's fancy." She's gotten dressed up, for her, in long jeans and a top with three-quarter sleeves the color of a cyclamen, which makes her skin look like it's been dusted with gold.

"Can I sit for a minute?"

"You can have *five* minutes if you want." She turns to the window that runs the full length of the room. "Look," she says. "This view is so much nicer than ours."

"When I can get up, I'll look." He sinks into the couch and then sinks some more. "Jesus," he says. "What is this, quicksand?"

"Isn't it *nice?*" Rose says. She's pulling the drapes all the way open so Rafferty can get the full effect of the panorama. "It's much softer than the one we've got, and it's so *pretty.*"

"It is?" The couch is covered in cream-colored cloth with broad, shiny crimson stripes running down it like gift-wrap ribbon. Fleurs-de-lis gleam here and there, woven with some reflective synthetic thread into the cream areas. Stand the couch on end and revolve it, he thinks, and you'd have a giant barber pole. Looking around the room, he realizes he had completely forgotten, perhaps in self-defense, what it looks like.

What it looks like is the waiting room for the Marie Antoinette Salon in an expensive brothel, where you sit until you're permitted to enter the queen's chamber, with the trick guillotine over the bed. The couch takes up much of the wall to the left of the door, giving him a good view of the huge, over-decorated living room, dominated by the long window. Fluffy Chinese approximations of Persian rugs smother the floor, and on the walls are pinkish paintings done in the kind of faux–French impressionist style so popular in convalescent hospitals the world around.

Rose, who has been waiting for his reaction, says, "You don't like it?"

"The whole place," he says, hearing the sourness in his voice, "looks like a starter mansion for a camel trader."

"I see," Rose says, and his heart plummets at her tone. He'd been too self-involved to hear the excitement at the view in her voice. He hadn't heard the yearning for a sofa like the one he's still sinking into.

"I'm sorry," he says, trying to get up. His apology, which was to have included bounding across the room and masterfully taking her in his arms, gets lost in an awkward attempt to free himself from the couch's embrace.

"I know I don't have very good taste," Rose begins.

"No, no," he says, trying to stand. "Please—"

"But I'm here—*we're* here—because of you, and you could at least let me try to enjoy it."

"Wait, I didn't mean—" He scoots as far forward on the cushion as he can, puts both palms flat on the table, leans over them, and pushes down, trying for leverage against the infinitely yielding couch.

"After the baby's born," Rose says, "and we have a new place, you can do *all* the decorating so he or she has a chance of developing your wonderful taste. We wouldn't want it to like the same awful things Miaow and I do."

"I'm sorry," he says, launching himself from the table, and to his surprise, he's standing. "I'm a snob and a jerk, and I feel terrible about what I just said, and I've had a wretched day, and . . . and, boy, you're right, that's quite a view, isn't it?" He edges left, between the couch and the table, which is too close to it to permit easy movement. "I'll just come on over there, and we'll look at it together."

Rose says something in Thai that translates roughly into "hopeless," but at least she seems a little less offended, and then, through the door that leads to the bedroom she chose, Miaow emerges and says, "What are you doing?"

"I'm escaping from the couch," he says, and looks up to see, behind Miaow, a teenage Caucasian boy of remarkable beauty with a flop of pale hair falling over his left eyebrow so perfectly that Rafferty figures a squad of angels sneaks into the kid's room every morning while he's asleep, just to arrange it. Rafferty says, "Hey there."

"This is my father," Miaow says, and it sounds like a confession. "This is Andrew—I mean, Ned. I *mean*," she concludes through her teeth, "*Edward.*"

"Nice to meet you, Ed," Rafferty says, getting away from the couch.

"Edward," Edward says.

"Right," Rafferty puts on a smile, because it allows him to bare his teeth. "And why are you here, Edward?"

"We're *rehearsing*, Dad," Miaow says. "We open on Thursday, remember?"

"You're *that* Ned," Rafferty says, "the Ned in the play."

"Yes, sir."

"I played Ned once, when I was your age."

"Yes?" Edward says with an absolutely total lack of interest.

"Miaow's got the good part, though." Rafferty is determined to keep the conversation going, if only to keep himself from throwing the kid through the window, into Rose's lovely view.

Edward's forehead wrinkles and he says, "Miaow?" just as Miaow says, "Mia. My name is—"

"Sorry. Mia. Of course, Mia." Moved by sheer malice, Rafferty says, "We call her Miaow sometimes, her mother and I, because she's our little kittycat. Maybe this time next month it'll be Moira." He sees Miaow's eyes widen in surprise. "It's like having triplets."

"Where did you—" Miaow begins.

"Sorry, Mia," Rafferty says. "In fact, I might as well apologize to everyone all at once. Make a clean sweep. We seem to have gotten off on the wrong foot." He heads for the door to usher the kid out. "But it's been great to meet you, Edward, and I hope you get home safely."

Edward looks at Miaow. Miaow closes her eyes against the reality of the moment and says, "Edward's going to dinner with us."

"Ahhh," Rafferty says. "Well. Great. Peachy. Should have thought of that myself."

Edward says, "Mia said you did." Miaow's face is flaming.

"Did she, now?" Rafferty says, happy that his daughter isn't armed. "Well, Ed, if the triplets said so, it must be true."

His phone warbles at him, and the readout says LEON. "You guys go ahead," he says. "I need to get this."

21

Three Questions

IT SAYS:

If you're worried about protecting her, ask yourself three questions:

Did you know that C-4 plastique, the explosive in Murphy's closet, can't be exploded by setting it on fire?

Did you know that all the gas burners on the stove and in the oven had been turned on high without engaging the pilot flames? By the time the fire reached it, the kitchen was a bomb.

The person who did this knew there were people in the house but she did it anyway. Who do you think that person was?

He's read it three times, and every time he reads it, he hears Treasure stammering over the story about Varney saying he wouldn't be able to smell escaping gas. Almost unable to finish the sentence.

"And you found this—" he begins.

"In here," Hofstedler says yet again, tugging at his shirt pocket. "I checked my money, and—"

"Did someone brush up against you?"

"But of course," Hofstedler says. "Wallace, you remember, I said to that man, 'Why you aren't looking where you are going?'"

"Word for word," Wallace says heavily. He's nursing a beer as though he plans to make it last. His eyes are cloudy and loose in their sockets, roaming the room but not really fixing on anything. He seems to be on the other side of an invisible wall. Down at the end of the bar, on his usual stool far from everyone, Campeau listens with interest.

"What did he look like?"

"Like anybody," Hofstedler says. Like the others in the bar, he pays close attention to the appearance of Thai females, but the males blend into a dark-skinned crowd, extras on the set, differentiated mainly by the color of their T-shirts. "Like a vendor, perhaps, or a tout."

"He was skinny, the way Thais are," Wallace says. "And dark. Combed his hair up into that stupid ridge in the center that guys do now. Looks like the flame on a match."

"Where was it?"

"Back there." Hofstedler gestures in the direction of Surawong.

"I know, Leon, but how *far* back there? How close to the bar? Was it obvious that you were coming in here?"

"Naw," Wallace says. "Farther back. And I know what you're thinking."

"What?" Hofstedler says. "What he is thinking?"

"He's thinking that whoever it was, he recognized you and knew you'd call Poke."

Hofstedler nods. "Aaahhhh."

"So what's the big deal?" Campeau says. "Varney knows what you look like."

Wallace says, "Varney wasn't there."

"How can you know?" Hofstedler demands. "You were talking to me."

"I was looking," Wallace says. "One thing I'm still good at, looking."

Hofstedler is shaking his head. "The street was full," he says. "If you could see him, I would have—"

"No disrespect," Wallace says, "but you could miss somebody in a closet. I did nothing for four years except look around." He moistens his lips with the beer, without swallowing. "And there was another one, farther up the block. He spotted us first. We were handed off, one to the other. There was probably another at the other end, in case we went in that way. How I'd do it anyways."

"I did not see *two*?" Hofstedler seems stricken.

"This is what I can do," Wallace says. "I kept people alive doing it." He puts the beer down and looks at it.

"Well, this makes me good and nervous," Rafferty says.

"It should," Wallace says.

Over him, Rafferty says, "The night that boy was killed. Someone saw Varney take a picture or two just before the boy ran by and I chased him."

Hofstedler says, "A picture of you?"

"Yeah. Problem is, when he took the picture, I was standing with you and Wallace."

"But this means—" Hofstedler begins. His face is all eyes.

"That he's got us, too," Wallace says. "And like I said, Poke, you should be nervous."

"And maybe so should we," Hofstedler says.

"He's never going to stop watching you," Wallace says to Poke. His words come slowly and evenly, almost without emphasis. "I figured out who he is. Ernie told me."

"Wallace," Hofstedler says, putting a hand on the man's arm. "Ernie is dead."

"Goddamn you, Leon, I know that." Wallace shrugs off Leon's hand so abruptly that he sloshes his beer onto the bar. Instantly Toots is there, mopping it up and saying, "Wallet, Wallet, no problem, Wallet."

"It *is* a fucking problem when your friends think you've lost it," Wallace says, pulling his glass out of Toots's reach, since she's trying to refill it. "I know he's dead, Leon. He told me in a dream."

"A dream," Leon says despairingly.

"Let him talk," Rafferty says. "Wallace, let Toots top you off, would you? Just to be polite."

"Sorry, Toots," Wallace says. "It was my goddamn dream, Leon, and it was Ernie I dreamed about because Ernie died like that, he was *gutshot*. That's why it was Ernie who reminded me about Hartley, this guy from 'Nam. Because Hartley and this asshole with the mustache are the same guy—no, no, not like that," he says to Poke, who shows signs of interrupting. "Not literally, but they might as well be. They like the same things. Before, I said Hartley was a back-shooter, and he was, but it was worse than that: he aimed low. He wanted to kill slow, and he wanted it to hurt, and that's who this other asshole, Varney, is. He's a back-shooter *and* a gut-shooter, I'd be willing to bet on it. You want to stay way far away from him."

"Too late for that," Rafferty says. "He's chosen me."

"Then I'll tell you what, Poke," Wallace says. "He's sighting you. Right now, all the time. He's got eyes on you, wherever you go. He *likes* sighting. Hartley shot like a son of a bitch, he could hit anything within a few square inches of where he aimed, and he'd wait longer to take a shot than anyone I ever saw. He'd miss good shots, just to stretch out the fun of waiting, and then he'd take exactly the shot he wanted to take, and what he wanted was the abdomen, where the most pain and the slowest, filthiest dying are. He brought down one VC after another, and he never got as high as the rib cage. He intends to hurt you before he kills you, Poke, and he'll wait for fucking ever to do it."

"Varney and Hartley," Poke says.

"Twins," Wallace says. "And you can't wait him out, because he likes the waiting. What you gotta do, you gotta dangle it in front of him. Whatever it is, you gotta dig a big pit, fill it with snakes and spikes, stand on the other side, and just dangle that fucker. Make him come to you and then cut him into little pieces."

"Can't do it."

Wallace sits back, visibly disengaging. "Up to you."

"I'm not blowing you off, Wallace. He wants two things. One of them I don't have, and the other is a person."

Wallace says, "I didn't tell you to *give* 'em to him. I said *dangle* 'em, or something that looks like them, to bring him up close. Because otherwise he's going to be behind you until you're trying to stuff your guts back into your shirt."

OUTSIDE THE BAR he stands, shifting from one foot to the other as he tries to spot whoever has been assigned to watch him. He supposes he was observed all the way down Patpong when he arrived, without even catching a hint.

He's got no idea how to protect Hofstedler and Wallace, if they need it. He's stretched pretty thin just looking after his family and Treasure.

Treasure.

Is Varney's note true or isn't it? Either way he needs to tell Arthit about it. Arthit needs to know that it's possible that the girl he's trying to adopt blew up that house believing that her father, her mother, Rafferty, and Rafferty's half sister, Ming Li, were inside it.

I'd believed she liked *me,* Rafferty thinks. Or maybe she couldn't like anybody. The way she grew up . . .

And if Varney is telling the truth about Murphy's kitchen, that's information he could have gotten only from someone officially connected with the investigation, which Arthit had mentioned as a possibility all those weeks—no, only *four days*—ago.

He punches up Arthit's number, so hard he nearly knocks the phone out of his hand, but before he can say a word, Arthit says, "Treasure didn't come home with Anna. Anna waited for her and Chalee, but they didn't come down, and now she can't find them."

"Maybe that's better," Rafferty says.

"Anna is at the shelter, crying. Doesn't feel better to me."

Scanning the street, Rafferty is sure he's located one of his watchers, a rickety-looking guy in a long gray coat three sizes too big, who's pawing without interest through a pile of women's clothes. "Did she tell the guy on watch to stay there?"

"She told mine," Arthit says. "She hasn't seen yours."

Rafferty feels a worm of uneasiness. The man in the gray coat catches him in mid-stare and turns away but shoots a look back over his shoulder. "He should have been there."

"Maybe he got a better offer," Arthit says. "Not the most dependable person in Bangkok."

"I need to talk to you about something," Rafferty says, searching the crowd for Varney. "But not now."

"When?"

"Maybe tomorrow. We'll see. Go take care of Anna."

"The only way to take care of Anna," Arthit says, "is to make this go right somehow."

22

Skritch-Skritch-Skritch

TREASURE ISN'T AWARE she's been asleep, but here's Dok, gently shaking her shoulder and whispering, "Shhhh." She opens her eyes wide against the darkness of the big room. There's no moon, and the curtains absorb the city's ambient light. A mosquito whines near her ear. She bats it away as she passes her tongue over her teeth to clean them.

She can hear and smell the sleeping girls. They breathe deeply and evenly, the sound coming from all directions as though the room itself were breathing. The air is edged with sweat, dirty clothes, and unwashed hair.

But not men.

She rolls over and sits up, and the cot creaks. She'd been sleeping on her left, and her clothes there are damp and cool with perspiration.

Dok hands her something. Her shoes. He whispers, "Don't put them on," and stands upright and begins to thread his way between the cots, heading toward the pale spill of light from the single fluorescent tube that hangs halfway down the stairs to the boy's level. She watches his silhouette, slender, straight-backed, narrow-hipped. Even at his age, he's obviously male. Still, whatever he'll be later, for now he's just Dok.

She's halfway across the room when someone seizes her wrist. She stifles a yelp and looks down at the new girl, the one with the dark skin and the mosquito bites. "Where are you going?" It's a hiss.

"Just out. We'll be back."

A girl nearby murmurs a protest in her sleep.

"Are you running away?"

"No."

"Are you going someplace better? I want to know. Tell me, or I'll shout."

She shakes her arm. "We're going to look for something to sell." That's what Dok and Chalee were doing when they found her. "Dumpsters."

The girl says, "I want half."

"Fine," Treasure says. She reaches down and pries the girl's fingers from her wrist.

"If you know someplace better," the girl says, "please take me with you."

"We're just going out for a while."

"If you don't come back, I'll tell."

Treasure brushes aside the reaching hand. "We'll be back." Dok waits at the top of the stairs, his body straining in impatience. Treasure walks toward him on the balls of her feet, the way she walked when she didn't want her father to hear her. She's good at this. Seeing her coming, Dok goes silently down the stairs.

Chalee waits below, stifling a yawn and holding a long-handled broom, a riot of ragged bristles at the bottom. She's wearing a sweatshirt with a hood and her old torn jeans. She waves Treasure to the side of the double door, locked only with a metal bar— hooked on one end—that runs through the two handles. "I looked out the windows," she says. Instinctively she glances at the opening to Boo's office even though it's dark now, since he's sleeping on the third floor with his girlfriend, Da, and the baby she was given as a prop when she was put on the sidewalk to beg. "I didn't see anyone."

"I'll go out first," Dok says. "Wait here. And don't lock the door." Chalee hands him the broom. He shoulders it like a rifle, pulls the heavy bar free, and passes it to Chalee. Then he takes a deep breath and strolls out as if there's nothing at all on his mind. He pushes the door closed from the outside, and Chalee eases it the rest of the way, the bar dangling from her hand.

Treasure goes to the window, standing a few feet back so her pale face won't emerge from the darkness for the benefit of anyone who might be watching, and waits for Dok to come into view. She says, hearing the tension in her voice, "Maybe we should have gone back to Mrs. Anna's."

"You can go," Chalee says. "I wouldn't blame you."

"I can't."

"Well," Chalee says, with a little flicker of anger in her voice, "that's not my fault. I can't be someplace they don't want me."

"They didn't have enough time to get to know you," Treasure says. "In a few days—"

"Never. And anyway, you don't really want to be there."

Treasure studies the floor at her feet. Then she says, "I'm—"

"You're afraid of him. Mrs. Anna's husband," Chalee says.

Treasure rubs at the skin on her upper arms. "I'm afraid of all of them."

"Not Boo."

"No, but Boo is . . . Boo is just a big boy." Treasure shifts to her right, looking out the window at an angle. "I *still* don't see him."

"If he doesn't want you to see him, you won't—"

"But there's only one way out of here, right? We're at the end of the alley, so he'd have to be right out there. What if somebody—" She can feel her voice rising, and she bites it off.

"There's nothing to worry about. He's okay."

"Maybe we should go upstairs," Treasure says. She feels the sting of Chalee's gaze and says, "We could see better from up there."

"Go where you want," Chalee says. "I'm staying where Dok thinks I am."

"It's just that—" She's suddenly shuddering, shivering to the center of her bones. "He should be out there, and he's . . . he's not. What if . . . I mean, what if—"

Chalee's arm goes around her shoulder. "He's fine, he's fine," she says. She hugs Treasure closer. "Come on, stop shaking. You're all right, we're all fine. He just wants to make sure we can get out of here without Poke's guy seeing us." She draws Treasure aside and looks through the window. "We'll see him any minute."

Treasure leans against Chalee, still shivering, and then a dark shape crosses the window, moving fast, and she gasps. Instantly Chalee clamps her free hand over Treasure's mouth. The door opens a few inches, and Dok peers in. He registers the picture in front of him—Treasure rigid and wide-eyed, Chalee behind her with the arm holding the bar wrapped around Treasure's neck and her other hand pressed over her mouth—and he frowns a question. Chalee loosens her hold on Treasure, who steps aside, looking out the window. Dok can hear her breathing, like someone who's just broken the surface after too long underwater.

"It's okay," he whispers. His eyes go beyond them to the sleeping boys, finding the two who are awake and watching, up on one elbow. "We'll be back," he whispers to them and then, to Chalee and Treasure, "Let's go." He ducks back outside, and a second later his arm snakes back in to catch the door and hold it open. Chalee hooks a finger in Treasure's sleeve, pulling her along. The sudden yank pulls Treasure off balance and nearly dislodges the stiff object, tightly wrapped in a napkin stolen from Anna's house, that's tucked into Treasure's waistband and covered by her shirt. She slaps a hand over it to hold it in place. A moment later she's outside, surrounded by the relative coolness of the night.

It's drizzled recently. Through a ragged hole in the cloud cover, part of the moon's face shines down, making the filthy concrete of the alley gleam like silver, momentarily redeemed by the wet night. Dok is already waiting at the bottom of the steps, shifting nervously from foot to foot and scanning the alley as Treasure, behind Chalee's back, secures the stiff, napkin-wrapped bundle tucked into her waistband and comes down to stand beside Chalee, who's still holding the iron bar that was used to lock the door.

The shelter is a few blocks uphill from the Chao Phraya. Treasure can smell the river and the port, a mixture of diesel fuel and mud, and she can almost hear the water's whisper as it glides by below. The building where they sleep blocks the end of an elbow-shaped alley between dark warehouses. Twenty meters from their front door, the alley takes a forty-five-degree right turn and eventually ends in a narrow, badly paved street. Looking up at the fast-moving clouds, framed by the flat black roofs of the warehouses, Treasure feels a disorienting sense of motion. The tattered hole that briefly bared the moon's gaze moves on, dulling the sheen on the concrete and plunging the night into a thicker, oilier darkness. Dok says, "We're going to show you a way out that most people don't know about, and a place to hide. This way."

She thinks he'll go forward, toward the point where the alley bends down toward the street, but instead he turns to his right, Chalee trotting along behind him. Treasure says, "Where are . . . ?" but Chalee loosens a sharp-edged "*Shhhh.*"

"This is a little scary," Dok says, not whispering but keeping his voice low. "Treasure, you get in the middle and hold on to my shirt. Chalee, okay if you go last?"

"I've done it before," Chalee says.

Dok says, "Are you all right, Treasure? Do you want to go back inside?"

"No." Over his shoulder she's located a narrow crack of absolute darkness between the edge of the shelter and the warehouse next door, barely wide enough for one adult to pass through. Dok, apparently thinking she's staring at the broom on his shoulder, hoists it and says, "For rats." He sweeps vigorously, back and forth in front of his feet.

"Dok is afraid of rats," Chalee says.

"This will clear the way," Dok says, licking his lips nervously, and something warms inside Treasure. He's braving a thing that terrifies him, and he's doing it for her sake.

"Me, too," she says. "You keep them away from us."

"Right," Dok says with a downward glance at the broom's broken, uneven bristles. "Right." He turns and walks to the black mouth of the alley, moving like he's climbing a hill. Chalee follows him, and Treasure hurries past her and takes hold of the back of Dok's shirt. A moment later she feels the weight of Chalee's hand gripping her own shirt.

"Swipe it up in the air every few steps," Chalee says. "Spiders."

"I'm not afraid of spiders," Treasure says. "There were big spiders in the hedge where I hid from my, my father. If I stayed in there overnight, they made webs to keep him away from me."

Chalee says to Dok, "Sweep anyway."

Dok pauses at the last step before the alley. Over his shoulder Treasure can see a dim rectangle, just bright enough to be visible. It seems to be an immeasurable distance away. "How far is that?" Treasure asks.

"Maybe fifteen meters." Dok takes a deep breath and squares his shoulders. "Maybe twenty." Treasure hears the scrabble of the broom's bristles over concrete, and he leads them in.

THE DARKNESS PRESSES in so closely that her ears pop. Her shoulders continually brush one rough wall or the other, and she fights down the panic that's been crouching low in her gut ever since the moment, in Boo's office, when Rafferty confirmed the shape of Paul's tattoo. It had been a huge somersault: since she'd gotten to the shelter, she'd felt that she had finally passed through some kind of doorway to a refuge, gasping in relief, only to learn that the door hadn't closed behind her. Paul is *out there*, and if he wants her, he'll get her. No one can stop him. She shivers again, and behind her, Chalee tucks the bar under one arm and uses her free hand to smooth Treasure's shoulder.

Chalee, she thinks, and the knot in her gut loosens a little. She focuses on the patch of almost-light at the end of the alley and the *skritch-skritch-skritch* of Dok's broom. Afraid of rats, she thinks, and Dok's leading her through this rat paradise. Dok and Chalee. Every now and then Dok grunts softly, and she thinks, *Rat*, but nothing scuttles back toward her or runs over or between her feet. What she has now, all she has in the world at this moment, is the patch of light, the *skritch* of Dok's broom, his rough T-shirt rubbing between her fingers, and the sharp but not-unpleasant smell of his sweat. Boy sweat, not man sweat. And Chalee hanging on to her from behind.

Chalee whispers, "Almost there."

"I'm fine," Treasure says, and is surprised to find that it's nearly true. Sandwiched between her . . . her *friends*, with walls practically touching her shoulders on both sides, with that dim patch at the end growing closer, with no silhouette making a man-shaped hole in the light, she feels almost safe, at least for the moment. *Running away*, she thinks suddenly, seeing herself living on the streets and in the odd corners of this enormous city, maybe even other cities, with friends who know how to survive. It would be something like freedom.

If she ran with Dok and Chalee, if they'd go with her, if she could find some way to get her hands on some of the money her father had left behind, they could hide forever. They could move from town to town, finding other kids to be with, always having enough baht for a meal or even a taxi and maybe some nice clothes once in a while. They might even ride a train. The three of them, kids with a little money and Dok and Chalee's maps of places to hide.

A little cold-water room somewhere tucked away in nowhere, a place no one would think to look for her, with a curtained shower in the corner and a door that locks. Maybe other kids in the building they could go places with, they could—she hesitates at even thinking the word—they could *play* with. "I never have," she says, and then she realizes she's speaking out loud.

"Never have what?" Dok says, the broom *skritch-skritching* beneath his voice.

"Played with anybody," she says, feeling her face redden in the darkness.

"I used to play," Chalee says, just making conversation. "In the village."

"What did you do?"

"We ran through the woods. Hid from each other. We jumped into the water in the paddies. We raced buffalo."

"I raced buffalo, too," Dok says.

Treasure says, "Is it exciting?"

"No," Chalee says. "It's funny, because buffalo are so slow. Everybody's jumping up and down and cheering, and it's like they're walking in their sleep."

"Then who wins?" Treasure asks.

"Nobody cares," Chalee says. "It's just fun."

Treasure says, "Oh." She thinks for a second about fun.

The dim rectangle marking the end of the passage is only a meter or two away, and Dok says, "Stay here while I look."

Treasure says, "Give me the broom."

"I need it," Dok says. "I'm not walking without it."

The broom makes its *skritching* noise as Dok moves slowly forward. As narrow as the passage is, he's slender enough to hug one wall so he can look out at an angle and then change walls to check the other side. Finally he stands in the center, waits for the space of a breath or two, and pokes his head out of the opening. He looks left and right, then steps all the way out. Then he turns and waves them forward.

Chalee lets out a rush of breath, and Treasure realizes that her friend has been frightened. Both she and Dok have been frightened. Who else had ever been frightened on her behalf? she asks herself, and instantly answers the question: *Poke.*

Coming through the mouth of the passageway, Treasure sees a narrow, sloping street running down to the river. It's a canyon, warehouses rising on either side, and she thinks, *Hard to get out of*, but Dok says, "This way," and turns left to lead them downhill.

Chalee gives Treasure her warm hand and says, "Let him be the boss. He likes it."

With Dok in the lead, they move down the street like people with a purpose. Treasure has seen hundreds of Thai girls holding hands with their friends, but she's never done it before, and the feel of Chalee's hand in hers makes her feel light-footed, almost giddy. The three of them, she thinks, with a little of her money and a whole country to play, or rather, *hide* in. She can't remember ever before visualizing a life she would actually like to live. With the money she could be free of Paul.

Except that what Paul really wants, of course, is the money.

After a few minutes of drifting downhill, they cross a street that Dok says is the same one their alley begins at, and Treasure tries to visualize it all: run this way, turn that way, and get back to the shelter. Just as she thinks she has it mapped in her mind, she hears something behind her. She whirls so fast that she yanks her hand out of Chalee's, but the street is empty.

"What?" Dok whispers.

She shakes her head. "Nothing. I just—"

Dok goes past her at a quick walk, all the way back to the cross street. He cranes his neck around and stands there, his hip thrown out and his weight on his right leg as though he thinks he might have to lift the left to run. But instead he evens his stance, takes a final look around, and ambles back down, shaking his head.

"The narrow alley," he says to Treasure as though continuing a discussion, "is the escape route, and it can be a hiding place, too. Most grown-ups don't even see it. And if they do, you can get out the other end." They start walking again. "Once you're out, you can run along down here, cross that street back there, and—come down just a little more—you can go in *there*."

Across the way there's a partially collapsed building, obviously once a warehouse, with a large word in Thai that translates to

"Prince," painted in graying letters. The rough surface of the wood has pushed its way through the paint, and Treasure has to squint to make out the word.

At that moment it begins to rain.

"Wait here," Chalee says. "Sometimes it's not empty." Treasure and Dok crowd back against the building behind them, sheltering from the slant of the rain, and Chalee runs across the street and does something to the building's door and steps back. She says a bad word that startles Treasure, not so much by the profanity as by the way her voice carries. The street is narrow and hedged by high walls, and sound travels even through the hiss of the rain.

Chalee goes at the door again and yanks outward, using both the iron bar and her free hand on the door. It emits a sustained bass note, like a sound played at half speed, that bounces back and forth across the street. By the time it fades, Chalee is standing beside the open door, leaning forward to peer in.

Treasure says, "What's she looking for?"

"People," Dok says. "It's a trick to get the door open, but some other people have figured it out."

Across the way, Chalee disappears into the darkness. A tiny flame flickers, throwing a rectangle of pale light onto the wet surface of the street. She reappears, a disposable lighter in one hand, and waves them in.

For reassurance Treasure taps her palm against the napkin-wrapped bundle at her waist and follows Dok.

The place reeks of mold and urine. They're in some kind of office, a small room, with a door in the right-hand wall that opens into a deeper darkness that suggests a much larger space beyond. Dok pulls the front door closed and secures it with a loop of heavy wire. To Chalee he says, "Back empty?"

Chalee holds out the lighter. "It looked empty to me."

"Okay," Dok says. He takes the lighter and holds it high, looking around. The floor is thick with dust and rat droppings and black termite sand. A couple of fallen roof beams, two-by-fours from the look of them, lean against the rear wall. There's a window to the left of the front door, but it's been boarded up. "They're as afraid of us as we are of them."

"Who?" Treasure whispers. She wants to go back into the street.

"If it's anybody, it's streeties," Dok says. "Like us, but some big ones."

"There's nobody there," Chalee says. "But if it makes you feel better . . ." She pushes the door to the dark area closed and wedges a fallen two-by-four against it at an acute angle.

A rusted metal desk with a missing front leg sags despondently in the middle of the room. Dok sits on it, bringing the legless corner all the way down to the floor with a bang. "This is another hiding place," he says, indicating the space with an open hand, like someone showing a room for rent. "If you want, Chalee can open that door to the storage area again and we'll show you how to get out that way. There's a wide alley back there, because they used to bring trucks right up to the rear doors to unload stuff."

The rain is making dull stuttering sounds against the wooden front of the building. From a corner comes the drip of a leak. Chalee sits next to Dok on the desk, and Treasure turns to face them, her back to the front door.

"Is there anyplace else?" she asks.

"Near here, one more," Dok says. "Near the docks. I think about hiding places in steps, nearest to farthest. The first step is the passageway next to our building. This is the second step, and there are a couple of places here in the back where you can get up, pretty high above the floor, and hide. People almost never look up. You can get out of here through the front and the back. Ow." He lets the lighter go out, giving his thumb a rest from the heat, and says, in the warm darkness, "And the third place is near the docks."

"How do you know about them?"

"The first thing I do," Dok says, "when I go anyplace, is be sure I know how to get out of it."

"You'll learn," Chalee says. "You'll have to if you don't go with Mrs. Anna."

Treasure says, "Could you light that thing again?"

"I don't know," Dok says. He tilts his chin at the wall behind her. "The boards over the window let a little light out."

"It's the middle of the night," Chalee says. "It's raining. No one's out there."

"Okay." The lighter sparks back into life, throwing Dok and Chalee's wavering shadows against the barricaded door.

After a moment's pause, Treasure says, "I have money, if I could figure out how to get it."

Neither Dok nor Chalee replies, but they're regarding her with interest.

"My, my father had a lot of money."

"You can tell," Chalee says. "All the kids can tell."

"How?"

Dok says, "Even when you were dirty, you were a different kind of dirty."

Chalee says, "And you're half-and-half, so there must have been someone with money sometime."

"But what I'm saying, what I'm trying to say, is that if I could get some of it . . ." Brought out into the light like this, her vision feels thin and implausible, a fairy tale or a pirate story.

"Then what?" Chalee says. Dok is looking at her, but he seems to have retreated to a point behind his eyes, as though he's regarding her through a mask a foot in front of his face.

"Then we could be together," Treasure says in a rush. "We could go where we want, we'd have food and clothes—not too much, but enough. We could go places. We could . . . we could be friends forever." She runs out of breath, almost seeing the words hanging in the air, waiting for a shaking head, a snicker. She grabs a new breath and says, "We could hide. *Together.*"

Chalee leans forward to speak but freezes. Treasure's head has whipped around, and her body follows until her back is to them, and then they hear her sniff the air, three or four sharp inhalations, and she retreats a step and moans, "*Noooo,*" and with a screech of nails pulling free from wood, the entire front door is yanked upward and away, and the lighter blows out, and the wet, shining, heavyset man standing where the door had been says, "*Treasure.* What a surprise."

23

There's Still the Gas

RAFFERTY'S CELL PHONE buzzes, bringing him out of deep sleep, and he reaches up and back, toward the headboard, but instead of finding the phone, he barks his knuckles on a wall covered in something that feels like fabric. Half conscious, he flails for a familiar surface, encountering instead mountains of pillows.

The hotel.

There's enough light through the window to let him make out the bedside table with the heavy crystal lamp on it and, blinking away at the lamp's base, his phone. He'd gone to sleep with it within reach, but he and Rose seem to have changed places during the night, as they sometimes do. He lifts himself on one elbow and leans across her to get his hand around the phone. Rose says something, but it takes more than a ringing phone and someone leaning on her to wake Rose up.

"Yeah."

"Poke," Arthit says, "Treasure is missing, definitely gone." In the background Rafferty can hear a stream of sound from Anna. "She left the shelter with Chalee and that boy—"

"Dok. What time?"

"Don't know exactly. My cop was at the mouth of the alley, and he swears they never came out. But about twenty minutes ago, a little girl woke Boo up. She said Treasure and the others left ten or fifteen minutes before that."

"Nobody came to get them? Nobody took them away?"

"Not according to her. She says Treasure told her they were going out looking for things to sell."

"She wouldn't, not with Varney out there somewhere."

Anna's voice scales up, and Arthit says to her, "One more minute."

"Where's my guy?" Rafferty says. "Sriyat?"

Arthit says, coolly, "I have no idea."

"It's been less than an hour. Maybe we should—"

"Up to you, but I'm going out to look for them now. Anna will wait here."

"Give me a little time. I'll meet you there." Awake at last, Rose sits up and yawns, and he leans over and kisses her and says, "I'll be back. Sometime."

TREASURE LAUGHS, A low, harsh rasp that brings Dok's gaze to her. She closes her eyes and laughs some more.

"What's funny?" the man says. He's produced a small penlight and trained it on them.

"Thought you were—" She starts to laugh again and then, abruptly, stops. "Thought you were somebody else."

The man in the doorway tilts his head back, surveying the room, and Treasure recognizes him. It's Sriyat or something like that, the man Rafferty hired to watch her. He says, "Glad you're happy to see me."

Dok says, "What are you doing here?"

"Shut up." Sriyat's voice is still soft, as it had been at Arthit's house, but there's force behind it. "Girl," he says to Chalee, "sit closer to your boyfriend."

Dok puts one foot on the floor, and the man says, "Don't do anything stupid, sonny."

"You're supposed to be protecting me," Treasure says. Now that the initial relief has worn off, her voice sounds childish in her ears.

"I've been thinking about that," Sriyat says. "You've got two men on you twenty-four hours a day, which costs a bundle. They're moving you back and forth, between nice houses and a slum, all very secret. What that says to me is that there's money somewhere. Who wants you, and why? Is the money yours? Is someone trying to get to it through you? And how *much* money?"

"I'm going to tell Poke."

"No, you're going to answer my question. And fast, or I'm going to shoot one of your friends." He reaches inside his coat and comes out with an automatic. "Which one?" he says. He points it at Chalee, and the penlight swivels with it.

"You wouldn't shoot her," Treasure says.

"No? You want to see me do it? Answer my questions. How much? Who has it?"

"My, my father. I don't know how much—"

"Not good enough. I need to know everything." He points the gun at Dok and waggles it side to side. "You might want to move away from her, kid, or your clothes'll get dirty."

"There's a . . . there's a letter," Treasure says. "It's from my . . . um, my father." She pushes herself past the word and keeps talking. Her eyes are lifted to the ceiling, but now she brings them back down to look at Sriyat. "He wants me back, and I don't want to go, and Poke is hiding me."

"Is your father rich?"

Treasure says, "Very."

"Why don't you want to go?"

"I hate him."

"Why is Rafferty involved?"

"I don't know exactly," Treasure says. "But I think everything is in the letter. I stole it from Poke."

Sriyat says, as though weighing it, "A letter. What's in it?"

"I can't read," Treasure says. "My father didn't send me to school. None of us went to school. We're just learning how to read now." She can feel Chalee's eyes on her.

"Where's the letter?"

"I have it." She widens her eyes. "Maybe *you* can read it."

"Is it in Thai?"

"I guess so."

"Give it to me."

"Will you give it back?" Treasure asks.

Sriyat smiles at her. "Sure, sure. It's your letter, right? Give it to me."

Treasure says, "I don't know."

Dok says to Treasure, "Don't give him anything. When he's got it, he'll kill Chalee and me and take you with him."

"Why would I hurt you?" Sriyat says. "It's not like you could do anything to me. Only reason I'd shoot you is if she won't give me that fucking *letter*." He takes a step farther into the room, ducking his head to avoid hitting it on top of the doorjamb. His smell, sweat and meat and tobacco, envelops Treasure, and she thinks she might choke. "This is how it goes," Sriyat says. "You hand me the letter, sweetie, and then we lock your friends in here to get a head start, and I take the letter to your father. You and me, we split the money. How's that sound?"

"She's not stupid," Dok says.

Treasure says, "You'll sell me to my father."

"No, I won't. And don't argue with me. Give me the letter."

Treasure takes a step toward him, glancing up for a second at the doorjamb behind Sriyat's head. "You promise you won't give me to my father?"

"I already said so. Give it. *Now*, or else your friends here *will* get hurt."

"All right," Treasure says, unfolding the white rectangle. She takes a step toward him and stops. "Will you read it out loud so I can hear it?"

"Whatever you want."

"That's what I want," Treasure says. "Please read it out loud," and she closes her hand around the wooden handle wrapped in the napkin, yanks it free, and lunges at Sriyat, lifting her right hand high and then dragging the edge of Noi's prized Japanese carving knife down on a diagonal, across the man's forehead and face, slicing into the side of his neck and continuing down as the blood rains around her, across his chest and stomach, opening his shirt and the skin beneath it, and at the same time Chalee leaps from the desk and brings the iron bar down on the wrist of the man's gun hand.

Sriyat yelps, spouting blood from his forehead and nose as the gun clatters to the floor, and he stretches both hands toward Treasure, reaching for her the way Paul had in her dream, and she shrills a high, taut-string sound and brings the knife's edge down again, over his left arm and hand this time, as Chalee swings the iron bar against his right elbow. Sriyat backs up fast and hits his head against the doorjamb. He can retreat no farther without turning around or bending down, and as he begins to fold himself at the waist, Dok comes at him through the air, feetfirst. Both feet slam into Sriyat's left kneecap, and Treasure, who has been screaming that same single note ever since Sriyat reached for her, takes the knife to her left, extending her right arm all the way across her chest, and then swings the blade right, slicing Sriyat across the abdomen. The man turns a quarter of the way around, dragging one useless leg, and goes down, so heavily that the floor shakes. He curls himself into a ball, whimpering.

The three children stand there gasping, looking down at him as the blood pools around him. Chalee kicks the gun away, toward the desk. After a few false starts, she manages to say, "Will he . . . will he die?"

"Maybe, maybe not." Dok says. "But he's bleeding pretty bad."

Treasure stares down at the man, her face slack and her mouth half open, and then she steps forward and kicks him with all her strength. Sriyat makes a sound like *whuff* and begins to moan again, and Treasure kicks him a second time and then a third. She's drawing back her leg again when Chalee puts her arm around Treasure's shoulders. Instantly all the force drains out of her body, and she sways as though she's going to collapse.

"You've been cut," Dok says. He and Chalee pull Treasure, as gently as possible, to the desk and sit her down.

"It's his," Treasure says, her voice a single rough edge. "All of it."

"Are you sure?"

"I'm not hurt." She nods toward the gun on the floor. "Take that," she says.

"For what? We can't keep it."

"*I want it!*" she screams, and she's halfway up before Dok grabs her arm and she sits back on the desk, hard, as Chalee goes and picks up the gun.

Sriyat says, "Help me."

Treasure bends forward at the waist, both hands gripping the edge of the desk, and says, "I'm going to watch you die."

"No you're not," Dok says. "We're getting out of here."

Treasure turns to look at him, and Dok realizes she has to reprocess his words to understand their meaning. In a moment she says, "Where?"

"You're covered in blood. You can't go anywhere except back to the shelter to clean up. Then we'll figure something out."

Chalee, her eyes wide, says, "*Ummm . . .*"

Sriyat has one arm up against the doorjamb, and he appears to be trying to pull himself upright. Treasure snatches the bar from Chalee's hand, crosses the office, and swings it into the back of Sriyat's hand, smashing bone and even denting the wood on the corner of the jamb. Sriyat screams hoarsely and snatches his hand back down to the floor. Lying on his side with his knees raised, he begins to rock back and forth, cradling the hand. He seems to be weeping.

Treasure clears her throat and spits on him.

"You don't know whether that story is true," Arthit says, with a glance at Anna. "Varney has lots of reasons to lie to you about her." Arthit looks weary, and the fluorescents put deep greenish circles beneath his eyes. To his left, leaning back against the desk in Boo's office as though she'd tip over backward without it, Anna watches Arthit's lips, her own lips the perfect circle of *no*. Crumpled in her hand is the note Hofstedler gave Poke. Although the boys in the other room are all awake, the three of them have been talking in whispers, trying to keep the news in the room.

Rafferty says, "I looked it up online. C-4 can't be detonated by fire."

"That doesn't—" Arthit stops, and his eyes go back to Anna, who is shaking her head in what could be disagreement or defeat. Behind her, on the whiteboard, is her last assignment of the day.

"I think it's true," Rafferty says. Anna looks like someone who has anticipated the worst possible news and is hearing it at last. "I know she lit the fire. It's not all that hard to see her turning on the gas, too."

Arthit says, "But *you* were in there." Anna squints with effort as she follows his words.

"So were her mother and Ming Li," Rafferty says. "But Treasure didn't have any affection for her mother, didn't know Ming Li. Didn't really know me either."

Anna raises the hand with the note in it. "Her *mother*—"

"Her mother was a zombie." He can't hold back a yawn, but it's nerves, not sleepiness. "Murphy had been abusing the girl for years, and her mother just sucked up the codeine. All I can say is, even if Treasure did it, which I think she did, you weren't in that house. It was a torture chamber. You have no idea how bad it was."

Turning away, Arthit draws an enormous breath, lets it out slowly, and says, "But I do know what murder is."

Anna springs from the desk, grabs his shoulders, and twists him to her. Says, "*Face* me when you talk."

"I said," Arthit says, and then he cups his face in his hands and rubs. When he takes his hands away, he says, "I said I know what murder is."

Pulling back, Anna says. "You've heard Poke. You know what she went through."

"I do. And if she did it, it doesn't matter what she went through. If that note is true, I can't have her in the house."

Anna rocks back as though ducking the words. Her face is rigid with control. "We need to talk about this."

"I don't think so."

"She needs *help*," Anna says.

"From doctors," Arthit says.

Anna says, "I'm not going to let you—I mean, I'm not going to let *her*—" and breaks off as Boo comes into the room towing a small dark girl with a bumpy face. The girl slides her palm under a runny nose and stares up at them, ready to deny everything.

"This is Apple," Boo says. He puts a hand on the child's shoulder and brings her forward a couple of reluctant steps. "Apple saw them leave."

After a moment of silence and a light double tap on her shoulder, Apple says, "Two of them." She wipes her nose again and studies her grimy palm. "The half-half and that skinny boy."

"What about the other girl?" Rafferty says. "Chalee?"

"Didn't see her," Apple says. Boo taps her again. "I *didn't*."

Anna says to Boo, "Are you sure Chalee went with them?"

Apple says, "You talk funny."

"You saw the three of them together earlier, didn't you?" Boo says.

"Talking," Apple says. She looks at all the faces in the room, trying to pick one, and then says to them all, "I'm hungry."

Arthit says, "I'll send someone to get you whatever you want. What would you like?"

"Tom yum koong," Apple says, very fast. "Som tam. Ice cream."

She opens her mouth to add something, but Arthit says, "Fine. Be right back." He leaves the room, presumably to go to the front steps, where his off-duty cop is waiting.

"What were they talking about?" Rafferty says.

"Running away, I think." Apple puts one foot in front of her, points her toe, ballet style, and lifts her heel so she can swivel it side to side. She watches the movement with interest. When no one replies, she glances up and finds them all looking down at her. "And about some man that the half-half, the one with the curly hair, was afraid of."

Arthit comes in and says to Apple, "Fifteen minutes. My man knows somewhere close by."

"And some people she didn't want to stay with," Apple says.

"Sorry?" Arthit goes and stands next to Anna. "I missed something."

"There were people the half-half didn't want to stay with," Apple says. "She could have gone back to their house, but she didn't want to. I told her she was crazy. She would have had her own bed. The other girl had stayed with them, too, but they didn't want her, they only wanted the fifty-fifty."

Anna blinks slowly and lowers her head. She says, "I never should have—"

"You were trying to help," Arthit says, putting an arm around her, but Anna shrugs it off.

"I don't need to be comforted," she says. "I need a *plan*." Then she asks Apple, "Why didn't she want to go back?"

Apple has been scratching the bites on her neck. "She was afraid of the man. She said he smelled like leather."

Arthit looks at Anna for a moment and then closes his eyes.

"This shouldn't surprise anybody," Rafferty says. "She's terrified at the thought of having another father."

Anna says, "And she's terrified of that man, whatever his name is, who's out there somewhere." She's looking at Poke but obviously speaking to Arthit. "You can't *begin* to understand how much pressure the girl is under. Even if she blew up that house, it was her *past* she was destroying. Damaged children wake up frightened, they go to sleep frightened. They don't believe there's anyone who will help them, anywhere in the world. And still they try to love their parents. When they finally realize that their parents aren't *worth* their love, the hate can be stronger than anything you or I have ever felt."

Apple volunteers, "I hate *my* father."

Arthit says, "But would you kill him?"

"No," Apple says.

Arthit glances at Anna and says, "Why not?"

Apple scratches her neck and says, "I'm not big enough."

DOK HAS TUCKED the automatic into his pants to free his hands for the broom, which is once again propped against his shoulder. He has to keep tugging on his waistband to keep his pants up.

After an agonizing forty-five minutes or so, watching Sriyat cough and try to move, the three of them finally worked up the nerve to jump over the man's body. His wheezing—a wet, irregular sound—frightened Chalee, although Treasure didn't even seem to hear it. Occasionally he made a surprising effort to get up. Not once had anyone spoken between the time Sriyat went down for good and the moment Dok said, "We have to jump over him."

Once they're outside, panting in the drizzle, Dok and Chalee pick up the door and lean it back in place, securing it the best they can with a twist of wire although they both know that, with its hinges gone, it will eventually sag to one side. It's obvious that Sriyat will be found soon.

Chalee leads them back up the hill. In a block or so, they'll be at the mouth of the passage. They're strung out in single file, farther apart than they had been on the way down, as though what's happened has physically come between them: Chalee, then Treasure, then Dok. Both Dok and Chalee look like they're studying the pavement, deep in thought. Treasure's eyes are everywhere. She seems to be rebalancing herself with every step, as though she needs to be ready to run in any direction. Watching her from behind, Dok sighs.

Chalee stops at the cross street and waits for them to catch up. Treasure gets there first, standing far enough from Chalee that the two of them could just barely graze each other's fingertips with their arms fully extended. They wait in silence, not looking at each other, for Dok to trudge up to them.

"Do you want to give me the broom, Dok?" Chalee asks. "I'll go first."

"No." Dok turns it upside down and looks at the bristles. "It's silly."

"It worked last time," Chalee says.

"If there even *were* any rats." Dok runs the flat of his hand over the tips of the bristles. "Useless," he says.

They hear a shoe scuff and see Treasure stepping off the curb and into the street. Her clothes are brown and stiff with Sriyat's blood, her hands so saturated that it looks like she's wearing gloves. The two of them trail behind until she comes to the passageway, and then she turns without a pause and goes in. The other two hurry to catch up.

For a moment they think they see a small silhouette at the far end of the passageway. Dok stops, but when he's blinked, the figure—if there had been a figure—is gone.

A BOY RUNS into the office, his face electric with news: "They're coming."

Rafferty, who had crammed himself onto one of the folding chairs, is up instantly. Boo goes straight to Apple and picks up the tray of food that she's been eating as fast as she can, and says, "Upstairs." Still chewing, she trails him out of the room, and by the time Rafferty reaches the door, Boo and Apple are five or six steps up. Rafferty pushes open the outer door, watched by a roomful of wide-awake boys, and jogs to the end of the building, where he slows, takes a very deep breath, and steps into the mouth of the passageway.

He hears the door to the shelter open behind him, but his attention is on the slight black figure, just a silhouette, coming toward him. He knows it's Treasure by the mop of hair, once again in rebellion against the brush. Behind her is another figure that, as it moves, resolves itself into two.

Treasure stops for a moment, probably surprised by the sight of someone standing there. He thinks she might turn and run, but the other two figures keep coming, and after they've taken a couple of steps, she seems to remember that they're back there and she continues toward him. Rafferty hears a *skritch-skritch* sound like that of someone using a stiff brush to clean a pair of shoes. He backs away from the alley to make himself look less threatening. There's a whispered argument going on behind him, Anna's voice overriding Arthit's and then rolling on, a stream of words. Rafferty tunes it out and watches the black figure advance, the two who are farther away leaning left and right to look over her shoulders and each other's. The brushing sound gets louder.

And Treasure steps from the mouth of the passageway. Her gaze slowly sweeps the area, pauses at his face and then continues its survey. He sees her register the people on the steps to the shelter, and then she looks back at him or, he thinks, through him. She's shaking. She hasn't taken another step since she emerged from the passageway, and the two children behind her have stopped, too, still in the narrow alley, just a few steps from the end.

She's covered in blood, her hands so thickly coated she could have been finger painting with it. Blood has saturated her clothes, dried in flakes on her face and arms, and clotted in her hair. He can smell it, the odor flowing off her like wet heat. He looks into her eyes and sees the emptiness of someone who may have just taken her final blow and doesn't know whether she can get up again or why she should bother, and all the revulsion he feels disappears. He opens his arms and kneels down, and, to his amazement, she comes.

She's burning hot. The moment his arms go around her, she begins to shiver violently, and then her breath starts to come in gasps and she seems to be trying to say something, but she can get no further than "I . . . I . . . I," and even that's all air, and as he tries to think of some way to comfort her, her legs buckle and collapse, and she turns to deadweight in his arms. It catches him completely unprepared and off balance. He's leaning forward, toward her, and her arms around his neck drag him down. The next thing he knows, they're both flat on the wet pavement with Arthit and Anna leaning down, Anna trying to help. Treasure's eyes are closed, and she's emitting a series of tiny wordless sounds, part sob, part yelp, like an injured animal.

Boo comes at a run, looks down at her, and says, "My office. I'll get the doctor."

Dok, who has emerged from the passageway with a broom in his hand, says, "It's not her blood." Behind him, Chalee's clothes are also smeared a dark reddish brown, and there are streaks of it on her forearms and forehead. She seems to have wiped her hands on the front of her T-shirt.

"Are you both all right?" Boo says.

Chalee says, "Yes. I don't know about her."

Arthit helps Poke up while Anna kneels beside Treasure. The child's eyes are still closed, and she's still making that whimpering sound. Anna says, "We have to get her inside, and she needs a sedative." To Arthit she says, "Go away," and Arthit backs up a few steps.

"I'll send someone to the compound to call the doctor," Boo says over his shoulder. He's already on his way back to the building, pulling his phone from his pocket as he runs. "And somebody will get the hospital bed ready."

Rafferty calls out, "I don't think she's been cut. *Please*, nobody except us, until we know what's happened." He kneels beside Treasure and slowly lifts her to a sitting position. Her head flops forward onto her chest. Waving Anna down on Treasure's other side, he takes the girl's near arm and wraps it over his shoulders, grasping her wrist with his other hand. He raises his eyebrows in Anna's direction, and she nods and gets Treasure's other arm around her neck. Rafferty says, "Up on three," and begins to count, the words separated by Treasure's yelping sounds. He ducks his head on three as an additional signal, since he's not certain that Anna has followed his lips, and the two of them stand, bringing the girl up with them. Treasure begins to scream, the same high, unwavering sound he'd heard the night she saw her father emerge, still alive, from the big burning house.

Rafferty says, "It's all right, it's all right, you're safe, it's all right," and the scream thins and drifts and breaks into the same spasmodic whimpering. With Treasure dangling between them, he and Anna get her up the steps and into the shelter, curious boys staring wide-eyed from their cots. One of them is Tip, the boy she'd scratched, who had developed a crush on her. When the boy next to him says something that makes a few other boys laugh, Tip punches the boy in the face. Instantly there's a knot of fighting boys, cots going over sideways, the smack of flesh on flesh, muffled grunts, and the occasional cry of pain.

Boo barrels past them, running into the room with the boys in it, and as Rafferty and Anna angle themselves and Treasure through the narrow entrance, Rafferty hears Boo bellowing and then the sound of a couple of slaps and something heavy—a cot, perhaps—hitting the wall. The room falls silent behind them.

Boo has lined up five folding chairs along one wall, and Poke and Anna half carry Treasure to them. They try to get her to lie down, but she resists mechanically and silently, without a word, her limbs rigid against their efforts. Ultimately they let her sit down. She slides to the middle chair, two empties on either side of her, and brings her knees up and hugs them, bending her neck until her forehead rests on top of her knees. She rocks back and forth. She's stopped whimpering, but there's a squeaky sound whenever she inhales. Rafferty sits beside her, saying, "Is it okay if I'm here, Treasure?" He gets no reply, but she doesn't move away, just clutches her knees and rocks.

Her T-shirt is pulled up because her back is so sharply curved, and protruding from the waist of her pants Rafferty sees what looks like a bloody napkin, tightly folded. He says, "I'm going to take this because it looks uncomfortable," and she doesn't resist as he pulls it free. He feels Anna's eyes on him as he unwraps it, and when she sees the knife, she sucks her breath in. A noise at the door makes him look up, and he sees Arthit staring at the knife.

Behind Arthit, Dok and Chalee come into the room. Chalee is bloodier and more disheveled than Dok. They both look at Treasure, with—it seems to Rafferty—more apprehension than affection. Dok's eyes go to the knife, and he bunches his mouth tightly. Rafferty wiggles a hand in the air to get Chalee's attention, and when she's looking at him, he says, "Whose blood?"

"The fat man you hired," Chalee says.

The squeak of Treasure's breathing scales up a couple of notes.

Arthit sidesteps the children and comes up to Poke, a hand extended. "Give it to me," he says, and after a moment's consideration Rafferty hands him the napkin and the knife. Arthit takes it, keeping his fingers off the surface of the knife, and very deliberately refolds the napkin around it. He turns and says to Chalee, "Where is he?"

Chalee's eyes go to Dok, and then to Poke, and then to Treasure, but all she can see of Treasure is the mat of bloody hair. "Out there," she says, gesturing vaguely in the direction of the passageway.

"Take me," Arthit says.

Rafferty says, "Goddamn it, Arthit, wait a minute."

Arthit says, "I don't actually need you with me to do my job."

Anna's snaps, "You stay here. You stay here until we know this child doesn't need a doctor."

"She doesn't need me," Arthit says.

"You have *no idea* what she needs," Anna says, biting off the words furiously. "Don't make this about you."

"I want to go with you, Arthit," Poke says.

Arthit waves the objection off. "For all you know, the man is still alive. What if he dies while I'm standing here?"

"He was going to shoot me," Chalee says. "And take her back to her father."

Arthit, turning toward the door, says, "Her father's dead."

"I know," Chalee says, scratching her head, "but that's what she said."

"Chalee, Anna," Rafferty says, getting up. "Please sit here with her." He bends down to Chalee, who has looked away, distancing herself from the request. "Please, Chalee? Dok, you take Arthit and me to where it happened."

THEY'VE TRAVERSED MORE than half of the passageway in silence, following Dok, when Arthit says, "What in hell am I supposed to do now?"

"I don't know what would be best for her," Rafferty says.

"I'm not thinking about *her*," Arthit says. "I'm thinking about Anna and me. I can't have that child in my house, but I know Anna's not going to give up so easily. Even in spite of what happened tonight."

"Deal with that when it comes up. If it does." Rafferty shortens his steps to avoid bumping into Dok, who has obviously slowed to listen to them, even though they're speaking English.

"I plan things," Arthit says. "I don't play it by ear like that. *And* I'm a cop." He shakes his head. "She took Noi's knife," he says, more to himself than to Poke.

"She felt like she needed it. And as it turned out, she did."

Dok reaches the end of the passageway, waits until they're both right behind him, and then turns left.

"Tell us what happened," Rafferty says in Thai.

"Treasure asked me to show her some hiding places," Dok says. "In case that man came, the one with the snake, you know? So I showed her a good place, and then that fat man broke the door and came in."

Arthit says to Rafferty, "He must have been watching that end of the passage. My guy was stationed at the end of the big alley."

"He wanted money," Dok says. They come to a cross street, and Dok steps down from the curb. "He had a gun," he says, tugging his shirt up to show them. "He was going to shoot Chalee."

Arthit sighs heavily and says, "Right. Of course. Slow down for a second." Dok does, and Arthit leans forward and lifts the gun out of Dok's waistband. Dok doesn't try to prevent him, although he gives the weapon a regretful parting glance.

"I'm sure that complicates things for you," Rafferty says, just barely muting his anger, "it being self-defense like that when you had your mind all made up, but still. Even you have to admit that it's better than not knowing."

"There's still the gas," Arthit says. They're heading downhill, warehouses to their left, and coming up on the other side, a sagging wooden building.

Dok says, "He's right in—" and stops, his arm still extended, pointing to the building. He swallows loudly.

The door is lying on the ground outside the building, the empty frame an entryway to darkness, and there's no one collapsed there.

"That's where he was," Dok says. "It's true. He was right there. Go look, you'll see all the blood. Honest. Go look."

24

Skin to Skin

WALLACE PRACTICALLY HAS to push him out the door, but *finally* Hofstedler leaves. He's still talking as Wallace shoulders the door closed, saying, "Yeah, Leon, really Leon, wow, how about *that?*" until the latch snaps into place. There's a moment long enough to light a cigarette in, and then Hofstedler's heavy footsteps echo down the hall. Wallace stays pressed against the door, listening, making sure Leon doesn't turn around, full of some new topic, eager to praise his ladyboys again, seized by the desire to lecture helpfully about the memory-strengthening properties of ginkgo biloba ("Just what you *need!*"), anxious to warn Wallace yet again to keep his eyes open for Varney's watchers. Like Hofstedler ever noticed anything in his life except a stein of beer.

The elevator groans at the far end of the hall. Wallace waits for the sliding doors to open and close again—they squeal in both directions—and then puts his life on hold for a count of ten to make sure Leon doesn't change his mind about riding down; there have been evenings, especially lately, when Leon left four or five times. Nam-Fon, the fierce little Thai woman Leon married all those years ago, who had administered every detail of his life for decades and had terrified the patrons of the Expat Bar with her vehemence about bar girls and the men who pay for them, left him a few months back. While she was with him, Hofstedler had complained about her endlessly. Now he hates to go home.

When he doesn't hear Leon returning, Wallace closes his eyes and presses his forehead against the door. He has more things than usual to think about.

For one there's Hartley, reborn. Oh, well, lately it seems like nobody ever really goes away. Ernie is practically at Wallace's elbow half the time, some of the other guys from the squad are popping up in his dreams, when he's in the bar he keeps seeing the younger faces of Campeau and Pinky Holland—they just push their way through the sags and wrinkles and *leer* at him—and recently he's been hearing his mother's voice, always muffled, chatting from the other room. Once or twice (or three times, or four), he actually changed rooms so he could hear what she was saying. It was one of those slap-your-forehead moments. He's been having a lot of them lately.

Did he drink that beer at the bar this evening or just nurse it? He runs his tongue inquisitively over his teeth. His mouth doesn't taste like beer.

So what it is, is that Hartley—no, Varney, *Varney*—took a picture of him and Leon, and people are using it to look for them in the hope that they'll lead the follower to Poke. It seems to Wallace, as he floats past the couch, foam exploding from its seams in popcorn shapes, that Varney should have been able to find Poke by now. Bangkok's not a small town, but if you know where someone hangs out and who his friends are, you should be able to find him easily in this much time.

Although, how much time has it actually *been*? This is—what?—Monday night, very early Tuesday morning? First time Leon talked about Varney and Poke was just a few nights back. Late Thursday sounds right, although who the hell knows anymore? So it's only three, four days. Not so long.

He's bathed in the light from the refrigerator, bending toward the beer, when he hears himself say aloud, "He likes to wait."

And there he is again, fresh as the moment, in Wallace's mind's eye: Hartley, his own eye pressed to that sight, the barrel of his

M16, complete with its hand-modified flash suppressor, doing a microdance as it follows the movements of someone with a short life expectancy three hundred, three hundred fifty, yards away. Hartley getting the shot lined up, grinning, then tilting the rifle up just to bring it down again a moment later. *Enjoying* himself, anticipating the distant death, delaying it to prolong the fun.

"Of all the cocksuckers in the world," Wallace says, popping the top, "Hartley." He turns off the kitchen light, his mind still in the heat and stink of Vietnam, and goes back in the living room, barking his left shin on a corner of the coffee table. Vietnam crowds the little rooms: the heat, the bugs, the leeches, the mud, the insufferable dust; the asshole sergeant, uniform fresh from the dry cleaner, who ordered them to search the tunnels before blowing them but who wouldn't go into them himself; the guy next to you going straight down like an imploding building, a tenth of a second before you hear the shot; the guys, the guys, the guys. All of them back, thanks to Hartley, all of them staking out spaces in his mind.

And then there's the one, he thinks as he sits on the edge of his bed, facing the watery window, the one who never comes back: Jah. Why can't he bring Jah back?

He's been told by the bar's self-appointed Alzheimer's experts that he's going to find himself living more and more in the past, gradually leaving the present behind like a closed-up room, full of things he can no longer get to. The prospect hadn't dismayed him. But now it's beginning to look as though the past he'll eventually be living in won't contain Jah, and that doesn't seem fair. She's the only thing from back there he wants.

Twice now he's awakened late at night, sufficiently unmoored in time to go visit her, to walk again on the Golden Mile, not as he dreamed it with Ernie but alive with music and lit up, with those impossibly wonderful girls, drop-ins from heaven, drifting up and down the road. But Jah was never there when he searched for it, the Mile was never there; it was buried beneath skyscrapers, and he'd wander, one foot in the 1960s, until he came to the shop-house, but now it was an apartment building, very fancy, complete with a uniformed doorman, and he'd linger there as though his strings had been cut until they sent him on his way. Wherever that led. But it never led to Jah. He had banished her, it appears, even from the small town of his past, and now she wasn't there any-more.

And he, only he, was responsible.

His fourth time here—*in Bangkok,* damn it, *Bangkok,* and he sticks a mental pin in the name to hold it in place—the fourth time he took R&R in Bangkok, he didn't catch the return flight to 'Nam. He just went AWOL. He'd been preparing for it, con-sciously and unconsciously, for more than a year. On his third leave, with Jah's help, he'd found an apartment in an airless con-crete building where the walls were unfinished plywood, the bathroom was at the end of the hall, and the door was secured with a padlock and a flimsy hasp. A single window opened onto an alley from which the reek of urine rose in waves so pungent they should have been visible, like yellow heat ripples. He'd opened a Thai bank account, and over the months back in 'Nam he slowly trans-ferred the money from his college account in Carlsbad into his new bank. Paving the way to escape.

And then Ernie had been killed, had fallen sideways in a tangle of his own entrails, and that was it. After they got Ernie, Wallace knew he wasn't going back, no matter what they did to him. They'd never find him anyway, he thought, not hiding in some cold-water apartment in an obscure corner of Bangkok. They had too much on their hands. They'd never find him.

And they didn't. At the end he found *them,* but not until he'd destroyed the one thing in the world that was worth having.

His first night back on that final fourth leave, he'd gone straight from the plane to Thai Heaven to find Jah. Her chair went over backward with a bang when she saw him across the room, and she'd let loose a scream of *"Wallet!"* that cut through the music and talk to make his heart blossom in his chest. He'd slapped down the money for her bar fine, and she'd leaped onto his back, slapping his shoulders and driving her heels into his sides to spur him into a gallop.

She had loved his hair, short as it was then. Wallace passes a hand over his scalp, feeling the skin with the long iron-gray strands clinging to it. Back then it had been thick enough for her to grab when they made love, for her to lock her teeth on and pull it from his head, laughing at his roar. *Locked.*

They were locked together, virtually never apart. He wouldn't let her work, not even dance, but she wouldn't quit entirely, because, she said, what would happen to her if he left? Who would take care of her mother and her sisters? He argued again and again that he would never leave her, that he was there for good; but that was the only topic that put a wedge between them. She wouldn't discuss it, just looked down, at her lap or the floor, politely disguising her disbelief until he was finished, and then she would say, "But what if you do?" So they found a compromise. After their day together, he took her to the bar every night when it was time for her to clock in and immediately bar-fined her. Then they'd flag a taxi so the two of them could flee the Golden Mile, free for another twenty-four hours. Through those long days and nights, he felt the way he had as a child when he found a new best friend: there was only one person in the world he wanted to see.

Locked. They were always touching, skin to skin or cloth to cloth; she pressed herself against him in her sleep and squeezed in beside him on the apartment's one narrow chair, throwing her smooth brown legs over his. She rested her head on his shoulder when they sat on the bed, sneaked her fingers down the back of his pants when they shared a seat on a bus. She grasped his hand whenever they left the apartment, as though she thought he might try to run away. Crossing streets against the anarchic traffic with her dragging him behind as she wove between the oncoming cars and trucks, he felt so free and so unburdened that he lost completely, for the space of a long moment, the knots of fear and anger 'Nam had tied in his heart and nerves.

She taught him where to buy street food, how to bargain in the sidewalk marketplaces, how to use the buses. She hauled him up to her village, all dirt roads and mangy dogs and slanting wooden houses, to meet her mother, whose eyes, above her smile, seemed to be doing arithmetic every time she looked at him. Her younger sisters stared at him with the kind of fascination they might have given to a five-legged dog and never got within arm's reach, huddling wide-eyed, their backs pressed against the thin walls, as far from him as they could get. When the train finally pulled away, after a long, long three days, he'd leaned back in his seat and sighed, and she'd doubled over with laughter, laughing until the tears slid down her cheeks, imitating how he'd walked in the tiny house, how he'd sat on the floor, how he'd pulled himself in to seem smaller, less *there.*

To his reflection in the mirror in the bathroom, which is where he seems to be, he says, "What a fucking idiot. What a total, colossal, balls-out, world-class fuckup."

Inevitably, the world began to push its way in. The apartment, cheap as it was, cost money. Her bar fines cost money, since she continued to refuse to quit altogether. "I quit, no one hire me after," she said. They ate the cheapest food, but it still cost money. His books, while he continued to buy them, cost money. The T-shirts he purchased after fierce bargains with sidewalk vendors cost money. He found and bought her the occasional present, nothing expensive, until she started taking them back to fight the sellers for refunds, which she handed him with irritation, the only time he ever saw her angry.

Eight months later, when the money was gone, she proposed a deal: she would work in the bar at night but not go with men. She'd just *talk* to them, she said—they all liked it when a girl talked to them. Until he could find some more money, he and she would live off her tips and the commissions she made from lady drinks, bought for her by the customers. Helplessly, Wallace agreed: he'd exhausted his college fund, his mother was furious about his desertion and refused to lend him money, and there was no way he could earn a living in Thailand, not without using the identity papers that would bring the army on the run.

But the lady drinks didn't pay enough. Her tips were minuscule. She'd gotten home late a few times, extra money in hand, to face his silence and withdrawal, and then, on a Saturday, the busiest night in the bar, she'd stayed out all night as he paced the floor and fumed. The next morning she came through the door with almost a hundred dollars and made it even worse by saying, as she handed it to him, "For rent." Wallace had bolted without a word and spent the day and all of the next night stalking the streets. He ended up on a bench in Lumphini Park, as though sitting in the dark all alone all night, deep-frying his own heart in shame and rage would *pay her back* somehow, although he couldn't have said for what. He couldn't find anything in the world that would compensate him for his humiliation, and this self-centered, all-about-*him* reaction would make him furious at himself for decades to come. When he got back, at eleven the next morning, she wasn't there. On the tidy, unrumpled bed was a bright new T-shirt for him, folded around a wilted orchid. The state of the flower made it obvious that it had been placed there the prior afternoon. She hadn't come back after work.

She arrived in the early afternoon, her eyes tight with anxiety and her arms full of his favorite Thai food, still hot. There was so much of it, cups and cartons of it, that she'd had to use the sawed-off bottom of a cardboard box as a tray. Two steps into the room she stopped, the open door behind her, her hands extended to put the box between them, an offering, her eyes locked on the center of his chest.

He didn't know what he was going to do until he'd done it: brought his hands straight up, fists clenched, under the bottom of the box. The food flew into the air, some of it hitting Jah in the chest and face. A big cardboard cup of hot soup struck her on the shoulder and exploded, soaking her in steaming broth and noodles. The box tumbled through the air, end over end, and bounced off the wall over their bed.

He slapped her, backhanded her, and she staggered backward until her shoulder hit the edge of the open doorway. Within the time it took her to blink twice, she made her decision. Without pause, without a parting glace, she took the couple of additional steps she needed to go all the way through the door, and he stood there, numb, almost choking on the fragrance of the food, listening to her footsteps on the stairs as she fled into the Bangkok day. The box was upside down on top of their pillow.

Slowly and meticulously, he cleaned the room. When he was finished, when the floor was washed and the linen on the bed changed and the pillow hung up to air and the box and cartons and cups of food thrown away, he sat on the edge of the bed and looked at the door. By seven o'clock that night, he knew she wasn't coming back.

He sat there for another hour, using the time to scrape at himself, to pick at his life, hating what he saw. A little after eight, he took the small wad of bills that had been in the cardboard box and tore them to tiny bits, scattering the pieces over the bed. He pulled the petals off the fading orchid and mixed the bright bits into the confetti of money. Then he walked out, leaving the door yawning wide, abandoning their home and everything they had put into it, taking only the clothes he was wearing and his empty wallet and passport. He walked for almost two hours. When the soldier at the gate of the US embassy looked up at him, he said, "I'm AWOL from 'Nam." The soldier picked up his phone, and Wallace said, "I give up. I give up, I give up, I give up, I *give up.*" He was weeping as they led him in.

He never saw her again. He was shipped home and served fourteen months at Fort Leavenworth, doing short time because of his valor in battle. During his imprisonment his mother died. When he came out, he owned the house in Carlsbad, which was worth a lot of money, as well as a substantial investment portfolio. It took him a few months to sell the house, liquidate the stocks, and send most of the money to Bangkok in small increments so as not to draw official attention, and then he grew impatient with how long the transfers were taking and he broke the law by getting on an airplane with almost a hundred thousand in cash, bills tucked absolutely everywhere.

She wasn't at Thai Heaven. Her friends in the bar avoided one another's eyes as they claimed they had no idea where she was. A few days after he arrived, he found the rooms over the shophouse, and over a period of weeks he decorated them in her favorite colors, buying the long body pillows she loved, the bright pastel sheets. At night he haunted Thai Heaven until they wouldn't let him in anymore, and then he made the rounds, dusk to dawn, night after night, of the other establishments on the Golden Mile, even Jack's American Bar, where the black soldiers who at first greeted him with stares gradually came to accept him, although the women, careful of their relationships with their black customers, wouldn't give him a glance.

He returned alone every night to the home he had made for her above the shophouse. Jah's place.

Patpong Road had just opened up, a strand of relatively flashy new bars siphoning customers from the Golden Mile, and he scouted that, too, every single bar every night for nights on end, but she wasn't working there either. One night on Patpong around 3 A.M., exhausted, half drunk, and unwilling to return to the home he had turned into a shrine to her, he walked into a tiny place called the Expat Bar. And he stayed there for forty-three years.

Getting old.

Part Three

SMALL TOWN

25

Shoveling Snow in a Blizzard

FOR THE NEXT couple of days, Rafferty is propelled by a numb, amorphous, centralized anxiety that seems to have plastered itself to his heart and lungs, with occasional forays southward to his gut. At unpredictable moments it gives him a squeeze, as though demanding attention.

It's worst at night, as he discovers the very first night after Treasure has been tranquilized and he finally climbs back into the soft hotel bed. Once Rose—who woke long enough to say hello—took her unvarying, unswerving dip into the deepest realms of sleep, he lay there stewing, staring at the ceiling and trying to see a clear way forward. They all either dead-end or lead him into useless loops. He feels like a man shoveling snow in a blizzard, clearing a path to the sidewalk at last only to turn and see that it's all filled in behind him.

He has lists, of course—he always has lists—and early the next morning he methodically goes over them, choosing the actions that might actually change things for the better. Some of those, unfortunately, depend on Arthit, and the affection between them is strained by what they left unsaid. Rafferty doesn't blame Arthit for anything that's happening, and he's certain that Arthit doesn't blame him, but the issue of Treasure—what Rafferty sees as Arthit's unsympathetic snap judgment about her and what Arthit undoubtedly sees as Rafferty's willful minimization of the facts that the girl tried to kill everyone in her house and then took a knife to Sriyat—seems to be uniquely undiscussable. The whole snarl comes down to feelings, and neither of them has any skill at talking about feelings. So, man style, they'll probably continue to avoid the entire issue.

Rafferty sits motionless at the hotel room's dining table for a moment and then adds to his list: *Fix things with Arthit.*

Treasure is back in the room at the shelter with the hospital bed in it, the room to which she was taken the night Chalee and Dok found her. Rafferty had checked on her the moment he gave up on sleep and got out of bed to text Anna, who spent the night in an adjoining room. This undoubtedly heightens Arthit's resentment, which had already deepened the previous evening when Anna insisted that he keep his two cops on protective duty.

So Treasure is protected, and she's getting visits from a doctor and is being kept mildly sedated, but she's back on that same damn bed. According to Anna, she doesn't move or speak, just lies on one side, her knees drawn up, one arm under her head. She'd lain there motionless, refusing to eat until about 11 A.M., when Chalee was finally persuaded to pay a visit. The two of them had shared the room in silence, Treasure still in that same withdrawn position, until she'd closed her eyes and begun silently to cry. After a long moment, Chalee pulled her chair closer and put a hand on Treasure's arm. Anna tactfully left the room.

Rafferty heaves a sigh that practically hollows him out. How much can happen to one kid? She hasn't spoken a word since she went down on the pavement the previous evening.

When he's not tormenting himself over Treasure's emotional state and his bad judgment in hiring Sriyat and Pradya, Rafferty is stewing about Varney, what to do about Varney. Unless Arthit's extensive check of hotels turns the man up, Rafferty's only plan is to continue making himself as visible as possible in the Patpong area in the hope that Varney will contact him to arrange a talk. He has to convince Varney that he doesn't have the money or

Treasure. Or, if there's no alternative, remove him from the picture somehow.

It's not much, but it's all he's got.

His worry about Sriyat's being dead fades a bit around 9 A.M., when Sriyat's partner, Pradya, fails to show up for his shift. A call to his cell phone gets a "not in use" recording. Rafferty can only theorize that Pradya was in on the scheme to grab Treasure from the beginning and was sufficiently nearby to come and haul Sriyat out in answer to a phone call for help.

So that's a very pale piece of good news: Arthit can't claim that Treasure killed Sriyat, self-defense or no self-defense. At least until the body turns up.

At the top of one of his lists is an enumeration of his weak spots. He's decided that his weakest—now that they're out of the apartment—is Miaow's school. It shouldn't be that difficult for Varney to find out where Miaow goes to school; he has to figure that Rafferty lives somewhere near Patpong, and there are only three international schools within reasonable driving distance. Miaow goes to the closest of them.

So on Tuesday morning at breakfast, after a sleepless night, a couple of hours spent with his lists, and two chats, via text, with Anna about Treasure's status, he announces to Miaow that as of now he's taking her to school. He gets an unexpected argument: Miaow wants to continue to use the school's private bus. Rafferty points out that she'd have to take a cab from the hotel to get to the bus's pickup point. Miaow's reaction is simple and sharp: she *wants to take the bus.*

"Why?" he says, trying to blink the sand from his eyes. She's sitting opposite him at the table in the suite's small dining room. She's ordered waffles—which she's not eating—an orange, which she is, and a Diet Coke, and he's gnawing on cardboard toast and avoiding the coffee, which is the color of tea.

Miaow says, "Because."

While he counts silently, waiting for additional information, he breaks off a corner of the toast and crumbles it onto his plate, then moistens his thumb, presses it into the pile of crumbs, and licks the crumbs off. When he's done and he's reached fifteen, he says, "Because why?"

"Because the kids are on the bus." She looks longingly over her shoulder in the direction of the bedroom where Rose is sleeping.

"Forget it," he says. "You couldn't wake her up with dynamite. I'm driving you to and from school, and that's the way it is."

"But . . ." Miaow says. She gives her attention to peeling the foil off a packet of strawberry jam that accompanied her waffles and then sticking her tongue directly into the packet. Normally this would earn her a mild verbal reprimand, but Rafferty just rests his chin in his hand and watches, as though it's the most interesting moment of the day.

Finally he says, "Aha."

She glances at him and then away. "Aha what?"

"Just aha."

Miaow drags her forefinger through the remainder of the jam and smears it in a circle on the end of her nose.

"Does *Edward* take the bus?" Rafferty asks with big-eyed innocence.

"I'm busy," Miaow says. She draws two strawberry cat whiskers on her right cheek.

"I'm going to pick you up and take you home, too."

"You can't," she says, working on her left cheek. "I don't know what time we'll finish." She licks the remaining jam off her finger.

"Why's that?"

"Today we do tech rehearsal," she says triumphantly. "The whole play twice, with all the lights and sound. It'll take *days*."

Rafferty says, "Do we have any more jam?"

"No." She puts her finger in her mouth. "I used it all up."

"I love tech rehearsals."

"How would you know?" If Miaow's tone of voice were a visible entity and using the Delsarte method, it would be leaning forward with its hands on its hips, elbows pulled back. "You don't even know what a tech rehearsal—"

"The first time I ever saw you act," Rafferty says, "was a tech rehearsal. Mrs. Shin called for the thunder and lightning and the sound of the wind, and then the follow spot went on, and there you were, way up on that rock, doing your first speech as Ariel." He has one hundred percent of her attention. "You were wonderful."

"How wonderful?"

"The hair on my arms stood straight up."

"Really." She leans her cheek on her right hand, but the jam is too slippery and she skids off it.

"You got it on your neck," he says.

"Who cares?" she says. "Did the hair on your arms really stand up?"

He extends his arm and runs his hand up and down it, a quarter inch from the skin. "Goosebumps."

"Okay," she says, getting up. "You can take me to school. But you have to talk some more about how good I was." She reaches into the pocket of her shirt and tosses an unopened packet of jam onto the table. "For you," she says, and as he watches her go, he remembers the abandoned, damaged, mistrustful child he'd first seen on the street, and when he thinks about how far she's come, with no therapy but love, a sudden surge of pity for Treasure almost rips his heart from his chest.

ABOUT 1 P.M. that day, Arthit calls to say that none of the hotels they've contacted has Varney's passport on record, and no one who's looked at their emails and faxes recognizes the face from the passport photo.

"Just out of curiosity, how many?" Rafferty says.

"There are more than a thousand Western-style hotels in Bangkok," Arthit says, sounding as though he's personally called every one of them, "of varying degrees of luxury or squalor. There's also an uncountable number of guesthouses and less formal, more downscale arrangements. Flophouses, by-the-hour hotbeds, and terrorist dens, in other words. Most of those are run by people with no fondness for the police, so we've been concentrating on the mainstream establishments, and it's a zero."

Rafferty says, "Well, shit," startling the waitress at his elbow.

"I think we've hit all the ones he's likely to be staying in," Arthit says. "It's hard to picture him on Khao San."

Rafferty is in the hotel's bright orange, ground-level coffee shop, clearly misnamed if the mystery fluid in his half-empty cup is any evidence. "So he's not staying anywhere. That's just great. Absolutely consistent with everything else."

"Well, this might brighten your day a bit. I got to thinking about what you said about Treasure maybe being Murphy's heir. Murphy wasn't a careless man, and I figured he probably made some arrangements for the disposition of his stuff. So I called a guy I know who worked the investigation into the explosion at the house and asked about a will, and he said there was a fireproof safe on the ground floor, and inside it was an 'in the event of my death' letter that directed people to a lawyer in Colorado Springs, which I suppose is in Colorado."

"That's where it is."

"Good place for it. So I called him—Hiram E. Bixby, a name from the age of buggy whips—and asked him to get his hands on the will and call me back. I was the first to tell him that Murphy was dead, so I sent him a link to the story that broke in the *Sun*."

"What reason did you give for asking about the will?"

"I said people are making greedy noises around the estate, and we think they might be fraudulent. Got his lawyer's blood pressure right up. But I've been waiting a few hours for him now."

"It's after midnight in Colorado."

"How thoughtless of them," Arthit says, "to have their own time zone." There's a pause. Then he says, "Bixby's wife is named Huldah. Not a name you hear often, so I looked it up. Huldah was a prophetess in the Old Testament, and the name seems to come from the word for 'weasel.' Not sure I'd hand it to a kid."

Anything about a child seems like an opening, and Rafferty jumps on it. "I want to apologize for ever having hired Sriyat. What happened last night was my fault. You warned me about him, and I didn't listen."

"I didn't suggest anything better."

"Well, he's apparently alive, Sriyat is, since his buddy, Pradya, can't be reached by phone."

"I suppose that's good," Arthit says grudgingly. "But it's hard to care about either of them. And as long as we're talking, I might as well say that I wouldn't be so stressed about Treasure if I weren't afraid she's going to cost me my relationship with Anna."

"I know."

"Anna sees herself as the girl's savior. She's convinced that she can keep Treasure from cutting her wrists someday."

"Might be true. So how are you doing?"

"I've only had one night alone, and I hate it. I'm making my own breakfast."

"And washing the dishes?" Rafferty says.

"We have a lot of dishes," Arthit says. "I'll wash one when they're all dirty."

"Would you like to come eat with us? We could call room service together. You could have a thirty-dollar hamburger."

"No thanks. I'll just nibble a couple of bad shrimp and feel sorry for myself."

"Okay, but the food here is—" He breaks it off. "You know what? It's awful. They put truffles on everything. I feel like I'm on the Gout Diet."

"This will distract you. According to the cop I talked to, Varney was right about the gas. Every burner, both ovens in the kitchen, on full."

"I probably would have done the same thing, in her shoes."

"Then I won't say anything about how much it bothers me that she took that knife out of our kitchen. Just relax. Sit back and enjoy your truffles. I'll call you when I hear from Mr. Bixby."

"I'm going to the state capital," Edward says.

Rafferty, sitting next to Mrs. Shin in the fourth row of the dim auditorium, mouths the words silently. In unison, he and Edward continue: "To go to college. There's no reason for me to stay here."

Rafferty knows the scene line for line—it's Ned's best moment in the play—but the way Edward (who is, of course, playing Ned) chews and swallows the last few words, they sound something like *nreezin frrme tstayheer,* causing Mrs. Shin to sigh discreetly and shake her head. While Rafferty, all those years ago, had belted his lines to the last row, Edward seems to have been told frequently that it's bad breeding to raise one's voice.

"Give us a little more volume, Ned," Mrs. Shin calls out. "Projection, remember?" When she's directing, she calls all the actors by their character names. Just imagine, she tells Edward, that Miaow—Julie—is thirty feet away instead of sitting directly across the small table that's doubling for the town's ice-cream shop. "One more time from the top," Mrs. Shin says, "and *audibly* this time. We've still got to do the technical run-through."

Throughout this exchange Miaow has sat motionless, as though she's in a bell jar that seals out everything that's not in the world of the play. She's hunched over the table, shoulders curved like a bow, neck stretched forward, awkwardness in every angle of her body, using her spoon to make tiny back-and-forth scribbles in the glass cup that's supposed to contain her ice cream. Rafferty recognizes it as something she does at dinner when the conversation wanders into an area that doesn't engage her. The moment Mrs. Shin says, "From the top," Miaow straightens, places the spoon precisely beside the cup, and gets up, clasping her elbows with her arms folded over her stomach and exits into the stage-left wings. Edward ambles behind her with his hands in his pockets.

Mrs. Shin has directed the scene to give Miaow the stage alone for a few seconds, a small present to her actress, which she has justified by telling Miaow that Julie always arrives early when she knows Ned will be somewhere. Mrs. Shin calls, "Let's go," and after a beat Miaow comes onstage down left like someone whose sentence is about to be pronounced. Her face is defenseless, her mouth slightly open, the image of someone who's moments away from having a nail driven into her one and only hope. She pulls out the chair and sits without seeming conscious of her actions, focused on something invisible just a few feet in front of her eyes. Rafferty realizes he's leaning forward in his seat.

When Edward enters, Miaow looks up at him and involuntarily starts to smile, then lowers her gaze to the tabletop, leans back in her chair, and puts her hands in her lap. Not until Edward is seated does she meet his eyes, and then only for a second. When the scene reaches Ned's announcement that he's leaving town, she slides down in her chair and her shoulders curve anxiously as she picks up her spoon and begins the scribbling motion in her cup. Edward seems to pick up her energy, and for a few moments they're just two shy, hapless adolescents from seventy years ago, adrift leagues apart on an ocean of feeling and unable to summon the words or the courage that would lead them to each other.

Rafferty thinks idly that he was probably a little better—or at least louder—as Ned than Edward is and that Miaow cuts to ribbons the high-school senior, three years older and a more experienced actress than Miaow, who had played Julie in his production. Movement at the edge of his vision attracts his attention, and he sees several cast members drift down the aisles to watch more closely. The one most intent on the action is Siri Lindstrom, the school beauty whom everyone thought would play Julie. She's got eyebrow-pencil lines drawn on her forehead and at the corners of her eyes to age her into Julie's mother, her glorious wheat-colored hair has been gathered up and stuffed almost maliciously into a gingham bonnet, and the expression in her eyes is one of the purest loss: someone who's always thought she had everything, seeing the one thing she'll never have.

Rafferty has never been particularly conscious of his age, but looking at all of them, both the kids onstage acting the play he once acted and the ones in auditorium watching, he's aware that he's seeing his own past, just as when he regards the men in the Expat Bar, he's looking at one of his possible futures. For a moment he feels adrift in time—much the way, he thinks, Wallace must often feel—and then the scene is over and the applause of the people in the aisles brings him back, and the lovelorn teenager on the stage is once again his daughter.

Mrs. Shin claps her hands twice, not applause but a demand for attention. "Clear the stage, everybody." She looks at her watch. "Lights ready?"

"Ready," someone calls from behind them.

"Sound?"

"Ready."

"Places, everybody. We're going double-time until there's a technical cue, and then we'll let the tech crew take it at their own speed." She glances over at Rafferty and then calls out, "One exception. Luther? Luther?"

A slender Chinese boy comes on from stage left. "Luther is our Narrator," Mrs. Shin tells Rafferty. "You'll remember him as Prospero in *The Tempest*."

"I certainly do," Rafferty says, trying to make it sound positive. Luther, a born actor and not a good one, is cured ham to the bone. He had impersonated age as Prospero by walking as though he'd been tied in a square knot for days and untied moments before taking the stage.

Mrs. Shin, who is holding back a smile, says, "We'll take your opening speech at the usual speed, Luther."

Luther says, "Thank you," in his prematurely deep and plummy voice, as though he's just been given a long-overdue Nobel Prize, and retreats back into the wings.

"Watch this," Mrs. Shin says. She actually elbows Rafferty in her excitement. Then she cups her hands to her mouth and says, "Let's go, let's go. *Lights*."

The stage brightens selectively, spots picking out the odds and ends that have been silhouetted there: furniture, a few partial walls with windows, a doorway or two, a couple of ladders—all of it strewn almost randomly across the space. Luther ambles in downstage, yawning and punching at the buttons on his phone, paying no attention to the audience, looking like a kid who's got a few spare minutes and nothing to do with them. He yawns and ambles upstage—his back to the audience—to a table, which he dusts with a couple of swipes of his palm. Turning to sit on the table's downstage corner, he freezes as he sees the audience. Instead of sitting, he comes a few steps downstage and cups his hands around his eyes to shield them from the lights, scans the auditorium, and says, "*Oh*." Immediately he shoves the phone into his pocket, tugs his shirt down, straightens, and begins to walk with a pronounced, stagy limp, working his elbows a little whenever he's on the bad leg. He stops, faces out, and says, apparently searching for his lines, "So . . ." He licks his lips and says, "Ummmm," and then looks at his palm as though something is written there, squints at it, and says, "Hilldale, *yes*, Hilldale. It isn't a very big town. 'Bout two hundred souls," and then he's limping again and talking at the same time, gathering momentum with the play's opening speech, and Rafferty is surprised to find that he's interested.

"Your daughter," Mrs. Shin whispers. She looks like she's being tickled. "We all know that Luther, despite that extra helping of voice, isn't the most convincing actor in Bangkok, so Miaow worked this out with him, didn't even tell me about it. Luther is playing a young actor who's not very good, and it's changed the whole production. Some of the actors are in the audience when we start, and they just get up and go onstage when it's time. Your daughter came up with the whole thing. "

Rafferty says, *"Miaow?"*

"You don't know what you've got there," Mrs. Shin says as Luther gathers steam onstage. "Everybody in the cast has picked it up. We've got a play about a play, and it's working. Oh, I almost forgot. Tell Miaow to keep her eyes on the newspapers for the next day or two. I think she's going to get a surprise." Then she raises her voice. "That was great, Luther, now double-time. Everyone *remain in place*. Lights, get on the ball. We've got to do this mon-ster *twice*."

"WHERE DO YOU get it?" he asks.

Miaow, leaning against the window on her side of the cab, says, "I don't know." She looks tired after the two run-throughs; she'd worked the part, even at double-time. But she also seems lighter inside, like she could almost float off the seat.

"You must have some idea. It's too . . . too strong for you not to have been aware of . . ." He tapers off. "Of *something*."

"Not really. I never thought about acting until Mrs. Shin made me try out for Ariel. Now it's practically all I think about."

This is a tone, direct and completely serious, he almost never hears her use. She'd grown so accustomed to disappointment before she joined them that she automatically distances herself from the things she feels most deeply about.

"But when you started to become Ariel," he says, "there must have been something in your past that you were leaning on. To imagine her the way you did and then, you know, to put it out there like that."

"All I can think of is when I was on the street," she says. She turns away as though to look out the window. "I saw so many people who weren't like me." For a moment he thinks she won't go on, but she says, "You know. People who had *everything*, I thought, and I didn't have anything. Mostly I watched kids. I tried to imagine what it must be like to be them, to have stuff, not to want all the time, to have a place to live and somebody who got upset if they . . . if they skinned their knee. I mean, I stepped on a *nail*—it went all the way through my foot and poked up on top, and no one even said, 'Poor little girl.' And I wanted all that, and I couldn't have it, but I wanted to know what it felt like. So I watched them and found little pieces of how they felt. I mean, I could see what the way . . . the way they walked or laughed or went into a store—what it said about how they felt, and I could practice moving like that when I was alone and sort of *build* that feeling a piece at a time, do you know what I mean?"

"Probably."

"I found out how it felt to move like I owned the whole sidewalk. Like what you were talking about, like Delsarte. What it felt like to look at things in stores and know I could have them. Like I'd earned it somehow. And how they felt when they looked at me, too. That was like eating matches," she says, "knowing the way they felt about me. It made me hate myself. So I pretended. I moved like I owned everything around me, only it was a secret and they weren't allowed to know it. I was like the king in disguise in all those stories you read to me when I was little. And that was true in a way, because I knew so much more than they did about what was actually happening all around them. How thin the walls around them really were. Does this make any sense?"

"Yes."

"It was a kind of acting, I guess. And that's what I've been doing ever since you put me in my school. I've been acting."

"It's not *all* acting, Miaow," he says. "The kids who like you aren't just falling for an act. Give them some credit. You think *Edward* is falling for an act?"

"Edward doesn't know me. No one at school knows me. I'm *good* at this," she says in a tone that closes the conversation.

"You've got a lot of talent."

She says, "It's what I want to do."

"We'll do what we can," Rafferty says, "to see that you do. And now I want you to do me a favor."

"Sure," Miaow says. "What?"

"I want you to tell me what someone is feeling." He leans forward and says to the driver, "Klong Toey. Near the river. I'll direct you."

26

You Have to Say Yes

ANNA LOOKS BLURRED with exhaustion, but the sight of Miaow brings her to her feet in the empty classroom, fumbling with her hands and then her thick, chopped hair as though she's been caught in the middle of doing the dishes. "What a surprise," she says, working too hard at the delight. She hasn't met Miaow more than a few times, Rafferty realizes.

Miaow's smile doesn't have much behind it; to her, Anna is the woman who tried to betray Poke to the police, back when Treasure's father was alive. Stepping in front of her, Rafferty says, "How is she?"

"The same." She finds her chair with the back of her leg, starts to sit, and then thinks better of it. "She won't talk or eat. She won't look at people. I don't think she's even turned over except the one time she had to get up to use the bathroom."

"Dok? Chalee?"

"They . . . they don't know how they feel about her. After what she did, even though she may have protected them from that man. Chalee says Treasure went crazy, kicking the man over and over when he was already hurt and then spitting on him." Her eyes go to Miaow, who doesn't look particularly surprised. "But Chalee's in there anyway."

"Good," Rafferty says. "Can you take us to her?"

"It's not locked," Anna says. "She's not going anywhere. Oh,

I'm sorry, you don't know. She's *here*. We moved the hospital bed here from the compound. Easier for everybody. And after what happened, no one wants to go into her room."

Anna leads them up the uneven stairs to the girls' floor, warmer than the ground floor even in this damp weather, and makes a left at the top of the stairs, away from the rows of cots, spottily populated by watching girls. Anna says, "Chalee still in there?" and gets a few affirmative mumbles. They go down a short corridor to a closed door. "Used to be for storage," she says, stepping aside.

When Rafferty opens the door, he finds himself looking at Chalee, who's facing him from across the bed. She's sitting in between the bed and the wall on a folding metal chair that's identical to the ones she and Dok sat on twenty-four hours at a time for days on end, after they found Treasure in the alleyway. The room, the hospital bed with the motionless girl on it, the chair, Chalee—Rafferty feels like he's back at the beginning of a story with a bad ending.

He lifts his eyebrows in a question for Chalee, and Chalee shrugs and gets up. He and Miaow go into the room as Chalee heads around the foot of the bed, toward the door. She and Miaow exchange curious glances, both of them turning back once they've passed each other. Chalee breaks the gaze and goes out, but Miaow watches her go, and Rafferty can see her mold her posture—stiffened spine, head held high—into an approximation of Chalee's. Miaow doesn't turn back to him until the door closes behind Chalee. As Anna said, Treasure is lying on her side, curled into a ball with her knees drawn tightly up, almost to her chest, and one arm folded under her head, as though she's trying to present as small a target as possible. Her back is to them. Two pillows have fallen or been pushed to the floor, where they lean crookedly against the legs of the bed. Miaow goes around the bed, with Rafferty following, and sits in the chair Chalee just vacated.

Treasure's face is waxy and damp-looking and her eyes are

closed, although the faint fluttering of her lashes says she's awake and aware of them. She sniffs the air a couple of times.

Miaow pulls the chair forward until she's no more than an arm's length from Treasure's face and stares at her. A handful of minutes—from Rafferty's perspective it could be anywhere from three to five—gets dealt from the deck, but Treasure gives no further indication that she's aware of them or interested in them.

Miaow leans in closer and blows on Treasure's face.

Treasure's eyes squeeze more tightly closed, but she doesn't open them or move her body. Miaow takes a deep breath and begins to blow softly, obviously intending to empty her lungs if need be. Rafferty puts a cautioning hand on her shoulder, but Miaow slaps it away, and the sharp sound of the slap brings Treasure's eyes wide, wide open.

Rafferty has backed quickly away from Miaow, hoping Treasure won't think that one of them struck the other.

"My name is Miaow." Miaow works the chair a little closer so she won't have to lean. "We met each other once before, over in that other building. Do you remember?"

Treasure closes her eyes again, and Miaow leans forward and blows again, harder this time, and Treasure opens her lids and stares at her.

"I'm not that easy," Miaow says. "Now, Poke, Poke is that easy. He'd fly halfway around the world if someone told him you were crying, but me, I'd probably make fun of you. Poke is much nicer than I am.

"I'm the girl Poke and Rose adopted," she says, settling into the chair. "*Don't close your eyes.* So why am I here? I'm here because Poke thinks I can see how people feel inside, and he wants to know how you feel. Because he's *worried* about you. Do you want to tell him how you *feel?*"

A slight movement to his right catches Rafferty's attention, and he sees that the door has opened about an inch and that Anna's face is pressed to the crack. Below her he sees, right against the opening, one of Chalee's eyes.

"I didn't think so," Miaow says. "If I felt like you, I wouldn't want anyone to know either. Think how embarrassing it would be, after you live through this, to have them know you felt this way. They'd *pity* you, and nothing is worse than that." She sits back in the chair, crosses her arms, and takes a deep breath.

"When I was three or four years old," she says, "my mother and father threw me away. Here's how they did it. They bought me a piece of candy, one of those big round, hard lemon balls that you don't chew, you suck on it, and then they tied a piece of brown string around my wrist, too tight to pull off, and tied the other end around part of a bus-stop bench—you know, the upright thing that separates the seat from the back. Then they went away." She stops and licks her lips, quickly, and says, "I thought they'd come back. I was *sure* they'd come back. I'm not certain about this, but I think I invented a game. They'd be back when the lemon was gone. I know even now that the lemon lasted a long time, because I kept tasting it and tasting it and moving it from one cheek to another. I sucked it really hard, rolling it around in my mouth, waiting for it to get smaller and go away so they'd come back. And it got dark, and some buses stopped, and a lot of people came and went, and my parents weren't with them, and then the candy was gone and the street was almost empty."

She puts one hand, with its chipped black fingernails, on the edge of the bed. "And I was crying, I guess, and leaning against the edge of the seat, because I wasn't big enough to climb up on it. I couldn't go anywhere, because, I mean, where would I have gone, and anyway I didn't know how to untie a knot. So I couldn't get up on the seat and I couldn't run away, and a big *soi* dog, bigger than I was, came up to me and stopped and looked at me. Its tongue was hanging out, and it had all these teeth. Then it went down on its front legs with its butt in the air and jumped at me. I screamed and waved the hand I could wave, the one that wasn't tied to the bench, but the dog went down again with its front legs spread out, and it jumped at me again. Now I know that's how a dog plays. The dog probably had a kid at home, and that was how they played, but I thought it wanted to kill me. Eat me, I don't know." Miaow begins absently to scrape at the nail polish on her thumb. "So it kept trying to play, and I yelled at it and kicked it, and after a while it turned around and left. And I stood there, leaning against the bench and wishing it would come back."

There's a rustle of bedclothes, and Treasure props herself up on one elbow.

"So I wanted the dog to come back, I wanted the lemon candy to come back, and I wanted my parents to come back. It's stupid that I wanted my parents to come back. My father slapped me a lot, one time so hard that my neck was sore for days. For years I only remembered two things about him, his loud voice and the way he slapped me that time. That was my father, that was every-thing I knew about my father. Two things. And then, when I was five or six and living on the street, I remembered one more thing about him. A man tried to catch me near Little India to . . . you know, do things to me, and he had been drinking whiskey. When I smelled that whiskey, I ran faster than I'd ever run in my life, because that smell was my father, and that's who I was running away from. And I got away from the man, but I've never smelled whiskey since without my neck hurting. That's how hard my father hit me. So that's the third thing I know about my father, that he drank whiskey. Do you want to hear more?"

It takes a full minute, maybe more, but Treasure says, "Yes."

"So I was . . . I was . . ." She scratches her head. "*Right,* I was tied to that bench, and the dog was gone. I don't know how long I was there, since little kids don't know how long things take, but it felt like a long, long time. I'd gotten cold. I was hungry. I'd wet myself—which made me even colder—I had snot all over my face, and a few people had walked by and looked down at me. I was ashamed to be tied to the bench, so I stood in front of the string, with my wrist behind me. So they wouldn't know that I was so bad that my parents had thrown me away. I'd figured out by then that they weren't coming back."

The door opens another half inch, as though someone has leaned against it, and then closes most of the way again. Anna and Chalee are still peeking around it. Neither Miaow nor Treasure seems to have registered it. "I was really tired of standing there, and I needed to try to sleep, but the string was too short for me to sit down on the sidewalk. If I sat, I had to hold my wrist in the air, which hurt after a while, and anyway it looked stupid. So I decided that everything would be all right if I could climb up onto the bench. Climbing on the bench would solve all my problems. If I could get up there, things would be fine. This must have been really late at night, because I don't think the buses were still running. So I got up on tiptoe and got part of my tummy on the edge of the bench and just tried to . . . you know, jump a little and flop onto it like a fish, but—" Miaow suddenly smiles, and Rafferty—who feels like he's hanging in space, listening to the story Miaow has never told him—realizes that she's returning a smile from Treasure. "But every time I tried to push off with my feet, *something*, my clothes or my tummy or something, would snag, and I'd fall hard, onto my knees. Really *hurts*, your knees hitting concrete. After three or four times, I gave up and sat on the sidewalk crying, holding my stupid arm in the air until my hand got numb, and I began banging it against the concrete bench and feeling how it didn't hurt, and then a boy came along, a few years older than I was, and he had a knife, and he cut the string and he took me away. That was Boo, by the way, the guy who runs this place now, that's how we know him. Boo came and found me, and after that I lived with the kids he bossed around. I did anything he said until he got into *yaa baa* and went crazy. We stole things, we beat up rich kids, we took food from drunk bums. We cut some purses. When I was five or six, I got a knife of my own. I cut people with it a few times. I cut one man pretty bad, and if I had to, I'd do it again right now."

There's a long silence in the room. Treasure has extended her neck toward Miaow so far that Rafferty can see her fine-boned profile through the frizz of hair that still has blood matted into it. He's certain she no longer even knows he's in the room.

"So here's what I'm saying," Miaow says. "You've got friends here, and they're really nice kids, my father worries about you all the time, and that deaf lady out there, the teacher, Anna? She's crazy in love with you, and she's with my father's best friend, who's a good man, and *you can have a life.* I have a life," she says, wiping one cheek with her palm, "and if I can have a life, anybody can. You know, people don't just throw love at you all the time. That's not how it works." She brushes her fingertips over her right eye, shaking her head. "They don't come back over and over again, and there aren't other people lined up behind them to throw more love at you. You have to say yes. You have to let them love you. Okay," she says, getting up and sniffling. "That's what I came to say. And oh, yeah, I hope we can be friends. That would make Poke happy."

She squares her shoulders and heads past Rafferty for the door, wiping her face in the crook of her arm, almost angrily. When she pulls the door open, Anna and Chalee back up fast, but then Anna stops and waits for Miaow to go through. Then she and Chalee come into the room. Rafferty catches the door as it closes and goes into the hall.

Poke hears Miaow at the bottom of the stairs, moving quickly, but he stays where he is, a foot propping the door open, looking into the room. For what seems to him like quite a long time, Anna stands by the chair looking down at Treasure, and then she sits. After a few more minutes, Anna's eyes slowly droop closed and her head falls onto her chest. Chalee, leaning back with one foot up against the wall, stares at Treasure, looking like someone trying to solve a puzzle. Then she sighs and goes to sit beside her on the bed.

27

Let Me See Your Teeth

"You saw the way she was, the way she was lying there," Miaow says as the hotel elevator doors close. Rafferty figures they've got about thirty seconds alone before they get to their floor.

"What about it?"

"How small she was making herself." Miaow is still working on the black nail polish. "What she wanted was to get smaller and smaller until she was like . . . I don't know, a seed. And then *pop*, just disappear."

Rafferty is looking at the top of her head as she worries at the nail polish. Compelled by sheer opportunity, he leans over and tousles her hair, which she immediately pats back into place. He says, "Why don't you part it in the middle again?"

Brushing it out of her face, she says, "Same reason you don't shave all yours off and grow a long beard. It looks stupid."

The bell on the other side of the door chimes softly to announce their arrival. He says, "I think you helped her."

"I don't know," Miaow says, heading into the corridor. "Nobody can help anybody who doesn't want help."

It's almost nine by the time he leaves Miaow and Rose to their evening stiff-upper-lip marathon, using the hotel's DVD player. On the way up Patpong, squinting through the drizzle and failing to spot his watcher, he ducks into the Expat Bar, where he finds only Leon, Campeau, and Toots in residence.

"It is early still," Hofstedler says a bit huffily, as though Rafferty's "Where is everybody?" had been a criticism. "Our friends here, they have lives, you know."

Rafferty says, "I'm sure they do,"

Hofstedler nods acceptance of Rafferty's contrition and glances down at his watch. "This is Tuesday," he announces to the room, as though he suspects they haven't been keeping up. "Miaow's play is Friday, yes?"

"It is. I watched the rehearsal today. It'll be good."

"I am coming, Pinky is coming, Louis is coming." It takes Rafferty a moment before he realizes that *Louis* is the Growing Younger man. "The one with the hair is coming," Leon concludes.

"Ron," Campeau says. "His name is Ron. Am I invited?"

"Of course you're invited, Bob," Rafferty says, wondering what will happen when Rose sees him. "Wouldn't be a first night without you."

Campeau says, "Should I dress up?"

Rafferty says, "I'm going to wear a clean shirt."

"Wow," Campeau says. "Semiformal."

"We've got, what, two, three days?" Rafferty says. "We can talk more about it later. Leon, did you keep your eyes open getting here?"

"There was a man looking at me," Hofstedler says. "The street was not yet crowded, so even I could see him."

"*Even* you?"

"Wallace tells me that I do not notice things."

"Well," Rafferty says, "compared to Wallace . . ."

"He is not so good tonight, Wallace," Hofstedler says. "In fact, he is very bad. When I knock on his door? First he does not answer, and then he calls me Ernie, through the door. Several times he calls me Ernie. I invite him to Miaow's play, and he does not reply. I knock several more times, substantially. I say, 'I come

to take you to the bar,' and he says, 'I have a date.'" Hofstedler has
hoisted his beer, but he puts it down in order to spread his hands
as though to say, *What can you do?* "It is a bad night, I think."

"He's seemed . . ." Rafferty searches for an accurate word, and
the one he comes up with seems sadly insufficient. "*Better* lately."

Toots says, "Sometime good, sometime no good."

"It is like the tide," Hofstedler says, wiping foam from his lip.
"It comes in and then it goes out."

"Except," Campeau says, "it goes out a little farther every time."

Looking up at him, Hofstedler says, "This is all of us, yes, Bob?"

THE RIFFRAFF IS dank with steam from the kitchen and loud
with the voices of men who are already well into their evening's
quota of beer. Here and there a bar girl twinkles like a rhine-
stone, sitting beside the man who paid her bar fine. Some of
them are working the job: listening, laughing, looking apprecia-
tive, keeping the current flowing with occasional touches on the
man's arm or the back of his hand. Others sit passively, just
waiting for the next stage of the transaction.

One of his favorite waitresses holds up two fingers for *Two
minutes* and inclines her head toward Rafferty's usual booth in
the window, where three heavyset Western men, one of them
black, are examining their money as though it were Kleenex and
sliding the check from hand to hand. The African-American guy
finally takes charge, squinting at the bills with the king's face on
them as he counts them out. When he's got a loose pile on top
of the check, he shrugs, and all three of them get up. On the way
out, one of them, looking over his shoulder at a woman in the
corner, bumps into the waitress. When Rafferty turns, curious
about who the man was looking at, he sees that it's Lutanh, who's
making adoring moon eyes at her customer. When she feels
Poke's gaze, she puts her hand to her forehead and, from behind
it, winks at him.

He sits while the table is still wet and orders some noodles with pork, basil, and chili, plus a small Singha. Still vibrating from the story that Miaow told Treasure, he's staring at the table as it dries and wondering whether she's shared it with Rose. The thought is broken when the waitress arrives and plunks down an oversize bottle of beer.

Rafferty starts to protest, and she says, "Big one. On the house because we don't see you too much and we want you come back. Boss think we give you free beer, you come back fast."

He says, "He figured me out." His attention is drawn by movement behind her, a Western guy with a shaved head, dressed entirely in black, who is escorting not one but two bar workers, one of whom—the older of the pair, by ten years or so—looks vaguely familiar. The man wears glasses with circular black lenses, the design of which owes a great deal to the old film *The Matrix*. Add it all up, Rafferty thinks, and it's a pathetic portrait of *Homo westernus* in Bangkok: shaving his head because he's balding and wearing black because he thinks it makes him look thinner, all to appeal to women whose only worry about his age would be that he might die on top of them and to whom the thickness of his mid-section takes a distant second place in importance to the thickness of his wallet. And the poor clown is topping it off with a pair of shades that were mildly hip, in a derivative way, maybe fifteen, sixteen years ago.

The man in black waves the two women to an empty table and does a peremptory little back-and-forth with his hand, index finger pointing at the women as he looks at the waitress, meaning *Give them whatever they want.* All pretty lordly, not likely to make friends. The man's upper lip looks a yard long.

Rafferty's lost in the tabletop again when the man in black slides into the seat opposite. He takes off the glasses to reveal bright blue eyes and says, as though continuing an interrupted conversation, "There's an informal interrogator's code about getting the information you need." He holds up a hand, palm out. "Stop me if you're already an expert in all this."

"No wonder you were wearing that dumb mustache," Rafferty says, trying to get his heartbeat under control. "I thought it was to make your teeth look white, but it wasn't. It was because you've got enough skin on your upper lip to make a pair of gloves."

Varney nods acknowledgment that Rafferty has spoken and ignores what he said. "So the first thing you have to do is get the subject's *attention*. Normally you do that by putting him or her in the room. The room is a great attention getter. You know which decorator touch makes for a great interrogation room?"

"You've actually forgotten the real first step—" Rafferty begins.

"A drain in the middle of the floor," Varney says. He's got his left hand flat on the table and the right is down, out of sight, which gives Rafferty a cold, sloshy feeling in his lower belly. "Raises all sorts of imaginative possibilities, that drain does. *Why do they need* that? *What gets hosed down* that *thing?*" He shakes his head as Rafferty begins to speak again. "I know, you've got a lot to say, but I have an agenda in mind, and I won't be here long. Nice-looking girls, aren't they? One of them anyway. The things bar girls learn to do—but hey, why am I telling *you* that? You're the expert."

Rafferty keeps his face blank while mentally running through four or five ways to kill him. The anger actually calms him.

"Aaaahhh, I'm sorry," Varney says, showing his big, square teeth in a grin. "Not worthy of me. Just a little payback for those things you said about the way I look, my teeth and all that. Let me see your teeth."

Rafferty says, "Fuck you."

"Let me see your teeth," Varney says again, in exactly the same tone. "And if you're asking yourself why you should, just look to your left, out through the nice window until you see Kiet. You'll recognize him. He's got that awful-looking long coat on, and he's been glued to your shoes whenever you were in the neighborhood. See him?"

Rafferty says, "I do." He *has* seen him before. In the glass he can also see Varney's reflection, and he watches Varney make a gesture like someone opening a door. Kiet obediently tugs the long coat aside for just a moment, showing Rafferty a short automatic rifle, probably an MP5 submachine gun. Then the coat swoops closed and the man gives him a big smile.

"He can take out this window and half the people in here, including that waitress you seem to like so much, in about three seconds and be up at Surawong and behind the motorcycle driver who's waiting for him while people out there are still looking for the bomb. And while he's firing, I'll use the gun in my right hand, the one down *here*"—he raps his knuckles on the table—"to blow your kneecap to pieces. Unless I miss and hit you in the balls. Show me your teeth."

Rafferty bares his teeth, fighting the impulse to lean over and bite off the man's nose.

"Not so great. Not much whiter than mine. Do you drink a lot of coffee?"

"Yes."

"That'll do it. You could drink it through a straw, you know."

"You came here to talk to me. Talk."

"At my own pace. And we're actually here so *you* can talk to *me*, since you have what I want. And that leads us back to the topic at hand. You haul the subject into the room, remember? Circumstances didn't permit me to drag you into a room, so I got your attention with a kind of metaphorical room, that first note, the question it implied: *Where's the money?* I always hope that a subject will be forthcoming and helpful, spare us all a lot of trouble, but it rarely works out that way."

"Maybe it's something about you," Rafferty says. "Maybe people just don't like—"

"So I asked you again, a different question, but on the same topic. The money, the girl."

"Well, if you ever do this again, let me make a suggestion. Give whoever it is a chance to answer."

"One school of thought says there's no point in letting the sub-ject answer early on. First answers are always lies. Anyhow, you knew perfectly well who sent those first two notes. There were any number of ways you could have signaled me. You could have said something to the people you saw watching you. Instead you got all clever, didn't you? When the subject gets dodgy, it means only one thing: the truth is not on tap."

"I don't have——"

Varney lets his hand drop, open and flat, onto the table. The bang it makes draws eyes from all over the room. "So the next step is to establish the subject's pain threshold. With some people, only thing you need is the drain on the floor. The world is full of people who would sell their mother to avoid learning what that drain is for. But most people—if the answer concerns something or someone they care about—need to scream a little first. Makes them feel better about themselves later."

"I *don't have the money.*"

"What money?" Varney's face is bland. "What money are we talking about?"

"The three million—"

"*That* money," Varney says. "Of course you do. So, as I was saying, we try to locate the pain threshold and then push just a *little* past it. In your case, since I couldn't grab you someplace where you weren't surrounded by people, physical pain wasn't in the cards, so I put you instead into an ethical dilemma that I thought would cause you *emotional* pain. But it seems I was mis-taken." He picks up the dark glasses in his free hand and holds them in front of his face, sighting Rafferty through the lenses. "See, I had you sized up as a good-hearted progressive, the way you put all those solid one-world principles into practice: marrying the bar girl, adopting the street kid, turning your whole life into a step up for the downtrodden. *Rescuing* the downtrodden, one beautiful woman at a time. I figured you for one of those moist souls who think we're all responsible for everything that goes wrong in the world. You know—a truckload of ignorant but devout dickwads shoot a schoolgirl in the face, and the progressives seize the blame and share it with the rest of us: 'Oh, it's the result of nineteenth-century European imperialism and our greed for oil. Shame on us, shame on us.'"

He sits back in the booth, puts the glasses down again, and rests his left arm on top of the seat back. Rafferty says, "Finished?"

"But you see, *I've* always read that reaction, shouldering all that guilt so selflessly, as cowards soothing their consciences. What's easier than accepting blame on some vague cosmic level when it's safe to do it and the killing is over?" He shrugs, overplaying it, hands palm up. "Where are all those good-hearted people when those things are being *planned*, when they're taking place? Why aren't these exquisitely attuned souls hauling their fine convictions behind them as they form a human shield around a girls' school in Afghanistan or protect villagers in Nigeria? I mean, that's the *basic question*, isn't it? Isn't that where the rubber meets the road on the whole *idea* of moral responsibility, the concept suggested by the phrase 'our fellow man'? *How much would you do to prevent the deaths of people you don't even know?*" He makes a loose fist and drums lightly on the table. "As it turns out, for you, not much."

Rafferty says again, "You can talk until sunrise. I don't have the money."

"I know, I know. No money, no girl." He looks up and smiles at the waitress as she brings Rafferty's food: the fragrant, oily, stir-fried mess of pork and basil and a neat, pristine mound of white rice. "Doesn't that look good," Varney says. "Dig in, dig in. Don't want to interfere with your meal."

"No matter who you kill," Rafferty says, pushing the plates away, "I can't give you what I don't have. And you *didn't* do the first thing a good interrogator always does, which is to make sure he's got the right person."

"Well," Varney says, and he taps the fingernails of his left hand on the tabletop, making a little snare-drum sound. "As to that point. My best estimate is that you spent about a hundred thousand bucks on that muzzy little drug addict, Neeni, what with her doctor and that apartment, and then maybe half that again on her unpleasant Vietnamese maid. Maybe, altogether, a hundred fifty, hundred sixty thousand US."

The bottom falls out of Rafferty's stomach. He says, reflexively, "I don't know what you're talking about."

"*And* you were in Murphy's house that night, and the money is gone. You haven't been facing facts. Like a lot of good-hearted people, you tend to avoid ideas with unpleasant consequences. You haven't asked yourself how do I know about the money you spent on Neeni."

Rafferty has to swallow against an upsurge of rage. "Did you hurt her?"

"Neeni? Don't be silly. She opened like a flower. All I had to do was show her a case of Corex, that cherry-flavored cough syrup with codeine. Her very favorite, from India. How I used to enjoy watching her knock it back and fall downstairs. She said you put her in a swell apartment for a few months, paid the maid to stay with her, had a doctor in from time to time, and now you send her money every month, regular as clockwork. So, see, you really *can* do some good in the world."

The smell of Rafferty's food is making him queasy. He moves it to the edge of the table and glances up for the waitress to signal her to come get it, but Varney says, "May I?" and grabs a spoon. "Naturally," he says around a mouthful of pork, "I was curious about the money you were being so generous with. Maybe, just maybe, you were rich. I looked you up online, had someone check the BookScan figures, which are amazingly easy to get, and near as I can figure, your income last year was in the lower third of the five-figure range. Burger-flipping sector. Your book on Thailand—hope you got the copy I left you—is your first new one in five years, and you're probably not seeing royalties from it yet. So it's obvious that the money came from old Murph's closet."

"I've been moonlighting," Rafferty says, "writing copy for a mail-order clothes catalog." He's talking just to give himself a little time. "The cutline on those nice gabardine pants, 'The Twill Is Gone'? That was me."

Varney deliberately puts another spoonful of food in his mouth, chews deliberately, an index finger raised in the *one-minute* sign, swallows, and says, "You really need to take this seriously."

"I'm sorry," Rafferty says, "but whenever I see a really big asshole, I just have to blow some smoke up it."

"That wasn't Murphy's money, it was mine," Varney says, unruffled. "And I *know* you took it. So that leaves the girl, doesn't it?"

"You're telling it."

"After Neeni," Varney says, "I went to see that cobra of a maid. She was a little more difficult, but she told me the most interesting thing of all: that you were going to put Neeni and Treasure back together, although that's a case of the halt leading the blind if I ever heard one." He puts down the spoon with a *clack*. "So, you see, even before I got here, I knew you had the money and the girl."

"I don't have the girl. And I only took one suitcase out of that closet."

"Right." He points his spoon at the beer. "You going to drink that? You stole six hundred K and left three million and change. That does not have the ring of truth. So here's the point. You remember this?" He swigs the beer and puts it down, then drags his forefinger through the oily gravy and writes *1*, *2*, and *3* on the tabletop. "How far did you get with this?"

"Don't be silly," Rafferty says, pointing at the number closest to him. "A halfwit could figure it out."

"You see," Varney says, digging around for a piece of pork, "this is the problem when you have to improvise. You get obvious.

None of this would have been necessary if I'd had a room with a floor that had a drain in it. Although you learn to take it on the fly when you're working in some of the shitholes Uncle Sam seems to covet. Camel World, you know, place like Afghanistan. Most structures don't even have a proper floor, much less a drain. Just dirt, probably swarming with the fecal bacteria of goats. So you make do. I can't tell you the effect you can achieve with a tin washing tub full of water and the blood a couple of chickens carry around. Splash it on the walls, drain some of it in the water, close the place up and let the heat hit it for a few hours. First time I did it, the guy started screaming the minute we hauled him through the door."

"I'm sure your mother is very proud."

"So," he says, tapping the chunk of pork on the oily numbers, "one with a check, two with a check, and three. It made the obvious point, that it was up to you to avoid a third killing, stepping up to your moral responsibility for the innocent, but it didn't drum up the atmosphere of dread you get with a tub and a little chicken blood. The dread that would lead you to what we've been hinting at all along: that those people, those innocent people who died because you want to keep a bunch of money that belongs to me, and a psychotic child who does, too—that they were surrogates for people who were close to you."

"That was painfully obvious."

"Yes, but I couldn't achieve the spin that would have told you the truth, which is, in fact the reason I'm sitting here. I failed to communicate that we're finished with surrogates. No more replacements."

Rafferty feels as though his body has vanished, as though he's just a point of consciousness floating a few feet above the table, focused on Varney.

"*Three,*" Varney says, scrabbling his forefinger back and forth through the slick number and then drawing an oily circle around it, "will be closer to you. As will four and five if they're necessary.

See the old bag over there?" He inclines his head toward the table with the two women at it. "She says she knows your wife."

Rafferty looks at her again; she's not all that old but she looks kind of beat up. While there's something familiar about her, he can't place her. "I don't know her," he says.

"Says her name is Nana," Varney says.

"Oh." Rafferty almost feels like laughing. "Well, do whatever you want to her. She cheated my wife, double-crossed her. Did her best to fuck her up. Nobody's going to miss her."

Varney shrugs. "Could be true, could be untrue. Anyway, I've got a block full of people to kill. Do you want to prevent it? Just tell me where the money is, tell me where the girl is." He leans forward, tapping a nail on the tabletop with each syllable. "And I mean that literally, any minute now."

"The cops took the money, the firemen took the money."

"And the girl? Why would they take her? For humanitarian purposes?"

"You can't get away with this," Rafferty says. "This country has a police force, they've got passport control—"

"Look, I'll tell you a little something about myself," Varney says, sliding to the end of the booth. "Between wars and the occasional intervals of peace, I've been living like this for almost thirty years, and I know how to do it. By the time anyone's really looking for me, I'll be fifteen thousand miles and three names from here." He struggles for a moment with his right arm, probably shoving the gun back into his pocket, and nods at the two bar workers. "So the old bag will get off," he says. "Not going to waste my time. But your friends had better keep their eyes open.

"And all you have to do to prevent all that," he says, getting up, "is give me what's mine. Just look around and spot old Kiet out there or whoever else is around, and hold up three fingers. Within, oh, ninety minutes." Turning away, he says, "'Scuse." He goes across the room to the women he abandoned and drops half a dozen thousand-baht notes on the table, kisses the tip of his index finger, and presses it against the center of the older woman's—Nana's—forehead, pushing just hard enough to rock her head back a few inches. Then he puts the round sunglasses on again and shoves his way out through the restaurant door. When Rafferty turns from the door back to the window, Varney is already gone, but Kiet is grinning at him, one hand inside his coat.

28

Teerak

THE ROAD IS far too wide.

He comes onto the sidewalk from the apartment house's single squealing elevator, feeling light on his feet, decisive, and clear-headed, as though he were back walking point in 'Nam. The Rolex says 1:44, plenty of time to get to Jah's bar. But as the door shuts behind him, he sees the road and takes a stumble that forces him to step forward quickly or fall on his face. It's six lanes wide, a Mekong River of lights, the demon red of taillights, the hard diamond yellow of headlights. He stands there for a second, loose-jointed and bewildered, as the narrow, lazy *soi* in front of the old shophouse thins, shimmers, and disappears, giving way to the clogged urban boulevard he lives on now.

He says, "Sukhumvit," aloud, identifying the street, and the kernel of dread in his chest softens at the name. His own voice reassures him. He says again, "Sukhumvit." Where was he going? Yes, Jah. Jah works at . . . Thai . . . Thai something. Thai Paradise?

Well, he knows where it is, even if the name eludes him. He steps to the curb, one arm upraised, palm down, a gesture of habit, blocking out the extraneous lanes of traffic and turning it back into that lost, earlier road. A couple of taxis slow, but he waves them by until he flags down a *tuk-tuk*. The driver, a skinny, dark kid with a shadowy mustache and a shoulder-length, center-parted fall of black hair, almost runs over Wallace's foot. Wallace climbs in, sits back, and says, "Golden Mile."

The *tuk-tuk* vibrates as its little two-stroke engine chugs and pops, but it doesn't move. The boy's eyes find Wallace's in the mirror. "You say where?"

"Golden Mile, the Golden Mile," Wallace says. He smiles so his sudden anger won't show but gets no smile in return.

"Hotel?" the boy asks.

"No, no, no. Golden *Mile*. Bars. New Petchburi Road."

"Okay," the boy says with a nod. "Golden Mile. Petchburi."

"Thai *Heaven*," Wallace says as the cab pulls out. Jah works at Thai Heaven. He knows something is wrong with that; the idea ripples for a moment, but then the boy hits the gas.

He sits back and closes his eyes. The exhaust is perfume, the *chuk-chuk* of the engine is music. For a moment he feels as though the seat has dissolved beneath him and he's falling through some kind of dark, undifferentiated space, but the *tuk-tuk* hits a bump and he's back, like a snapped finger: *tuk-tuk*, Golden Mile, Jah. Waiting for him. For a second he thinks he remembers someone on the sidewalk outside his apartment, looking at him as he flagged down the *tuk-tuk*, but when he turns to check behind him, he sees a dense, almost blinding curtain of headlights, and in his surprise at the sight the concern evaporates.

The second night she stayed in the hotel with him—just the two of them this time—she'd raised herself onto one elbow just as he'd been about to drop off and said, "This room. How much?"

He'd told her, naming a sum that seemed insubstantial to him, especially when it was paid in this dreamy, ornate money. Her eyes had gone round and her mouth had dropped open, and she'd emitted a sound like a puff of steam, and then she was up and pulling on her clothes, her shoulders rigid with determination. A moment later the door closed behind her.

He thought, *I didn't pay her.* He panicked briefly, thinking she might have taken the money from the pocket of his pants on the sofa, but when he checked, it was right there. He had refolded his trousers and was sitting on the bed, wondering how he'd offended her, when the phone rang and the desk clerk said, "Mr. Palmer? The young lady has pointed out that you have accidentally been overcharged, and she's renegotiated your room rate. You've been given a discount of thirty percent." And then she'd knocked on the door, and when he'd turned away after closing it, she'd whipped her T-shirt over her head and flogged him with it all the way back to the bed.

She's going to be so happy. He'll walk into the club, and she'll scream "*Wallet!*" and abandon whoever she was sitting with and run across the dance floor to him. With that smile, brighter than Liberty's torch . . .

"Okay," the driver says. "Golden Mile."

The *tuk-tuk* stops. Wallace has his hand in his pocket when the boy says, "One hundred twenty baht."

"*One hundred twenty?*" Wallace sits there, a wad of money in his hand. "*Twenty*, twenty baht."

"One-twenty," the boy says. "Twenty baht, one hundred year ago, maybe."

"Forty," Wallace snaps. "And that's it." He drops two twenties over the back of the seat, feeling the rudeness of the gesture, and climbs down onto the pavement, tuning out the boy's yells. He finds himself on a narrow street, nowhere near as wide as New Petchburi. A couple of cars, each with a wheel up on the sidewalk, are almost too close together to allow him to pass, but he turns sideways and hears the *tuk-tuk* sputter away, the boy still shouting angrily.

Once onto the sidewalk, he stops, looking up as though he's walked into a tree.

It *is* a hotel. Huge letters on the side of the building read CASTLE SUITES. Up and down the street are buildings, some new, mostly old and in disrepair. Nothing he recognizes.

A uniformed doorman comes through the revolving door,

eyebrows raised inquiringly, and says, "Sir?" No more than mild politeness.

Wallace says, "The Golden Mile?"

The doorman lifts a hand, palm up, and brings it shoulder height, fingers pointed back to indicate the hotel behind him. "Hotel," he says. "Owned by Golden Mile."

Wallace is already shaking his head. "No, no. No, not a hotel. *The Golden Mile.* Bars, restaurants . . ." He runs out of words. "*Bars.*"

"Sorry, sorry. Don't know. Maybe . . ." The doorman points down the street to his left, in the general direction of what must be New Petchburi Road, gleaming long, dark blocks away. The hotel is on a narrow *soi*, the building sprouting from a row of shorter, darker structures, here and there a filthy chain-link fence. "Over there maybe. Other side."

"No," Wallace says, but he's already turning, already forgetting the doorman. "It's on this side. I'm sure it's on this side." Down the block a taxi backs up illegally, trying to get out of the *soi*, and the interior light comes on for a moment as a man gets out. Wallace glances at it, something tapping for attention on the side of his head. Now, though, he's completely lost, and he crosses the *soi* at an angle, leaving behind him the taxi and whoever got out of it. Once across, he lowers his head to shut out the confusion of the unfamiliar neighborhood and strikes out at a brisk walk with the lights of New Petchburi behind him, half certain that in a hundred yards or so there will be light and music and the sound of English being spoken.

But there isn't. Thinking about Jah, hanging on to the vision of Jah, he passes a narrow cross street, almost turning in to it, but it's too dark. *Bars are off the main drag. The* tuk-tuk *driver brought me to the wrong place and tried to cheat me. Bangkok is changing.* He walks more rapidly, his boots hitting the pavement with a noise like a slap, leaving New Petchburi farther behind, moving in the certainty that sheer decisiveness will get him where he wants to go.

It isn't hard for him to imagine, in front of him, Thai Heaven's vertical strings of lights and the scattering of neon, the neon not as ornate or as vulgar as at Patpong but bright enough to suggest warmth and friendliness, the smell of beer, the music of women's voices. Jah's voice, Jah's face, the slightly overlong upper lip, the permanent upward curl at the corners of her mouth that makes her look like she's always suppressing a laugh. The sea-salt taste of her skin.

Another cross street approaches, promising in its furtiveness, but he stops, the street slipping from his mind as he registers the floating ribbon of concrete suspended against the dark sky far, far in front of him: an elevated highway. *That's why I'm turned around,* he thinks. *That wasn't there before,* and the moment he articulates the thought, he sees the boys.

Three of them, maybe eighteen or nineteen years old, facing inward in a tight circle around a faint glow of light, as though they're warming themselves at a candle. Wallace feels his chest expand, feels his lungs fill with air as certainty courses through him. Boys always know where the action is. And he likes Thai teenagers, so open and friendly, unlike the sour, angry, overprivileged American kids with their long, dirty hair and thrift-store clothes who had sneered at him, shouted at him, when he went home. At the sight of the Thai kids, he feels a smile stake claim to his face.

As he approaches, he calls out, "*Sawatdee!*"

And time goes wrong. The comfort and assurance and youth drain out of him as the boys turn and separate, and he sees their faces—despite his efforts to keep them young and friendly—turn older than he'd expected. He sees, in one blunt-force glance, the glittering eyes, the crumpled tinfoil pipe, the disposable lighter with something jammed into the jet to create a thin blue needle of flame. Smells the sweet methamphetamine smoke curling from the sizzling pills at the bottom of the pipe.

"Hey, Papa!" one of the boys calls. Smoke snakes out of his mouth, and he squints against it.

"Never mind," Wallace says, shaking his head. "No problem." He steps off the sidewalk, intending to cross the road. The block is dark and deserted, no cars in sight. Nowhere to go.

"Papa!" the boy calls, following. Maybe twenty-three, twenty-four, gaunt and dirty, with lank, greasy hair and a smile that looks stolen. "Papa, got money for friends? Got baht, got dollar?"

"No." Wallace sees the other two boys floating along behind the leader, one of them with the foil pipe at his lips, a red glow lighting the upper half of a misshapen face, crimped on one side as though someone had pressed it in with the heel of a hand before the bones hardened. "Go away." Behind the boys Wallace sees a man round the corner, coming in the same direction he had been taking, and his hopes soar, but the man turns in to a doorway.

"Nowhere here to go," the leader says, picking up his pace and angling across the *soi* toward Wallace. "Give money, we take taxi, go. Okay, Papa?" He spreads his hands to show they're empty. "Then no problem, yes?"

Wallace feels a flare of young man's anger. He says, "Fuck off. Get your own money and leave me alone."

"Ooooohhhhh, Papa," the boy says. He calls something in Thai, and the other two boys laugh. The one with the crimped head sticks out his chest and beats it, gorilla style, and they all laugh again. The two who had been farther away are closing in, and inside a few seconds all three of them will be within striking distance.

Always move toward trouble, Wallace thinks, and he drifts toward the closest boy, saying, "What is it? What is it you want?" He cups his ear and leans toward the boy, whose grin hardens as he comes directly beside Wallace . . .

. . . Who puts every ounce of strength he possesses into a much-practiced but very rusty foot smasher, jumping straight into the air and bringing all his weight, all his velocity down onto the fragile bird's nest of bones at the top of the boy's foot, mangling them with the edge of his boot heel and then leaping aside as the boy yanks the injured foot up, cradling it in one hand, yelling disbelievingly in pain and shock, and then, when he puts the foot down, going over sideways as though that leg were much shorter than the other. Before the boy lands on the pavement, Wallace is running.

The *soi* judders by as he strains, hoisting leaden legs: he's an old man, after all, only ten or fifteen yards along and already winded for Christ's sake, but hearing no feet behind him. He dares a glance over his shoulder and sees the two other boys lifting the leader off the pavement, the leader screaming after him, pointing an outstretched hand like a rifle, hopping on one leg, with the other leg, the one Wallace had damaged, lifted and bent like a stork's. Wallace faces forward again and finds a burst of speed from somewhere, although he knows in the part of his mind that's keeping score that two of them could catch up to him in a minute or less if they abandon the injured boy and give chase.

He comes to a cross street and slows. From somewhere in the past, information assembles itself: he's running on a back street near Petchburi. To his left the cross street goes only a short way and hooks left again, back toward the big road. To the right he has no idea.

Thai Heaven had been nowhere near here.

If he goes left and then left again, trying to get to the bright lights of New Petchburi Road, they might split up and go in opposite directions around the block until one is in front of him and the other behind. He's laboring now. His lungs feel like he's inhaled fire, and his heart seems to be trying to punch its way out of his chest. There has to be *something* to the right.

Right it is.

And he hears flip-flops slapping pavement behind him.

It's the jolt he needs. Some ancient, long-stored reserve of strength flames into being, the soldier's training overcoming, even if only for a few moments, the old man's body. He stretches his stride, feeling like he can fly, angles across the empty street, leaps for the curb, and snags a foot on it, pitching forward, fighting to get his arms down to break the fall. He lands heavily on his right elbow and knee, knowing immediately that the elbow is a problem, and rolls over twice until he can push himself to his feet with the arm he can still bend, and then he begins to move, as much at a limp as a run.

Laughter floats toward him from the boys behind.

The knee of his pants tore on impact. There's blood on the cloth, making it stick to his leg. His right elbow is an independent sphere of pain with a demonic halo of heat around it that seems to have seized his nervous system by sheer force. It squeezes off a machine-gun tangle of agony every time his heart beats. Looking down at it, he sees for the first time that the stinging he'd been feeling in his right forearm is a neat slice, the sleeve of his shirt looking like it had been cut with scissors. The boy he kicked must have gotten to him with a blade as he went down.

He doesn't have it in him to go much farther. They can . . . they can have him.

But the young man inside flares up again and says, *Fuck that*, and Ernie calls him a pussy, and Wallace is running again, feeling like he's leaving red streaks of pain in the air behind him. Doorways and dark windows flow by, and then, up ahead to the left, on his side of the street, he sees light: yellowish, bright, as harsh as a snapped word, but *light*.

A paved area, a parking lot, but not many cars. Instead, from knotted wires, carrying electricity stolen from the high-voltage lines above, a crop of clear, naked bulbs dangle, spherical as oranges, hanging over little stands. A few cars are parked along one edge as though they've been swept aside to make room for this little cluster of carts selling cooked food and produce. Many of the cart operators are packing up, closing the glass doors that kept the flies away, sprinkling water on charcoal. Among the few remaining shoppers, Wallace sees some *farang*, solitary men as old as he, coaxed by the vendors from their apartments. Old, stooped, balding, left behind when the Golden Mile disappeared.

The cart farthest from the street is a big one with glass sides and a long piece of plywood laid across it, perhaps seven or eight feet long. Four stools are pulled up to it, three of them occupied: a bent-spined man in a blindingly white shirt sitting beside a woman with hair too black even for Thailand, and on the third stool a plump woman in her late fifties or early sixties, her body popping out of a black cocktail dress that might have fit her twenty years earlier. At one end of the plywood plank, a small boom box is playing something from the seventies. Of course, what else? "Hotel California."

A portable bar. Wallace has seen a few of these, but fancier, on the sidewalks of Sukhumvit, but this one is as unexpected as an oasis with camels and palm trees. He looks behind him, sees the shoppers thinning and the merchants closing, and goes to the empty stool and sits. He couldn't run another yard if there were wolves chasing him.

"Beer Singha," he says, trying to steady his breathing. Now that he's sitting, he feels his legs trembling violently. His elbow sends up a neural yelp of pain, and the plump woman, who had gotten up to get his beer, takes a second look at him and straightens. The powder on her face looks like chalk in the hard light.

"Honey," she says. Her eyes drop to the cut shirt, the blood on the cloth. "What happen?"

"Some kids," he says, hearing the quaver in his voice. "It's okay. I just need to sit a minute."

"Poor baby, poor baby," she says. "Kid no good now. Not like before." She reaches into the glass case and pulls out a relatively clean dish towel, scooping up a handful of melting ice and wrapping the towel around it. She lifts the dripping mess in both hands, gives it a professional-looking squeeze, and holds it out. "Here," she says. "For . . ." She flexes her own right elbow and points at it.

He presses the wet, cold cloth to his arm, and the fire of pain banks slightly. A few of the vendors are reaching up with towels or pot holders to unscrew the bulbs over their carts, which sets him looking around anxiously, but the kids are nowhere in sight.

"You say kid," the woman in black ventures. She pops the cap on a Singha. At her end of the bar is a big Chinese cleaver on a circular wooden cutting board, piled with limes. She grabs the cleaver and cuts a delicate slice of lime. "Glass?"

He shakes his head.

"Kid how old? How many?" She drops the lime slice back onto the board and puts the bottle in front of him, then hoists herself onto the stool to his left, resting her hand on his thigh with the eternal familiarity of bar girls everywhere.

"Three. In their twenties. Smoking—" He mimes the little pipe with his left hand.

"I see before," she says. "Bangkok now no good."

A fat Thai man with a Chinese face waddles out of the darkness, abandoning an aluminum lawn chaise with a blanket on it. "Close soon," the man says. "Order last drink, please."

"Aaaaahhhhhh," the man with the bent spine says. "I'll quit now." He puts a couple of bills down, drops some coins on top, and pushes his stool back. Standing, he's no taller than he was sitting, his back as crooked as a question mark. "You," he says to Wallace. "That arm's busted."

"I think so, too," Wallace says.

"Little shits around here," the other man says. "Know we're old. Know what days the pension checks arrive. Little fuckers. Oughta carry a gun if you're gonna come here."

Behind the man with the bent spine, Wallace sees another man come into sight on the street, emerging from the same direction he had run in. The man glances for a moment at the bright lights and then walks on, moving faster, and Wallace's attention is drawn downward by a lightning bolt of pain from his arm. When he looks back up, the man on the street is gone and the one with the bent spine is waiting for a reply. "I won't be back," Wallace says.

"Smart guy. Get that arm looked at, hear?" To the woman beside him, he says, "Coming?"

"I go with you?" the woman says, doing her best to look surprised and pleased.

"Sure, sure. We talk money later, okay?"

"No problem." She grabs a tiny purse and darts a quick, victorious glance at the woman beside Wallace, then takes the bent man's arm, and the two of them head for the street.

"Why you come?" asks the woman in the tight dress.

"Golden Mile," Wallace says.

"Ah," she says, her face softening. "Golden Mile, yes. Very good."

"You know a girl named Jah?" Wallace asks.

He gets a moment of silence as she gnaws her lower lip. "I know many Jah."

"At Thai Heaven."

"No," she says. "I no work Thai Heaven. Work California bar."

"Mmmm," Wallace says, and knocks back half the beer. With the bottle most of the way down, he freezes.

She follows his gaze, and there they are, the three of them, in a loose triangle at the edge of the lot. She points at them with a tilt of her chin. "*Those* boy?"

"Yes," Wallace says.

"You stay," the plump woman says, and faster than he would have thought possible, she's at the end of the bar and she's grabbed the cleaver. Raising it high in the air, she runs toward the boys, small strides because of the tight dress, but a run nevertheless. The boys step back, one of them limping badly, and when she shows no sign of slowing, they turn and retreat, up the street and out of sight. The woman with the cleaver follows.

Wallace's hand trembles as he downs the rest of the beer. He wants very badly to close his eyes.

And perhaps he does, because when he opens them again, she's trotting back into sight, hair slightly disarranged. She sinks the cleaver's edge into the side of the cutting board and says, "They go, but maybe not far. You pay, you come with me. I take you home. We go." She waits, not sitting, until he's put the money on the plywood, and then she laces her right arm through his uninjured left and leads him toward the street, in the direction opposite the one the boys took.

She wears a light floral perfume, a fragrance that brings to Wallace's mind the wildflowers in a place he and his friends had played each spring in the hills above Carlsbad, a sloping stretch of blue lupines above the hard, bright sun wrinkles of the sea. Looking for the messages they had left there the previous fall, when the hills grew dry and prickly. Answers to secret questions they'd asked each other, maps to things they'd hidden.

Maps.

They're on the sidewalk now, the lights receding behind them. Wallace's knee has stiffened, and he's limping. He says, "How can you take me home? You don't know where I live."

"No problem," she says. "I take you where you can get taxi, get *tuk-tuk*. Take you home."

The shophouse, he thinks. *No, no, that's not right.*

"Have taxi up here," she says. "Come little bit more." They pass beneath a streetlight, her face suddenly blossoming from the dark.

"Jah?" Wallace says, studying her, and then she looks back over her shoulder and he hears them.

"In here." She shoves him into a narrow space between two buildings, half illuminated by the streetlight, with chunks of rubble underfoot. She pushes him in front of her, and then a blue flame ignites ahead of them: the boy with the crimp in his head. The other two come into the alley behind them. The woman backs away from him.

He's turned to face the two who had just come in when he hears the grit of a step behind him, and then something enormously hard slams the side of his head, and his vision fills with flares as the thing hits him again, driving the other side of his head into the wall of the building. He's sliding, sliding somewhere, feeling a rough surface against his arm and shoulder, and then something rises up from below, very fast, and strikes him on the underside of the chin, and his head snaps back so hard he thinks he hears something break.

The woman is screaming in Thai, sounding not frightened but furious, and one of the boys barks a string of syllables like rocks, and she falls silent. Someone kicks Wallace in the ribs, but he barely feels it. He's on his back, not feeling much of anything.

There are *stars* up there, pale ones, at the top of the narrow canyon between the buildings. He hasn't seen stars in Bangkok for decades. When he first came, the stars were . . . He and Jah had . . .

A hand under his head, lifting it up, putting it on something soft, her leg. The woman, looking down at him, fat and powdered, her face shining with sweat. He sees the eyes, the bones, the skin; and the fat melts away, and the corners of her mouth curl up, and the lacquered hair falls loose and long, and he says, "Jah."

"I'm here, *teerak*," she says. "You okay now, I'm here."

"I looked for you," Wallace said. The world dips sharply down for an instant, everything going sideways, but he forces it back the way it should have been.

"You found me," she says. "You found me." She wipes his face gently with her hand. "Always I wait for you."

He feels another hand in his pocket, but when Wallace tries to look down at it, the world tilts again, and this time it keeps tilting and the streetlight goes down like the sun. He's alone in an empty room, the walls rushing away from him, the space growing bigger and emptier and darker until the only light is him, whatever *he* is, a sharp point of white light, narrowing to a pinpoint, and he says again, "*Jah*," and the light blinks out.

"Who's Jah?" asks the boy with the crimped head, fanning the wad of bills.

"How would I know?" the woman says. "Some *teerak* from a hundred years ago. Why'd you hit him so hard?"

"He hurt Beer's foot," says the boy with the crimped head.

"*Hee mah,*" the woman says. "Dog pussy. Hurt by an old *farang.*" She eases Wallace's head off her leg and lowers it softly to the pavement. "Give me a hand."

The boy called Beer limps forward and helps her up. She says, "You should be ashamed." She holds out her palm, and the boy with the crimped head passes her a tight crumple of bills. She tucks them into the front of her dress, brushes cement dust from the black fabric, and looks down at Wallace.

"Long time ago," she says in English, not even aware she's speaking it, "he was probably handsome man." The boys are already filing out of the alley, and after a last downward look she follows.

Silence. A rat runs across the alley, pausing briefly beside Wallace and then careening away toward the street, but a foot or two from the entrance it makes a fast left and disappears. A man, bald, dressed in black, scuffs his way in, pausing for a second to give the alley a once-over, and then comes forward to stand above Wallace's body.

"You old clown," Varney says. "You didn't even get laid."

He reaches into his shirt pocket and pulls out something small and circular, a stiff piece of paper, then bends and slips it into Wallace's own shirt pocket. "Ahhh, well," he declaims, turning. "'He was a man, take him for all in all. I shall not look upon his like again.'" He kicks a rock in front of him as he goes. "If I'm lucky."

A minute passes, maybe two. The rat reappears and saunters out through the mouth of the alley. The woman in the tight dress ducks back in, looking anxiously down the road in the direction Varney took. Reassured, she hurries to Wallace's side, kneels, and begins to fish in his pockets. She finds the circular piece of paper, glances at it, and puts it back. Picks up the wallet on the pavement and flips through it. Satisfied that it's empty and that nothing remains in his pockets, she lifts his left wrist and bends forward to peer at the Rolex.

"Fake," she says, and Wallace groans.

She doesn't even remember straightening up and leaping backward, but the next thing she knows, her back is pressed against the side of the alley and she's trying to swallow a scream. But Wallace doesn't sit up. No spirit materializes above him. He just groans again, and the broken arm, partially bent at the elbow, slides a few inches over the gravel and dust of the alley floor.

The woman backs away toward the street, turning suddenly to make sure there's no one or nothing waiting behind her, and then she hurries onto the sidewalk. After a few quick steps, she slows, then slows again, then stops. She stands there, doing nothing. A passerby would probably say she's looking at her feet. Then she says, in English, "Shit," and opens her purse to take out her cell phone.

29

It Doesn't Much Matter Who They Are

HOFSTEDLER'S SPARSE HAIR stands out in stiff, thorny wisps, his eyes are crusted with sleep, and his pendulous lower lip is shaking, making him seem frail and infirm. It's 4:40 A.M., and the hospital's chalk-white light turns the veins at the sides of his forehead almost ink blue.

"I should have kicked his door down," he says for the fourth or fifth time. "After you came to the bar tonight to tell us about that man, I should have kicked his door down. I knew he was in there."

"It's not your fault, Leon," Rafferty says, rubbing his face with the palms of both hands. "If it's anyone's, it's mine."

"Why?" Hofstedler says. "You invited this man? No, he *came*, he was *looking* for you, and we all, all of us, we talked and *talked* about you, told him you would come some night. Like *children* we talked, happy for the attention. Happy someone was *interested* in us. Useless, stupid. *Quatschköpfe*, babbling old idiots."

The room has pale gray walls, a scuffed brown tile floor, and, shoved up against one wall, six bolted-together plastic chairs in colors so bright they look angry. One of the room's doors, permanently open, leads to the hallway that connects to the hospital's entrance and public areas. The other door, permanently closed, seals off the secret chambers where the doctors perform their mysteries. Mounted on the wall opposite the chairs is a flat-screen TV, mercifully dark. Someone has cleaned it wrong, probably with ammonia, and the wet cloth has left long streaks that pull rainbows from the fluorescent light, like a film of oil on a puddle. Rafferty has been studying the rainbows off and on ever since he joined Hofstedler in this awful room. The rainbows offer Rafferty a kind of refuge from what's happened to Wallace.

"Come on, Leon," Rafferty says, leading him toward the garish chairs. Despite his three hundred–plus pounds, Hofstedler follows with virtually no resistance; it's like towing a balloon. Rafferty gets him to the fire-engine-red chair at the left end of the row, and Hofstedler sits, although he seems barely to be aware he's doing it. He's blinking semaphores, his lower lip continuing its meaningless movements. Rafferty sits beside him and puts an arm around his mountainous shoulders, feeling the shivers running through his frame. Hofstedler has always seemed so solid, the boulder that anchored the entire structure of the Expat Bar, held it in place, and now he's a quivering old man, muttering in German.

"So," Rafferty says, both to get it straight and also to try to bring Hofstedler out of himself, "some woman called the hospital and reported a *farang* who'd been beaten up, over near Petchburi, and when the ambulance crew got there—"

"Crews," Hofstedler says. "Three of them. Competing, like always."

"Okay, three. When they got—"

"They all wanted to be paid," Hofstedler says, his voice finding support in his anger. "All three came to the hospital. Shouting for my money. This *city*," he says. "Why am I in this city?"

"When they got him here, they found your phone number in his wallet?"

"Yes. And the picture of him, the one the police have now. You have not seen it, but it was taken in front of the bar. That swine cut his face out in a circle and put that piece in Wallace's pocket, but behind him you can see the Christmas lights in the window. Until they showed the picture to me, I thought he had been burglarized and beaten, but this photo comes from Varney.

And also they found the number for Louis. They called Louis also."

"Louis?" Rafferty says, and into the room comes the Growing Younger Man.

To Hofstedler the Growing Younger Man says, "How is he?" And then, "Hello, Poke."

"Hey . . . uh, Louis," Rafferty says.

"How he *is?*" Hofstedler says, more loudly. "He is beaten and cut, broken *bones* he has, he does not talk, he does not open his eyes. How he is? He could be dying."

"We don't know that, Leon," Rafferty says. To the Growing Younger Man he says, "They're working on him."

"When he's out of here," the Growing Younger Man says, sitting in the chair next to Poke, "I'll put him on a regimen of holistic supplements, clean out his system. The stuff they give you in hospitals is poison."

"You will give him your . . . your *goofus dust when* he is out of here?" Hofstedler says. "We will be lucky *if* he is out of here." He leans forward, plants his palms on the edge of his chair, and lifts himself, with a grunt, to his feet. "This is too much," he says as though to a large group of listeners. "It is not bad enough that we're old and foolish, that people think we are laughingstocks who have thrown our lives away so we can be old alone." To Poke he says, "Do you know I'm alone now? Do you know that Nam-Fon has left me? Twenty years we are together, and now she . . . she . . ." He makes a violent sideways gesture with his arm, as though batting something away. "It is not good to be old alone. But this is not about me. This is about Wallace, this is about *us.* All of us. We are who we are. We will never be young again, but I will not let this man treat us so. I will *not.*"

His voice has increased in volume, and his face is reddening. Rafferty remembers his heart attack and starts to say something calming, but Hofstedler makes that same sideways arm sweep, knocking Rafferty's words into some imaginary corner. "Wallace is . . . is a noble soul. He has been sad, a man of sadness, his whole life that I have known him, and he has been *dignified* in his sadness, he did not wrap himself in his sorrows like some romantic hero and *parade* in them like a black cape for everyone to say *aaawwwww*, and if my English sounds like a book, well, fuck the book and its mother. This *cannot* stand."

Both Rafferty and the Growing Younger Man are on their feet now, trying to calm him, but Hofstedler is in full flood.

"I am swearing to you, Poke, that I will do what I can do, I mean *all* I can do, to help you stop this terrible man. We will all help, yes, Louis? All of us—Pinky, Bob, that man with the hair. We are not in the second childhood yet, are we? We can do something, we can think, we can have ideas, we know Bangkok better then he does, that swine. I know you, Poke. You will go *after* him, and you must let me help. You must let all of us help."

"I'm in," says the Growing Younger Man. "We're all—" And the door to the inner sanctum opens to admit a tired-looking doctor in his late thirties or early forties. He might be Indian, with deep, probably permanent, circles beneath his eyes, dark skin, and straight, thick, black hair bristling from beneath a plastic hairnet. There's a Japanese brushstroke of dried blood on the front of his scrubs.

"You're the one they called, is that right?" he says to Hofstedler. He speaks accented English.

"Me, too," says the Growing Younger Man. Hofstedler, absolutely still, looks as though he's hanging by a string from the ceiling.

"Yes or no?" the doctor says impatiently.

"Yes, yes," Hofstedler says, blinking in time to the words. "Yes, yes, yes."

"Fine, I heard it the first time. Well, then, he'll be all right."

Hofstedler makes a choking sound.

"He has a broken arm, which we've set and put in a cast, and two broken teeth we can't do anything about here. A dentist, later.

What looks like a knife cut on the broken arm, which I've stitched up. The stitches are going to itch under the cast. And a concussion, certainly a concussion."

Hofstedler says, "He is alive." He seems to be unaware that he is weeping.

The doctor shakes his head impatiently. "Of course he's alive. Would I do all this to a dead man?"

Rafferty says, "Is he awake?"

"You're joking," the doctor says. "I can't get him to go to sleep. He wants to go home."

Hofstedler is still weeping, but somehow he's also smiling when he says, "This is not a good idea." He sniffles hugely.

"No," the doctor says. "We're going to keep him here for at least twenty-four hours to watch that concussion, make sure he's not bleeding in there, building pressure on the brain. One thing, though. I'm not sure he knows where he is. He couldn't tell me what year it is."

"This is not new," Hofstedler says, wiping his nose on his shirt-sleeve. "He has trouble lately with . . . with all that. That's why my phone number was in his pocket."

The doctor narrows his eyes at Hofstedler. "Weren't you a patient here?"

"My heart," Hofstedler says. "I am surprised you remember."

The doctor gives him a sudden, broad smile. "You made a dramatic entrance. That squad of *katoey* who carried you in took over the whole hospital."

Hofstedler says solemnly, "They are good friends."

"We all need friends at times," the doctor says. "Doesn't much matter who they are."

RAFFERTY INSISTS ON getting a cab and taking Leon home. He's afraid to leave him wandering around in Bangkok; the man's thought processes are erratic, and he seems unmoored. It's a surprise to Rafferty when the cab stops in front of a run-down four-story apartment house in a sketchy area, the kind of building that Bangkok developers demolish in their imaginations twenty times a day. The only other time he went to Leon's place, it was an expensive condominium near the river.

"This is where I am living now," Hofstedler says, seeing the look on Rafferty's face. "I gave Nam-Fon, my wife, the condominium. She . . . she cares where she lives. I do not." He opens the door but doesn't get out. "It is— What time is it, Poke?

"Six twenty A.M. Where's your watch?" Poke has never seen Hofstedler without his three-pound Swiss watch.

"I forget," Hofstedler says. "When the call comes, I can think only of Wallace." He leans to one side as though about to climb out of the cab, but instead says, "Would you like some coffee, please? Maybe a sweet roll? I have sweet rolls—they are only two days old or maybe three."

"I have to go home, Leon. I need to get cleaned up and drive Miaow to school. I can't let her take the bus now, not with—"

"Of course, of course," Hofstedler says, nodding more often than is necessary.

"But I'll tell you," Rafferty says, putting a hand on Hofstedler's arm, "the minute Wallace feels up to it, the three of us will go out for the best dinner in Bangkok."

"This is good," Hofstedler says, and he sits there gazing at nothing until the cabbie turns around to look at him. "Is good," he says again. "Okay. I go home." He grabs the edge of the open door and hauls himself out of the cab, then starts lumbering across the sidewalk.

"Can we go?" the driver says.

"Just a minute." Hofstedler navigates the sidewalk and climbs the steps without mishap, but trying to fit his key into the door, he drops it. His shoulders sag. He gazes down at it so long that Rafferty starts to climb out, but then the big man bends down stiffly, picks up the key ring, and manages the lock. He disappears into the darkness of the hallway as the door slowly swings closed behind him, and then he's gone.

Rafferty says to the driver, "Have you ever wanted seriously to kill someone?"

THE HOTEL IS out of oranges, so Miaow is rolling into little balls the threads she's peeled from inside the skins of the tangerines that were sent as a substitute. Once they're rolled tightly, she flicks them at Rafferty. She has splendid aim; she's hit his nose twice, and one of the pellets is stuck to his right cheek. He can see it at the lower periphery of his vision, but she's so delighted that he lets her go on thinking he doesn't know it's there.

His cell phone rings as another fragrant little wad of tangerine thread hits the center of his forehead and bounces onto his plate. Miaow raises a single clenched fist and says, "Three points."

He looks at the phone: Arthit. Getting up, he says to Miaow, "Do you have any idea how much I love you?" and then leaves her there, looking one-upped with another little tangerine ball in her hand, and takes the phone into the living room.

"Well, *this* is interesting," Arthit says. "But is it too early for you?"

"I've been up since three." Because he knows Miaow is listening, he gives Arthit a compressed and sanitized version of his evening, complete with the scrap of photograph in Wallace's pocket. Arthit says, "He shows up to go *boo* at you and goes after Wallace the same night. He knows he hasn't got much time. Despite all his posturing, you can't get away with this sort of wholesale mayhem, not in Bangkok."

Rafferty says, politely, "I'm absolutely certain you're right."

"Let's see if I can distract you. Mr. Bixby called me back last night. He opened a window on the whole thing. It's all about the will, but not quite the way you thought."

"I hadn't thought much of anything. I was just guessing."

"Here's the will: Everything goes to Treasure. Stocks, bonds, bank accounts, not enumerated but presumably all over Southeast Asia, totaling more than twenty million US, and that was five years ago, when the will was made. Here's the interesting part." He pauses. "Sorry, trying to read my notes. First, Treasure gets absolutely everything when she turns eighteen."

"When's that?"

"In . . ." Rafferty hears paper being rustled. "Oh, my. She's got a . . . um, she's got a birthday coming up." There's a silence, and Rafferty hears him swallow. "In ten days," he says, "she'll be . . . she'll be fourteen. Jesus, she'll be fourteen. I'll have to tell Anna about that."

"We'll all plan something nice," Rafferty says, adding mentally, *If we're still alive.*

"Good," Arthit says. "Hard to believe so much terrible stuff can be packed into fourteen years." There's another silence, and as much as Rafferty wants to know about the will, he lets Arthit stew in it. Finally Arthit says, "Anna told me what Miaow said last night. To Treasure, I mean."

"Yeah," Rafferty says. "I just told her I love her." At the table Miaow is making a pile of tangerine pills, and she looks up and flicks one toward him.

"Right," Arthit says. He clears his throat. "So she gets everything when she's eighteen. Here's the interesting part. Until then the estate will be administered by an executor, one Gerald Terwilliger, which seems to be Varney's real name. And you can bet he's kept *those* papers up to date, because here's the deal. Once every calendar year between Murphy's death and the day Treasure turns eighteen, the executor is entitled to withdraw any amount up to two million, to care for Treasure and/or, in the exact words of the will, 'to spend as he sees fit.' The only condition is that Mr. Terwilliger *must* be personally accompanied by Treasure, the ultimate heir, to make the withdrawal. The banks have all received a photograph of Treasure and her thumbprint."

Rafferty says, "Hold it." Miaow wiggles her eyebrows at him, and he realizes he's been staring at her. He turns away. "For Murphy," he says, "this is almost human. He found a way to take care of her. He knew she couldn't survive without him and that Neeni was useless, so he turned her over to Varney, but in a way that forces Varney to keep her alive and well instead of just . . . you know, pushing her out of a plane."

"Until she's eighteen," Arthit says.

"Even then, he'll have to use her to get the rest of the money. But you know what this means. The last thing in the *world* Varney wants is for something to happen to Treasure."

"If I were in his shoes," Arthit says, "I'd have her cushioned in bubble-wrap. I'd keep her in a vault."

Rafferty feels like he's been hit on the head with a down pillow. "He's *not going to hurt Treasure.*"

"I think we've covered that."

But Rafferty's still talking. "Someone said—Wallace, it was Wallace—that I needed to dangle, out in plain sight, the thing that Varney wants and let him come try to take it."

"But you can't do that. He still wants to take her. And, Poke, I made a couple of other calls, starting with the mercenary outfit we know Murphy worked for at times. Terwilliger has been all over the Middle East. He was charged with murder in Iraq for a small massacre in what turned out to be the wrong village, and he was yanked out of the country to avoid an Iraqi trial and then fired. No wonder Murphy built that insurance policy into his will. Varney is too bad for *those* guys, Poke, and those guys are awful."

Despite his distraction, Rafferty hears the concern in Arthit's tone. He says, "I know. He . . . he talked about Afghanistan last night. But still—knowing that he won't actually hurt Treasure. Well, this changes things."

30

Sub-Saharan Africa

NEW RULES.

New rules for Miaow, who's obviously at even greater risk. He'll arrange it with Mrs. Shin to take Miaow to school in her car, on the floor in the backseat, and go home the same way. Rafferty will drop her off at Mrs. Shin's in the morning and pick her up at night. There's no way, he thinks, even if Varney figures out which school Miaow goes to, that he'll be looking at Mrs. Shin, one teacher out of seventy, at the school.

As long as he doesn't go anywhere near the school, as long as Miaow is being ferried in by someone with no visible connection to him, then everything should be fine. As far as Varney's concerned, it'll be as though Miaow's going to school in sub-Saharan Africa.

That pleasant certainty lasts until early Thursday afternoon.

Making his rounds, he drops by the Expat Bar to double-check that everyone's still alive and to ask Leon what's new with Wallace. The gray drizzle has yielded to damp breezes that move the carbon monoxide around in a manner that would probably be pleasant, he thinks, to some species that drinks gasoline. Halfway down the relatively empty street, the boys who will erect the night market huddle to smoke and tell jokes, waiting for someone to unlock the storage area where the bones and the fabrics of the booths are stored.

More of the colored bulbs in the bar's window have burned out; now only four remain. The last of the red ones has given up the ghost, which eliminates Christmas from the arrangement and turns it into a meaningless straggle of unevenly spaced green lights. "You need to get some new lights," he says to Toots as he goes in.

"Have," Toots says. She's sitting on a stool with a newspaper in front of her, folded tightly around the story she's reading. "Maybe I do tomorrow." Also in the room are Campeau, who might as well sleep there, and Pinky Holland. The overhead fixtures are off, and the gray light coming through the window seems damp and spectral.

"This is not a room that would cure depression," Rafferty says. "What's the word on Wallace?"

Pinky says, "He's getting out today. He made a fuss. Leon's taking him home. Leon's home, I mean."

"Good," Rafferty says. "Probably good for Leon, too. He seems pretty lonely."

"Tell the man what you're reading, Toots," Campeau says.

"You are . . . bestseller?" Toots says to Rafferty.

"I turned it into a question when I read it, too," Campeau says.

"What?" Rafferty says. "When you read what?"

Toots holds the paper out to him. "English," she says. "Cannot read too good."

It's the *Bangkok Sun*. "SMALL TOWN" HAS BIG CAST, the headline runs. Beneath it Rafferty reads:

> The first production in Thailand of William Thurgood's classic American play, "Small Town," will open tomorrow night (Friday) at Regent International School, Sathorn. The drama, a semirealistic depiction of daily life in a tiny town in the American Midwest, won a Pulitzer Prize when it debuted on Broadway in 1948.
>
> "This play has special meaning to our students," says drama teacher and director Kyung-Hee Shin. "It's about home and

family and life and death, and two young people who fall in love."

The cast, made up entirely of Regent International students, is headed by Luther So, the son of Taiwanese Consul-General Chih-Ming So, as the Narrator. The two young lovers are played by Mia Rafferty, daughter of bestselling travel writer Poke Rafferty, and Edward Dell Jr., son of an American Bangkok resident. The role of Mrs. Withers is played by tenth-grade student and professional model Siri Lindstrom, daughter of Swedish hotelier Andreas Lindstrom and his wife, the actress Pia Vogler.

"Small Town" will be presented in English on Friday, Saturday, and Sunday evenings at 8 PM. Tickets can be purchased by telephone from the school.

"Mother of God," Rafferty says. He suddenly remembers Mrs. Shin suggesting he tell Miaow to check the papers. He'd forgotten all about it. "This is a disaster."

"Look very nice to me," Toots says. "What it say about you."

"We're all going, right?" Pinky says. "I'm planning on it. I bought a tie."

"I don't know," Rafferty says, his head spinning. "I mean, I have no idea."

"Thought we talked about it," Campeau says.

The door opens, and the Growing Younger Man comes in, carrying an umbrella despite the fact that it's not raining. "Morning pick-me-up, okay, Toots? Heavy on the chlorella. Hey, famous writer, look at this." He extends a newspaper that's been folded beneath his arm.

"I've seen it."

"Really?" the Growing Younger Man says. "You read the *Polyglot*?" The *Polyglot* is a new enterprise, a slapped-together sheet of computer translations from the Thai-language press, printed in English, Japanese, and German editions, plus Russian for the gangsters in Pattaya.

"You're shitting me." Rafferty extends his hand and takes the paper, and there it is, word for word. "Is this in everything?

"I don't *read* everything," the Growing Younger Man says. Rafferty hands him the *Sun*. "Hey, you and Miaow are both famous."

"Which is exactly what I didn't need," Rafferty says. He gets up. "Did Leon say how Wallace was?"

"Bandaged and walking," Pinky says.

"I may be back," Rafferty says. "Or I may leave for South America." He goes out and turns left, picking up Varney's designated watcher, Kiet, about halfway to Surawong and waving at him. Kiet, still wearing the long gray coat, mimes a long-distance high five. Rafferty crosses Surawong and goes into the Montien Hotel—still working at fancy but getting shiny at the knees and elbows—and into the bookshop, where he buys the other English-language papers. The story—almost word for word, with *Small Town*, Miaow's name, and his own—is in all of them, along with the name of her school and even the area of Bangkok, Sathorn, where it's located. And, of course, the identity of the teacher he had planned to ask to chauffeur Miaow to and from school.

It's two thirty when he finishes reading the papers in the Montien's lobby, time to go pick up Miaow, which no longer seems like a good idea. As he sits in the armchair, aimlessly sorting and resorting what's happened, three possible courses of action present themselves. He can pull Miaow out of the play and stay away from the school tomorrow night, which would outrage his daughter, spark a war in his family, and probably ruin the production. He can ignore the story and hope for the best, hedging his bets by showing up heavily armed. Or, since the story is already out there and it might be the only chance he'll get to draw Varney to him, he can try to take advantage of it.

And instantly he has an idea. It's complete and almost fully formed, with a beginning, a middle, and about six endings, only one of which isn't irredeemably disastrous. He dismisses it and gets up.

And sits down again. He brings up a map of the Sathorn area on his phone. With his forefinger he traces on the arm of the chair the streets that matter. *Maybe*, he thinks. *Maybe someone can talk me out of it.*

He calls Mrs. Shin and asks her to take Miaow home with her.

31

Nowhere to Go

VARNEY'S FIRST REACTION is, *It's a setup.*

He's been up for a couple of hours, essentially seething. There's been nothing on the television news about the old guy those clowns killed down near Petchburi, which means Rafferty might not even know about it, son of a *bitch*. So, after he makes his instant coffee, he spends twenty minutes returning the furnished condominium to its "unoccupied" state—all the used paper cups and plates, plus the take-out-food containers, in a small trash bag, his clothes and toiletry kit folded tightly into the big computer bag with the shoulder strap, all the porcelain surfaces wiped down and spotless, the shower stall dry, the bedclothes stretched to military tautness, not a wrinkle anywhere. Then he picks up the trash bag and hangs the computer case from his shoulder and lets himself out of the condo. On the way to the elevator, he drops the trash bag down the chute, as he does each time he leaves, and totes the computer bag onto the sidewalk.

He needs to look at a paper. He's checked the *Bangkok Sun* and the *World* on his cell phone, but not all stories make the cut for the online edition, which means the old guy still might be in the print version. So now he steps into yet another hot, cloudy, damp day and heads for the nearest Starbucks. First, though, he ducks into an Asia Books store and buys the papers. Then it's back into the world of crowded sidewalks and sweat.

How he hates this city. He hates the wetness, the smell—the rank stew of exhaust and people, plus the occasional seep of sewage. He hates the Third World power lines overhead even in some of the most expensive neighborhoods, tangles of black that remind him he's still a prisoner of money, still scrambling for the final score that will put him permanently back in Prague, the only city on earth he loves. The hot countries are the places where the gold can still be seen glittering on the walls of the mines, there for the taking if your hands are fast enough and your knife sharp enough, but he yearns for cold, still winters and silence and the tidiness of several centuries of rigorous, tightly organized civilization.

The overpriced coffee and sweet roll, naturally, require a long wait in line, listening to the Thais quack at each other, watching the meaningless smiles, wishing he could just blow away everyone in the place and help himself to whatever he wants. Sit down among the bodies for a nice hot cup of coffee and a Danish, basking in the silence of the dead. Somewhere he saw an engraving of Vlad the Impaler having a picnic at a formally set table—white tablecloth and all the other trappings of aristocracy—in the center of a forest of impaled people, Vlad tucking in heartily while a henchman in front of the table uses a hatchet to disassemble some nameless bystander chosen to provide the meal's entertainment. Vlad, Varney once read, put a solid-gold cup beside a public fountain in the city of Târgoviște so passersby could refresh themselves. During the years of his rule, the cup was never stolen.

Now, that's *order*, Varney thinks. He grabs a tiny table beside the window and sits with his back to the street, shutting out the perpetual crowd, the slow tropical stride. He's wished passionately at times for a cannon to precede him through these dawdling throngs, cutting a swath for walking at a purposeful pace.

The papers disappoint him. Nothing about the man in Petchburi. He folds the *World*, wondering whether it's possible the old fart survived. The murder of a *farang* would be reported; a mugging, even a brutal one, might not be. Bad for tourism. He should have checked the man's pulse.

Although what does it matter? He's gradually accepting the pos-sibility that Rafferty might not actually have Treasure. The money, yes, he's clearly lying about the money. No one would steal $600K and leave $3 million behind. But maybe, just maybe, when Rafferty talked to that dragon of a maid about bringing mother and daughter back together, maybe he was simply *close* to finding her. Maybe he was being optimistic. Rafferty has the simplicity at his core that often distinguishes optimists and other types who usually lose at the long game. Romantics, idealists.

And whether Rafferty's an idealist or not, it's hard for Varney to believe that the man would put himself and the people he loves at risk for a murderous kid he barely knows. For $3 million, sure. But a girl who tried to blow up a house with him inside it? Doesn't compute.

As much as he'd like to get the three mil, and as badly as he needs it, the money in the closet is small change compared to the fortune Treasure could unlock for him, money he's planned on for years. Money he put up with Murphy for, flattered Murphy for. *His* money.

But maybe Rafferty actually doesn't have her.

He sighs and unfolds the paper again, looking for the Life-style section, where they put the photos of the rich girls. He's always liked rich girls, if only because their idea of how life works is so breathtakingly wrong. He regrets sometimes that he was born too late for all the *great* revolutions, when he might have had the opportunity to drag some brittle princess into that room with the drain in the floor and break the world open for her like an old glass Christmas ornament.

And there are two of them, right on the front page: a pair of fine-looking debutantes, with that expression that says as far as they're concerned, their shit smells like doughnuts and yours doesn't, and then a word detaches itself from the bottom of the page, blinks on and off a couple of times, and virtually punches him in the eye. *Rafferty*, it says. And then *SMALL TOWN*.

He says aloud, "Bullshit," earning him a few reproving glances that he doesn't notice. He reads it twice, almost laughing at its transparency. *Sure*, he'll go to check out that school, *sure*, he'll loiter around on the sidewalk with a sign taped to his back saying ARREST ME.

He reads it again. Flips through another paper and finds it.

Pulls out his phone and brings up the website for Regent International School, Sathorn, Bangkok. Full address duly noted. My, my, the Korean woman, kind of butch-looking, is actually listed as a faculty member. How neat, how *plausible*. Just for the hell of it, he dials the school and asks to be transferred to whoever is handling tickets. When the woman comes on the line, speaking Thai-accented English, he confirms the dates and the times of the production. She asks how many tickets he needs and how he'll pay for them, and he disconnects.

They've put real *effort* into this, he thinks. Hitchhiking on an actual school production.

This time when he reads the story, he sees the bit he missed. *Mia*.

It takes him about twenty seconds to find her Tumblr page. He'd looked for her online once or twice as Miaow, but there she is, Mia Rafferty, a dark-skinned, apparently short, ordinary-looking Thai girl with intelligent, watchful eyes and a bad haircut. In a couple of pictures, she's with a skinny, big-headed Viet geek in glasses whom the captions identify as Andrew Nguyen. And then, *mirabile dictu*, there she is, looking a little spoony, a tad adoring, with a ridiculously handsome *farang* kid named Edward Dell. The caption reads, *OMG, Edward is going to play "Ned" in "Small Town."* The picture went up on Tumblr twelve days ago, more than a week before Rafferty had ever heard the name Arthur Varney.

So.

He sits absolutely still, looking at the photo of the two teenagers. Rafferty might not have Treasure, but he's got Mia. Seems like a fair trade: one little girl for another or, at a bare minimum, the three million from Murphy's closet. The newspaper story might still be a setup, but the information it contains is too valuable to ignore. *Whatever* Rafferty has, he'll want to trade it for Miaow. *Mia*.

UNLIKE MOST THAI women, Lamai has hair with a natural curl in it. It's not much of a curl, but it's enough to create frizz when the weather is damp.

The weather is always damp.

She's smoothing her hair with the palms of her hands as she strides into the condominium's lobby, her high heels tick-tocking on the composite-stone floor. She's short, although she prefers to think of herself as "compact," and briskly energetic. A spark plug, her husband calls her. It's the right temperament for Bangkok real estate, where every deal has nine prices and an infinite number of negotiables, plus built-in dodges and hidden trapdoors for both sides in the transaction.

She has a spare half hour, which is unusual for her, and she's decided to use it to check on the condo unit that Mr. Terwilliger, who's supposed to arrive from Malaysia in three days, reserved for two weeks. In this market if a customer who's planning to come to Bangkok sees a suitable unit on an agent's website, he or she is well advised to put a hold on it by paying a month's rent for a two-week hold or two months' rent for a month. If the deal goes through, if the customer sees the place and likes it, a percentage of the money is put against the rent after the lease is signed, and in the meantime the unit is off the market: not advertised, not shown.

But a unit left alone, even in a nice building, can get musty and stale-smelling. The damp has its way with things just as it has its way with Lamai's hair. In her big purse, she's got a bunch of clean, folded hand towels and an aerosol can of something that's supposed to erase all unpleasant scents and replace them with the fragrance of an open meadow, although to Lamai it smells like ironing. Still, a pleasant smell.

The moment she opens the door, she knows that something is wrong.

There's a very slight scent, clothes that have been worn once or twice too often in a hot, wet climate—socks, maybe, or shirts. And it's too cool; the air-con was on only a few hours ago. As the door closes behind her, she thinks about opening it right back up again and leaving. Someone has been in here. *The lock,* she thinks. *It's cheap crap. Should have changed the lock. I should leave.*

But Lamai didn't get where she is, didn't buy the big four-bedroom unit by the river and the place on the beach in Rayong by being meek. After she stands and listens long enough to convince herself that no one else is in the place, she slips off a shoe and cracks the door open, sliding the shoe into place so the latch won't engage. Just in case she has to make a quick exit.

Carrying her other shoe in her hand, she checks the place out. The refrigerator is empty, but there's a little spill of something on the second of its glass shelves. It's sticky and smells of oranges, so it's juice. The glass-topped table in the dining nook has been wiped sloppily; there are grains of salt near one edge. *Things,* Lamai thinks, *a woman wouldn't miss.*

Going into the bedrooms suddenly seems less like a good idea, but she squares her shoulders and does it anyway. The small one seems untouched, but the big one has definitely been used. Lamai employs one cleaning crew for all her rental units. They make a bed the way she tells them to, and this isn't it. The closets are empty, but there are black markings, like graphite, on the top of the white horizontal wooden rods, and Lamai has cleaned them often enough to recognize them as having been made by clothes hangers sliding back and forth. When her crew finishes a job, those are scoured away. In the bathroom sink near the drain, a few tiny hairs, very short, the kind left by someone who shaves his face or his head.

Lamai runs her finger around the drain and peers at its tip. Black hairs.

It seems like an excellent idea to leave. Let her office's strong-arm guys, kept in reserve for renters who don't pay, handle it. She pulls out her phone.

HE'S HALFWAY DOWN the hall when he sees the shoe.

The newspapers under his arm crackle when he moves. Standing stock-still, he transfers them to his left hand. In the computer case, he has both a small automatic and a Cold Steel Black Bear fighting knife, almost six hundred dollars retail, with an eight-inch blade that can cut through thick leather as though it were cheese.

He hears a woman's voice from inside the unit and slowly unzips the case.

The light coming around the open edge of the door dims and brightens and dims again: someone moving between it and the window. He makes a decision and closes the bag. A death here will be a problem. The doormen know him by sight. The real-estate agent has his name. Whoever is inside won't be a sex worker or a street child or even a half-senile *farang*. Whoever is inside will belong here. Someone with juice.

By the time Lamai slips her foot back into the shoe and comes through the door, he's barreling down the fire stairs. Half an hour later, he's walking the sidewalk outside Regent International School and thinking, *Perfect.*

32

Nein, Nein, Nein

"IT'S PERFECT," RAFFERTY says, trying to convince himself.

Arthit looks down at the diagram that Rafferty has made. Miaow's school takes up most of a short block, with a scattering of commercial establishments on each side. The entrance sits at the apex of a T-junction, running along the horizontal stroke of the *T*. It's an Italicized *T* because the vertical stroke runs into the horizontal at an angle of about eighty percent.

"One-way," Rafferty says, running a pencil along the street at the top of the *T*. "The kids get dropped in front, *here*." He taps the juncture of the two streets, only a few yards from the school's entrance. "*This* street," he says, indicating the vertical part of the *T*, "is also one-way, traffic coming toward the school. You can only arrive from these two directions, and you can only leave in this *one* direction." He runs the pencil along the street the school is on. "It's like Anna's fish traps—easy to get in, hard to get out. If you need the quickest route to a two-way street, you have to keep going past the school and turn right, *here*. Then it's two blocks to Sathorn Road." He draws a line along the narrow street, four shops and a couple of restaurants away from the school. "One car could block it."

"Blocking streets," Arthit says neutrally. He picks up his hotel coffee and puts it down untasted. The two of them are at the small dining-room table in the hotel suite. It's midmorning, Friday. Rose is down in the hotel coffee shop, letting her pregnancy-sharpened food preferences guide her through the menu, and Miaow, who has been excused from the first few hours of school, is on an assignment from Rafferty, talking to Treasure at the shelter. It keeps her out of school for the time being, which seems wise, and will also allow her to run a second errand for Rafferty in an hour or two. She's being driven and guarded by Arthit's former cop.

Rafferty says, "You probably won't need to block it."

"Well, good. Because that's official stuff, closing streets, and we're not out to draw attention. It's a small operation to catch the guy who committed that murder in Pattaya, and that's all. If you and Treasure and Murphy and Murphy's money get brought up, warning lights are going to blink all over the place, and they'll wake up the Thai antiterror people, the Americans, and whichever cops or firemen stole the rest of Murphy's cash. You'll have new problems."

Rafferty nods, but he's barely listening, lost in his diagram. "There's no other usable entrance to the campus," he says. "Everybody has to come in here, in front, between the administration building and this first block of classrooms." He slides the diagram aside to reveal an overhead view from Google Earth, fuzzy but readable. "This is the auditorium, about forty meters from the entrance. At an angle, linked by this sidewalk. The sidewalk is exposed. Anyone stationed in front of the auditorium would see Varney coming, if he's not in a big group. Your plainclothesman with the picture from the Pattaya passport will be at the entry door, looking at everyone who comes in, and then he'll go out and watch the sidewalk. And one of your people is making a new picture, right? Without the mustache and the hair."

Arthit says, "Yes, but he's not going to come into the auditorium. Whatever happens, it'll happen on the perimeter of the school. Out front."

"I agree, but still. So look. If you're facing the place from the front, the sides of the campus to the left and right butt up against solid blocks of shops and restaurants all the way down to the next street. See? Here and here, with no space between them. The only way to get into the school that way is over the shops' roofs, and even then you'd hit the chain-link fence that surrounds everything except the front entrance. The only other functional way is a gate at the back of the school, opening onto the block behind, to the lot where the teachers and administrators park." He makes an X on the far side of the diagram. "About twenty spaces. You get in through a remote-keyed gate, just a sliding section of the chain-link. The gate is the same height as the fence, which is about ten feet, so even if someone climbs over it to get into the school, he's not going to be able to leave that way hauling someone else along. He'll have to come out through the front."

"And if he's got a remote?" Arthit says.

"He still has to use that sidewalk to get into the auditorium."

Arthit says, "Everything always looks so neat on paper. Still, I think you're right. It'll happen in front."

"So that's the where," Rafferty says, "and I think the *when* is after the play."

"My guy will take Miaow into the school, through the back, when she's finished with Treasure," Arthit says. "He's got a remote. She'll be on the floor of the car, and he'll bundle her out and take her inside to her homeroom teacher. Once she's safely inside the school, she stays there all day, out of sight from the sidewalks. No in and out, no chance to get snatched until evening. I think the period before the play, when the audience is arriving, is safe, because we're going to have Anand, in uniform, directing traffic as people come in. After everyone is gone, he'll take off, creating a nice, police-free zone. So that leaves after the play."

"And we'll control the exposure of the audience at that point," Rafferty says. "We'll go back and congratulate Miaow and stand around for fifteen or twenty minutes until most of the parents are gone, and then we'll hold people back for a few minutes so we go can out alone. That has to be when he'll make his move."

"It still frightens me to death," Arthit says. "The man is crazy."

"Me, too. But we're forcing the action to a specific time and place. We'll have Anand, *out* of uniform, waiting around the corner. Your off-duty guys will have done a couple of very discreet street sweeps, nothing to frighten him away, and then they'll be on call and close at hand."

Arthit says, "I think we should do more street surveillance. Who knows? Maybe they'll spot him and grab him."

"Here's my problem. He's going to *kill* someone. He promised me he would, and that very night he either beat up Wallace and left him for dead or stood back while someone else did it, if the woman who called the hospital got it right. If he spots surveillance and leaves, someone is going to die."

"I wish I liked it better."

Rafferty puts the pencil down. "Both of us do."

Arthit says, "And we can't just leave him out there, sniffing after Treasure, because eventually he'll find her. If there were a way to draw him anywhere else, I'd cancel this whole thing."

"We'd have to set that up. This is perfect. If he saw the story, he verified that the play was running and who is in it. We couldn't have created it, not without months of preparation."

"Maybe he didn't even see the newspaper story."

"I did. You did. Everybody I know did. Mrs. Shin says the father of one of the kids is part owner of the *World*, and he calls in favors for the school once or twice a year."

"I still hate the whole thing," Arthit says.

The two of them sit there, their eyes on the map Rafferty has drawn. It looks imprecise and amateurish, a diagram of disaster.

"We haven't got an alternative," Arthit says. "But it's stupid to get innocent people hurt." He tucks his forefinger under his thumb and then flicks Rafferty's map. "We've taken care of the audience members, but do *all* those old guys have to come?"

"*You* try to talk them out of it," Rafferty says.

* * *

"No," Hofstedler says. "No, no, *nein, nein, nein.*"

Campeau says from his stool, "We're going."

"I bought a *tie*," Pinky Holland says.

Hofstedler says, "And *Wallace* is going. This he is not missing."

"We're all going," says Campeau. "Son of a bitch screwed with the wrong bunch."

There are manly mutters from around the bar. Hofstedler says, "We go with you or we go without you."

"Then I'm telling all of you," Rafferty says, "to be at the hotel at seven. Anyone who's not there will be left behind. And if you show up solo, you'll be arrested." This claim is sheer bravado; they're not going to run around arresting people if there's a chance Varney is watching.

"I was going to go from home," Hofstedler complains. "With Wallace. It is not so far."

"You're going with me," Rafferty says, "or you're not going."

Arthit stands on the rungs of his stool, clears his throat, and waits for everyone to look at him. "I haven't met most of you," he says, "so you don't know, first, that this is a police operation and, second, that I'm the ranking cop. This man has killed three people we know of—a tourist, a woman, and a child—and we're sure there are more. The only reason you're invited is that you're pig stubborn and this is the only way we can control you. But I warn you, Mr. Rafferty's view on how the operation should run is also the official police view. Arrive with the group or stay home. If you don't all arrive together at the proper time, if you straggle in individually, there's the chance that Varney or one of his thugs could grab you and turn it into a hostage situation. You *will* arrive in the two cars Mr. Rafferty has arranged. Once you're on the school grounds, you'll follow the directions you're about to hear. If things start going wrong, Mr. Rafferty and I have the weight of the law on our side, and you will do what we tell you to, and quickly. Now, is there anyone who can't live with that?"

No one says anything.

Behind the bar, Toots applauds the speech.

"Great, I guess," Arthit says. He looks at his watch. "Almost three." To Rafferty he says. "Try to make this sound good."

Rafferty explains the rules.

HE'S ALREADY HOT and tired and angry, and he has hours and hours to go.

He's been there since the middle of the night, except for a couple of hours' sleep at a "number hotel," that fading Bangkok tradition for adulterous liaisons: the room is directly above the garage, with a stairway going up into it, so once the room is rented there's no need to go to the front desk or to haul your honey down a hallway. There's a curtain that can be rolled down in the garage to hide the customer's car from prying eyes. Checking in, he'd used the Étienne Bressac passport, acquired from a Frenchman he'd met in Phnom Penh and with whom he'd returned to Bangkok, so Bressac's visa is still as valid as Varney's. Bressac is in no position to complain.

The number hotel is a perfect place to take a hostage, which is what he intends to have at the end of the day. He can't understand why he didn't think of it before.

Rafferty is just another *farang* without influence, so it's unlikely his plight would interest the police sufficiently for them to give him a hand. Still, Varney is certain that *someone*, probably an amateur or amateurs, will be watching for him, and even if by some miracle they're not, it's better to behave as though they are. So his first priorities were to survey the landscape, which he did Thursday immediately after leaving the condominium, and arrange places from which he can watch without drawing attention.

As a longtime hunter of animals and people, he recognizes the importance of a blind. After his first look at the somewhat down-scale neighborhood that houses the Regent International School, he'd burned through a lot of time and energy to buy a cheap Nissan compact in Bang Na, paying in cash with a bit extra to compensate for the fact that Étienne Bressac hadn't held an international driver's license. The car's body looks okay, and the windows are darkly tinted, which is essential, but the engine is a wreck. He'd driven the area for hours, the valves hammering, until he managed, in the middle of the night, to park it facing the school about halfway up the one-way street that runs up to the narrower street that forms the top of the T-junction. Then he took advantage of the darkness to pull out the Black Bear and slash the front tire on the traffic side to explain its being stuck there. Finally he put one of those folding reflective sunshades under the windshield. He's cut several pop-out holes into the sunshade so he'll be able to sit there without presenting a human silhouette, in an apparently disabled car, which any cop would look at once or twice and automatically discard as a potential escape vehicle. Blind number one.

He's also located his second and third blinds, two small restaurants that have plate-glass windows through which he can look down the slanting street toward the front of the school. One of them is only a few yards from the car and faces west, which means the owners have thoughtfully tinted their own window against the afternoon heat.

And he's changed his appearance: he's now a slimmer, shorter man with light brown hair and rimless glasses. He's been wearing shoes with lifts in them since his first appearance in the Expat Bar, so he's now almost three inches shorter than he was. He's also discarded the outsize clothing and the light cotton padding he'd worn under it. Silhouette is about half of a person's visual signature from more than eight or ten meters away, and his silhouette is much less imposing than when Rafferty last saw him. Facially he's not worried, since, in the unlikely event that someone he hasn't met is looking for him—if Rafferty has somehow interested the police—that someone will probably be trying to match the face in Varney's passport or some cocked-up Photoshop of a broad-shouldered bald guy.

That leaves patterns to worry about. Anyone who's watching will be waiting for someone, anyone, who keeps popping up or appears to be loitering. So he's packed into his computer bag two clean shirts of different colors and a jacket so he can change his color pattern two or three times over the course of the day, and he's also stashed a baseball cap and a pair of sunglasses in the glove compartment of the car. None of this will be enough, probably, if they've got half a dozen people looking out for him, but he doesn't think they will; Rafferty couldn't muster that much support, and even if he could, they'd be afraid of chasing him away.

He has Kiet ready to go, gun and long coat and all, within five minutes of here. He has a driver with a small car who will drive slow loops very close to, but not in front of, the school, until he gets the call, and then he'll do what they've gone over a dozen times. Both Kiet and the driver have been booked from early morning to late at night. The driver is the weak link, because he might just floor it and take off if things get hot, so Varney has introduced him to Kiet and made it very clear what will happen if he, Varney, gets stranded. However it shakes out, the whole key is speed: go in fast, inflict blunt force fast, make the grab fast, and get away from the scene while people are still trying to figure out what just happened.

When he looked at the possibilities and at the school layout late Thursday afternoon, he identified five, or possibly six, potential opportunities to grab Miaow, four in daylight and one, possibly two, at night.

So far the day has been a grave disappointment.

He'd been sitting in the car at 7:30 A.M., waiting for the first opportunity—the likelihood, however remote, that Miaow would be brought to school between eight and nine. The opening of the school day was guaranteed to be a mob scene, with the entire student body arriving at once, but he knows how to turn a mob scene into an advantage. He'd sat there, peering through holes in the sunshade with the getaway car idling half a block away, until ten, but he never sighted Miaow. This gave him a moment of uneasiness: was it possible the newspaper story *wasn't* a plant? Was it possible that it had surprised and horrified Rafferty and that he'd pulled her out of the play? Or had someone brought her in through the parking area in back?

That, he decided, as a sudden flare of pure white fury subsided, was what they'd done. It would have made no sense for him to keep an eye on that back area. The gate was so slow to open and close that once he was inside it, getting out would have been like needing to skate to safety in November and having to wait for the lake to freeze.

So he had calmed his nerves, changed shirts, put on a cap, and positioned himself in his second blind, at the table in the window of the nearer restaurant in time for what he saw as the second and third possible opportunities of the day, before and after lunch. The neighborhood was full of restaurants. Maybe she'd go out to eat.

He was pretty certain she wouldn't; odds were twenty to one that she'd been ordered not to leave the campus. But . . . kids were kids. Or maybe they *hadn't* ordered her, but in any case it would be stupid to ignore the opportunity, no matter how remote—especially since, as he'd visualized it, it would have been a snap. Miaow would be leaving school to eat in one of the nearby cafés, maybe with a few friends in attendance, and the car with him and Kiet in it would have materialized out of nowhere as she left the restaurant to go back to school: a screech of brakes, Kiet applying a little maximum force on the other kid while he snatched Miaow—all of them back in the car and out of the neighborhood in less than two minutes. They'd have been at the number hotel twenty minutes later.

But she didn't show. Although dozens and dozens of kids had poured out of the school and filtered through the neighborhood and then dutifully returned at one, Miaow hadn't been among them. So scratch daylight opportunities two and three, going to and coming from lunch.

The hope he'd been clinging to, without much faith that it would be rewarded, was that the entire evening exercise, which he instinctively saw as the most dangerous of all the scenarios, might prove to be unnecessary. But now, with most of the daylight possibilities gone, he begins to wonder again whether she really is coming at all.

Well, there's still one more daylight possibility: at 3 P.M. classes will end. If she's actually inside the school, and if she's not staying there until the play begins, she'll come out with the rest of the kids, and probably Rafferty will be waiting to pick her up. It's equally probable, Varney thinks, that Rafferty will have backup in tow.

He makes a sudden decision. If she comes out at three and Rafferty picks her up, he'll have the driver follow Rafferty to wherever they're staying. That will mean engineering a second snatch, but this one isn't feeling good. So at two forty-five, his driver is waiting in front of the school, along with dozens of parents in taxis, as Varney watches from the restaurant, phone to his ear to identify her the moment she comes out, and Kiet is behind the school, across the street from the teachers' parking lot, to alert him with a call-waiting signal if any teacher gets into his or her car accompanied by a student.

By three thirty it's clear that Miaow has not left the school by either route.

Blocks away now, back on the sidewalk to stretch his legs, and trying to shrug off both his anger and another swirl of anxiety, he begins to wonder again whether they really *did* pull her out of the play.

If they did, he'll have to engineer a second snatch or keep his threat to tighten the spiral, and people will probably be watching the obvious candidates, those clowns in the bar. Barring an enormous stroke of luck, he's not going to be able to find out where Rafferty's got the wife and Miaow stashed. And he, Varney, is running out of time. Hotels are out of bounds, and he's not likely to score another empty condo.

That means it might be tonight or not at all. The simple trade: Miaow for Treasure. If Rafferty has Treasure, he'll make the swap in an instant. The key to all of Haskell Murphy's fortune, almost $30 million, counting the money from the house, will be delivered to him either tonight or tomorrow, or not at all. If Rafferty doesn't have Treasure, then Miaow for the money from the closet. Tonight or tomorrow, or not at all.

If it turns out to be *not at all*, though, he vows, he *will* kill Rafferty before he leaves Bangkok.

33

Opening Night

"ANAND IS THERE," Arthit says, putting his phone in his pocket. "In uniform and directing traffic, although so far there's not much traffic to direct."

"Good," Rafferty says. "I mean, good that he's there." He's perspiring even in the air-conditioned hotel lobby, and he has stomach cramps that have hauled him into the bathroom several times already.

"As soon as people are inside the auditorium and the doors are closed," Arthit says, "Anand will get into his car and drive off, in plain sight. He'll go to the hotel, just a few minutes away, and change into civilian clothes. As soon as it's completely dark, he'll take up his position."

"The guy I'm most worried about is almost as tall as Anand and usually wears a long gray jacket. Name is Kiet."

"Anand knows that," Arthit says. "He's good, Poke. You've worked with him before. If that man is there, Anand will have him."

Poke says, "And the plainclothesman in the lobby of the auditorium?"

"He's got the picture from Varney's passport and the one we monkeyed up to your description, and he'll be facing the door as the audience comes in. But chances are, as I said, Varney's not going into the auditorium. He'd have to tote her almost forty meters to get her to the street. He needs to hit fast and get out fast."

"Okay." Rafferty looks out through the hotel's glass doors at the two waiting black town cars. Their windows are deeply tinted, and the doors are closed to keep the air-con in. It's been drizzling, so the wipers have left clear half circles where they swiped the rain away and diamonds of water, reflecting the hotel lights, everywhere else. The drizzle is the only thing Rafferty is happy about at the moment: anything that reduces Varney's visibility for an additional moment or two, that might make him delay for a few seconds out of uncertainty, is a small item in their favor.

Arthit says, "You can still call it off."

"And get him when?"

"There's that, of course," Arthit says.

"So what do you think?"

"If I could think of anything else, I'd do it. We're doing everything we can to protect the audience and any other bystanders, but that doesn't mean nothing can go wrong."

"No," Rafferty says. "Of course not." He looks across the lobby. "And then there's them."

Standing bunched together around a huge ceramic jar shaped like a giant's funeral urn are Hofstedler, Pinky Holland, and Campeau. They look vulnerable outside their natural habitat. Beside Hofstedler, his head wrapped in bandages, is Wallace, wearing a light blue sport coat and a sling around his neck to support the cast on his right arm. He's slipped his good arm into the sleeve of the coat and draped the other side over his shoulder so the right sleeve hangs empty. The arm in the cast is invisible. He's leaning on a crutch propped under his left arm. The Growing Younger Man is a no-show.

Arthit says, "Send them home."

"They won't go. They've got their damn tickets, they're going to see the play no matter what I say, and they're actually *hoping* Varney makes a move. They're all heroes. If I tell them to go away, they'll just come on their own, and then we won't have any control at all."

Arthit says, "Well, then. It's time."

"Could you shoehorn them all into the car in front?" Rafferty says. He takes a deep, deep breath. "I'll go to the bathroom one more time. Then I'll go upstairs and get her."

THE POLICEMAN DIRECTING traffic is a surprise.

He's tall and young and efficient. He stands in the middle of the road, separating cars right and left, waving along those who aren't going to the play and sending to the curb those who are. There's a backup of taxicabs carrying audience members, and the cop works his way down the line, ordering the drivers to inch forward until they're closer to the entrance to let their passengers out. He seems to be completely engrossed in his job, keeping traffic moving and organizing the drop-offs.

It's a rich school, Varney thinks, sitting in the damaged car. It can afford a cop for special occasions. So it looks plausible.

But he doesn't buy it, and a little spark kindles just behind his eyes. If there's a cop here, Miaow is here, too. He's still got a chance at her.

He'd considered skipping the arrival of the audience, if only to reduce his exposure to anyone who might be on the lookout. If Miaow is actually going to appear in the play, she's been inside the school all day. But what if Rafferty doesn't show? If he comes, will his wife be with him? She'll present another target. Will there be a group? Every possibility has its advantages. Group confusion can be the most valuable asset: get a bunch of people running into one another, rolling around like balls on a table, and you can waltz away untouched.

He's reasonably certain he can pull it off and get clear. He's done harder things. What infuriates him is that it's *Rafferty* who's brought him to this point. It had seemed so easy at the outset; Rafferty was a *writer*, for Christ's sake. Spook him a little bit and hold out your arms for him to unload everything you want. Nothing about the man set off alarms. He seemed like a typical, woman-dominated American wisp of smoke, driven out of his own house by his wife and daughter, hanging with a bunch of mummies because he's comfortable with people who are weaker, physically, than he is. In other words, a pushover.

And yet here I am, Varney thinks, *with all my experience, and I don't even know whether he's got the fucking girl.*

He's squinting through the drizzle on the windshield as the cop turns his back and leans down to argue with a taxi driver, and he risks reaching out to wipe away the water. Much better. The parents are about what he'd expect: largely white and North Asian, a sprinkling of Africans, not many Thais. They're in their forties mostly, obviously well-off, the women hiding their nice clothes under umbrellas. He's got his own umbrella lying on the backseat. An umbrella, used right, is a portable blind.

The light is beginning to fail. It'll drop almost imperceptibly for the next thirty minutes or so, and then, with tropical swiftness, it will go dark. For right now, though, it's bright enough to see. He's getting bored when the two black cars pull up, the cop ushering them to the head of the line with the deference shown to money all over this city.

He sits up straight. The fat kraut from the bar, Leon something, has climbed out of the front seat of the first car, and here come the rest of the Incontinence Patrol: that little bald one with the shiny head, the prune-faced skinny guy—*Bob*, the famous *Bob*—who always sits at the end. And now the kraut is leaning forward, helping someone out of the backseat, someone wearing . . . what? A turban? No, it's bandages, and Jesus fucking Christ, it's the guy from the alley. Taller, when seen standing among the others, than he'd seemed before, and moving pretty stiffly on one crutch, which should come as no surprise. *Well, at least now*, Varney thinks, *I know why it didn't make the news.*

The driver of the second car hops out and runs around to open the rear door, which makes it clear which car contains the person who's paying for everything. First out is a Thai man of medium height in a dark suit, no tie. He's got dark skin and a round belly, but despite the belly there's nothing cozy-looking about him. Just the way he scans the area is enough to say cop. The back of Varney's neck prickles. He resists the impulse to check his rearview mirror. The cop leans down and says something, and Rafferty gets out. Like the cop, Rafferty takes a deliberate look around, and then he steps away from the car door and extends a helping hand as a third person emerges into the fading light, maybe the wife, but no, it's not the wife, it's—

Varney's heart stops.

His first reaction is, *That son of a bitch.* His second reaction is, *Everything just got easier.* His third reaction is sheer, unmitigated joy as he takes in the slight frame, the pale face, the stiff, anxious position of the shoulders, the tangle of reddish brown hair. He'd have recognized her even without seeing the hair and the nocturnal pallor of her skin, just by the way she walks, as though there might be unexploded mines beneath her feet, and the way she twists her head back and forth in the habit of a lifetime, looking, *looking* for her awful father.

With one of his hands supporting her elbow and with the old guys trailing behind, Rafferty leads Treasure into the crowd, and they disappear from sight.

AFTER THE FACT, Rafferty's recollections of Miaow's opening night are swirled together and formless, like colors applied over one another while wet and then smeared with a sleeve. The plain-clothes cop watching each face as its owner comes in, Rose's hand landing on his arm, the news that Andrew has sent flowers all the way from Vietnam, that Rose has met Edward's father and one of his bar girls, and the father is *awful.* Poke has the feeling that everything is too bright, the way it is sometimes in dreams, and that he's squinting painfully against the glare, never completely sure that what he's seeing is what he seems to be seeing. Even the noise level seems to rise and fall at random.

Rose, leading the old guys and the girl down the aisle, and he and Arthit taking seats on the aisle in the last row. The first laugh of the evening—thirty seconds in—when Luther, limping as if one of his legs is made out of sponge, reads his lines off his palm. The leap of Poke's heart when Miaow blossoms out of the darkness of the wings and moves center stage, and the realization that the man who immediately stands and comes up the aisle can only be doing one thing, the bitterness of his satisfaction when, standing with the door to the lobby open an inch, he hears the man say into a cell phone, in English, "She's in it. The girl in the picture is—" and then sees the man snap the phone closed and leave through the front doors. Arthit's brisk nod when he hears the news, and the endless internal recycling of the plan, running through checks and cross-checks, possible surprises and responses. Looking up again—feeling like he's missed only a few minutes but realizing that it must have been longer—to see Julie and Ned taking their seats in that imaginary soda shop to talk about the future, and losing himself completely in what Miaow is doing up there.

The two of them get a hand as they leave the stage. For the rest of the performance, he's in that small town.

In the middle of Miaow's long and beautiful closing speech, the farewell of a girl brought back from the dead for one last wistful look at the beauty of the life she hadn't appreciated, Arthit's phone vibrates and Rafferty looks down at a text from Anand: WE'VE GOT KIET, BUT VARNEY NOT IN PLACES KIET SAID: OLD CAR, CAFE.

Arthit keys in HOLD HIM OUT OF SIGHT AROUND CORNER and waits until the end of the standing ovation at the curtain call, all the parents up and cheering and the kids on the stage red-faced and grinning, before he shows Rafferty the rest of the exchange.

Rafferty says, "Tell them not to search for him. I want Varney to be confident."

Arthit says, "I'd say he has good reason to be confident."

* * *

IN THE BACKSEAT of the car, as it's driven slowly past the school, Varney sees the audience filing between the two buildings at the front of the campus. Some of the parents have private chauffeured cars or taxis waiting, but others are hiking down the diagonal street in search of a cab. The sprinkle has become a light rain now, still soft enough that the driver can flick the wipers on and off, but it's dark and everyone's umbrella is up, so Varney can't see any faces.

Better and better. He has the driver pull over, just past the biggest cluster of proud parents and family members, and he gets out, holding the umbrella at a tilt that obscures his face. As the car angles back into traffic, he does the "Excuse me" routine of someone who's looking for the person he's come to meet, threading his way politely through the crowd. Most of the people seem to be talking about the play, and he hears someone say, "The little Rafferty girl," and the name snags at him, almost makes him miss his step, but he shrugs it off and keeps moving toward the administration building, just to the right of the entrance to the campus. Several people climb into cars, and doors slam, and the crowd moves forward, away from the front of the building and the dark, less-than-shoulder-high bushes that crowd up against it, and he moves forward with them, not wanting to stand out.

The crowd slows and stops again, and Varney stops with them. The woman next to him, blonde and elegantly forty-something in an Hermès scarf from twenty years ago, gives him a quick look and then a smile. "It was good, wasn't it?" she says, briskly British.

"It was," he says. "I thought the little Rafferty girl was great."

"They all were." Her smile broadens a bit. "Is one of your children in the cast?"

"No," he says. "I'm not married. I just *love* the play. It's so *American.*" He puts just enough emphasis into the words to make her pull her face back half an inch or so, and then she says, "I see my car."

"Well, ta," Varney says, "nice chatting with you."

She holds her umbrella high so she can get through the crowd, and almost simultaneously the next big group of people arrives from the auditorium, clustered together beneath a nearly solid roof of umbrellas. Varney waves at an imaginary companion among them, lowers his own umbrella in front of him, and walks toward the crowd, past the administration building. Then he turns and falls in with them, moving back toward the street, and when he reaches his final blind, he simply steps aside and disappears from sight.

Settling in to wait, he thinks, *Six or seven minutes now.*

THE BACKSTAGE AREA is crowded with families, and the three of them are intertwined in one tight knot. Rafferty hugs them both so close that Miaow squeaks. He steps back and says, "You were wonderful." His heart is thumping in his ears.

"Really?" Her face is so flushed she might have a fever. "Was I?"

"Tell her," he says to Rose.

"I was crying," Rose says.

Miaow says, "You're a hard cry."

"I was crying, too," Rafferty says.

"You," Miaow says. "You cry at commercials." She glances past him and says, "Look at Treasure. Isn't she amazing?" The girl stands a few yards away, with Hofstedler and Wallace beside her.

"She looks phenomenal," Rafferty says, and the knots reclaim his stomach. There doesn't seem to be any way around the next steps, which suddenly loom in front of him like a dark doorway he'd rather not go through. "Thanks to you."

Miaow says. "Did you *really* cry?"

"Like the world's biggest, ugliest baby." He feels Rose's gaze on him and consciously lightens the expression on his face. "Tell you what," he says, manufacturing a smile. "See you in ten or fifteen minutes."

Miaow surprises him by closing the distance between them and wrapping her arms around his middle, something she never does. She says, "I love you."

He tries to kiss her on the forehead but misses and gets her hair. He hugs Rose, holding it for a few extra seconds. Stepping away, he turns to Arthit and the guys from the bar, who are standing in a semicircle a few steps off, and says "Pinky, you and Wallace stay here, please, with Rose and Miaow, just in case." To the others he says, "Let's go."

Wallace says, "I'm going."

"Okay, okay. Bob, you stay with them, please." He follows Wallace, who's already limping toward the stage apron. As they descend the five steps to the auditorium floor, he hears Campeau say, "Hello, Rose." He's never heard Campeau sound so tremulous. Then the plainclothes cop says loudly, "Ladies and gentlemen, we've got a little situation in front, nothing to worry about, but please let these folks go out alone. Enjoy yourselves here for a few minutes, and then anyone who wants to leave can go. Anyway, it's raining out there."

HE THINKS, *They look like bowling pins.* They're moving in a more or less triangular formation, with Rafferty and Treasure in the lead. She's on his left as he holds her arm—apparently lightly, although she moves like a prisoner, lagging very slightly and being tugged along, looking down at the sidewalk as though she thinks someone might have set up something for her to trip over. The cop is directly behind Rafferty and slightly to his right, scanning the scene in all directions, and a bit farther back on the cop's left are the fat kraut, holding an umbrella so small it looks like a comic prop, and the guy with the crutch—Wallace, his name is. They're moving slowly so that Wallace, who's putting a lot of weight on the crutch, can keep up. Watching them come, Varney draws an imaginary trajectory; in about thirty seconds, when Rafferty and Treasure have just passed him, Treasure will be on his side of the group, just a few feet away, and the old fart with the crutch will be right behind her. He couldn't have choreographed it better.

Should he go for a strike or a spare? He could probably work out the geometry to take them all down at once, except the fat guy, who's probably got too much mass to go off balance, but he decides against it. He wants Treasure to be standing. Once the trap closes, he needs everything to be fast: the distraction, the violence, the confusion, the snatch, the exit. No stooping awkwardly and trying to lift a squalling, terrified girl. No. Leave Treasure and Rafferty upright, as many as possible of the others down on the pavement, and the gun in his left hand so he'll have the right free to deal with Treasure. She is not going to be pleased to see him.

There's almost no one around—fewer people, actually, than he'd hoped. As Varney had figured he might, Rafferty spent some time inside with his daughter while the crowd outside thinned. Varney's irritation returns like a hand squeezing his throat; it would actually be easier for him if there were more people close by, more confusion, more potential collateral damage to slow the reactions and to give them second thoughts. He takes one more look at the approaching party. Maybe twenty, twenty-five seconds. He says into his cell phone, open and waiting, "Right now."

ARTHIT SAYS, "ANAND has passed Kiet to one of the plainclothes, who's hauling him off. Anand is just around the corner to the right. I'm telling him to move in but stay out of sight behind the classroom building."

"If he can see us, he needs to duck back," Rafferty says. "If anyone's coming by road, it's got to be from the left. It's a one-way street, and he definitely won't come up *this* way," he says, nodding at the street that forms the vertical stroke of the *T*. "He'd be visible for more than a block."

They follow the sidewalk leading between the administration building and the classroom block, and all the free-floating doubts and fears Rafferty's been batting down one by one gather in his gut and accrete, as though by the pull of gravity, into one massive, planetary black certainty: this is wrong, this is stupid. Someone is going to die.

The thought strikes him with almost physical force as they come between the buildings and into the open, and he pushes his way through the feeling, turning his head to scan the low bushes in front of the administration building, and at that moment there's a flare of light, a grinding of gears, and a squeal of tires, and he snaps his head around to stare into the glare of a pair of high-beam headlights as a small car jumps the curb, fishtails, and heads straight for them.

He's dragging Treasure backward, fast, hearing the others scrambling to retreat behind him as the car closes in on them, and then something slams against his back and he stumbles forward, grabbing frantically to keep the girl's arm in his grasp, and Wallace pitches face-first onto the pavement with a crack and a shout as his cast hits the concrete, and Arthit grunts and drops to his knees. Hofstedler, knocked off balance, stumbles past Rafferty, barely keeping his feet. And there's Varney, stepping around Treasure with a gun in his hand, pointed straight at her, and Treasure presses both hands to her face and emits a high, shrill, unvarying tone, as unwavering as the shriek of a teakettle, and takes a panicky step back, away from Varney, away from Poke as he instinctively reaches out and snags her elbow.

"Stay down there, cop," Varney says to Arthit. "If I can't have her, I'll shoot her." Behind Arthit the door to the car opens from inside and remains open, waiting for Varney.

The gun barrel flicks to Rafferty, and Varney says, "You've got exactly one second to let go of her." Rafferty takes his hand off Treasure's arm and the shrill noise scales up a tone or two. With the gun pointed at Poke, Varney snatches at Treasure's sleeve, but she yanks it away, and he swears something that's mainly a snarl and grabs her by the hair.

And takes a quick stagger step backward when there's no

resistance, and he looks down at the hair in his hand, staring at it, unable for a half second or so add it all up, and then the shrilling sound ceases, and out of the corner of his eye he sees Treasure's hands come down from her face, and he brings his head up to find himself looking at a delicate Thai ladyboy wearing layers of pale powder. The ladyboy winks at him and gives him an air kiss, and Varney emits a furious howl and punches her in the face, driving her back two steps. Far beyond the constraint of logic, he brings the gun up and points it at her but hears a hoarse bellow behind him, and when he turns to face it, a shouting, enraged Leon Hofstedler barrels into him. Hofstedler's three hundred pounds knock Varney back, one step and then two, and Varney manages to bring his gun around and fire it one time, and Leon grunts from someplace very deep, but then Varney's feet tangle in something that's been thrust between them—the injured man's crutch—and they go down, both of them, toppling over, Varney backward and Leon forward. They land heavily about four feet from the fallen Wallace, Hofstedler smothering Varney with his bulk.

Varney is kicking and shoving to get Hofstedler off him as Poke leans down and tries to heave Hofstedler away, out of Arthit's line of fire as Arthit circles, shouting, trying to find a shot. Pulling at Hofstedler, Rafferty is vaguely aware of the car door slamming behind him, screeching tires as it accelerates away, and then Varney's gun goes off again, the sound muffled by Hofstedler's body, and Rafferty hears Wallace, stretched full length on the pavement, say, "Got him, Ernie," and sees Wallace use his good hand to point an old, rusty revolver at the side of Varney's head from little more than arm's length and put two bullets dead center into the man's left ear.

Wallace lets go of the gun as though it's red-hot and says, "Leon. *Leon?*"

34

We Open Now

IT'S ALMOST THREE thirty, and the sign hanging from the string of green lights says CLOSED.

Standing there with his back to the street and the day yawning open and stale and empty behind him, potentially free of human encounters, Rafferty allows himself a brief flash of hope: maybe he can just go home and get back into bed, maybe he won't have to see any of them. Won't have to say anything to anyone. He can't imagine what he can say. He's spent most of the past four days in bed, alone in the apartment while Miaow and Rose, at his insistence, remain in the hotel. The one time Rose visited, she tried to talk to him for a few minutes and then said, "It isn't really about you, you know," and left.

He hasn't been answering his phone. He disconnected when Arthit was explaining that the cops had decided there was no profit, either financial or prestigious, in investigating what really happened and quite a lot in claiming credit for catching and killing a man who'd murdered at least two expats, the Australian Arthur Varney and the Frenchman Étienne Bressac.

If Toots hadn't called repeatedly for almost an hour beginning at nine this morning, a ring every minute or so, he wouldn't have spoken to her, and when he did, he told her he wasn't going to come. Her response had been silence, stretching out for several minutes as they both held the line. When he heard her begin to weep, he said he'd be there.

But the sign says that the bar is closed. He can go away again and maybe stop somewhere for a drink. A dozen drinks.

When he pushes at the door, however, it opens a few inches. He steps back onto the sidewalk and lets it swing shut, breathes deeply several times, and then shakes his head from side to side to loosen the iron rod in his neck. It seems to take him forever to open the door the rest of the way.

The door closes behind him as his eyes adjust to the dimness. The overhead lights are off.

The first person he sees, the person closest to him, is Toots. She's sitting in front of the bar with Hofstedler's special stool tilted on two legs so the seat rests in her lap. She's got the back facing up so she can work on it. He smells the metal polish she's been rubbing onto the nameplate that says LEON HOFSTEDLER. She looks up at him just long enough to see who he is and returns to her task, which is working a Q-tip into the incised letters, getting out the last clots of polish. As Rafferty nears, he sees her finish the *f* and move the Q-tip to the bottom of the *s*.

Beyond Toots he sees Campeau, the Growing Younger Man, Pinky Holland, and the guy with the hair. Except for Campeau, who's in his usual chair, the others are seated at random, each separated from the others by an empty stool or two on either side. Pinky, who usually sits in a booth, is at the bar, occupying the stool Wallace usually claims. No one says anything

Toots says, "What you want, you get." She sniffles. "Today everything free. Leon say."

"No thanks," Rafferty says. "I don't—"

"Yes you do," Toots says, almost a snap. "Leon want."

"*Leon* wants?" Rafferty asks. He goes behind the bar, gets a glass, feeling their eyes on him, and uses the fountain nozzle to fill it with club soda.

"I tell you after," Toots says, digging away with the Q-tip. "Tell you everything after."

He's never been on this side of the bar before. It's cramped, with barely enough room to move sideways, and oddly isolating, with the wide wall of wood between himself and everyone else. Toots has been standing back here for something like forty years. He decides he likes the distance the bar gives him from the others, so he tosses the soda and pours himself a beer. The silence in the room presses against his ears.

"Since Toots is busy," he says, mainly to get past opening the conversation, "does anyone need anything? That okay, Toots?"

"Okay," Toots says, swiveling her barstool so the light coming through the window falls directly on Leon's newly bright name-plate. She makes tiny swabbing gestures with the Q-tip. Rafferty sees that a shining red ribbon, about two inches wide, has been stretched tightly from one armrest of Leon's stool to the other, making it impossible for anyone to sit in it.

Rafferty says again, "Anyone?" No one answers. He looks down at the bar's stained surface for a moment, fighting the impulse to flee, to yank the door open and run into the street, but instead he looks at his watch, clears his throat, and says, "Am I early or is she late?"

After a few seconds, the guy with the hair says, "What we can say with certainty at this point is that you're early. She may also be late, but we can't know that yet, can we?" He slides his glass over the bar. "I'd like a refill. Rum and Coke?"

"Sure." Grateful to be doing something, Rafferty splashes some Coke into the glass and turns to locate the rum.

Toots says, "On left," and he picks up the bottle.

"Mekong for me," Pinky says behind him, and he hears a glass being slid across the bar. "This time the bottle with the Jack Daniel's label."

Campeau says to Pinky, "Live it up."

Rafferty says, "Anything for you, Bob? Toots?" And the door opens, ringing the bell.

All their heads turn in unison. Lutanh and Betty come in, Betty puffy-eyed and tragic-looking in black from head to toe, in a cocktail dress that looks like it was designed in the 1960s. Lutanh wears a loose-fitting white one-piece sheath with a high Chinese neck. Her left eye is swollen closed, the color of a Bloody Mary, and her nose is swathed in white padding, held in place by crisscrossed adhesive tape, startlingly white against the skin on her cheeks. Campeau looks at Lutanh twice and then lets his head droop.

Lutanh and Betty go to Toots and look over her shoulder at what she's doing. The sight of the bandages brings the silence back into the room for eight or ten seconds. Then Campeau says, "Beer Sing." He adds, "Please."

"Scotch for big *katoey*," Toots says, her hand wrapped in the sleeve of her shirt so she can buff the metal. "For little one, Orangina. Leon buy for her." She stops, swallows, and continues. "Keep in small refrigerator down there."

Rafferty barely hears it. He can't take his eyes off Lutanh's damaged face. Then the translation of what Toots said presents itself to him, and he gives an abrupt nod and says, "Sure." He pours the rum into the Coke and hands it to the guy with the hair. Taking refuge in being busy, he fills a glass with ersatz Jack and pops the top from a Singha, then gives the Singha to Pinky and the Jack to Campeau. The two of them glance at each other and then drink without complaint. Idle for a moment, Rafferty finds himself looking at Lutanh again and on the verge of breaking into tears.

Feeling his gaze, Lutanh says, "No problem. I want small nose, right? Want to make small, and now have." She smiles brightly. "Doctor, he fix bambam on my nose and make nose small, same time. Now very good, very small. Before, Leon say he pay for doctor—" She breaks off, blinking. She brushes her cheeks with an open palm, sniffles, and, without thinking, wipes her nose with the back of her hand, and says, "*Yiiiiiiiiii,*" in a very high voice, and Betty puts an arm around her shoulders and Toots covers the nameplate with her hand and says to Lutanh, "Don't drip."

The bell rings as the door opens. Miaow comes in, looking everywhere at once, as though she's entered the garden of the beasts, before her eyes settle on Lutanh. Behind Miaow is Rose.

"Look, everybody," Lutanh says, wincing as she touches the padding covering her nose in a very gingerly fashion, "my acting teacher."

"Isn't she beautiful?" Miaow says to Rose, who is regarding Rafferty with the air of someone working toward a diagnosis. "Even with all this stuff on her nose." She puts her fingertips beneath Lutanh's chin and turns her face slightly. "I want to see. Wow, look at that eye. Poke always says to put raw steak on one of those."

"I vegetarian," Lutanh says. "It go away. Tomorrow I look okay. Tomorrow I very okay."

The door behind Miaow opens, and she and Rose and Lutanh step aside to make room for Arthit.

Miaow nods hello at Arthit and says, "Poke," glances around the room and changes it to, "Dad. Lutanh wants to take an acting class. We talked about it when I was teaching her to move . . . you know, like Treasure."

"I very want," Lutanh says. "Want to play Little Mermaid."

Betty says to Poke, "*Scotch*, please? Orangina?"

"Acting is a good idea," Rafferty says dutifully, bending down to open the refrigerator.

"She was fucking great," Campeau says. His eyes go automatically to the tip jar, and then he closes them. When he opens them again, he looks at Miaow and Rose and says, "Sorry."

"With Dr. Srisai," Miaow says. "I told her about Dr. Srisai, and—"

"If he can take her," Rafferty says, popping the cap from the big orange bottle.

"He said he can," Miaow announces with the air of someone who's sneaked a peek behind Door Number Two.

"In afternoon," Lutanh says, her hands clasped together

imploringly, making her look like someone who's about to sing. "Before I go bar."

Mid-pour, Rafferty sees where this is going. "Dr. Srisai is . . . ummm, kind of expensive."

"I know," Miaow says, "but we were hoping—"

"I'll pay for it," Arthit says. "That's the least I can do." Lutanh lets out a small, delighted squeal as the door opens again and Anna slips in, leading Treasure by the hand. Treasure is wearing the clothes Anna bought her the night they went shopping, and the sight of the clothes seems to roll everything that's happened since he last saw them into a giant ball of solid regret, and for a moment Rafferty thinks he will simply break down in front of everyone. Treasure looks at all the men in the room and sidles closer to Anna.

Arthit says to Anna and Treasure, "We're going to send Lutanh to acting school." He ignores the puzzlement on Anna's face and says, "Is my watch right? Is she late?"

"She's late," the Growing Younger Man says. He's looking a bit shamefaced, probably because he hadn't shown up on the night everything changed forever.

Picking up the bottle of Betty's scotch and clearing his throat to get rid of the lump in it, Rafferty says, "According to my watch, she should be here at any minute. Miaow, you want a Coke?"

"You work here now?" Miaow says.

Betty says to Poke, "Your wife? Your daughter?" Poke nods and pours the scotch, and Betty, shaking her head, says, "No. No ladyboy."

"I don't know about that," Rose says. To Lutanh she says, "You really *are* pretty."

"She try with him already," Betty says.

"Everybody tries with Poke," Rose says, studying Poke again. "I don't know why he comes home at night."

Rafferty dredges up a smile and says, "I get hungry. Do you want something?" Rose shakes her head.

Arthit shoos Anna and Treasure toward the booth Pinky usually sits in, and they settle. Treasure says to Miaow in a half whisper, "*What* are you going to drink?"

"Coke."

"Then can I have a Coke, too?"

Arthit says, "What do you want, Anna?" and Anna says she'd like one of the orange things Lutanh is drinking, and Arthit says, "Beer for me, I don't care what kind."

Campeau says, "He can't handle all this by himself," and gets up. On his way to the bar, he swaps drinks with Pinky and then slides in behind the counter, next to Rafferty. "Tight back here," he says. He grabs a glass and hits the Coca-Cola spigot.

"It is," Rafferty says, more pleased than he'd ever thought he'd be to have Campeau's company. He hears Miaow and Lutanh talking, two very different voices in the same approximate register, and when he turns around with Anna's Orangina, he sees Campeau offering him a Coke. Taking the drink, he says, "What a team," and as he totes the drinks over, Miaow and Lutanh beat him to the booth, both of them talking to Treasure. Seated, Treasure tilts her head up to them, reserved but listening. Rafferty gives the drink to her, and Anna turns back to the bar to get Miaow's Coke and Arthit's beer, and Lutanh says something that has both Miaow and Treasure laughing, and then he hears Anna laugh, too.

He hasn't heard Anna laugh very often.

Rose snags his arm as he passes and tilts her head inquisitively. He shrugs in equivocation: he has no idea how he actually feels.

The door opens yet again, and Wallace comes in, his cast patched with some kind of composition the color of cooked salmon. He looks at his watch and says, "Where is she?"

"She late," Toots says with finality. She gets up and straightens Leon's stool, the red ribbon in place, the brass shining. "She say she come three thirty, but maybe not come. She very angry everything, always angry too much. Maybe she not come."

She pushes the stool into its accustomed place. "This Leon," she says. "This always Leon, okay? Leon always here." She looks around the room. "Now. Everybody sit same places, same place you sit at night. You and you," she says to Campeau and Rafferty, waving them from behind the bar, "Out, out. Get stool."

She goes briskly behind the bar and draws a tap beer for Wallace, plunks it down, and then pulls Leon's big stein from beneath the bar. "Always he think I don't make this full enough," she says. She blows off the foam and fills it to the brim, then slides it gently across the bar, dead center in front of Leon's stool. "Forty-two year," she say, "and I never make full enough." She lifts her shirt from the neck and blots her cheeks and looks at them defiantly. "Okay. Everybody right place."

For the first time since he began to come into the bar, Rafferty sees Toots pour herself a glass of whiskey, from the Jack Daniel's bottle. She holds it at the center of her chest, looking down at it, as though the words she wants are there.

"Leon own this bar," she says at last. "He buy many, many year before, tell me not to talk about it, so I not talk about it. He pay money for police every month, pay money for land every month. Cannot own land because Patpong family own land, but he own bar." She takes a first sip. "Real Jack," she says. "Now *my* bar, now I own bar, we have real Jack. Leon give me, some kind of paper for when he dead."

"A will," the Growing Younger Man says.

"Maybe," Toots says. "Nam-Fon, wife of Leon, she get house, get money. Me, I get bar and small money for police and land. And Leon's ashes. Nam-Fon, she very angry. Want bar, want everything. When I call you to come here, I think she bring Leon's ashes, I think we say goodbye to him, but now she late. No problem." She lifts her glass in the direction of Leon's stool. "Leon here now, we can say goodbye anyway."

People around the room lift their glasses. Wallace and Campeau say, "Goodbye, Leon," and Rafferty finds himself on his feet.

"I just . . . I don't know how, but I have to say how much I . . . how deeply I—" He's weeping, and he sees Wallace stand up, but he goes on, saying, "A hundred times a day, I try to change what I did. I go over and over and . . ."

"It was my fault," Arthit says, getting up. "I was the cop in charge, and I screwed it up. I should have had more men there, should have had them everywhere, but I thought he'd spot them, so I—"

There's a bang as loud as a shot, and they all turn to see Wallace standing at the bar with beer all over his hand. He says, "I'm going to say what Leon would have said if he was here, and if I get lost, one of you guys can take over, because we all know what he would have said. He would have said we're old, we're all going to die soon, in a hospital or alone, or maybe next to someone we're paying, but however it happens, it'll be soon. And we're just counting time here, in here, trying to, trying to . . ."

"Figure it out," Campeau suggests.

"Trying to figure it the fuck out," Wallace says. "And trying not to look like clowns. And that Varney or whatever his name was, that son of a bitch came in here and made fools out of us all. Laughed at us while he used us to get to Poke, used us to try to hurt one of these precious little girls here, killed people. Left me to die.

"I *went* with you that night, Poke, we *all* went with you. I didn't care if I lived or died, long as I was doing something to fuck up that human tumor. Leon felt the same. He was old, he was fat, he wasn't *doing* anything. This was a chance to do something, and he did. He showed up, he knocked that fucker ass over teakettle, and I can guarantee he felt great when he did it. You know what? It was quick, it was exciting, and it probably didn't even hurt very much. So I'm here to say fuck you to your guilt, and if I can't say goodbye to Leon's goddamn ashes because that bitch hasn't showed up, then I'll just do this, because this is what he'd want me to do." He comes around Leon's stool and wraps his arms around Poke. To Arthit he says, "You, too, damn it," and

Poke hears Arthit get up and come across the room, and then Arthit is behind him and Wallace's arm goes around Arthit as well.

Then Rose is beside him, and Miaow, and all over the room people are getting up. Rafferty hears a squeal to his left and turns to see Campeau pushing his stool back and getting up, rigid with duty, his mouth as downturned as a trout's, and Rafferty is grinding his teeth at the prospect of being hugged by Campeau when the bell rings, so sharp and hard that someone might have hit it with a hammer. The door strikes the wall with a bang, and a furious-looking woman, with the assertive emaciation of those who live on anger, stalks into the room. She slaps onto the bar an urn, thin, cheap tin, badly plated with something meant to suggest gold, and already dented. Without a word she wheels around and leaves. The door sighs shut behind her.

On the other side of the bar, Toots tilts her face downward and brings up her hands, palm to palm in a prayerlike *wai*, and says, "Hello, Leon," with Rafferty half a tight-throated syllable behind her, and then everyone else says hello to Leon.

The silence fills the room until Toots says to Campeau, "Turn on lights, please, Bob. We open now."

Afterword

The Hot Countries is the final book in an informal trilogy that
explores the evil caused (and left behind) by the villain of *The
Fear Artist*, Haskell Murphy. The second of the "Murphy" books,
For the Dead, concerned itself in part with Rafferty's effort to sort
out the wreckage within Murphy's nightmarish household, especially the fate of his badly damaged daughter, Treasure. At the end
of *The Hot Countries*, I feel we've reached a kind of resolution on
that front, even if it turns out to be temporary.

One of the interesting things about writing as I do, which is
to say by the seat of my pants, is that I never have the faintest
idea what I'm getting into. Even when it became obvious to me
at the end of *The Fear Artist* that I needed to find a way to complete the story of Murphy and Treasure, I had no idea that Miaow
would prove to be so central as I pursued Treasure's tale. This
development has been a source of delight to me. A confession: If
I were told that in the future I could write about only one of my
characters, I'd choose Miaow. She's come so far from the defiantly
terrified street child Poke and Rose adopted, and yet I think at her
core she's still the same person. As someone who's never had a
daughter and has obviously never been a Thai street child, I find
it fascinating and somewhat bewildering that Miaow is the only
character I write whose next action, next words, are never in
doubt: I write them as though I'm taking dictation, and then I
have to sit around and figure out what the other characters are
doing.

I also want to give Miaow credit for my favorite fan interaction.
From the first Rafferty book onward, I received mail from people
who had chosen to follow the sometimes difficult path of

intercultural adoption and who wrote to tell me that when they read the books they felt as though I'd been hiding in their closets, taking notes. I corresponded for several years with a couple in the Midwest who had adopted a little Thai girl, Tippawan, who was about Miaow's age and who, in a sense, grew up in their household as Miaow grew up in the books. When I'd finished a bookstore event last year, a young girl came up to me, gave me a *wai*, and said, "I'm Tippawan." Behind her were her parents, both wearing enormous grins. Their obvious happiness put me on the edge of bliss to think that my little fictional family might have contributed something to Tippawan's very real family finding their way to one another, across some very forbidding cultural gulfs.

Finally, and probably most important, a word about all the help I had in writing about the guys in the Expat Bar. I knew from the very beginning of the series that I wanted to write a book about the first American expats in Thailand, the ones who found their way there from the killing fields of Vietnam and stayed. (In *A Nail Through the Heart*, the first book, it's Leon Hofstedler who tells Poke that someone needs his services, setting the main plot of the book into action.) For quite a while I'd been thinking about a guy who's beginning to have cognitive problems and who lives part of the time in a Bangkok that was paved over decades ago. I had roughed out a story line for him when I was contacted by the Bangkok novelist Christopher G. Moore to submit a short story to a collection to be called *Bangkok Noir*. I developed one fateful night of Wallace's story and sent it to Chris, and I'm happy to say it got very nice reviews.

But I wasn't finished with the Expat Bar or the Bangkok of the Golden Mile. To reconstruct it for this book, I needed the assistance of people who had actually been there. Bangkok author Dean Barrett, whose books I've always enjoyed, talked to me about the period and gave some names and email addresses. Both in person and via email these men brought to life the Bangkok of the late 1960s. Anything that's accurate and evocative of that era I owe to their generosity with their time and memories. (Anything that's wrong is my fault.) So the final thank-you and the biggest of all goes to Dean Barrett, John McBeth, Tommy A. Odiorne (O.D.), and Norm Smith. You guys are amazing.

About the Music

I LISTENED TO a lot of Vietnam-era stuff during the writing of this book, especially Creedence Clearwater, Marvin Gaye, Edwin Starr, Buffalo Springfield, The Rolling Stones, Country Joe, and so forth. In what I initially saw as a courageous sacrifice to art I overcame a lifelong aversion to The Doors, and I have to admit that they provided a lot of fuel. I've even put "Whiskey Bar" and "Roadhouse Blues" on some playlists. How could you not like a song that contains the line, "Woke up this morning and I got myself a beer."?

But the majority of the music was more contemporary. I listened to a mostly-female playlist of about 600 songs that had big chunks of Lake Street Dive, Broods, Ingrid Michaelson, Alabama Shakes, Imogen Heap, Rachel Yamagata (thanks, Ed!), Parker Millsap, Langhorne Slim, mid-career Dylan, Ashley Monroe, Dwight Yoakam, the great James McMurtry, the immortal Little Feat, Lucius, Van Morrison's "Astral Weeks," and a lot of string quartets, mainly Beethoven's later ones.

As always, feel free to contact me at www.timothyhallinan.com to clue me in on music you think is better than the stuff I've listed here.

And thanks for getting all the way to this page.